What Reviewers Are Saying About

The Big Ray Elmore Novels

Their Feet Run to Evil

A *US Review of Books* **Recommended Read**

A *Book Readers Appreciation Group* **Medallion Honoree Selection**

"A solid addition to Holland's impressive oeuvre . . . a thrilling Southern whodunit anchored by a grizzled, whip-smart main character." —*Kirkus Reviews*

"Thomas D. Holland excels in crafting not just a mystery, but the Southern culture and milieu backing it . . . Readers who look for nonstop action will find plenty to like; but Holland also takes the time to weave solid character development into this story, as well as social and political inspection . . . Historical truths wind into the story to provide realistic, thought-provoking suspense and action . . ."—D. Donovan, Senior Reviewer, *Midwest Book Review*

"[A] Southern-fried whodunit . . . that is both clearly told and enjoyable to read . . . a well-told period piece that reflects the tensions of a small Southern town." —*Publishers Weekly / The BookLife Prize*

"Holland sweeps readers into a world of pride, prejudice, recriminations, and regret as he fills page after page with smile-inducing metaphors, similes, and down-home descriptive prose that graciously lightens the load of a harrowing event at the heart of this compelling mystery. This is the kind of book one doesn't want to stop reading. Holland's plot initially seems standard, but it isn't. His characters are drawn vividly . . . This author's style brings to mind the best of Pete Dexter, but both the story and the voice are all Holland, a truly excellent writer."—Joe Kilgore / a *US Review of Books* Recommendation

---

Grind Slowly, Grind Small

Also by Thomas Holland

The Dr. Kel McKelvey Novels

One Drop of Blood

K.I.A.

UnHoly Ghost

The Big Ray Elmore Novels

Their Feet Run to Evil

Grind Slowly, Grind Small

Vessels of Wrath

VESSELS OF WRATH

A Big Ray Elmore Novel

THOMAS D. HOLLAND

ISBN: 9798392970841

For Susan Stevens Cowan

"What if God, willing to shew his wrath, and to make his power known, endured with much long suffering the vessels of wrath fitted to destruction?"

Romans, 9:22

VESSELS OF WRATH

AUTHOR'S NOTE

Raymond Sallis Elmore was born on July 4, 1916, on a small, hardscrabble cotton farm in the delta community of Split Tree, in Locust County, Arkansas. He served in the U.S. Navy as a corpsman attached to the Fifth Marine Division in the Pacific, where he was gravely wounded. Upon his return to Split Tree after the war, Ray "Big Ray" Elmore was hired as the town's chief of police, a position he held until his untimely death from injuries sustained while in the line of duty on November 12, 1987.

What follows is the third installment of a multi-part oral history conducted with Big Ray shortly before his death. The interviews were taped over a three-week period at the Split Tree Community Center. The reader is cautioned that the account is presented in Big Ray's own words, and while the transcript has been edited some for length and readability, it retains some graphic language and images that some may find disturbing or offensive. Additionally, the author has included some explanatory information gleaned from external sources, including newspaper accounts, county and municipal records, and separate interviews conducted with Big Ray's sons, coworkers, and his many friends. These editorial insertions are kept to a minimum and are provided solely for the purpose of providing additional context.

This work was funded in part by the East Delta State University's Southern History Program and a grant from the Arkansas Commission for the Preservation of Folkways and Culture.

TDH
Canefield, Arkansas

PROLOGUE

Pulaski County, Arkansas
Thursday, July 28, 1960

*W*ho'd have t'ought dat man's head, she come off so easy? *Mon Dieu! Da' ting, she roll like da bowlin' ball*, Gilbert Gervais thought to himself. Who'd have thought it'd come off so easily? Gilbert had no intention of killing the man; certainly not pulling his head off its stalk like a damn ripe tomato. *Maudit. Damn.* He was just trying to send the man a message. *Maudit. Maudit. Damn. Damn.*

The gentleman without his head was named Clyde Martin. He was from Poteau, Oklahoma, and was in Little Rock for a convention with some army buddies. Nothing wrong with that. Where he got on Gilbert's wrong side was when he'd hired Gilbert's girlfriend for the evening. Actually, she wasn't his girlfriend, although Gilbert found himself developing feelings for her that he didn't quite understand, but Lidia Fernandez wasn't officially his girl in that sort of way. No, she was more like a co-worker. She entertained lonely men for a living, men like Clyde Martin from Poteau, and Gilbert made sure that the lonely men paid their bills and didn't depreciate the merchandise. Gilbert Gervais was good at that. He was six five and built like an iron wedge set on its point, with a brain to match. He wasn't the sort that you'd ask for help if you were working on a crossword puzzle, but if you needed someone to break an arm or stomp a man unconscious, you'd be hard pressed to find a person better suited for the task.

What led up to the man losing his head is that the night before, Clyde Martin from Poteau had retained Lidia's services for a few hours. She'd shown up at his hotel on time, and Gilbert escorted her there and watched from the end of the hallway as the man opened his door and invited her in. There was no reason for Lidia or Gilbert to assume that there'd be any problems. Mr. Clyde Martin from Poteau certainly didn't look like trouble. He was middle-aged and over-weight, and didn't appear to have much on his mind that Lidia wouldn't be able to resolve in a couple of minutes. The problem is that he wasn't visiting Little Rock by himself, and three of his army buddies decided that they were lonely too. Even then, the problem was not so much the numbers as the fact that the other three somehow got it into their brains that they should get a group discount.

That was the problem. Doing what she did for a living, with men like Clyde Martin, was unpleasant enough, but Lidia Fernandez hadn't fled Castro's Cuba only to practice socialism in the Land of Opportunity. When the men refused to pay up, and then tried to laughingly throw her out the door, she wouldn't have it, and she pulled a straight razor that she carried in her small purse for just such occasions. That might have worked too if it had been only middle-aged and over-weight Clyde Martin from Poteau, Oklahoma, but it didn't work so well with four grown men. One of them, the same one who'd been particularly rough with her in the first place, took the razor away and began rearranging the room with her. In fact, he seemed to enjoy that even more than he'd enjoyed the earlier activities. He beat her pretty badly and even sliced off part of her ear, and then laughed as he flushed it down the toilet like a chewed plug of tobacco.

When Gilbert found out later that night, he decided that something needed to be done about it. Going to the police wasn't an option given Lidia's line of work, and in fact, she begged him to let the matter go; she figured that she'd learned a valuable lesson and didn't think that there was much to be gained by trying to settle a score. Gilbert however, thought it was bad for business. It also bothered him to see Lidia hurt. Despite her pleading with him to let it be, he decided to send the man a message.

Gilbert parked outside the hotel almost all day, watching. Clyde Martin had stayed indoors almost the whole day, and a less patient man would have given up waiting, but Gilbert Gervais was nothing if not single-minded. And abidingly patient. About ten thirty that night, Clyde Martin from Poteau finally emerged from his hotel and began leisurely walking down the sidewalk. Where he was headed, Gilbert didn't know or care; he started up his car and followed the man for about a block before pulling alongside him. He got out and walked toward him. Clyde Martin didn't pay him any attention at first, he didn't recall ever meeting the tall man and had no reason to assume that they were about to meet now, but that changed when Gilbert grabbed Clyde Martin by the back of his shirt collar, and in one quick motion, slammed his head into a metal lamppost.

Gilbert then pulled the stunned and cussing Clyde Martin to the rear of his car. He had a length of clothesline cord that he'd purchased earlier in the day, and he quickly tied it around the man's wrists and then the free end to the rear bumper of his 1959 Cadillac Eldorado. While Clyde Martin was still cussing and struggling with the knotted cord around his wrists, Gilbert Gervais got back into his car, put it into gear, and proceeded down West Capitol Avenue. He drove slowly at first, but fast enough that the man would have to dog-trot to stay upright. That was the whole idea. Gilbert knew that sooner or later, the man would trip and fall, and then Gilbert would continue driving for a little bit, just enough to take some of the hide off of Mr. Clyde Martin from Poteau, Oklahoma. Just enough to send the message that you can't mistreat Lidia Fernandez.

Gilbert Gervais was thinking about Lidia, and his feelings for her, the ones that he didn't really understand, when he glanced in the rearview mirror. It took him a minute to understand what he was seeing. In fact, he didn't fully understand what he was seeing, and he had to pull to the curb and stop and get out to take a closer look.

Somewhere in the last half block, the clothesline apparently had gotten looped around Mr. Clyde Martin's neck, and his head had popped off and rolled like an unbalanced bowling ball into the front yard of a local dentist and his horrified wife, who watched it all happen from the lazy evening comfort of their front porch swing.

Maudit, Gilbert thought. *Who knew dat da head she come off dat easy?*

CHAPTER 1

Split Tree, Arkansas
Friday, August 16, 1963

I've spent my whole life here; just about. Forty-seven years last July Fourth. I was born on a small farm in Locust County, just on the eastern edge of Split Tree, Arkansas, and I've been here the whole time except for a trip that I made to the South Pacific at the request of the U.S. Navy in 1944. Even that was short. It ended in February 1945, when a two-inch fragment of Jap shrapnel shattered my right thigh like it was made out of glass, and that was that. It took me a while to find my way home; I spent the better part of a year in different Navy hospitals, learning to walk all over again. But other than that, I've been here the whole time; as had my parents, and their parents before them, and theirs before them.

I've got no plans to leave again.

Split Tree's a small town with even smaller aspirations. Its population is 506; that's according to the 1960 census, though neither of the town's two signs has been updated in the last three years to reflect that. One still reads 416, and the other says 472; which one you see depends on which direction you're driving. Which one you believe depends on your sense of optimism. I don't know which is closer to the truth, but I know that both signs have been stuck on those numbers since before the war. I'm the chief of police for the town; have been since I limped home in late 1945. The position opened up shortly after I got back, and somehow I ended up in it; for better or worse. I suppose it sounds more important than it is, especially once you know that there're only four of us to be the chief of. I have two officers. Ricky Forrest is one of them; he's been with me for four years now. I trust that boy with my life. The other spot was vacant for almost six years due to a lack of money in the town's budget, but I finally got to fill it last February, though I didn't have much say in who I got to fill it with. Charley Dunn Skinner is the second cousin of the head of the town council, and I got the money for the position if I took Charley Dunn along with it. I'm not entirely sure what to think about him. He's not from around here originally, he's from up in Lee County, and I can't say I know him much, but I do know his cousin, Carl Trimble; he is from around here, and I don't think much of him. We'll see how it works out. I also have a part-time secretary, Jewell Faye Ivey. She works three days a week and spends the rest of her time patiently sitting in her husband's Jon boat reading romance novels and listening to him cuss more than a Baptist man should. She's been managing the office for almost thirty-five years, and she's seen her share of the town's police chiefs come and go.

I was sitting at my desk smoking a Lucky Strike, looking out the window, when I saw the sheriff come out the front door of the Locust County courthouse across the street from the police station. The Sheriff's Department is on the second floor. As I watched, he got into his car and drove the hundred or so feet over to my office and parked. He does that routinely. You can walk it faster, but Cecil Ben Cooper firmly believes that God blew life into the automobile on either the fourth or fifth day of Creation, and gave man dominion over it for a purpose, and he doesn't figure it's really his place to argue the matter. A minute or two later, I heard him come in the front door. He always makes a loud entrance when he does, and I could hear him exchanging morning greetings with Jewell Faye. He always stops to check on how her husband's fishing had worked out the previous day, and that takes a few minutes, but soon he appeared in my doorway. "Big Ray," he said by way of announcement. "Big Ray Elmore. How you doin' this fine mornin'? Another hot one today."

"Fair to middlin', Ben. How you doin'?" I answered.

"Good as a yeller tom cat with two hairy peckers," he replied. That's his standard reply, at least if you're a male; he'd have said it at his momma's funeral if you'd greeted him nicely in between hymns. Ricky Forrest was out on patrol, and Ben tossed his hat onto Ricky's desk and pulled a chair over and sat down across from me. He leaned the chair back on two legs and held up both hands like a baseball catcher to indicate that he'd be ready if I was inclined to toss him my pack of smokes.

I did, and I waited for him to get a cigarette lit before I asked, "What can I do for you, Cecil Ben? Almost ten thirty, you about to wrap things up for the day?"

He made a show of looking at his wristwatch. "Don't I wish. I suspect I can hold out till lunchtime. Jewell Faye says Clement did all right yesterday afternoon; couple big ol' cats, some crappie. Figure I'll give it a go this afternoon. I just got me one of them new fiberglass Sport King castin' rods from Montgomery Ward; came in last Monday. Hasn't even touched the water yet. Cork handle. Stainless steel line guides. I tell you what, it's a beaut. I was lookin' to try my luck out at McKelvey Lake."

"So, what's holdin' you up?"

He made a face like that was about the dumbest thing he'd ever heard. "Don't you know?"

"That you got yourself a new fishin' pole? Sorry. Haven't gotten to the second page of the newspaper yet this mornin'."

"No. No. Ain't you heard about that Colored preacher?"

I shook my head.

Ben Cooper made the same that's-the-dumbest-thing face again. "Charley Dunn didn't tell you?"

I took a final drag on my cigarette and flicked the butt out of the window behind my desk. I blew the smoke up and into the room where a lens of blue-grey undulated at shoulder height, and I shook my head again. "No. Haven't seen Officer Skinner yet this mornin'. What should he have told me? What preacher?"

Ben Cooper laughed. "Dang Colored preacher says he's here to register some voters."

"Hadn't heard."

"Yeah. Name's Jackson. Leonidas Jackson. *LEO-neye-dus*. Some name, don't you think?"

"Can't all be named Cecil Ben," I said.

"Ain't that the truth? No, this old boy showed up a couple-three days ago. Blew in from Missouri, I hear. St. Louis or somewhere up there. Got hisself these plans to register all the Coloreds around the county. Lord knows, that's what we need; more people votin' for that Kennedy jackass again. That's all we need. That man will have us all kneelin' at church and worshippin' the dang Pope before he's out of office. Mark my words. Goddamn Catholics."

"Give you a good excuse to eat catfish on Fridays."

"Don't need an excuse to do that. Never have."

"You know the blacks around here will vote for Kennedy, do you?" I asked.

"Makes sense. Who else they got? They sure ain't goin' to vote for that son-of-a-bitch Goldwater. That's who everyone says is goin' to run." Ben Cooper took a long drag on his smoke and let it out slowly through his nose before continuing. "What I don't get is, how dang stupid can a man be? Ain't been but hardly a month since that old boy went and got hisself shot over in Jackson, Mississippi, doin' the same dang thing. Registerin' Colored voters. Dang. Shot in his own garage to boot, and now this *LEO-neye-dus* Jackson shows up around here. Dang. How stupid is that?"

"Maybe he knows this isn't Mississippi. Could be he has more confidence that the sheriff of Locust County won't let that sort of thing happen here."

Ben Cooper snorted. "The fuck—" He stopped short and glanced at the direction of the outer office, worried that Jewell Faye might have overheard his profanity. He lowered his voice. "Well, you're right about this not bein' Mississippi, but that don't mean he won't rub some folk's fur the wrong ways around here. We're just fine without that sort of outside trouble makin', thank you very much."

I lit another smoke. "He doin' that? Makin' trouble?"

Ben Cooper laughed. "You tell me. It was your deputy that up and arrested him this mornin'."

CHAPTER 2

Split Tree, Arkansas
Friday, August 16, 1963

I had a general idea where Charley Dunn would be, so I made a quick phone call to the jail, told Jewel Faye where I was headed, and then went out to find him. He was at the Spur gas station a few blocks away, sitting in the office with the owner, Jim Bevins.

"Hey, Big Ray," Jim Bevins greeted me when I walked in.

Charley Dunn nodded at me.

"Jimbo," I replied. I flipped him a nickel and went to the drink cooler and got a bottle of grape Nehi. It's a funny thing, I don't much like grape pop, don't really like it at all, but I find myself always selecting it. I guess it reminds me of my tenth birthday, when my father took me and my younger brother to town. To this day, I have no idea why he did it, but he bought us each an ice cream and a bottle of grape Nehi to share. That was 1926, and he never did it again, but that just might have been the best time in my life. I reckon drinking a grape Nehi nowadays reminds me of that one summer afternoon. I opened it and took a swallow before acknowledging Charley Dunn's presence. "Officer Skinner," I said.

Jim Bevins put the nickel in his desk drawer. "Remember to leave the bottle," he said.

"Of course," I replied.

He nodded at a vacant chair in front of a display of truck tires. "What's up, Big Ray?" he asked. "This a social call, or is the Old Horseshoe in need of somethin'?"

I sat down and looked out the window at my police cruiser. It was twelve years old and looked every day of it. It was dented and scratched and the paint was starting to fade, but most noticeably, the front bumper was bent into a pronounced U-shape, the result of one of my former officers driving it into a tree and the department not having the money to fix it. In fairness, the former officer was in the middle of a fatal heart attack at the time, and that led to the unfortunate encounter with the tree, so I can't really hold it against him. He's dead and gone now, but the car still runs, even if everyone in town jokingly calls it the *Old Horseshoe.*

"What doesn't it need?" I replied. "But no, I just dropped in for the company and the refreshments."

Jim Bevins leaned back in his chair and put his feet on his desk. "Charley Dunn here was just tellin' me about some Negro preacher he had to arrest. An *agitator* from up north."

"That right?" I said, looking at my officer. I didn't indicate that I'd already talked with Ben Cooper. "Why don't you tell me all about it? If you don't mind chewin' your tobacco twice." I took another swallow of Nehi and got my smokes out and lit up.

Charley Dunn leaned forward and cleared his throat and shrugged, trying to appear nonchalant. "Was gonna make a report when I got back to the station."

"Understood. You're busy," I said.

"Not all that much to tell, really," he replied.

"Is that right?" I said. "Arrestin' someone seems like it'd be worth tellin' me. Especially an *agitator.* We don't seem to get too many of them."

He shrugged again and looked quickly at Jim Bevins, who offered no support. "Yeah. Arrested this preacher."

"So I hear. We in the habit of arrestin' preachers now, are we?"

"When they start makin' trouble, we are," he replied. There was a bit more lip to his tone than was good for his long-term health.

"Just what kind of trouble was he makin'?"

"You know, general trouble makin'. Tellin' them people they should be unhappy with the way things are. Tellin' them they should be changin' things. Rilin' them up."

"Wouldn't want that. People need to be happy with the way things are," I said, as I took a drink of my Nehi. "And just where was he doin' all this?"

"All over the county, but I found him down in the *Bottoms*."

"Unless we've gone and annexed some land recently, the Bottoms are in Sheriff Cooper's jurisdiction. You got business out there, do you?" The Bottoms referred to a sunken floodplain area south and east of town along the Cotton Belt Railroad spur that runs parallel to the river. Before the war it was a line of the Chicago-Rock Island Railroad that connected Split Tree to Helena and Memphis, and from there, just about anywhere else in the United States. Trains came and went all day and night back then and that meant work crews, and work crews meant lonely men away from home with money, and more, bulging in their pockets. A little community grew up around the tracks, with its inhabitants intent on providing solace to those lonely men. Today it's considerably reduced in size and activity, but there are still maybe five or six shacks out that way, where for the right price you can still find solace if you're lonely, or drink if you're dry, or both if you can afford it. It's outside Split Tree's corporate limits, and as long as folks keep their doings outside of our town, I leave it be.

"Law breakin' don't know no boundaries," Charley Dunn said.

"No, but the law does. He threaten anyone? Hurt anyone?"

"My cousin Carl told me—"

I held my hand up to stop him. "First, I don't particularly care what Carl Trimble told you. Understand? He may be head of the town council, but you still work for me, not him. And second, if Sheriff Cooper needs our help policin' the county, I'm sure he'll ask for it." I took a drink of my Nehi and followed it with a long draw on my cigarette, to keep him waiting, before I continued. "We clear on that, or do I need to repeat myself? Because I don't want to have to repeat myself. Not to you." Normally I wouldn't have done that. If someone needs dressing down, it's best to do it in private, but Charley Dunn doesn't bring out the best in me.

Charley Dunn looked like he'd just bitten into a rancid pecan. "You're the boss," he said.

"Yeah, I am. From what I hear, this preacher didn't break any laws."

He stood up. I suspect to make it appear as if he still had some say in the conversation. "I guess you'll be wantin' that boy released then."

"I already took care of that."

CHAPTER 3

Split Tree, Arkansas
Friday, August 16, 1963

I was leaving the gas station when my other officer, Ricky Forrest, drove up. It was his day off, and I didn't expect to see him, but the way he stopped short and hopped out of his car, it was clear he was looking for me.

"Ricky," I said as I walked over to his car. "You look like a man with the dogs after him."

"Chief. Sorry to bother you, but we got a situation."

"Then I should apologize to you. It's your day off. What is it?"

"I got a call from the jail. Johnnie tried to get hold of you but couldn't, and he called me." Johnnie Young is the county jailer. The town of Split Tree pays Locust County to use some of its cells on the rare occasion that we need one. "He says that he's got a prisoner; some black preacher that Charley Dunn arrested this morning."

I glanced back through the window of the gas station. Charley Dunn was still talking with Jimbo Bevins. "I know all about it." I looked back at Ricky. "Sorry they had to get you involved. I called over to the jail almost a half-hour or so ago and told Johnnie to let that man go."

"Well, that's the problem," Ricky replied. "Johnnie says that the prisoner won't leave. I was headed over there to try and get it fixed when I saw your car here."

It was all I could do not to laugh. "What do you mean, he won't leave? Who doesn't want to get out of jail?"

"Got me, Ray. Johnnie says the man refuses to leave his cell."

"I swear," I muttered. "If it's not one goddamn thing . . ."

"Don't worry about it, Chief. I'll go take care of it."

"No. No, you won't. It's your day off; you get on home to your family or whatever it was you were plannin' on doin' today," I told him.

He nodded, and we each got back into our cars. It was a short drive to the courthouse, and when I looked in my rearview mirror, I saw that he hadn't listened to me and instead was following me in his car. We both parked in front of the police station and walked over to the courthouse together.

"You don't listen so good," I said.

"My mother used to say the same thing. So'd my First Sergeant."

"Well, I can't say I mind the company," I said.

"Wouldn't want to miss this," he replied.

When we got to the basement, where the cells are, Johnnie Young was leaning against the booking counter as if he'd been waiting on us to arrive. I suspect he was. Johnnie's an old man, though I can't even start to tell you how old. He did some farm work for my father back in the thirties, and he seemed old even then. He's a bit crippled up, but not enough to keep him from getting around, provided there's no hurry involved with it. The story I always heard was that he'd gotten kicked by a horse as a boy, and it busted up his hipbone pretty bad. When he finally healed up, one leg was a good two or three inches shorter than the other. He used to nail a two-inch block of hickory wood to the bottom of his boot to compensate, but a few years back, he found a shoe-repairman over in Canefield who made him a proper leather heel. But even with the wood block, his limp drew a sharp line around job opportunities, at least until the war opened up all sorts of vacancies. He's been the Locust County jailer for over twenty years now.

"Mister Johnnie," I greeted him.

"Mister Big Ray," he responded. "Deputy Forrest."

"Mister Johnnie," Ricky returned the greeting.

"Mister Johnnie, what's this I hear about that preacher still bein' here?" I asked. In addition to being gimped up, Johnnie Young is not an overly smart person. He always means well, but sometimes the follow-through on common sense can be lacking. "I thought we understood each other on the phone. I want that man released."

Johnnie Young grinned and looked at Ricky and then back at me. "Don't I know it, Mister Big Ray. I understood you. I got two workin' ears. It's that man back there who don't hear so good, and I can't make a man leave if he ain't got a mind to."

"I don't follow. You let him go?"

"I did."

And you're sayin' he won't leave?"

The jailer shook his head but kept grinning. "That's exactly what I'm tellin' you. That man won't budge nary an inch. Says he wants to make his phone call. Long distance. Won't leave till he gets it."

"No need for a phone call, Mister Johnnie. There are no charges bein' filed. He's free to go."

"But he ain't leavin' without you givin' him a phone call to New York City, that's what I'm sayin'. And I can't let him, Mister Big Ray. Long distance phone call. Lord, the county don't got the money for that sort of extravagance. But he says he has a *Conversational* right to a call." Johnnie Young made a face as if further talking wasn't going to be any more productive, and he turned and started walking toward the rear of the building, where the cells were located, determined to show me the problem in person. He made a waving motion with his arm to indicate that we should follow. "Long distance. New York City," he muttered. "New York City. Can you even imagine?"

We found Leonidas Jackson sitting in the first cell. The other cells were empty. He was seated on the cot, with his arms crossed and his back against the wall. He didn't look mad, but he didn't look happy either. He looked like a man with an intention.

"Mister Jackson," I said, as I motioned for Johnnie Young to open the cell door. "I'm Ray Elmore. I'm chief of police for Split Tree. There seems to have been a bad mistake made. My apology. You're free to go, sir." I stepped back to emphasize that the path was clear.

Leonidas Jackson was a spare man, about my age—midforties—and relatively light-skinned and sharp boned. He wasn't what they used to call a high yellow, he was darker than that, but still light-skinned with mostly white features, except for his hair, which was conked and combed straight back from his forehead so that it resembled a shiny black helmet. He stood up slowly, without saying a word, and bowed a kink out of his back, and then he took two steps forward, grabbed the cell door and pulled it closed. With that accomplished, he returned to the bunk and sat back down and refolded his arms. Only then did he speak. "I believe I'm allowed a phone call, or does the Constitution of the United States not apply down here."

I looked at Ricky, who shrugged.

I looked at Johnnie Young, who smiled.

I looked at Leonidas Jackson. "You understand that you're free to go," I said.

"I understand that I am demanding my phone call," he replied. "Only then will I depart."

"Mister Jackson, I've been out of school for a while now, but I don't recall anythin' in the Constitution of the United States, or the Constitution of the State of Arkansas, that says a word about phone calls. What I do remember is that you're entitled to an attorney. Legal representation. That's what you're entitled to. But since you aren't charged with anythin', there's no need for a lawyer, and that means there's no need for a phone call." I motioned for Johnnie Young to open the door again.

Johnnie slowly shook his head and chuckled and opened the door. "He'll just shut it again, Big Ray. I'm tellin' you."

Leonidas Jackson stood up, but didn't step forward. I suspect he was waiting to see how I was going to respond.

"You got some handcuffs, Mister Johnnie?" I asked.

He smiled, and almost smacked his lips. "Up at the front counter, where they always is."

I turned to Ricky. "Go grab me a pair, will you?"

Johnnie Young, Leonidas Jackson, and I all stood quietly looking at each other while we waited on Ricky to retrieve the handcuffs. He was soon back, and he held the cuffs, waiting for my instructions.

Leonidas Jackson stepped forward slightly and extended his hands. "I suppose I'm to be beaten once you've restrained me," Leonidas Jackson said. He straightened his back and bowed up like a rooster, as if to show resolve.

"What?" I asked.

"I believe you heard me."

"I hope I didn't."

"I asked if I should expect to be beaten once you have me restrained?" he replied.

"You reckon I need to cuff you before I beat you?" I asked. "Because I don't." I shouldn't have said it, but it'd been a long three minutes, and I was losing patience with the man.

For the first time in the conversation, Leonidas Jackson looked uncertain at how the situation was playing out. His eyes flashed back and forth from Ricky to Johnnie Young to me. He took a half step backward and pulled his arms across his chest, as if he was bracing for a blow.

I turned and took the cuffs from Ricky and looped them through the bars of the cell and then through the bars of the door, and clicked them together; chaining the door open. Then I turned to Johnnie Young. "This man is free to go. We don't seem to have any other business today, and neither does the county, so we don't need this cell. Town's already paid for it, so if he wants to stay here all day, that's his choice. Understand?"

Johnnie Young nodded, though I'm not sure he fully understood what was happening.

"In fact, if Mister Jackson wants to sleep here tonight, that's his choice as well," I said. "You just make sure this door stays open at all times." I turned to Leonidas Jackson. "As I said, sir, you've my sincere apology for any inconvenience we've caused you. You're free to go, and I sincerely hope you will."

I nodded an understanding to Johnnie Young and then left without further engaging with Mr. Jackson.

Ricky didn't say anything until we left the building, but once we were outside, he chuckled. "I'm not sure I've ever heard of that. You ever recall a man refusing to leave a jail cell?"

I got my smokes out and lit up. Ricky declined the offer of one. "He gets hungry enough, he'll leave," I said. "I just hope Mister Johnnie has enough sense to not let him back in once he's out."

"What do you suppose he wants? I mean really. Besides a free phone call to New York. He's after something."

"No idea," I answered. "But you're right, he's up to somethin'. I just don't know what."

"And here I thought it was going to be a quiet Friday," Ricky said, as we got to his car, and he started to get in. "You want me to check back in later?"

"No," I responded. "No, I want you to do like I've already told you. Go on home. This is your day off."

CHAPTER 4

Split Tree, Arkansas
Friday, November 8, 1963

W hat was left of the summer went quietly, and quickly. That preacher, Mr. Jackson, had moved on to somewhere else, and we hadn't had any more problems with him. Charley Dunn Skinner remained a splinter under my fingernail, but to be honest, even he'd stayed more or less out of trouble. I was starting to think that things were back to normal as we drifted into fall weather, when, about nine o'clock, I looked out of my office window and saw the sheriff come out of the courthouse building across the street. He didn't seem to have the usual spring in his step, and he walked like a man with a big lump of worry in his shoes. As I watched, he got into his car and drove the hundred or so feet to my office; a minute later, I heard him come in the door and exchange greetings with Jewell Faye, though he was noticeably quieter than usual, and he didn't seem overly interested in how her husband's fishing had gone. Shortly, he made his way into my office, and I knew immediately that the day was about to turn sour.

"Big Ray, you got a minute?" he asked me as he sat down next to my desk. He put his hat on his knee. His voice was turned down a couple of notches from his regular volume, and his leg was humming nervously, and it made his hat hop around like a jumping bean.

"Of course," I replied. He looked a little bit like someone had just run over his favorite dog. Mainly, he wasn't smiling, and that said a lot. I've known Ben Cooper my whole life and usually you can't beat the smile off of his face if you used a long stick cut for that purpose. There was something bearing heavy on him. "You look like Marley's ghost there, Cecil Ben," I said. "All weighed down and all. What's the matter?"

He hesitated. "You heard anythin' about Ring Johnson?"

"Ring? No. Can't say I have. I haven't seen him for a while. Somethin' wrong with him?"

Ben fidgeted with the brim of his hat. "And just when was it you seen him last?"

I shrugged. "I don't know. Couple weeks probably. Saw him at the hardware store a while back. He was buyin' a tack hammer and some rabbit wire, I think. That was probably the last time. You got a reason for askin'?"

He hesitated. "Looks like he went and killed hisself."

"Ring did? Damn." I hesitated. "When'd that happen?"

"Not sure." He shrugged.

"What do you mean, you're not sure?"

"I just found out myself. Looks like it was a little while ago. That's all I know. That's why I was curious when you seen him last. I can't say I've seen him any more recent."

"Sorry to hear that. I know you two were close."

"Yeah. Can't necessarily say close, but we're friends. Damn shame."

The window behind my desk was opened a couple of inches to let in some air, and I flicked my cigarette butt out into the yard and leaned back in my chair. "Granville know?" Granville Begley is one of the town's three doctors. He's one of my best friends, and also one of the best people I've ever known. He's also as the Locust County Coroner.

"Called him as soon as I heard. Got his wife. She said she'd get ahold of him, and send him along as soon as she could. I sent a deputy out to Ring's place already, and I'm goin' out there now myself."

"How'd it happen?"

"Looks like he blew his dang head off with a shotgun. Can you believe that? I haven't been out there yet. Just heard about it myself, not twenty minutes ago."

"Damn. Who found him?"

"Jack Tyler. That's who reported it. Ring's been lookin' to buy Jack's truck. That old Chevy of his. Ring said he'd get back to him with an offer, but Jack says he hasn't heard anythin' for a while, so he stopped by to give him a nudge on it."

"But no real idea when it happened?"

"Hell, didn't you just ask me that?" he snapped, and then he caught himself. "Sorry, Big Ray. No, I don't know. I'm hopin' Doc can tell us. Weren't in the last couple of days, I know that. From what Jack was tellin' me, I guess it's a damn holy mess. All kinds of bugs had time to get after him. Week, maybe a couple, but I'm just guessin' here."

"And Jo?"

Ben fidgeted more with his hat. "That's why I'm here? Mostly. About her."

"Why's that?"

He shook his head and leaned forward. "We don't know where she is. Jack says there weren't no sign of her anywhere, and he says he checked the place pretty damn good. You know, just to make sure she was okay. She ain't answerin' the phone neither. I tried."

"That's no good."

"Nossir."

"And the boy?"

"Neither of them."

"Damn, Ben. Jo's some kind of kin, isn't she?"

"Yeah. Wife's cousin's niece," Ben answered. "By marriage."

"And the family hasn't heard from her? You checked with them, I guess."

"She ain't that close to them." He looked down at his hat and then up at me. "I hate to ask you this, Ray, but . . . would you mind comin' out there with me? I'm headin' out there now, and I . . . I mean . . ."

"Of course, Ben."

"It's just . . ."

I stood and picked up my hat. I felt my hip pop from sitting too long. "You don't need to tell me your reasons. You asked, and that's good enough."

He stood up at the same time. "No it ain't. Truth is, I'm not sure what's goin' on with this, but I'm afraid somethin' ain't right. Got a feelin', you know? Right here." He tapped at his gut.

"Ben—"

He held up a hand to quiet me. "I've been elected sheriff of Locust County for goin' on nineteen years now, but I know what I am, Ray. I may bullshit a good line come election time, but deep down I know my limitations. I'm good at overseein' a tax sale or executin' a summons, maybe catchin' some high school kids hot-roddin' on a back road, but not for somethin' like this. Somethin' just ain't right about this. Don't feel right. Maybe old Ring just up and blew his head off. Maybe that's all there is to it, and maybe Jo and the boy are off somewhere; on a holiday or somethin', but . . ."

"It's all right, Ben," I said, as I started walking toward the door. "Want to take one car?"

Ben followed me. "I wouldn't ask but for this feelin' I got. If there's somethin' wrong here, there ain't a better person in this world to figure it out than Big Ray Elmore."

CHAPTER 5

Locust County, Arkansas
Friday, November 15, 1963

Ring Johnson has about fifty acres a few miles due west of town; about thirty of those in cotton and the remainder in beans and cowpeas and occasionally, when the forecast is favorable, a little sorghum. He's not a big farmer by today's measure, but he manages to break even most years. He also has a clean little three-bedroom house with a garage and a barn and a workshop and tool shed in the back. The house was built about four years ago after a tornado picked up his old one and deposited it on the other side of the road one April afternoon. Ring and Jo and their son, Joe Dennis, had been at a church picnic at the time, otherwise they might have been deposited across the street as well. Ring'll tell you that them not being in the house when it happened is just another example of God's boundless mercy. I think before I started handing out the accolades, I'd be inclined to ask God just whose idea it was to pick up my house in the first place, but that's just me.

Ben Cooper rode with me. He was silent for a good while before he spoke up.

"Cotton's about ready," Ben finally said. He was looking out the window at Ring's fields as we drove past. "Goin' need harvestin' soon."

I have serious doubts that Ben Cooper really cared about the state of the cotton crop, but he obviously needed to talk, and so I tried to oblige. "It is ready," I answered. "What little there is of it. Pretty poor showin' this year. Beans are a little late, but the cotton's ready to go."

"Well, it don't look ready."

"May not, but it is. Trust me. Past ready, and it's not goin' to get any better for waitin' longer. Needs to be brought in before it rains."

"Not much chance of that. They say this is the driest year on record."

"I think they say that about every year."

"I think you're right."

"Last few years have been bad, though. No denyin' that. Haven't had a good spell of rain in five or six years," I said.

"Ever since we had that rainmaker in here. The one that hung hisself," Ben said.

The Rainmaker's death isn't something I like to think about if I don't have to, and I was near the end of my store of small talk, so I didn't respond further. Ben finally shifted the conversation closer to what was bothering him. "Who you suppose is goin' take care of Ring's crop now?"

"I reckon that's the least of his problems." Despite myself, I was still thinking about the Rainmaker case, and my response came out harsher than I'd intended.

"I suppose you might be right," Ben responded. He hadn't taken offense at my tone. "I guess I was really thinkin' about Jo. How could someone do a thing like that? What makes a man do that?" He continued looking out the window, but he went silent again and didn't say another word.

We got to the house two or three minutes later. There was a Locust County Sheriff's car parked by the mailbox, and one of Ben's deputies was sitting on the hood, presumably controlling access to the property. He was a young kid, and his name is Chester Bean, but he answers to *Pinto*. I've dealt with him a few times, and I've always found him to be as thick as a gum stump in winter. The Beans come to stupid naturally. He nodded and grinned and waved as we pulled into the driveway.

Ben got out of the car and adjusted his hat and his belt, and then his hat again. Some of it was habit; some of it was stalling off the inevitable of dealing with what happened to Ring.

We stood quietly for a moment, doing nothing. "We waitin' on Granville?" I finally nudged him.

He shrugged reluctantly and adjusted his belt again. "I don't know. Not sure when he'll show." He looked around and then out to the road. He paused and then walked down the driveway to talk to his deputy.

While he did that, I went over to the garage and opened the door. It was empty, or at least Ring's car was gone. I left the door ajar and walked back to my own car and leaned against the quarter panel and smoked a cigarette while Cecil Ben continued to exchange a few words with Pinto. I watched Ben clap his deputy on the arm and give him instructions of some sort, and then he slowly walked back towards me, shaking his head the whole way.

"Sounds like Granville was here but went on home to change clothes. He'll be back shortly," Cecil Ben said.

I took another long drag on my cigarette. Maybe I was stalling off the inevitable as well. I pointed at the garage. "His car's gone," I finally said.

Ben Cooper looked and nodded. "Yessir. So I see. Don't know what to make of that."

"Jo doesn't drive, does she?"

"Not that I've ever known. I think Ring's tried to teach her a couple of times, but he don't got no patience. If I had to bet money, I'd say the teachin' probably didn't go well. As far as I know, she never learned."

"So she probably isn't drivin' it."

He nodded some more. "Probably not."

"Worth puttin' the word out to be lookin' for it."

"Good idea."

"Probably should tell the sheriffs in Lee and Phillips counties. Desha County too."

"Yeah."

"Across the river as well."

"Soon as we get back."

We both went silent again.

I finished my smoke before I spoke up. "So, what now? You want to wait on Granville or not?" I asked.

"I don't want to do any of this at all if I'm bein' honest, but I don't think what I want much matters."

"Fair enough. Mind if I have a quick look-see in the house?" I asked.

"Go ahead."

"Why don't you come with me? We'll hear Granville when he drives up. Maybe you can set your mind at ease about Jo and the boy. Maybe we'll see somethin' that Jack Tyler missed."

He agreed. We looked around the house, quickly, upstairs and down, but we found nothing to indicate where Jo Johnson or her son may have gone. That was the bad news. The good news was that nothing suggested a struggle or that anyone had left in a hurry or against their will, but it did little to set Ben's mind at ease.

We went back outside to wait on Granville, and we both leaned against the back of my car, and I smoked another cigarette.

"It's bad enough as is, Ben," I said, after a minute or two of silence. "I won't try to tell you that it's not, but let's not imagine the worst. Let's wait and see what we have first."

"But it's got to be him," he replied. "Jack knows Ring as good as anybody. Somethin' ain't right."

I listened to Ben repeat himself several times about how his gut told him something was wrong. We were still doing that seven or eight minutes later when Granville's old Ford Fairlane pulled in and stopped behind my car. I looked at my watch. It was almost nine thirty. I figured the news would be all over town by now.

It took Granville another minute or two to get out of his car. He turned seventy-eight a few months back, and it's definitely starting to show. He can still outwork men a third his age, but he's slower, and I've been noting for the last couple of years that he's starting to move like an old man whose back and knees hadn't paced themselves for the whole journey.

"Boys," he said. "Awful damn way to end a good week." He was from western Tennessee originally, and he still had a soft, rubber-band twang to his voice that fifty years living in the Arkansas Delta hadn't smoothed out. He slowly worked himself free from the front seat of his car. Granville's not an overly tall man, but he projects big. I'm six four or so, but I don't think of myself as being taller than him. In his day, before age started to kink him up, he may have been a solid six-foot tall, probably no more than that, but like I say, you think of him as being much bigger, and watching him unlimber from the driver's side of his car, you'd still think a giant was emerging. Just an aging one.

"Granville," I responded.

Ben didn't say anything, but he nodded a greeting. The fact that Ben was quiet didn't go unnoticed by Granville.

"Sorry about this, Cecil Ben," Granville said. "I know you two were close."

Ben nodded again and swallowed hard. "Not necessarily close, but friends."

"The Donnies not here?" Granville asked. The Donnies referred to Donnie Hawk and his son, Donnie Junior. Donnie runs the largest funeral home in Split Tree, and his son is learning the business now that he's out of high school. Donnie Senior is about the closest thing to a brother that I have left in the world.

"Not yet," I responded.

"We got us a damn mess on our hands, Raymond," Granville looked at me and said. He pointed to the rear of the property, where the tool shed stood. "Been back there yet?"

"Waitin' on you," I replied. I got my Luckies out and chain lit another one.

Granville got his own cigarettes out. He smokes unfiltered Camels like R. J. Reynolds pays him to do it for a living. He lit one up and blew the first lungful of smoke away before he responded. "Well, it's enough of a mess that I went home and changed clothes. I wasn't dressed for this. I was out at the Dumas place. One of their brood broke his arm for about the tenth time." He took another long drag on his smoke and exhaled. "I tell you this as a fact, I've never seen a family that breaks as many bones as that bunch of monkeys."

"What do you think about Ring?" I asked. Aside from slowing down physically the last few years, Granville's mind was also getting more prone to straying if you didn't keep a firm string on it. I tugged him back.

"Hmm. Oh. Well, as I said, a mess. Damn mess," he replied. "That's what I think. If it's even him."

"You ain't sure?" Ben Cooper finally wedged into the conversation. There was a hopeful tone to the question, as if maybe this whole thing was a misunderstanding somehow.

"Not sure of anything at this point. Wait until you've seen him, Cecil Ben," Granville answered. "No reason to doubt it, but whoever is back there, he could have stuck his head in a cotton bailer, and he'd be more recognizable than he is now." He looked at his watch and made a face. "I guess there's no point waiting on the Donnies. They'll come when they come. Always do." With that, Granville started walking toward the rear of the property.

Ben and I followed. I'd leaned against the side of my car too long, and my right leg had stiffened, and it was slow to want to work right. I limped the first few steps. I have a seven-inch plate and sixteen stainless steel screws holding my right thigh bone together. The Navy docs who patched me together did a remarkable job, and I know that

I'm lucky to even have a leg to complain about, but with each passing year it gets a little more stiff and the pain almost never leaves me alone anymore. If I were prone to drink, it'd be a problem.

"Any sign of Josephine and the boy?" Granville asked. "What do we know about them?"

"Nothin'," Ben answered. "We searched the house. No sign of them. That's got me worried. Got me worried plenty."

"Well, first things first," Granville responded. "First things first. Let's deal with what we do have, and that happens to be a dead body. I haven't talked to Jack Tyler yet. I understand correctly that he's the one who found him? Can I assume he didn't touch anything he shouldn't have?" he asked over his shoulder as we walked. "Either of you heard anything different?"

"He said he didn't mess with nothin'," Ben replied. "He told me he'd come straight from here when he was in my office. I asked him that specifically. He said he didn't touch nothin'."

"You may want to light up a cigarette before we get much closer," Granville said to Ben.

Ben shook his head. "Not much in the mood for a smoke," he said quietly. "Maybe later."

"It isn't about the nicotine," Granville answered. "It's pretty aromatic back there."

"I hear you," Ben said.

"Have it your way. I don't think you do, but don't say I didn't warn you."

"You know where Jack Tyler is now?" I interrupted them.

"No, but he said he'd meet us out here. I'm surprised he's not here yet," Ben answered. "I hope he's not spreadin' the news about town. I told him not to. That'll happen soon enough as is."

Granville was right; you could smell Ring Johnson long before you could see him. The nights had been dipping down into the thirties, but the days were still hitting the upper sixties and lower seventies, and inside the tool shed, it was considerably warmer than that. From the smell, even with the door closed, it was clear that he'd been cooking for a while. The whole building buzzed with flies.

Granville opened the door and stood aside. I'd been to enough of these that I knew he was letting the first wave of hot air and smell out and not just being polite for us. Ben either didn't understand, or didn't think, and he started in first, without waiting, and just as fast, backed up like he'd been smacked in the forehead with a stiff board.

"Holy Jesus and pancakes," he said, as he staggered backward. "Jack Tyler told me it was a mess, but I . . ."

Granville waited a few seconds longer and then pushed in past Ben, who obviously had no intention of going back in, but who remained rooted in front of the door. "A shotgun will do that to you, Cecil Ben. That's why I always tell people not to point one at their head," Granville said. "Tends to be messy."

I went in behind Granville, but Ben stayed just outside, his arm up across his face and his nose buried in the crook of his elbow. It wasn't entirely clear what was harder for Ben to contend with, the sight of his friend or the dripping stink that immediately covered you like a thin oily film.

It was dark inside the tool shed. There was a light hanging from the ceiling, but it didn't come on when I pulled the chain. The open door provided some illumination, and a small cracked-pane window let in some more, enough anyhow that you could see all the way to the back, once you let your eyes adjust. It was cramped inside, and the flies were thick and as noisy as a shook beehive, and not in the least way happy that the door had been opened. Ring Johnson was seated with his back pressed against the rear wall of the tool shed, looking like he was taking a break from work; except for the fact that he had no head and his belly was a mass of roiling maggots. He was wearing a pair of overalls and what looked to have been a white shirt once upon a time. He'd slumped a bit to his right and was leaning against a workbench that ran along the side wall. With the bugs, and with the heat, he was well into decomposing. He had a bolt-action shotgun on his lap, the long, tapered barrel angled off to the side. What was left of his right hand, which wasn't much, was curled around the grip, the bony stub of his index finger on the trigger.

"You know guns better than I do, Raymond. What can you tell me?" Granville asked.

I hooked the toe of my boot under the barrel and lifted it slightly so that I could see the end of the muzzle. "Looks like a sixteen gauge. Full choke," I replied. "Mind?"

"Go ahead."

I reached down and picked the gun up, careful to avoid handling it more than I had to. Ring Johnson's arm fell stiffly back into his lap. I shook a couple of fat maggots off of the stock. "Looks like a Mossberg. Model One Ninety, I think."

Ben Cooper heard me and poked his head partially into the open doorway. "Ring has a Mossberg One Ninety," he said into the crook of his arm. "I've been duck huntin' with him before. He likes that one. Is it him?"

I turned the gun over in my hands. "Well, that's what this looks to be. Mossberg. Good lookin' gun."

"Is it him?" Ben repeated.

"Patience," Granville replied to him. He puffed a thick cloud of cigarette smoke. It helped to mask the smell and kept all but the most-adventurous flies out of his face. He slowly knelt down and looked at the body from different angles, while he poked and prodded with his fingertip.

I set the shotgun on the work bench and turned back to Granville. "How do we want to do this?" I puffed my own cloud of blue smoke.

Granville shook his head as he slowly stood up, his knees popping loudly. "If you mean manhandling this mess, then the answer is *we* don't. We'll let the Donnies take care of this. I've seen enough for now. Why don't we go outside in the fresh air while we wait? Get away from these damnable flies if nothing else."

We moved outside, and Granville started up a new smoke. Ben had backed a few feet further away. He was no longer breathing into his elbow, but I also noticed that he was taking shallow breaths through his mouth rather than his nose. Granville noticed as well.

"Cecil Ben, we won't know if it's Reginald for sure until I get him back to the funeral home, and we damn sure won't know what exactly happened until I can examine him properly. I wish I could tell you more now," Granville said. "I suspect it's him, but it's hard to know for sure. I will say though, if it's not Ring, then he'll have some serious explaining to do when we do find him. But first things first, we need to deal with this body, and that means waiting on the Donnies. In fact, why don't you do me a favor and go out to the road and look for them. They should be here by now. Send them on back this way when they show up," Granville said.

"You sure?" Ben asked.

"Yes. Yes. Raymond and I can watch over this. I doubt this old boy is going anywhere."

Ben didn't have to be prompted more than once. He adjusted his hat and belt and then quickly walked back to the front of the house happy to feel useful, and to get away from the sight and the smell.

Once he was out of earshot, Granville smiled sympathetically. "I don't think old Cecil Ben much appreciates the fragrance of decay."

I put out my smoke and lit up a new one as well. "It's an acquired taste," I replied.

"I'm sure you've seen more than your share."

I shrugged at that and redirected the conversation back to the matter in front of us. "This one cuts closer to home for Ben than most."

"I know it does. That why you're here? We're in Ben's jurisdiction now; you don't have to be."

"He asked."

"Well, I'm glad he did. So, what's your first impression?"

"My first impression is that Ben's got a big problem on his hands."

"I don't know that I disagree, but why do you say that?"

I took a long drag on my cigarette while I thought about what I was going to say. "I don't have any reason to doubt that's Ring Johnson in there, despite the condition of the body."

"Me either. But? I detect a *but*."

I looked around the yard and at the house, and then back to the tool shed. "But whoever it is, he sure didn't shoot himself."

CHAPTER 6

Locust County, Arkansas
Friday, November 15, 1963

D onnie Hawk and his son arrived around ten thirty. Granville and I smoked some cigarettes and talked, and tried to stay out of their way so that they could do their job. Donnie mostly directed his son, who wrapped Ring's body in a sheet and then in a waterproof canvas tarp, and then I helped them carry the bundle to Donnie's truck. Ordinarily, Donnie uses his hearse to pick up bodies, but for cases like this he prefers the open-air bed of an old truck he acquired a few years back. It's not dignified, but it's practical.

Ben Cooper stood a few feet further back from us, the whole time hovering on the fringe, shifting weight from one foot to the other like a schoolboy needing badly to pee, and repeating to himself that he couldn't understand how a man could do such a thing. I watched him, and finally suggested that he take another look around the inside of the house. I didn't think there was much to find, but I didn't say that, and I certainly didn't think that even if there was something to find that Ben would recognize it if he saw it, but I didn't say that either; he was working himself into a state, and he needed the diversion.

I guess I look at these things different. I have my own slab of scar tissue that shades the way I see things. I've never fully told anyone about what I saw in the war, and when I have, it's not been in much detail. Not many people would understand. I've told Sam Green some of the story. Sam Green is an old friend. He's a Negro preacher with a church out east of town. I've known him my whole life; he was my father's friend, and now he's mine. He'd gone off to his own Great War to make the world free, and then he came home, lungs scarred from chlorine gas, only to find that his service to democracy mattered very little to his neighbors, most of whom still held a serious grudge against Mr. Lincoln. I'd say if anyone does, Sam has all the reason in the world to have a case of the ass for his fellow men, but he doesn't. Instead, he came back home and buttoned on a white collar and committed himself to trying to save souls. I wish him well, but I can't say that I share his optimism. I've come to the conclusion that not many of us are worth the effort to save. But, I also know that Sam's seen more evil than most men should have to see in ten lifetimes, and I know that if anyone could come close to understanding what I saw, and did, and why I did it, it'd be him. So I've told him some of my story.

Actually, it's not that complicated. I was a corpsman in the navy in February 1945 when I washed ashore with the Fifth Marine Division on a small Jap-held island. Goddamn flyspeck that our generals thought they wanted as much as the Jap generals thought they did. I guess, compared to some of the other slaughterhouses, it wasn't as bloody as it could have been those first couple of days, but it was bloody enough for me and the men I was with; that's all I know. That's the thing about dying. If you're the one doing it, the numbers don't matter, not if there are a dozen others dying with you, or a hundred, or a thousand. Or just one.

We'd landed in the morning and gotten off the beach as quickly as we could, just like we were trained to do. They drilled that into you, but you didn't need to be told. Getting off that damn beach was what you wanted to do more than anything; no one in their right mind wanted to remain exposed out there like that. All that soft, glassy sand that sucked at each step you tried to take, like it wanted you to take root and stay.

That was nineteen years ago next February.

I can't say I know what kind of casualties they were taking anywhere else, but on our little piece of the island that day, we soon had more than we could handle. Kids were dropping like dry leaves without a breeze to blow them, and soon we had a too many down and nowhere to shelter them. One would drop, and then another. And another. After a while, I remember looking around that morning and realizing that I was one of the few men still walking. I remember thinking that something needed to be done and that there weren't many options. There was a shallow blast crater nearby; it didn't really provide much in the way of shelter at all, but it was all that there was. Just this shallow depression in the soft, sucking sand. So, I pulled some dead bodies together and stacked them up two and three high around the lip of the crater to form a partial wall around the wounded. I didn't really think about it; just did it. Some were Jap dead, most were ours. The color of the uniforms didn't matter. Neither did the color of the skin. At that point, they were just human sandbags to me. Red and green sandbags. And I stacked them up. It worked. After all these years, I can still hear that dull wet slap of bullets burying into the bodies of those poor souls; all these years later I still know there's a forgotten corner in Hell that's reserved just for me.

I also remember all of the boys I tended to that morning; their faces anyhow, every one of them, but there's one who particularly sticks out. He was a skinny eighteen-year-old kid, not much bigger than a large sack of red potatoes, and I didn't know him from Adam's house cat other than I'd met him on the troop ship coming over. He'd gotten a tattoo in some back alley off of Hotel Street in Honolulu. It was a seahorse, I remember, and it got infected, and I gave him some antiseptic salve a few days before we landed. Dolski was his name. Polack, I guess. He was from Wisconsin or Ohio; some sad place like that. He was big-toothed and all anxious to kill him some yellow Japs for God and country; anxious to earn himself a medal and get on home; probably to some freckle-faced girl who he'd known since grade school. One who'd wait for him, and who'd fix his meals and iron his clothes and bear his babies, but would never be able to understand why it was he'd changed or what it was that changed him. The problem for kids like Dolski is that the Japs had their own God and country, their own medals and their own young girls waiting at home, and one of them Japs just got to him first. No more complicated than that. I don't know what it was, a bullet or a piece of shrapnel, but whatever came zipping out of the jungle with his name on it that morning took his left arm clean off right below the shoulder. He was standing next to our bomb crater when it happened, and I heard something like a tree branch snapping off, and when I looked up, I saw him spin like a top a couple of times and then drop; spurting blood like a fountain in a park. I crawled over to him and got him pulled behind the wall of bodies so I could work on him without getting him shot up even more. He was bleeding out so fast that I didn't even take time to give him any morphine. I should have; I wish now I had. Instead, I let that boy suffer. In my arrogance, I was God; I could save him.

That's what it was: Arrogance. Pure and simple. I recognize that now.

He was bleeding badly, the brachial artery had snapped back into the stub of his arm, and I had a hard time trying to get hold of it and tie it off. In fact, it was so shredded that I never could get it completely closed down, and there wasn't much left of his arm to put a tourniquet on. I did finally get my belt partly around what remained of it, and I slowed the loss of blood some, and there was a wounded Marine in the crater, he was from another unit and I didn't know him at the time, but he had a chest wound that I'd treated, and he was still mobile; he helped me cinch the belt tight, and he laid on that boy's shoulder to try to keep pressure on the wound while I got a line into his other arm.

In my arrogance, I was cocksure I could save him. I gave him what little plasma I had left, but he soaked that up like a hot board on a dry boat dock, and it was gone almost in the time it took me to find his vein. He was bleeding out so fast, and I was losing him even faster, and there wasn't time to go looking for more plasma. All the time he kept looking at me; looking up at me and calling me *Pop*; asking about his mother; telling me how cold he was and asking me to help him. He was cold. That's the part that I remember most. As hot as it was, and it was hot; the sort of heat where you can't take a breath without it feeling like you have a sack of wet concrete on your chest; the sort where the air sticks to your skin like it was blackstrap. It was so hot, and he was cold. Maybe if you're an eighteen-year-old kid, your arm blown off at the root, losing blood like you're pissing it away into a ditch, maybe you think it's cold. Maybe it really was to him. Maybe it doesn't matter, but it still sticks out in my mind. I remember that soft, squeaky voice like he's standing at my shoulder right now, whispering in my ear. *I'm cold, Pop. I'm cold. I'm so cold.*

I let that boy suffer. And for what?

I can't tell you why I did it. I can't be that honest with myself. I should have jabbed him with some morphine and let him go, but I didn't. I should have just released the tourniquet and let him go quickly. But I didn't. Arrogance. I was God. I could save him. Instead, I jerked the tube from the plasma bag and got another needle fixed to the other end, and I plugged him into my own arm. I'm O-negative; what they call a universal donor, so I knew he could take my blood if I could just get it into him. The problem is that his veins were shutting down and not wanting to take anything. I had to raise up and lean over him to get enough gravity to make it flow into him. But he was losing blood fast, and so I kept rising up, higher and higher, until I was l almost standing over him. He kept telling me how cold he was; his voice getting quieter and more childlike, like he was giving up on me. Dying is like that. It often doesn't come with a gasp or a moan or a rattle. Sometimes, it's more like a campfire burning out. The embers slowly fade and all of a sudden you realize that it's not throwing off heat any more, but instead it's sucking the warmth out of you. I stood over that boy and felt him sucking the heat out of me, and all the while he looked at me like he knew I was going to fail him.

He was right. I did fail him. I'm not God.

I never heard the explosion or saw the blast, or if I did, I don't recall it. The last thing I remember is standing over him, getting cold myself and light-headed, bracing myself against my make-shift wall of bodies and wondering which one of us was going to bleed out first. They told me later that a Jap mortar round went off behind me. I also heard it was one of those damn Kamikaze nuts. I kind of doubt that, but that's what they wrote; I'm sure it made for a better story in *Stars and Stripes*. I know one thing; I don't remember it. It doesn't matter either way really. I guess the wall of bodies that I'd stacked up caught most of the shrapnel, because none of the wounded were hit, and I'll take credit for that, but standing up like I was, I caught a piece of iron in my right thigh. I woke up a couple of days later on a hospital ship.

They said my war was over.

Even then I knew that was bullshit. It'll never be over.

I lost fourteen men that day. Boys. Kids. Men. Dolski was one of them. The last of them. Fourteen. All in one day. All in one hour. I've heard people say that there are no atheists in foxholes. I wouldn't know about that, but what I do know for damn certain is that there's no God hanging around in foxholes either. And I can also tell you that for eighteen years those fourteen men have visited me every night, eager to know why I'm not among them like I should be. Why I failed them like I did. Why I thought I was God. How I could be so arrogant and yet so lacking. Dolski is always at the front of the line, and he's always cold. And he's still suffering. And he's no longer smiling.

And so, when I hear men like Ben Cooper ask how someone could blow their own head off, I don't wonder. Not for one minute. I could tell him, if he really wanted to know. I can give him at least fourteen good reasons. In fact, sometimes it's waking up in the morning and finding the one good reason not to do it that takes all the effort that you can muster. It's waking up each morning and forcing yourself to earn your right to keep on living that takes all the will power that you have.

But that wasn't the case here. Ring Johnson hadn't blown his own head off, he'd had help with that, and watching Ben Cooper, it was fast becoming clear that it was going to be up to me to figure out who it was.

CHAPTER 7

Split Tree, Arkansas
Friday, November 15, 1963

Donnie and his boy drove the truck back to their place, and Ben Cooper rode back to town with his deputy, Pinto. To Ben's mind, Ring Johnson's death was a suicide, clear and simple, and while there was still significant uncertainty as to the whereabouts of Jo Johnson and her son, Ben didn't feel that their house required a guard to be posted in the driveway. I didn't agree with him, but I didn't argue with him either.

I followed Donnie and Granville and stopped long enough at the funeral parlor to watch Donnie Junior unload the body and get it wheeled inside. Donnie remodeled his place a few years back, and he added a new embalming room when he did, but he kept the old one in the back of his place in workable condition, and he uses it for decomposed and messy cases like this. He also lets Granville use it whenever there's a need for an autopsy, which, to be honest, in this county is pretty rare.

Granville and I stood around outside for a few minutes, tidying up our earlier conversation before we went inside. He told me he'd make a quick inspection of the body, but that he wasn't convinced that much in the way of an autopsy was needed. There wasn't any doubt in either his mind or mine as to what killed Ring Johnson; it was the *who* that we needed to figure out, but whatever clues there might be to that question, they were long past being detected by a medical doctor. He told me he'd stop by and fill me in later, and with that I drove back to my office.

It was shortly after noon when I got to the police station. As I got out, I spotted my office manager, Jewell Faye, sitting across the street on a bench on the courthouse lawn. I waved to her, and she responded with a wave of her own. She's had her lunch at that same bench three days a week for as long as I've known her, probably not missing more than a dozen days over the stretch, always eating a pimento-cheese sandwich and a yellow apple. About the only change to her routine is that she's recently swapped out her grape Nehi soda for something they're calling *Tab*. She tells me that it's a new diet drink of some sort, just like a girdle in a bottle; she says it tastes like it too.

Ricky Forrest looked up when I walked in. "Afternoon, Chief. You just getting back from the Johnsons' place?"

"Afraid so," I replied. "I stopped at Donnie's for a couple of minutes, but, yeah. Took longer than I thought it would."

"Jewell Faye told me about it. As bad as you expected?"

I put my hat down on my desk and opened the window a couple of inches to let in some fresh air; I still had Ring Johnson in my nose. I would for at least a day or two. I sat down and lit up a smoke. "Don't know if it was as bad as I expected, but only because I didn't know what to expect. It was some bad, though. Looks like that old boy was murdered at least a week ago; maybe longer."

Ricky Forrest was at his desk, more-or-less parallel to mine, about five feet away. He'd been working on some paperwork when I walked in. Prior to hiring on with me a couple of years ago, he'd done a short stint as a deputy for Ben Cooper, and before that he'd spent the better part of two years with the First Cavalry in North Korea, killing Red Chinese as fast as he could pull the trigger on his BAR. Now he's married and the father of a little boy. He deals with what he saw over there better than I do. Maybe because he killed his hundred or so men at a distance. I killed all fourteen of mine up close.

"You're not one to use words for no reason," he said. "Murdered? Not a suicide?"

I blew some smoke in the direction of the open window before I answered. "Let me ask you. You know Ring Johnson. If I told you to describe him, how'd you do it? Physically, that is."

Ricky leaned back in his chair and got his own smokes out and lit up. "Ring Johnson. Well, I'd say he's maybe mid-to-late thirties. Not much in the good looks department, but acceptable, I'd say. Light-brown eyes. Mud-brown hair; starting to thin on top. Real stubby arms and short legs. Medium build. Fairly muscular, but probably not more than most farmers around here. Shorter than most though. That whole family tends that way, but he's five-two, three, maybe, with his boots on.   One-thirty; one-thirty-five; though he's starting to show some extra around the middle. I've heard that Missus Johnson's a pretty good cook, so that shouldn't be a surprise."

I nodded. That was pretty much on the mark. "At least that's the way he used to look. We found him sittin' against the back wall of his tool shed. Head blowed off like you'd put a half-stick of dynamite in his mouth. He had a Mossberg One Ninety across his lap; what was left of his index finger in the trigger guard. The barrel was pointin' away to the right."

Ricky was nodding. Taking it all in, while I spoke. "I know that gun. I thought once about buying it from him, but he wanted more than I was willing to pay. Walnut stock. Variable choke. Sixteen gauge, right?"

"Yep. Ben Cooper's got it now." I didn't say anything else, but I watched Ricky begin processing the information. I don't know that I've met many men who can connect the dots faster than that boy. I gave him time, and it didn't take long.

Ricky leaned forward in his chair and flicked some ash onto the floor, and then parked the cigarette in the corner of his mouth. He held his hands out in front of himself, about two feet apart. "Barrel on that gun's got to be what, twenty-six, twenty-seven inches," he said, as much to himself as to me. He widened the distance between his hands. "With the stock . . . about . . . so." He took a long draw on his cigarette and turned his head and exhaled out into the room and then looked back at me. "Shot in the head?"

I nodded. "Under the chin or in the mouth, most likely."

"And he was seated on the floor?"

"He was."

We looked at each other for a moment.

"So you see the point," I continued. "That's more than Ben did."

"Sheriff Cooper has some emotional involvement that I don't," he responded graciously.

"Ben Cooper's got shit for brains most days," I responded less graciously. "But you're right. I'm more interested in what you think. How do you see it?"

He nodded. "What I see is that it wouldn't be easy. Not under the chin. Not sitting on the floor anyhow, and at least not if he was using his index finger to pull the trigger. That's a heavy weapon, it'd be hard to hold that way. You could do it, but not easily. Barrel's too long, and his arms are way too short to do it with much control. You could, but it'd be difficult. Awkward. But even then . . ."

"Go on."

"Well, mainly, I'd say, even if he did manage it somehow, a bolt-action sixteen gauge like that one kicks like a young mule. If he somehow was able to get the muzzle in his mouth, or under his chin, he couldn't have had much of a grip on it. The damn recoil would have sent it flying half way across the room. No way it'd be laying in his lap with the muzzle pointing away."

"Which means he probably didn't do it. And that means somebody arranged all that for us to find and hoped that Ben Cooper wouldn't ask any more questions than he had to."

"Which he didn't."

"Which he didn't."

"And no sign of his wife? Jewell Faye said that Sheriff Cooper was worried about her and the boy."

"No. Ben and I searched the house while we were waitin' on Granville to get there. I'm goin' to go back out there again later, but, no, not a sign. That's good and bad, I guess. At least there's no sign of a struggle of any sort. Of course, that may also mean that she left on her own doin', and that may mean she had a reason for doin' so. Their car's gone, but she doesn't drive."

Ricky shook his head. He was still working through it. "Missus Johnson's not a big woman, and that Mossberg's not for light-weights. I'm not saying she couldn't have done it, but it wouldn't be my first choice if I were her."

"Might not be a first choice, but it did a fine enough job."

"I'm sure it did, I'm just saying that if Kitty wanted to do me in, and believe me, there are some days that she gives it serious thought, I know she could find a dozen ways to do it without having to wield a six-pound shotgun that would knock her on her rear end. And Kitty's a bigger woman than Missus Johnson."

I flicked the butt of my cigarette out of the window. "I won't tell her you said that, but I agree."

"So where does that leave us?"

"At the beginnin', Ricky. Where else?"

CHAPTER 8

Split Tree, Arkansas
Friday, November 15, 1963

Ricky and I were still talking when we heard Jewell Faye Ivey and my other officer, Charley Dunn Skinner, come in the front door. That meant it was 12:55; Jewell Faye doesn't vary her schedule by hardly a minute or two, and she's always sure to be back at her desk by one o'clock. It was also time for Charley Dunn to check in. We only have two police cruisers that are working, and I take one, which means that Ricky and Charley Dunn share the other one. Charley Dunn had been driving around town making the morning rounds until he stopped for lunch; now he was checking back in at the station.

Jewell Faye made a predictable beeline to the coffee pot. She drinks coffee continuously, without regard to time or temperature, taking a break only for lunch and her new *Tab* colas, and now back to work, she was tanking up for the start of the afternoon. Charley Dunn came into the side office where Ricky and I were sitting. He has a small desk next to Ricky's, and he sat on the corner of it and lit up a cigarette. He wore a lot more smug on his face than is becoming on a man of his untested abilities.

"Big Ray. Ricky," he greeted us. "Lots of commotion this mornin'."

Ricky and I both nodded enough to acknowledge his greeting, but not enough to encourage him.

I waited while he got his smoke going. "How bad is it?" I asked. "The story made two loops around town yet, or is it still on its first go around?"

Charley Dunn laughed. "Definitely two. Maybe three already. Jack Tyler's holdin' court over at the barbershop right now. He says there are parts of Ring Johnson splattered all the way onto the ceilin'. That true? I'd like to see that."

"Son of a bitch," I said.

Ricky started to get up. "You want me to go over there?"

I motioned for him to sit back down. "No. Damage is done. I was hopin' to talk to folks before what they know gets all muddied up with what they've heard. Probably doesn't matter now; can't put the juice back in the tobacco." I looked at Charley Dunn. "So, what are other people sayin'? I don't care about what Jack Tyler's spreadin'. Not yet anyhow."

He shrugged. "Not too much. I'd say folks are mostly listenin'; not sayin' much."

"Any talk of a motive?"

"Couple versions," Jewell Faye said. She was standing in the doorway, holding her coffee mug between her two hands and blowing on it over the rim.

"That right? What are you hearin', Miss Jewell? Folks gettin' this sorted out in their minds?" I asked. Jewell Faye Ivey is possessed of an extraordinary memory. Moreover, she's a magnet for information. I suppose every town has someone like her; in our town, she's the one person that you can count on to remember almost every version of every story and piece of gossip that has been told in the city limits within her lifetime.

"Well, I can tell you all you need to know there, Big Ray," Charley Dunn started. He'd moved to his chair and propped his feet loudly on the desk as he turned and looked over his shoulder. "Jewell Faye, why don't you fetch me a cup of that coffee? Couple of sugars." He winked at her.

She didn't move.

"You know where the pot is. We each get our own coffee around here," I said quickly. Had I been close enough to backhand him, I would have. I have a low tolerance for rudeness. I suppose I have a low tolerance for Charley Dunn. I didn't look at him, and so I have no idea how he took it. Instead, I kept my eyes on Jewell Faye, and I nodded at her to continue.

Jewell Faye is more than capable of fighting her own fights, but she smiled at me anyhow. "Well, Chief, most people are still in the listenin' stage of this story, but that'll change soon enough. There's a couple versions startin' up already." She took a loud slurp of coffee. She has good manners, and I suspect it was meant for Charley Dunn's benefit.

"That was fast," I responded.

"Give it until tomorrow mornin'," she said. "You'll have a good half-a-dozen by then."

"So what's the award winner?"

She wrinkled her forehead and took another sip of coffee while she sorted out the details. "Well, the short version is that Jo and their new hired man ran off together, and Ring killed hisself over it. End of story."

"Ran off? They havin' trouble, were they?"

"Some say."

"Some?"

"Some."

"You don't?"

She shrugged. "I know what I've heard. They say Ring's been drinkin' more than he should the last few months. More than a few, really."

"I've heard that."

"I also know that Jo's not much for that. She was raised Pentecostal. Though her family thinks she strayed from the path when she married Ring."

"Marryin' a Baptist will do that." Jewell Faye was raised Methodist, but her husband Clement, when he's not fishing, is a Baptist, so I said that for her benefit.

"Don't I know it. No, the problem isn't so much the drinkin' as what comes from it. Some of the women also say Ring's become a mean drunk. Wasn't always, but is now." She took a long sip of coffee, quietly this time, and watched me over the lip of the mug.

"Not sure I'd agree with that. I'd say he was always bad at holding his liquor," I replied. "I know I've seen that side of him more than a couple-three times. What else?"

"Some say that he's started takin' it out on Jo and little Joe Dennis."

"Words or fists?"

"Both."

I looked at Ricky. *"You heard any of that?"* I asked.

He shook his head, and I looked back at Jewell Faye. "That I hadn't heard. She ever report it?" The Johnsons live out in the county, and she was related to Ben Cooper. If she'd reported it, I suspect it'd have been to the sheriff's office and not me. Even so, I like to think I'd have heard something.

"Not that I know. It's not really in her nature to air her laundry."

"Gettin' slapped around is exactly the sort of laundry that needs airin'. Any truth to it?"

"May just be gossip," Jewell Faye said. "But I think there is."

"How about the rest of it?"

She nodded and smelled her coffee. "If you ask me, I think Jo may have been steppin' out some on her own."

"That right? With this hired man you mentioned?"

"Some say."

"Who is he? I didn't see any sign of anyone else at the farm. He from around here?"

"No one seems to know much about him," she replied. "He just showed up, and Ring hired him to help to get the crops in. You know how it is this time of year. Temporary. Just for a few weeks."

"When was that? Because from what I saw today, Ring hasn't gotten his money's worth. His cotton doesn't look to have been touched. Neither have his cowpeas. If he has help, it doesn't show. But you don't know anythin' about him?"

She shook her head.

"But not from around here?" I repeated.

"Not from here," Charley Dunn spoke up, as if I'd asked his opinion. He was still leaning back in his chair, feet still on his desk, still looking pleased with himself, like he had a mouth full of thin molasses and no immediate plan to swallow. If he'd taken offense to my dismissing him earlier, he was making up for it by wedging back into the conversation.

"You know somethin' about this man, do you?" I asked him. I didn't want to involve him, but if he did know something, I wanted to hear it.

"I hear things too," he replied.

"Last I checked, you work for me. You hear things, I need to know it. How about sharin' them?"

He took a long draw on his cigarette and let the smoke out slowly. He clearly planned to share what he'd heard, but only on his terms. "I know what my cousin Carl says."

"Ring Johnson's temporary farm help seems like a funny thing for Carl Trimble to know anythin' about," I said.

Charley Dunn put his hands behind his head, and he leaned further back in his chair. "He knows lots of things. He has his sources. Carl Trimble's an important man in town. Probably the most important."

"He is at that," I said. *Carl Trimble is an ass*, is what I wanted to say. Carl Trimble is about the most worthless person I've ever met, and I've met my share, and the only thing that keeps him from being the undisputed king of the shit pile is that he had a father and an older brother who perfected being shitbags into an art form. They're both dead now, which leaves Carl with a good claim to being the most worthless person still alive.

Now, Carl's wife, Grace Louise Davis, she may be the best thing that God ever created. She and I were supposed to be married, but the war, and life in general, got in the way. After I was wounded, the initial reports that filtered home said that I was dead. Sadly, for many of us, that turned out to not be the case, but it took a good while for the real story to make its way back to Split Tree, and it took me even longer to make it back in person, and by then it was too late for us two. By the time Odysseus limped home, his Penelope had married Carl Trimble and had a son, Jimmie Carl. Part of me can't blame her. Her father, Judge Davis, was always charitable to a fault, and had died without much left in the bank, and her mother was bad ill, and that left Grace with more than her share of responsibilities to shoulder by herself. She needed security, and I was nowhere to be found. Another person I failed. I was mad at myself and bitter about it for a long time, in some ways I reckon I still am, but I guess I understand what Grace had to do. Doesn't make it one bit easier to accept. That's not why I think so poorly of Carl Trimble, though; my feelings for him go back long before that.

I looked at Jewell Faye. I was fixing to ask her more about Jo Johnson and the hired man when the phone in the outer office rang. She nodded for me to wait, and then stepped away to answer it, and I reluctantly returned my attention to Charley Dunn and picked up where I'd left off. "I find it interestin' that Carl Trimble would take much interest in who Ring Johnson hires as temporary help. Tell me, Officer Skinner, Carl got a reason for knowin' about this man, does he?"

"Like I said, he knows people. I think Jo Johnson told him herself."

Before I could respond, Jewell Faye called out from the other room. "Chief, you got phone call. Says it's long-distance."

"Long-distance?" I called back. "Not sure I know anyone long distance. Who is it?"

"Well, he says he knows you. Says his name's Art Hennig. He's with the state police in Little Rock. Says it's important. Says he's a friend of yours."

"I'll take it," I said.

CHAPTER 9

Split Tree, Arkansas
Friday, November 15, 1963

I guess you could call Art Hennig an old friend of mine. We've known each other now for almost nineteen years, though I've only met him in person twice. He used to be a firearms examiner for the Arkansas State Police over in Little Rock; now he's the director of their whole crime lab. Split Tree is a small place, and neither the sheriff's office nor my little department has the capability to do any real laboratory testing. Fortunately, we don't have much call to do that sort of thing, but on those few times over the years that we have, Art has helped me out.

The first time I met him was in 1945. He was with me that day in the bomb crater. He was the wounded Marine who helped me put the tourniquet on that kid's arm. The second time was a few years later when he hunted me down out of the blue. He showed up on my front porch one afternoon; said he wanted to thank me for patching him up. Despite my argument to the contrary, he thinks he owes me somehow. Truth is, I owe him. For not being among the ones who visit me at night.

"Doc," Art said when I picked up the phone. "Your old buddy Art Hennig here. How you been, bubba?"

"Fair to middlin', Art. How you been yourself?"

"Well, thanks to you and the good Lord, I'm alive."

"Aside from that?"

"Can't complain, can't complain," he answered. "Watchin' the calendar. One day closer to retirin'."

"That right? I'd think you're too young for that. I can't imagine what you'd do with yourself if you retired, besides drive your wife crazy that is."

"There's that. You're right about that part, but you see, there's these fish in a pond not far from here that are just beggin' me to come catch them. Just beggin', if you follow."

Ricky Forrest caught my eye.

"*Tell him I said hello,*" Ricky slowly mouthed the words.

"I'll bet they don't have to beg you too hard," I said into the phone. "Hey, before we go any further, I got Ricky Forrest sittin' here in the office. He wants to make sure I pass along his hello."

"Well, I'll be damned. I was wonderin' about him the other day. Still with you, huh? You tell him Art says hello back. Tell him also that we still have a job waitin' for him over in the big city just as soon as he gets tired of puttin' up with your grumpy old ass all day long."

I laughed and said, "I'll pass along your hello. Not sure he needs to hear the rest of that, though. I need him here too much." I winked at Ricky, and he nodded a response. Ricky got to know Art a few years ago when we had a case that required some bullet slugs being tested, and Ricky had to make numerous trips to Little Rock to carry the evidence back and forth. He'd impressed the state police, and Art made him a job offer. Fortunately for me, his roots are deep here, and neither Ricky nor his wife have any desire to leave Split Tree.

"Say, Doc, I know you must be busy over there in the buzzin' metropolis of yours, so I won't keep you but another minute; I got some news that you might want to know about. Check that. You need to know about even if you don't want it."

"That right? What kind of news?"

"Name John Christian mean anythin' to you? From Magnolia."

"No. Should it?"

"He turned up dead a few weeks back. Head bashed in like someone took a baseball bat to a ripe watermelon, if you follow."

"I don't follow. I'm sorry to hear that, but you're goin' to have to fatten that hog up a bit if you want me to buy it."

"How about Clyde Martin from Poteau, Oklahoma? Ringin' bells yet?"

"Afraid not. Battin' oh-for-two."

"All right. Here comes the fastball. You ready for it? How about Gilbert Gervais? That one should."

I nodded to myself as he said the last name. "Yeah. Yeah. Now, that one does. He's that old boy from Little Rock a couple of years back, isn't he? The one that drug that conventioneer behind his car. Took the man's head off."

"Bingo. And the unlucky conventioneer was named . . . ?"

"Well, I'll wager it was probably *Martin*," I answered, the name suddenly coming into context.

"That's right. Clyde Martin. He was one of the four. The unlucky one. One of the unlucky ones. See, Doc, senility hasn't quite got hold of you yet."

"No, but it's reachin' out for me with both arms. So what's the news? Aren't they about ready to put that Gervais fella down? His time's got to be comin' up soon."

"Well, that's why I'm callin'. Gervais, Gilbert, one each, broke out of Tucker Prison about two months ago, if you follow."

"Broke out?"

"More like ran off. He was on a work-farm crew. Out in the county for God's sake. Smuggled hisself out of there on a produce truck buried under a load of God dang melons is what I hear. Why they let someone on death-row out onto work crews, I have no friggin' idea, but I suspect they're rethinkin' that policy right about now. Don't seem too smart to me, but what do I know? I'm just a dumb state cop."

"Who wants to retire."

"Retire and catch fish. That's right. Anyway, Gervais got clean away before anyone knew it. Fortunately, as it turns out, he had hisself some help from a couple-three prison trusties, who I'll wager my next paycheck are no longer trusties. Well, it seems as if the friendly prison staff there at Tucker managed to persuade them trusties to tell all that they knew about the escape."

"I'll bet they did."

Art Hennig laughed. "You know, they tell me it's all in the way you ask," he said. "If you follow."

"That, and how many times you turn the crank," I responded. Tucker Prison Farm is famous for using an old crank telephone wired to a man's testicles to facilitate frank and candid discussions. I hope whatever motivated them to help Gervais was worth it to those boys.

"I'm guessin' it didn't take too many long-distance calls," Art continued. "Anyhow, a couple of those old peckerwoods admitted that Gervais' girlfriend, now I'm usin' that term politely, went and arranged it all. You remember her? She's that cute little Cuban gal that got roughed up by Martin and his three buddies. Remember her?. She's the one that started that whole mess."

"I only followed that case from a distance, but I do, sort of. From what I recall, I'm not sure you can say she started it, but go on."

"You're probably right about that; she may not have started it, but it looks like maybe she and Gervais damn well plan to finish it anyhow, if you follow. At least that's what one of the trusties on the other end of the telephone told them at Tucker. I asked you about John Christian; he was another one of the four amigos. Police down there in Magnolia say that neighbors saw a man matchin' Gervais' general description hangin' around Christian's house the same day he turned up beat to applesauce."

"Is that right? What a coincidence. Any sign of the woman?"

"Lidia Fernandez? Nope. Not that anyone's reported anyhow, but the concern around here is that that old coonass Gervais has got hisself a score to settle, if you follow. We've been asked to coordinate a statewide manhunt; that's how serious everyone's takin' this. That's why I'm callin' you. I wanted to notify you personal. Be-on-the-lookout, if you follow. We think they may be drivin' a seafoam green, nineteen sixty-one, four-door Chevy Impala. There was one reported stolen about two blocks from the murder scene; about the same time. We think they may have taken it. I also sent some photos of Gervais and the girl to you a little while ago. I put them on a Greyhound, so have one of your men check at the station in a few hours for an envelope. I figured that was faster than the mail. The photos are a couple of years old, but they'll do."

"I need photos, do I?"

"To recognize them?" He laughed. "A little Cuban gal and a Coonass the size of a tobacco barn? I doubt it."

"Then why?"

"You might want to post them around. The thinkin' at the head shed here is that Gervais is likely workin' his way over to your neck of the woods. The other two men involved in that Little Rock incident were from Split Tree, ain't that right? If this son-of-a-bitch Gervais is evenin' up the score, that's where he'll need to go to do it." There was the sound of some papers being shuffled. "Trimble. Carl Trimble and his brother. Have I got those names right?"

"Jay Trimble," I said, completing the thought. "The brother was named Jay. Only one of them was from here. Carl is. His brother Jay moved away years ago and lived up in Blytheville."

Art Hennig paused. "Lives or lived? You say *lived*? Where is he now? I probably need to get in touch with him."

"He disappeared not long after the killin' over in Little Rock. Been gone three years now."

"Gone? His disappearance don't got nothin' to do with Gervais and his girl, does it?"

"No. I'm sure of that."

"So, is this Jay Trimble just missin' or worse? Because I need to get hold of him if I can."

I hesitated. "Depends what you mean by *worse*. I think you can count on him bein' dead," I replied. "In fact, I'm sure of it."

Art Hennig paused. "Sounds like there's more to the story."

"Maybe there is."

"Maybe I'll ask you sometime."

"Maybe I'll tell you sometime."

He paused again, but didn't press. He shifted gears. "Well, that makes things a bit easier, don't it? If you're Gervais, you'll figure that out soon enough, and that makes three down and only one to go. For us, that's only one to watch. Is this Carl Trimble still around your area, or is he dead too?"

"No, he's alive. Unfortunately." I looked at Charley Dunn, who was still leaning back in his chair, still looking satisfied with himself. He obviously wasn't tracking my conversation.

"Sounds like there's more to that story, too." Art Hennig hesitated. "Maybe I'll ask about it sometime."

"Maybe I'll tell you sometime."

CHAPTER 10

Split Tree, Arkansas
Friday, November 15, 1963

I sent Charley Dunn back to find out what folks in town were saying about Ring Johnson. While he was busy doing that, I planned to take Ricky Forrest and go out to the Johnson house again and have another look around, but Ricky said he had another half-hour or so of paperwork to do, and he looked like he wanted to get it finished, and I wasn't in that big a hurry. We have to send our crime statistics to the FBI every year for inclusion in some sort of national report they put out. I'm not sure what the purpose of it is other than to show how bad it is to live in places like New York City. I'm sure their report is worthwhile for budgeting and planning in big cities like that, but for us, it takes longer to fill out and mail in the forms than we spend time solving the types of crimes we usually deal with. Situations like Ring Johnson are a rarity, and for the most part, what passes for a crime spree around here probably has more to do with some high-school seniors spray painting girls' initials on the town's water tank than anything else. I usually find a dozen or so reasons to avoid filling out the forms, but Ricky recently got himself a college degree in psychology, and he seems to have a real interest in the report that the FBI puts out, so when he volunteers to tackle it, I'm happy to let him do it.

While he tallied up how many cows got tipped over last Halloween, I decided to walk the couple of blocks home and check on my wife. I've known Ellen Mae my whole life; we were married shortly after I returned home from the war; shortly after I got back to learn that Grace Louise had married Carl Trimble. Ellen Mae is a fine woman, but she has a problem, and I don't mean being married to me. I don't know what it is exactly, and no one has been able to fully explain to me. I don't reckon it's really a disease as such, but it might as well be. Actually, it's more that sometimes she's like two different people, or maybe two different versions of the same person. She's always herself, but sometimes she's like a house on fire. She doesn't need to sleep or eat, and she'll talk an endless stream whether anyone's listening or not. The other Ellen Mae is tired and weepy and has no desire to do anything or talk with anyone. Sometimes she'll be like that for days; maybe a week or so. It usually comes on the heels of her other self. She calls the weepy times having one of her *spells*. Her last one was almost a month ago, and it lasted the better part of a week and left her wrung out like an old dish towel. Granville says there isn't anything to be done about it but to show patience. Kind of like hitting a slick patch of black ice; all you can do is grip the steering wheel tighter and hope you come out straight on the back end of it. Her mother had it too, but they covered for it better, I guess. She called it her *darkness*, which answers the mail about as well as calling it a spell. Folks used to always attribute her mother's problem to Ellen Mae's father running off with his young secretary. He got killed when his car stalled out on a railroad crossing up near Paragould. I don't know, but maybe her father's death affected Ellen Mae too. Maybe it did; maybe it didn't. She was just a young girl when it happened, and it must have been awful hard, but I have difficulty believing that's the sole root; mainly because it's getting worse with time not better. In fact, I think Ellen Mae's trouble started right after my twin boys were born, or at least that's when it got to a point where she couldn't hide it easily or joke it away. I don't know why that'd do anything, but that's when I think it started. That was seventeen years ago, and while it got better there for a few years, now it seems to be getting worse again; more frequent and lasting longer each time.

Mostly on account of it, I try to get home each day for lunch with her, especially during the school year when our boys aren't around as much. Sometimes, when she's way down in the bottom of a deep hole, she's not even aware that I'm there, but generally she does even during the worst spells, and I think she appreciates my presence, even if she's not in the mood to talk. Just having my company seems to help. She's a good woman and good mother, and I owe her my life. I was in bad shape when I got back from the war and the stay in the hospitals, and I would have done myself some harm were it not for her.

Ellen Mae was sitting on the sofa in the living room when I got there, folding laundry and watching *Search for Tomorrow* or *The Guiding Light* or something equally indistinguishable to me. She was well on the mend from her last tumble down the well, it showed in her eyes, but there was still something of a dry thinness to her. Brittle, like the cast-off shell of a summer cicada. I sat with her for a while and helped fold some pillowcases and some boy's underwear, the value of doing which escapes me. We didn't speak much, mostly out of deference to the young woman on the television who appeared to be crying at the news that she was adopted and that her fiancé might just in fact be her brother. Ellen Mae seemed to be taking the news considerably harder than the woman on the television. So we folded and commiserated quietly.

As soon as the credits began running, we moved to the kitchen and had lunch. Ellen Mae fixed us some fried egg sandwiches and opened a jar of pickled okra. I decided to tell her about the Johnsons.

"Ben Cooper came by the office this mornin'," I said.

"Is that right? And how is Cecil Ben?"

"Well, he's been better. He got some bad news this mornin'. Ring Johnson's dead."

"Ring Johnson?" she said. She wiped her mouth with a napkin and sat back in her chair. "Oh, my. Poor Jo. And little Joe Dennis. Oh, my. I need to fix somethin'. What happened? Was he sick?"

I shook my head. "Maybe, but that isn't what happened. Shotgun. Ben thinks it's a suicide."

"Oh, my dear Lord. *Suicide*," she repeated. Then she must have seen something in my face that I hadn't intended to put there. "You say Ben says that, but you don't?"

I took a long sip of tea and wiped my mouth with the back of my hand. "Too early to tell, I suppose. Granville's doin' an autopsy right about now, but . . ." I shrugged and let the thought trail off. I was walking a bit of a fine line. I wanted to tell Ellen Mae as much as I could, and I would, eventually, but I wanted to skip around some of the details for now. Other than Jewell Faye's retelling of town gossip, I had no real reason to suspect any marital trouble between Ring and his wife, but because of how Ellen Mae's father ran off, tales of marital infidelity, even when they are mostly baseless gossip, can be an emotional tripwire best avoided. And she was still getting over the news about the woman on the television being adopted.

She looked at me for a moment before she spoke. "If you don't think it was a suicide, then it wasn't. You don't need Granville to tell you that." She said that with some finality, and then paused again. "And I guess it wasn't an accident either."

"No."

"Where's Jo? And Joe Dennis?" she asked after a pause; the full implications starting to firm up in her mind. "Are they all right? I need to make a casserole."

I shook my head again. "Don't know. Ben and I went out to their place this mornin', soon after Jack Tyler reported it. He's the one who found Ring. We searched the house but didn't find any sign of her or the boy. I'm hopin' she's off visitin' friends." I didn't tell Ellen Mae that Ring looked to have been dead for some time.

Ellen Mae dropped her eyes to her half-eaten sandwich and slowly nodded. "Not suicide. That means . . . Oh my. Oh, my. In Split

Tree," she said quietly. Then she shifted gears. "Dear Lord. I don't know Jo Johnson well, but she doesn't deserve that. And the poor little boy. Dear, dear Lord." She shook her head slowly. "Here in Locust County. What are you goin' to do?"

"Ben was pretty shook up this mornin' when we were out there," I said, partly to keep the conversation headed away from discussing the Johnsons' marriage.

"His wife's kin to Jo, I think. You remember that?" she asked.

"I know. I do. He's takin' it harder than he lets on. I understand that, but it also means that he's not necessarily the best person to be investigatin' this. If it turns out to need investigatin', that is."

"You need to do it, Ray. Cecil Ben Cooper is a nice enough man, most days, but he's not up to somethin' like this on his best day. You don't need me to tell you that. If it's not a suicide, then . . ."

I sighed. "I know. I do. Ricky and I are headed out there in . . ." I looked at my watch. "Actually, he should be here any minute."

Ellen Mae stood up and took her plate to the sink. She still had several bites of her sandwich, but I'd managed to kill her appetite.

"You okay?" I asked.

She didn't respond.

"Ella Mae?"

She was looking out the window into the back yard. "Men can be selfish to the point of bein' cruel."

"They can." I knew it was only a matter of time before we got there.

"They say Ring has started drinkin'," she said after a moment.

"So I've heard. I also heard this mornin' that maybe he's been takin' it out on Jo."

Her back was still to me. She was nodding but said nothing. I don't know if she was nodding because it made sense somehow or because she'd heard it as well or because nodding just seemed like the thing to do.

"Well, one way or the other, it's an unfortunate thing," I said. "Bad all around. And gossip and speculation won't help it any. The sooner we get the facts sorted out, the sooner folks can get back to mindin' their own business."

"Folks here won't ever be satisfied mindin' their own business. That's not the way it works around this town. Never has been," she said quietly.

CHAPTER 11

Locust County, Arkansas
Friday, November 15, 1963

Ricky showed up right at one, and I left Ellen Mae cleaning the lunch dishes and staring out the rear window; though what she saw, I couldn't tell you. She'd turned quiet and had tucked into herself some, but whatever thoughts Ring Johnson was stirring in her mind, they didn't seem likely to trip the start of another one of her spells. Not yet, still, it bears keeping an eye on. I felt better knowing that our two boys would be home from school in a couple of hours, and while they'd quickly head back out with their friends, they'd stay long enough to eat a baloney sandwich and change out of their school clothes, and that would perk up her spirits again.

Ricky and I got to the Johnson place, and we went first to the tool shed. Donnie Hawk had propped the door open with a cement block earlier, to let the room air out some, and he said he'd send Donnie Junior back with some bleach and some pine cleaner, but that hadn't happened yet, and even with the door having been left open for a couple of hours, the stink was still pretty strong, and the flies were still thick when we got there.

I described for Ricky where the body had been, and how it had been positioned, though the stains in the wood and the rosette of dried blood and tissue told the story about as good as I could. I didn't tell him any more than I thought was necessary. I wanted his opinion, not mine. Ricky took it all in.

"I guess Jack Tyler was telling the truth," Ricky finally said. He was looking up at the ceiling as he did. "He's telling folks that there's residue as high as the ceiling."

"*Residue*? Jack Tyler said that?"

Ricky smiled. He'd gone to college, and he sometimes gets embarrassed when he uses a big word. "Sorry. No, but I'm not sure what else to call it."

"No. No. Good name. *Residue*. Yeah, there's *residue* all over, that's for damn sure, but then, that's a shotgun for you; it'll blow the *residue* clean out of your head." I lit a cigarette and offered Ricky one. He lit up.

"Seems odd, though," Ricky said. He exhaled a lungful of smoke forcefully, to chase off some curious flies.

"How so?"

He looked at the wall and back at the ceiling and back at the wall. "You'd think there'd be more. Wouldn't you? At least it'd be spread out more."

"More *residue*?"

He smiled and pointed to the wall. "Most of it's here, just like you'd expect, but it's pretty concentrated. If he was sitting here, like we think, and he tucked that Mossberg under his chin—"

"Which we know he probably didn't."

"Which we know he probably didn't, but if he did, you'd expect the res . . . the *shit* to be sprayed more upwards. Wouldn't you? I mean, I'd expect more up on the ceiling. At least further up the wall here. Instead . . ."

I exhaled my own cloud of smoke and waved some flies out of my face. "Which adds up to what?" I asked.

He shrugged. "I guess it just confirms what we already knew. He didn't sit down here and eat the end of that gun."

"Not willingly. But he was sittin' there when it happened."

Ricky nodded and leaned down to look at where some of the buckshot was buried in the wall. "I guess so, but I'd say the gun was more or less level. It sure wasn't pointed upward. Does that make sense?"

"It does if someone was standin' about where we are and leveled it at his head."

"Pretty damn cold, if you ask me. Shooting a man while he's sitting down."

"Not sure it's any less cold blooded to shoot a man who's standin' up."

"Probably right."

"You seen enough here?"

"For now. If you have."

"We'll leave these flies to their business. How about a look-see around inside the house? Remind me though to get a photograph of that wall before Donnie Junior cleans this mess up. Let's get a shot of the *residue*. Don't know if we'll need it or not, but better to have it than be sorry."

"I got it. I'll come back later and do it. I'll borrow a camera from the sheriff. He's got better ones than we do," Ricky said as we walked out into the fresh air. He unbuttoned his shirt pocket and took out a small note pad that he carries most of the time. He scribbled a note to Donnie Junior, telling him to not clean the walls without checking with him first, and then he pinned the note onto a nail protruding from the door.

We finished our smokes and then went inside the house. To be honest, I wasn't sure what else there was to see that I hadn't caught the first time around, but I also knew that I had a better pair of additional eyes with me this time. We checked the living room and the dining room. Both were relatively clean and didn't suggest that anything out of the ordinary might have taken place. The kitchen was a bit more cluttered, and I'm sure Jo Johnson wouldn't have wanted visitors to see it that way. There were a couple of dirty dishes in the sink, and the last of a loaf of store-bought bread was on the table, the wrapper open and the remaining slices dry. The lights in the house weren't working, and the refrigerator, which was mostly empty, was dark and warm. There were candles on the counter and table. The power was off.

The main bedroom had been slept in, though how recently was anyone's guess. The left side was wrinkled and soiled, and a light, summer-weight blanket and cover were pulled back. The bottom sheet had come out at the foot end, and the mattress was partially exposed, and the pillow was soiled and dented from the weight of a head. There was a copy of *True Danger* magazine on the nightstand on that side, a pair of men's glasses resting on the cover, and an opened package of Cannon Ball chewing tobacco. And more candles. The other side of the bed was made up and didn't look to have been disturbed recently. I pulled the bedspread down. The pillow was plumped and clean but didn't appear freshly washed. It looked as if someone had made the bed one morning but only half of it got slept in.

The closet had clothes in it, both men's and women's. I don't know either Ring or Jo well enough to be familiar with their wardrobe, so I couldn't tell whether much, if anything, was missing. There was clutter on the shelves above the hanging clothes: some hats, what looked to be a photo album, a shoebox of bank records, a jar of loose change. There also were several boxes of ammunition. A half-empty box of .38-caliber pistol rounds, and two boxes of sixteen gauge; one bird-shot and one of number-four buckshot. Both had a couple of shells missing. There was a box of twelve-gauge as well, and a Winchester twelve-gauge was standing up in the corner of the closet behind some pants. There was nothing else that seemed to warrant much attention.

The bathroom didn't tell us any more about what happened. The toilet seat was up, and it was unflushed, and there were some cigarette butts floating in a pool of dark, stale urine that smelled like old molasses. The boy's room, Joe Dennis's, also didn't appear out of the ordinary. There were clothes in the closet and the bed was made, but not freshly laundered. There were some toy trucks and painted-wood animals on the floor in front of the dresser.

The door to the third bedroom was closed, but we opened it and went in. It looked to be a spare guest room. The bed was made and the dresser was empty, as was the closet except for some cardboard boxes that had *Xmas Decs* written on them with a black grease pencil.

Ricky and I went back downstairs. Ring Johnson was dead and wouldn't care if we were there, and we had no idea about the whereabouts of Jo Johnson and her son, but still it felt like it was an intrusion, poking around in their belongings, looking in their underwear drawers and in their medicine cabinet. It needed to be done, but it wasn't pleasant, and I think both Ricky and I felt better going back to the more public part of the house to talk.

"What do you make of it?" Ricky asked me when we were downstairs in the living room. He sat on the arm of the couch.

"Goin' to ask you the same thing." I leaned against a worn upholstered chair. There was a stained sheet of newspaper on the floor and an old coffee can was on top of it, dried tobacco spit in the bottom of it. The paper was dated over two months earlier.

"I wonder how long the power's been off?" he said.

"Electric company can tell us. What else?" I asked.

"I'd like to know where his thirty-eight is."

"Could be anywhere. Glovebox of his car, maybe, if we knew where that was, or on his tractor. We always kept a snake gun close when we were workin' the fields. Why your interest?" I asked.

"It'd be more support that it wasn't suicide. Why use a heavy sixteen-gauge shotgun when you have a handgun?" he asked.

"To make sure. A thirty-eight isn't the most lethal round, and you got one shot to get it right. Screw it up and you're left a cripple, or a half-wit. A shotgun does the trick even if you flinch at the last minute. I saw more than one man in the war, with half his brains blown out, who couldn't die."

Ricky nodded. "Yeah, me too."

"So, what are you thinkin'?"

Ricky shrugged at that. "Just working through the details. Eliminating all the contingencies."

"*Contingencies*? Damn, son, you're full of big words today. Okay, what else you see?"

He got out his cigarettes and offered me one. We both lit up while he formed his response.

"I'd say Missus Johnson hasn't been here for a while."

"I'd say you're right, but I'm curious to hear your reasons."

"You mean aside from her husband decomposing noticeably next door?"

"Aside from that."

"Well, the beds are made. At least the boy's and her side of their bed. It looks like Ring might have been sleeping alone for a while."

"Doesn't mean she's gone. Maybe she just doesn't want to share a bed with him if he's takin' to drinkin' like they say. Especially if he's been abusive. All sorts of reasons to sleep apart."

Ricky almost laughed. "That's true, Chief. There's been more than one occasion when Kitty has me sleeping on the couch."

"But you're right. That's more the pattern, isn't it? The man moves, and yet, he's the one sleepin' in the bed. How often is it that you get the bedroom and Kitty's the one that moves out to the couch?"

Ricky nodded while he thought. "I believe that would be never. Sometimes she'll sleep in Eddie's room, if he's sick or having trouble sleeping, but never when we've been fighting. I do the moving."

I gestured to the top of the stairs, in the general direction of the bedrooms. "I agree with you. I don't reckon she's been in Ring's bed in quite a while. And I'm reasonably sure that he didn't make up her side of it, so that means that the last time she was in it, she made it up the next morning and hasn't been back." I took a long drag on my cigarette and let the smoke out slowly through my nose before I continued. I still had the smell of Ring Johnson in my nostrils. "What's your record for time spent on the couch?"

Ricky smiled. "Maybe three days. Usually it's just one. Sometimes not even the full night, but there was this one time . . ." He grinned. "She was madder than a wet cat. I think I spent three solid nights in the den."

"You probably deserved it."

"I did. There's no probably to it."

"Wait till you've been married longer. You're still an amateur. My record's a full week. Six nights, anyhow. And to this day, I don't know what it was that I did."

"Damn, Ray. I guess I've got something to look forward to."

I shifted back to the problem in front of us. "No, I just don't see Jo Johnson sleepin' on the couch; not even for one night. I don't know them all that well, but I just don't. She'd make Ring move. Maybe if it was bad enough, if he was into drinkin', maybe she might temporarily move to another room, another part of the house; son's room most likely, but I don't see her doin' that for any length of time."

"The bed in the boy's room is hardly big enough for him."

"She's a small woman."

"How about that spare room upstairs?" Ricky asked. "We didn't look that close. You and Sheriff Cooper spend any time in there?"

"No. Just enough to make sure there wasn't a body on the floor."

Ricky shrugged and headed back upstairs to take a better look in the guest room. I followed him, a little slower. Stairs are about the hardest thing for me to negotiate with my bad leg. I was still in the hallway when Ricky opened the door and looked in. "Bed's definitely big enough for two, if you're friendly. It's been made up though." He went on inside.

"So was her side of the bed. That doesn't tell us much," I said, when I finally joined him. I stood in the doorway while Ricky pulled the thin bedspread back.

"Made up, but it doesn't look to have been laundered recently. Two pillows. Both are a bit soiled; one more so than the other," he said. "Someone's used it. Goldilocks, maybe."

I joined him by the side of the daybed and pointed at one of the pillows. "Dirty. Almost like the one in the other room. Looks oily."

Ricky picked the pillow up and sniffed at it. "Sweet. Sort of."

"Perfume?"

He shook his head and made a face. "Not really. Could be hairspray maybe." He sniffed it again and held it out for me to smell. "What do you think?" he asked.

"Sorry." I shook my head. "All I can smell is Ring Johnson," I replied.

CHAPTER 12

Split Tree, Arkansas
Friday, November 15, 1963

We got back to town a little after three, and I had Ricky drop me off at Donnie Hawk's funeral parlor. I wanted to talk to Granville and see if he'd found out anything else from looking at the body. I told Ricky to check in at the office and then to go on home. We split weekend duty among the three of us, and tomorrow was Charley Dunn's day to work, so I told Ricky to get an early start on his Friday evening. He thanked me but said he'd swing by the Greyhound station first and check to see if the bus from Little Rock had come through yet. If so, he'd pick up the photographs that Art Hennig had sent over and leave them on my desk.

I stood on the walkway and looked at the street. Despite Donnie having a good-sized parking lot for visiting mourners, Granville always parks out front, by the mailbox. I've never known him to park anywhere else, and the fact that his Ford wasn't there meant that he wasn't either. I went on inside anyway.

Donnie Junior was running the vacuum cleaner in the foyer. He waved and smiled, and I saw him start to switch it off so that we could talk, but I shook my head to indicate there was no need.

"Where's the old man?" I asked over the noise of the vacuum.

Donnie Junior grinned knowingly and pointed off to the side, in the direction of the viewing room. I knew Donnie Senior wasn't in the viewing room but in the small office adjoining it. It's not really an office; certainly not the main office that you go to when you have funeral business to transact, but it's more of a hideaway where he can go to get away from his wife for a while to scratch in private and pretend to work. It has a window for venting cigar smoke, and he has a small desk with a drawer full of gentlemen's magazines in there, and a solid office chair that leans way back and is well suited for short naps.

I nodded my thanks and clapped the boy on the shoulder as I walked by him.

I knocked and opened the office door all in one motion. As expected, Donnie Senior had his chair tilted back and his feet propped up on the desk. His eyes were closed, and his mouth was slack, but he didn't seem to be asleep. "Donnie Junior told me you'd be in here," I said.

"Yeah," Donnie replied. He didn't seem surprised, and he didn't startle or immediately open his eyes. "Heard you two hollerin' over the Hoover. I'm tryin' to get some serious work done here."

"So I see."

"What's up with Big Ray Elmore this afternoon?" He dropped his feet to the floor and swiveled his chair in my direction and wiped some spittle from his mouth with the back of his hand. "You just missed Granville."

I nodded and got my smokes out. Donnie took one, and we both lit up. I leaned against the doorframe. "Afraid of that. I noticed his car was gone. He get finished with Ring's body?"

"As much as he could do. Yeah. He had to run out to the Dumas place. It's his second or third trip out there today. Another one of them boys got hurt somehow."

"That right?"

"Yessir. What a bunch. Anyway, we determined it's old Ring for sure. That much we know. He has that long scar on his right calf; where he fell into a stove when he was a kid. You remember it?"

"Not really. I didn't know him the way you did, but I trust you. I guess I'm just surprised there's enough left of his calf to see a scar. From what I saw, he looked pretty far gone."

Donnie stood up and adjusted his pants and then motioned for me to follow him down the hall. "His face and belly are gone, you're right about that," he said as we walked through the viewing room. Donnie Junior was still vacuuming and Donnie Senior had to raise his voice above the Hoover. "Mercy. Yessir, that part of him is a mess, but the rest of him ain't so bad. I'm startin' to think he may not have been dead as long as all that."

We cut through a small room that had some model caskets on display in it and then went down another short hallway that led to the old embalming room. You could feel a sting in your eyes from the formaldehyde fumes well before you could smell them. Donnie opened the door. It was cool. The windows were open, and he had the attic fan on to exhaust the smells and the fumes outside. The porcelain table that Granville uses for autopsies was empty, but wet, as if it had been recently rinsed off, and we walked past it to an old claw-foot bathtub that Donnie had installed next to the sink.

He pointed at it. "Can't embalm him very good given the shape of his head and belly. Major veins are shot, so I got him soaking in twenty-five percent formaldehyde and fifty percent ethanol," he said. "You might want to step back with that cigarette."

I did.

Donnie continued. "I figure I'll let him soak a while. Probably all night, and then I'll have Donnie Junior dry him out tomorrow and cover him with some hardening compound. Wrap him up in a mile of gauze and cotton, and he'll be as good as a smoked ham by this time Sunday. That's about the best we can do. He won't be pretty, but as long as you don't crack open the lid on the casket, you'll be able to wheel him into a church without anyone complainin' and holdin' their noses."

I leaned forward and looked in. Ring Johnson's body was partially curled up in the tub. The liquid covered all but a few patches of skin that protruded like islands from a dirty yellow-brown sea. "Hard to see much," I said.

"Hmmm," Donnie replied. He handed me his cigarette and then leaned over and reached into the tub, grabbing Ring's right leg and pulling it out of the liquid. Unlike the wrists and hands that had been little more than bone and ligaments when we first found the body, the legs were stilled fleshed and plump. Donnie turned the leg slightly, exposing the pale purple calf. "See? There's that old burn scar. Actually, pretty much from the belly on down he's in passable shape."

"Unlike you."

"Hey now. Watch it. Watch it, now," he laughed. He let go of the leg and it slowly sank back beneath the surface. "I tell you what, though, if them maggots had had another day to work on him, it'd be a whole different story altogether. Mercy."

"So how long you think he's been dead?" I asked. "You said you're rethinkin' that."

Donnie stepped back and wiped his hand on his pants leg and then retrieved his cigarette from me. He took a puff and blew the smoke in the direction of the attic fan. "Hard to tell with a case like this," he said after a minute. "Nights are cool enough. Days aren't, but the nights are. The tool shed was pretty closed up. The real problem is the head and belly, don't you know. You open a man up like that, and the damn flies get to him a dang sight easier. Get a head start; no pun intended. They can work some serious mischief in a short time. Makes it hard to tell."

"A week?"

Donnie shrugged. "Maybe. Could be less; could be more."

"Doesn't help much."

"Ain't a science."

"Granville find anythin' worth notin'?" I asked.

"He said Ring's head was blowed off."

"I think we knew that."

"Yeah. We did. But me and you knowin' it, and Granville Begley, Locust County Coroner, sayin' it are two different things entirely. It's official now."

"I was hopin' for more."

"I'm sure you were, Ray. You go on hopin' all you want, but don't expect much more. What's that old sayin' about shittin' in one hand and hopin' in the other? Just ain't much you can tell from a mess like this. But look on the bright side, at least we know for sure that it's Ring."

CHAPTER 13

Split Tree, Arkansas
Friday, November 15, 1963

I swung back by the office before I went on home for the day. Charley Dunn was out, but Jewell Faye was still there; she had a few things she was working on, but none that couldn't wait until Monday, and I told her to tidy up her desk and get on home. Instead of listening to me, she filed a few papers away and poured another cup of coffee, and sat back down, and we talked for a while, long enough for her to drink her coffee and pour another cup. We discussed a few scattered things, but mostly we talked about Ring and Jo Johnson. She said that she hadn't wanted to say too much in front of Charley Dunn, but she'd heard that they'd been having some marital troubles for a good while, and even before the talk about the hired man, there'd been gossip that she might be stepping out on Ring. Jewell Faye didn't know whether there was anything backing up the loose talk, but she also admitted that she wasn't surprised that something had happened; she said that she'd been expecting as much, though she sure didn't think it'd involve Ring ending up with his brains as wallpaper. She also seemed fair certain that sooner or later Jo would turn up all right, though she couldn't really say why, but I've come to trust Jewell Faye's gut instincts. I hoped she was right.

I finally got her shooed out the door about four o'clock, and I went back to my desk. Ricky had done like he'd said he would, and he'd picked up the packet of photos from the bus station: eight-by-tens, two copies of each. I looked at them briefly; Art Hennig's hand-written notes were paper-clipped to each one. I decided I'd study them later, but I left a copy of each photo on Charley Dunn's desk, along with a note for him to take them to King's Rexall Drug across the square from our office and have ten copies made in the morning. Bob King runs a small photo lab in the back of his store, and he does good work.

I got home at four forty-five. Ellen Mae had started dinner but was at a point where she could step away for a few minutes, and she joined me on the porch swing as the shadows overtook us. It was cool, but not unpleasantly so, and I smoked some cigarettes, and we talked about the shortening days and how our sons were growing up fast. It's a regular source of conversation for us nowadays. We have twin boys. Just turned seventeen. Identical to look at, but nothing at all alike. They'll be seniors next year, and then maybe college. Who knows? The oldest, Raymond Junior will get some scholarship offers for sure. Baseball, football, track. You name it; he's a born athlete, and coaches from some of the smaller colleges in the state have been keeping an eye on him for several years now. His brother, W.R., is the way smarter of the two, and more level-headed, and I have no doubt that he'd make the most of a college education, but paying for it will be his problem. Our boys have been the center of our marriage from the beginning, the glue really, and as we approach the day when they strike out on their own, I think both Ellen Mae and I catch ourselves wondering what that means for the two of us afterwards. I suspect that thought was lurking under the surface, unspoken, as it always is nowadays, because without being aware of when or how it happened, I realized that we'd shifted gears and found ourselves discussing Ring and Jo Johnson and the state of their marriage. I'm sure we'd have gotten there eventually, but the fact that it happened without a noticeable bump in the road probably says more about us than about the Johnsons.

I told Ellen Mae more details of what I'd heard. I told her what Jewell Faye had said about their marital troubles, though I still went easy on the talk of Jo Johnson having an affair. She hadn't heard any of that, or if she had, she'd chosen to ignore it. I suspect she hadn't. The Johnsons are a few years younger than we are. We'd both known Ring growing up, but only in the way that you tend to know everyone in a small town. He was closer to my brother's age, but even then, I don't recall my brother having much to do with him one way or the other. He grew up west of town on the same farm that he and Jo have now, and my father's farm was to the east. Locust County isn't big, nor is Split Tree, but even so, we didn't have much call to know the Johnsons then or now. Same for Jo. In fact, she wasn't from around here at all growing up. Her family is from up in Crittenden County, and she didn't show up around here until shortly before the war, about the time I was shipping out. Her father moved down here to work for Carl Trimble at the Western Auto for a short spell. Even now I don't really know her much more than to tip my hat when we pass on the street.

Ellen Mae and I got quieter the more we talked. After about an hour we'd bottomed out with things to say, or things that we were willing to say, and we simply swung silently, both staring out into the street without really seeing anything except what was in our heads. It was quiet, but it wasn't unpleasant. A little before six thirty, a beige Ford Galaxie station wagon pulled up by our mailbox and killed its engine. Even in the growing dark I recognized it as Ricky Forrest's car. He'd bought it a year or two earlier from his father-in-law.

Ricky got out and waved as he walked around to the rear door and opened it. A large black dog, resembling a fifty-pound bag of charcoal briquettes with four short legs, hopped out quickly.

"That looks like Ring Johnson's dog," I called out as the two of them started up our sidewalk. In a town like Split Tree, you might not know everyone well, but you tend to know their dogs by sight.

"You'd be right," Ricky responded as he reached the porch steps. "*Missus Elmore*," he said to Ellen Mae as he got closer.

Ellen Mae smiled and stood up. "Evenin' Ricky. I don't see the rest of your family. Now, don't you dare tell me you've stopped by and didn't bring your wife and that baby of yours."

Ricky reached down and tugged on one of the dog's ears. "I'm afraid so. Just me and Todd, here. Kitty and Eddie are over at her folks' place. Friday dinners. I'm due there shortly."

"Where'd you find him?" I asked, nodding at the dog.

Before Ricky could answer, Ellen Mae interrupted. "Oh, my Lord. Dinner. That reminds me. I have a supper casserole that needs some attention. If it's burned, we may all be askin' to eat at your in-law's. *Here, you come up here and sit down,*" she said to Ricky.

Ellen Mae went inside, and Ricky stepped up on the porch and took a seat in the rocking chair next to the swing. "I can't stay, boss," he said. He got out his smokes and offered me one, and we both lit up. Picking up my question about the dog, he nodded at Todd. "Found him out at the Johnson farm."

"So I figured. Just now?"

"Little while ago. I went back out there to take those photos of the tool shed before it got too dark. As I was leaving, old Todd showed up."

"Doesn't look too worse for wear. He seem hungry?"

Ricky shrugged. "From the looks of him, I suspect he always seems hungry, but no, not like you'd expect if no one was feeding him regularly." The dog had laid down next to Ricky's chair, and Ricky leaned over and patted him on the belly. "Couldn't really leave him out there."

"Suspect not. Wonder who's been feedin' him."

"No idea."

"You plan to keep him?"

"I guess. At least until Missus Johnson shows up."

"Assumin' she does."

"Yes, sir."

"Kitty gonna get a say in the matter?"

Ricky laughed. "Now, you understand how it is; she gets the only say that does matter. That's sort of why I'm here. You mind if he stays with you until I can discuss it with her? She'll come around, but I'd rather not just show up with him without getting the lay of the battlefield first."

"Course not. Trip's inside," I said, referring to our own dog. "In fact, I'm surprised he hasn't figured out he has company. He's probably asleep on one of the furnace grates. He'll figure it out soon enough. Suppose he's house broke?"

"No idea. I figured you could put him in the back yard for one night."

"We'll see how he and Trip get along. Either way, don't worry."

"By the way, did you get by the office to see those photos Sergeant Hennig sent?"

"I did," I replied. I held up the brown envelope that was on the porch swing next to me. "Right here. I looked at them briefly, but that's about all. I'm fixin' to study them a bit more after dinner. I put a copy of each one on Charley Dunn's desk and asked him to have some more made tomorrow."

"Already did that."

"Did what?"

"Arranged to get more made."

"Damn, son."

Ricky shrugged. "Sergeant Hennig sent three of each. I had to take the film from the Johnsons' tool shed over to King's Drugs to get it processed anyway, and I thought they could make some copies of them while they're at it."

I laughed. "Should have figured you'd be one step ahead of me."

"That'll be the day."

"Like hell. Well good, but it'll still give Charley Dunn somethin' to do in the mornin'. It's best to keep him busy, and we can always use a few extra copies."

Ricky smiled but didn't comment on his coworker. He launched his cigarette butt into the yard in a high glowing arc. "Well, I should be heading out. I know you've got better things to do than entertain me. And, I'm late for dinner."

It was my turn to laugh. "I'm not sure I ever have anythin' better to do than talk with you. You're good for my mental health. If I wasn't sittin' out here, I'd be inside watchin' the evenin' news. Seein' what went wrong in the world today. Gettin' depressed about it."

"It's a mess isn't it?"

I shook my head slowly. I wish I could have told him otherwise. "Everywhere you turn, just one mess after another," I answered. It did seem the world was trying hard to go crazy again. Germany. Vietnam. Cuba. I read the other day that the president had to put in a special phone to the Soviets just to make sure we don't blow each other up by mistake. And it's not just overseas either. Things aren't much better back here at home. Blacks marching on the Capitol. That nutcase governor blocking the schoolhouse door over in Alabama, like he didn't learn anything from our governor trying it a few years back. And it's getting worse. Just a few months ago some Mississippi cracker killed an NAACP leader in his own carport over in Jackson. Not more than three-hours east from here. And on the same day that the president gave a speech on civil rights. And then, two months ago someone blew up a church in Birmingham and killed a bunch of little black girls. No, the world is coming apart at the seams every which way you look.

We sat quietly for a minute or two, and then Ricky turned to me, and in a low voice intended to not carry inside the house, said, "It's probably not my place to say this, but I worry about your boys."

I looked at him in the dark. Ellen Mae had turned the lights on in the living room and there was a weak yellow glow coming out of the front door that served to silhouette Ricky's head without illuminating much of his face. "I do too, but what are you referrin' to specifically?"

"You following what's happening over in Vietnam?"

I nodded. "Some. Can't say I like what I'm seein'."

"That's what I'm talking about."

"I guess you saw that religious monk fella burn himself up a few months back?" I asked.

"Yes, sir. That was something."

"You can call it that, I suppose; I lean more to callin' it crazy. I thought the damn Japs were fanatical, but to set yourself on fire like that . . ." I flicked my own cigarette into the yard and got out my Lucky Strikes and lit up another. Ricky declined my offer of one. "You know, Ricky, I came back from the war eighteen years ago. Eighteen years. Seems more like eighteen months some days. I came home hearin' about how we had us the A-bomb. And now the H-bomb. I came home hearin' how we wouldn't be fightin' any more wars with young men. No need, they said. The next one would be a couple of generals pushin' a button or two. How about that? Isn't that what you heard?"

Ricky nodded. He must have changed his mind about leaving, because he got his own smokes out and lit up. "Yes, sir. That fairy tale lasted all of five years, didn't it?"

"That's right. Five years. Five years and then they had you boys over in Korea fightin' hand-to-hand; stabbin' and clubbin' each other like you were back in the damn Stone Age. I can't imagine what you saw."

"Neither can I, and I saw it. But then, so did you. You saw the same. You saw more. Different terrain; different weather. Same crazy. Killing is killing."

"I reckon you're right," I replied.

"I am, and that's why I'm worried about your boys. There isn't any such thing as a push-button war, Ray. You and I know that. Killing is a personal thing. As personal as it can get. Always has been. I suspect it always will be, and it's always the young men that we ask to do it for us. You and me had our turn. That's what worries me. I don't like what the president is saying about coming to Vietnam's aid. I've heard that Siren's song before. He's talking about supporting them, and your boys are at that age where someone's going to ask them to do the next round."

I nodded in the dark. There wasn't an answer to be made.

"Sorry," he continued after I didn't respond. "I guess you don't need me bringing it up. You mentioned the news and I . . . it's just that I worry about them when I see what's happening."

I shook my head. "No apology necessary. I appreciate the fact you care about them."

"Of course. They're good young men. You and Missus Elmore saw to that. When I look at my own boy, I just . . ." he let his thought trail off.

We both went silent again.

"Well," Ricky said after a minute. "I need to be going. I'm late already. Not going to solve the world's problems tonight." He stood up and took a long draw on his smoke. "Thanks again for keeping the dog. Shouldn't be more than a day."

"Sure thing. Tell Kitty and her folks I said hey, and hug that son of yours while he'll still let you. They tend to grow shy of that before you know it."

"I will." He smiled. He started to step off of the porch when he pivoted on one foot and swung back in my direction. He reached into his pocket and pulled something out. "Damn. Almost forgot. Got talking about the dog and the rosy future of the world and everything. I found this out at the Johnson's place; when I was taking the photos."

"Hell is it?" I asked. It was too dark for me to see what he was holding in his hand.

"Probably nothing," he replied as he tossed whatever it was towards me.

I caught it. It was a book of paper matches.

CHAPTER 14

Split Tree, Arkansas
Friday, November 15, 1963

Ricky stepped back up onto the porch. "I doubt it means much of anything," he said. "Still, we don't have much to work with, and it just sort of seemed like it was out of place. I figured you could make sense out of it. Or not."

"Hmmm." I opened the green paper matchbook cover. Most of the matches were gone, and the strike pad was well worn. "Where'd you find it?"

"Floor of the tool shed. Under the workbench. I photographed the wall and the blood pattern, but I also took shots of the bench top and the tools on the wall. I made sort of an inventory; just in case."

"Good thinkin'."

"I took a couple of rolls inside the house as well."

"Even better thinkin'."

"Nothing much struck me as out of place or odd in the tool shed," he said. "It was fairly orderly as work sheds go, but when I got down on the floor, and looked under the bench, I saw that." He nodded at the matchbook in my hands. "It wasn't far under; more like it got dropped and then accidentally kicked maybe. It's really the only thing that seemed like it shouldn't be there."

"Except for Ring's brains on the walls. What'd you call it? His *residue*."

"Yes, sir. Except for that."

"*Gofer* matches," I said, more or less to myself.

"What?"

"Hmmm. Oh. Sorry. I was just thinkin' of somethin'. *Gofer* matches. That's what some of the Marines called them anyhow. You doggies never call them that?"

Ricky shook his head. "Not that I ever heard. Sounds like a swab jockey name. Gopher?"

I shrugged. "I reckon you're right. Maybe it's just a Marine thing. Navy. Maybe just that bunch I was with, or maybe it's just a Pacific island thing." I looked up at him. "It was so damn humid everywhere. You'd pull a match and strike it, and it'd just sputter out like you were botherin' it and it had better things to do that catch fire for your damn benefit. You always had to *gofer* another. And *gofer* another. Usually took two or three to get a cigarette lit, and by then the damn Japs had you sighted in. That was one reason you learned to chain smoke. It was easier to light the next one off the old butt than with one of these."

"Hadn't heard them called that."

"Hang around me more; you'll learn all sorts of useless shit." I leaned to the side and held the match cover in the little illumination that was coming out of the doorway. "General Fagan Motor Lodge," I read. "Not placin' it. It's not in Locust County, is it? Is that the one the other side of the Desha County line?"

Ricky shook his head. "No, sir. I think you're thinking of the Rest-Mor Motel. It's down that way. I'm not for certain, but I think the General Fagan is the one up there in Lee County. Up Highway One, like you're going up toward Marianna. Just across the line a few miles; over on the west side." He paused. "I think."

"Bullshit. If I know you, you've already checked where this is."

He smiled and shrugged.

"Hmm. Maybe it rings a bell. Sort of," I said. "I used to go that way regular; I had an old aunt I'd visit on Sundays, but I haven't been up there in a couple of years now. General Fagan." I handed the matchbook back to Ricky and watched him look at it and put it back into his pocket.

"Want me to log it in or not?" he asked.

"I reckon you should. Just in case."

"I'll do it tomorrow if that's okay. Like I said, I doubt it means anything, but it does seem like maybe it's an odd place for Ring Johnson to have matches from. I'm thinking we ought to check it out."

"Yeah, probably nothin'. Ellen Mae has matches from all over the place. Collects them. Can't take a trip without her pickin' up a book of gofer matches. Keeps them in a big jar on the bookshelf. We've still got a couple from the Peabody up in Memphis, and we haven't been there since our honeymoon."

"Ring Johnson doesn't strike me as the type to collect souvenir matchbooks."

"Probably right. And you're probably right that it's worth takin' a drive up there. It's not like we have any other leads."

"I'll do it tomorrow as well."

"Like hell," I said as I stood up. I'd sat too long and my leg had stiffened, and it took a little effort to manage. Once I had my balance, I clapped Ricky on the shoulder and urged him to get going. As I walked with him back to his car, I continued with my thought. "I didn't mean to suggest that you do it. I'm with you on this; I can't imagine that book of matches is much more than a book of matches, but what I do know is that tomorrow's your day off."

"You know I don't mind."

"I know you don't, and you know that I do, and I suspect Kitty does as well. It can wait, and if it can't, then I'll drive on up there myself." Todd, Ring's dog, had followed us to the car, anxious for an opportunity for another ride. He started to follow Ricky, but I grabbed a handful of skin around his neck and held him back on the sidewalk while Ricky walked around the front of his car and opened the driver's door. "Besides," I continued, "you're likely to be in enough hot water for hangin' around here talkin' to me when you're supposed to be at your in-law's for dinner. You may be busy tomorrow buildin' a dog house for both you and Todd to sleep in."

"First rule of a firefight, always keep your sights on the closest target. It's where I'm sleeping *tonight* that I have to worry about," he laughed. "Thanks for keeping him; I'll be by to get him tomorrow."

"Not a problem."

Ricky started to get into the car, and a thought came into my head. "Ricky," I said.

He stopped and stood up and looked at me over the hood of the car. "Chief?"

"I was just thinkin'. We have any idea if Ring Johnson smoked?"

CHAPTER 15

Split Tree, Arkansas
Friday, November 15, 1963

After Ricky left, Todd inspected the front yard and tended to a couple of azalea bushes in a way Ellen Mae likely wouldn't appreciate if she'd known. I went back to the porch and sat down and smoked a couple more cigarettes. I tried to sort through my thoughts but after a few minutes gave up and went inside to find our dog, Trip. As I suspected, he was laying on one of the furnace grates in the kitchen, and while there was no heat coming through it, he seemed to think that he was deriving some comfort from it. If nothing else the location gave him a good view of Ellen Mae and the plates of food as she worked on dinner. Against his better judgment, I got him to follow me outside to meet Todd, and I refereed the two of them for five to ten minutes until they arrived at a general agreement as to whose yard it was, and then I went back inside and left them on the porch to work out some of the finer arrangements. Trip can be rather detail oriented when it comes to other dogs.

While I was washing up, our two boys came home. They'd had basketball practice, and it had run late. After they got cleaned up, we sat down and had supper. Right off, they wanted to know about Ring Johnson, particularly the condition of his body, the somewhat imaginative details having raced through the high school like a bad odor. Ellen Mae didn't particularly want to hear any more than I'd already told her about it, but she also knew that going with the stream is less exhausting than swimming against it, and two teenage boys intent upon stories of blood and gore can be a powerful current to overcome. I steered a middle course and gave them an abbreviated recitation of what I knew, which, to be honest, wasn't all that much. Predictably, they were disappointed with the limited details I had to offer, having gotten their appetites for a more graphic version of events whetted by talk in gym class, but their interests in prodding me any further about it soon gave way to other topics, the likes of which Ellen Mae was only slightly more comfortable with. I told them about Gervais and his escape from Tucker Prison, and that seemed like an acceptable alternative topic for them. They remembered when the murder happened in the summer of 1960, and the idea that a notorious killer might be working his way to Split Tree was like an early Christmas present for them. My two boys and Grace Trimble's son, Jimmie Carl, couldn't be any closer if they'd been whelped from the same litter. Jimmie Carl is a few years older, but those three have been inseparable since they could walk, and the fact that the man who lost his head happened to be an old army buddy of Jimmie Carl's uncle made a particularly big impression on my sons at the time.

All of that is true, but it's also the case that Ellen Mae has had seventeen years of experience in dinnertime conversations of this sort, and she's learned not to be deterred easily from her efforts at decorum. She sat patiently and rearranged the food on her plate with her fork and let the line on that topic spool out for a while, and then, without any of us being fully aware of it, she artfully reeled the mealtime discussion firmly back onto something more acceptable, and for the most part, the rest of dinner was spent talking about school and how basketball practice had gone and what chores needed to be completed before the weekend was over, and who the boys were planning to meet later that evening, and whether there'd be girls there, and—most importantly—what girls those might be. After dinner, the boys helped their mother clean the supper dishes, but they soon relapsed into a very enthusiastic discussion of how the electric chair works and whether your eyes really do catch fire and pop out of your head when the voltage first hits you. Whether it was planned or not, it had the effect of prompting Ellen Mae to excuse them early, telling them that they had done enough to help and that they were free to head on out to join their friends who were likely already gathering at the drive-in. I speeded up their exit by helping her finish the dishes, and then I let the dogs in, and we both went to the den and sat down on the couch, and she started reading a magazine while I opened the envelope from Art Hennig.

Art was right, the photographs were a few years old. Both had been taken at police bookings. Lidia Fernandez looked young and small. Pretty in a self-confident way. She was holding a nameplate dated April 3, 1960, which read NOPD. There wasn't a rap sheet with the photos, but I remember Art first telling me back in the summer of 1960, when Gervais killed that conventioneer, that Cuban girls were turning up in Arkansas as prostitutes. They'd fled Castro, along with thousands of other folks, and many of them got to the U.S. with no applicable job skills. What happened then was not entirely unpredictable, and some of them had found themselves in the working-girl circuit, moving frequently from one city to the next in hopes of staying one day ahead of their court appearances. From the nameplate, I had to guess that Lidia Fernandez must have spent some time in New Orleans before showing up in Little Rock.

The photo of Gervais was dated almost three months later, June 29, 1960. That was the day that he pulled that conventioneer's head off in Little Rock and started the whole thing in motion; as I recall they picked him up at the scene and he'd made no effort to flee, so the photo likely was taken that same night. To be honest, he looked like a thousand other big, raw-boned peckerwoods that I've known; muscular, but not more so than most of the men you could have pulled randomly from the local feed store on a Saturday morning. What did stick out was the confused look on his face, as if he wasn't entirely sure why he was standing against a wall holding a chalkboard with his name and date written on it. I suspect that if you asked him, he'd have told you that the conventioneer had it coming to him, and to a simple man like Gervais, the response of the police must have seemed like a bit of an overreaction.

"Is that those two?" Ellen Mae finally asked. We'd been sitting quietly for a while, and she'd been watching me.

"What?"

She nodded at the photos in my hand. "Those the photographs you mentioned?"

"Yeah. You remember Art Hennig? State police over in Little Rock?"

She smiled. "The one whose life you saved? Of course I do."

I sighed. "Ella, I wish you wouldn't—" I started to say, but I caught myself. My lifesaving skills was not a conversation that I wanted to wade into right now. Or ever, for that matter. Instead, I took a breath and started again. "Art sent these over this afternoon. He thought they might prove useful if Gervais does head this way." I handed them to Ellen Mae. "They're a few years old, but he seems to believe they still look pretty much the same."

"You think there's really much chance of that?" she asked.

"Of what? Of him showin' up here?" I shrugged. "I doubt it. Maybe, but my guess is that he's a long ways away from here by now. No need to worry."

She looked at me for a second and then turned her attention to the photograph of Lidia Fernandez. She studied it closely. "She's pretty. Sort of. Don't you think?"

Ellen Mae can sometimes be a bit of a puzzle. She's a wonderful woman, but she has this thick vein of jealousy that threads deep through her core. It's not tied to anything reasonable, and it's about the most unattractive thing you'd ever want to experience when it shows its face. I guess what happened with her father when she was young, him running off with his secretary and getting killed, scarred her in a way that I'll never quite understand. She was also engaged to a good man when the war started. He got killed overseas, and that took a toll on her as well. He didn't cheat on her, but he also went away and didn't come back, and that's what seems to matter. I think that's the part that she really fears; being left. She knows he didn't willingly abandon her. She knows I won't abandon her either, but sometimes knowing something and feeling something don't quite mesh up in the thinking part of our brains like they should. It's as if she needs constant reassurance. It used to be worse. In fact, there was a time when if I so much as tipped my hat to another woman, that vein would start to pulse. Things are much better now, even as her spells have gotten worse and more frequent, she manages to keep her jealousy in a box better. Still, I'm wary around questions like that.

"If you like that kind of look, I suppose," I responded safely.

"Hmmm. Most men would, I'd think. She's got that . . . that *exotic* sort of look. Like Rita Moreno." There was no edge to it. Like I said, there was a time when there might have been. This was light-hearted; almost matter-of-fact.

"Well, most men aren't married to one of the prettiest women in this county." That seemed like another safe response. And an honest one. And I congratulated myself.

"One?"

"What?"

"Nothin'. I just thought you said *one of.*"

It took me a moment to realize that she was joking with me. "No, ma'am. I'm fairly sure I said *the. The* prettiest," I said.

She smiled. "Why, thank you. That's awfully sweet of you," she said in a Southern belle voice. Then she let out an exaggerated sigh. "Of course, I guess this county is rather small. As counties go." She was in a good mood.

"Who said county? I'm pretty sure I said *state. The whole state.*"

"I'm sure you did," she laughed. She turned her attention back to the photo, but her smile was even bigger. "She looks young."

"I think she was. Is. Those are a couple-three years old."

She looked at it a minute longer and then slid the photo of Lidia Fernandez behind the one of Gervais. "Oh, my. So this is him. The *killer*."

"Gilbert Gervais."

"And he's a Cuban? I guess he looks like it, with his hair all slicked back like that and all." She tilted her head and looked at the photo from a different angle. "Is that why they call them wetbacks?"

I laughed.

"What? *What?*" she asked. She elbowed me in the ribs. "Don't laugh at me." It came out almost as a giggle. "*What?*"

"You're what. You are. First of all, he's not Cuban. The girl is; he's just some local redneck from Louisiana. And two, I don't know of anyone who calls Cubans wetbacks. You're thinkin' of Mexicans. Cubans are like Desi Arnaz. And three, even if he was a Cuban, or a Mexican, they don't call them that because they slick their hair back. Men all over this county slick their hair back."

She didn't seem overly inclined to argue the matter. She looped a lock of her own hair behind her ear and looked at me out the corner of her eye as she replied. "Well, whatever he is, whatever *you* call him, I'd just as soon he not come to our little town. No matter how he combs his hair."

I laughed again. "Well, that's good to know, and if I have the opportunity to speak with him, I'll be sure to pass that along. *Mrs. Ellen Mae Elmore of Split Tree kindly requests that you not come to our town.* I'll tell him. That way he can't say he wasn't properly warned."

"Bless his heart," she said, and she meant it, at least in that Southern-woman half-pity, half-reproach sort of way. I've known plenty of Marines who tack a *fuck-you* on the end of their sentences for much the same purpose, but without having nearly as much effect. She handed the photos back to me. "Bless yours, too."

"If it makes you feel better, I suspect Carl Trimble agrees with you about Gervais not bein' welcome here."

"Carl Trimble is a pig; if you ask me," she said. It came out before she had a chance to reel it back in, and it almost seemed to catch her by surprise, like an unexpected hiccup. I waited for her to follow it up with another apologetic *bless his heart*, but she didn't. Instead, she reached out and touched my thigh with her fingertips. "I suppose you have to warn him though?"

"Who?"

"Carl the pig."

"I reckon so. Ben Cooper probably should, but . . ."

"But you need to."

I sighed again. "Reckon so. I'll go by the Western Auto tomorrow. I suspect he'll be workin'."

"And Grace."

There it was again. Another one of those questions that can take a leg off if you stepped on it wrong. Despite her getting a better handle on her jealousy, if there is anything that will bring out the worst in Ellen Mae, it's the thought of Grace Trimble and me occupying her brain at the same moment. That's a particular sore that will scab over but never quite heal up. And I suppose there's good cause. I still love Grace, and that won't never change. I don't suppose that's much of a secret; certainly not to either Grace or Ellen Mae. Or me. Not much I can do about it. If the war hadn't intervened, Ellen Mae would be married to Tommy Dobson and I'd be with Grace, and we'd probably all be going to each other's homes for dinner on Sundays and talking about Razorback football and the falling price of soybeans and how fast our boys are outgrowing their clothes. Instead, Tommy disappeared somewhere over in New Guinea, and I disappeared on an island in the Pacific. Don't get me wrong; I love Ellen Mae with all my heart. She's a wonderful woman, and I'm maybe the luckiest man in the world to have her. I know that. That isn't a secret either. It's just that we've had to make the best of the hands that we were dealt, and there's no drawing cards from the deck, but all three of us, Ellen Mae, Grace, and me, we all got a glimpse of what might have been. It's sort of like when you see something bright and the image of it continues to float across your vison even after you close your eyes. I think that's what it's like for the three of us. The image gets more and more blurry, and it fades with time, but it continues to dance across the back of our eyelids, forever teasing us with a vague what-might-have-been. But with Ellen Mae, sometimes it can provoke darker visions.

I treaded lightly; stepping to the side. "I'll talk to Carl Trimble tomorrow," I repeated.

She nodded slowly and looked at the photos in my hand. "Grace needs to know too. She needs to protect Jimmie Carl. Don't leave that to Carl to tell her."

I nodded without clearly agreeing. "I don't believe this Gervais fella is a threat, but if he is, he has no issue with Grace Trimble or Jimmie Carl. It'll be Carl Trimble he's after."

She didn't seem reassured. "And if he does show up? What then?"

Her fingers were still resting on my thigh. I put my free hand on hers and squeezed it gently. "Then I'll deal with him."

She leaned into me and rested her head on my shoulder. She was quiet for a minute, and then she said, "I know you will. I may not know a Cuban from a Mexican, but I know one thing; it'll be the biggest mistake of his life if he shows up here."

I leaned into her. She was warm and good. I hoped I was right. I hoped Gervais stayed a long way away from all of us. I looked at his photograph again. I've seen the eyes of killers; I've seen my share of the angry dregs left in the bottom of the glass.

I hoped I was right.

CHAPTER 16

Split Tree, Arkansas
Saturday, November 16, 1963

I slept late. Normally, I'm up well before Ellen Mae or the boys; I can seldom sleep through the nights anymore; the hardware in my leg makes sure of that if nothing else. Sometimes I just toss and turn and adjust my weight and manage to fall back asleep for short spits of time; sometimes I get up and go downstairs and read so that I don't bother Ellen Mae. Last night I went out and sat on the cool porch and smoked cigarettes and thought about Ring Johnson and Jo and the General Fagan Motor Lodge. I stayed out a long time, and when I finally went back to bed, I unexpectedly slept until almost nine o'clock.

The boys were gone by the time I got downstairs. They had morning basketball practice, and the house was quiet except for the sound of a pot of coffee percolating on the kitchen counter. I poured a cup and drank it as I stood at the sink and looked out of the kitchen window; Ellen Mae was at the back fence talking to our neighbor, and Trip, our dog, was sitting at her side, facing the house. Todd was about six feet away, sitting and looking at Trip, still adjusting to the complex rules of the yard.

I didn't particularly want to talk to my neighbor, so I sat at the kitchen table and had a smoke and finished my coffee and waited. Ellen Mae came in while I was doing it.

"There you are," she said. She leaned down and kissed me on the cheek. "Not like you to stay in bed so long. You have trouble sleepin'?"

"Some. Hope I didn't keep you awake."

She poured herself some coffee and sat down opposite of me. "I slept fine. You get up?"

I nodded and took a sip from my cup. "Around two, I guess. Two thirty. Didn't want to bother you, so I went and sat on the porch until almost sunup."

"Oh, my. I'm so sorry. I guess that's why I didn't know you were restless; you weren't there to be restless. Your leg?"

I shrugged. "Maybe. Plenty to think about as well."

"I'm sure. So, what's first?"

"Today? I don't know. Just workin' that out now. I reckon I'll go talk to Carl Trimble. Get that pleasant piece of business over with." I lit another cigarette and took in a deep lungful of smoke and let it out slowly. "I need to talk to Ben Cooper at some point; I've got a couple-three questions for him. I may swing by his house later. And after that, I'm not sure." I specifically didn't include a talk with Grace in the discussion. I nodded at the two dogs, who were now standing side-by-side at the screen door looking in. "I may load up those two and drive out to the Johnson's place later."

"What for?"

"Probably nothin'. Ricky said that when he found Todd yesterday, he didn't seem hungry."

She laughed. "Good Lord, I can't imagine that. He's been at my heels all mornin' beggin' for somethin' to eat."

"You give him anythin'?"

"Of course I did. Bacon, eggs, even some pancakes," she laughed again. "There's nothin' much left for you. Every time I turn around, he wants more."

I joined her in laughing. "That's sort of my point. Animal like him, I expect he gets hungry every few hours, but he wasn't when Ricky found him. Makes me think that somebody must have been feedin' him all that time." I took a sip of coffee and another drag on my Lucky Strike before I continued. "And we know it wasn't Ring. Not for a while anyways. And we assume it wasn't Jo." I paused. "If she were around to feed the dog, then it'd mean she knew somethin' about her husband."

"So probably not her?"

"Probably not. For her sake anyway."

Ellen Mae was nodding as I talked, and she looked at the dogs at the back door. "Someone fed him. You think one of the neighbors?"

"Figures so. Fixin' to start with them anyway. See where that leads. Probably nowhere."

"That's my husband," she laughed. "The glass is always half empty."

"I've come to believe that pessimists are seldom disappointed."

She got up and let the dogs in. They both blew in like they'd been shot out of a circus cannon, and Trip immediately sat down on the furnace grate; Todd stood a few feet away, watching Ellen Mae and me and Trip. He seemed to be wondering when it'd be his turn to sit on the furnace grate.

"And you're goin' to take them?"

"Yeah. Figure they'll enjoy the ride, and seein' Todd may prompt someone to remember somethin' that they might not otherwise. But, first things first, I need to go see Carl Trimble and Cecil Ben. Get that out of the way."

We talked some more and Ellen Mae fixed me some toast to go with my coffee. About ten o'clock I grabbed the envelope with the photos, got into my car, and drove into town to the Western Auto store. I saw Trimble's black Buick Riviera parked out front, so I knew he was there.

Carl Trimble's father, Frank Trimble, opened a general hardware store in 1904 or 1905. It was a modest business, but in the twenties he and his brother had the good sense to buy into the Western Auto chain, and their store really took off. He died in 1931; not a day too soon as far as I'm concerned. Frank Trimble was a monster in just about every way you can think of to measure monsters, including raising two sons with the moral character of something best scraped off the bottom of a barn boot. The oldest son, Jay Trimble, had aspirations beyond Split Tree, and he married himself into the ownership of a dry goods business up in Blytheville and moved away. He seems to have studied the hardest and learned the most about being a monster from his father. Fortunately for all of us, he's dead now too; unfortunately, little brother, Carl, is still with us. Carl was always the considerably dimmer of the two Trimble lightbulbs, and I don't think that the limits of his brain could expand past Split Tree's. Not even a world war managed to pry him loose from the city limits; a doctor's letter attesting to his flat feet kept him at home. I don't think he could imagine anything more ambitious than taking over his father's business, moving into his father's house, marrying Judge Davis's daughter, and hanging her on the wall of his den like a deer head mounted for all the town to see. He and I have had our share of run-ins over the years, and I've even had the pleasure of breaking his jaw a couple of times, so I can't really say that we're on the best of terms. In the last few years we've managed to avoid each other more than you'd think possible in a town this size.

I parked at my office and walked across the square to Trimble's store. It was about as busy as you'd expect on a pleasant November Saturday morning, but not overly crowded. I visited with a few folks briefly as I worked my way to the sporting goods counter in the back left corner of the building, where the firearms are sold. Ever since he graduated from high school a couple of years ago, Jimmie Carl has been working at the store, ostensibly to learn the ropes, but I suspect it's more about earning some money to fix up his car than it is learning to carry on the Trimble family business. He works weekdays and most Saturday and Sunday mornings. I saw him behind the gun counter.

He was finishing up with a customer when I walked up. I leaned on the other end of the counter and waited while he made change and bagged up a couple boxes of twelve-gauge shotgun shells. He saw me and responded with a large toothy smile and a nod to indicate he'd be right with me.

"Big Ray," he said as his customer departed.

"Jimmie Carl. How you doin', boy?"

"Super, Big Ray. Super."

"The boys tell me that y'all just about got that old Bel Air runnin'."

"Yes, sir. We do. Runs like a top," he paused and smiled again. "If you can just get it to start. But once she starts . . . I named her *Maggie Jean*."

I smiled back. When he gets excited about something, especially when he grins big, Jimmie Carl reminds me for all the world of my younger brother, Reuel. "Well, I don't reckon it'd be much fun if it didn't need work."

"Yes, sir. You're right about that; that's where the fun is." He paused. "But I'm learnin' sometimes you can have too much fun."

"You can at that," I replied. Carl's office is on the second floor, and he's installed a window so that he can look out onto the store, the better to keep an eye on the young women that he has a habit of hiring. I glanced at the window. "He in?" I asked.

The boy stopped smiling. Or maybe I imagined he did. "Yes, sir. He should be upstairs. At least I haven't seen him come down all morning."

I nodded. "He alone?"

Now I was positive that he'd stopped smiling. Carl Trimble doesn't just hire young females to work behind the counters, rumors have it that he also has a habit of working with them alone in his office; even in the middle of the day. "Not sure," Jimmie Carl answered. "I try not to know."

"I hear you. Hate to ask you this, son, but I need to see him. Suppose you can you call him for me?"

He nodded and picked up the phone beside the cash register and pushed one of the round translucent buttons below the dial. It connected to an internal line, and I heard it ring and the sound of a voice bark on the other end. "Dad?" Jimmie Carl said in response to the bark. He paused while something was barked back. "Yes, sir. I know, but Big Ray—, I mean, Chief Elmore is here. He—"

There was an even louder response that cut him off, and Jimmie Carl reflexively pulled the receiver slightly away from his ear. I took the phone from him. I could hear Trimble still bellowing a blue streak at his son.

"Carl Trimble, this is Ray Elmore. You shut up and listen, I need to talk with you," I said sharply into the phone. "I can come up there, or you can come down here to the gun counter, or I'll be happy to meet you somewhere in between; after that you can go straight to hell for all I care, but I got somethin' to tell you, and you need to hear it, and I don't figure to make two trips to get it done."

"Fuck you, Elmore," he shouted. "Get the fuck out of my store before I—" he caught himself and pumped the brakes. He went momentarily silent.

I started to ask *before you what?*, but I held up. There was no need. "I'll repeat myself one time, in case your ears are stopped up with wax," I said, before he could start mouthing off again. "I have somethin' you need to hear, and I aim to tell you. After that, I'll be more than happy to leave. Now, which is it? Do I come up there, or do you come down here?"

"Screw you," he said as he hung up.

From another man, that response may have been less than illuminating, but I know Carl Trimble, and I knew that he'd be down shortly. He knew that I wouldn't leave without doing what I'd said I'd come to do, and he sure didn't want me to meet whoever it was up in his office with him, so he'd be down. I handed the phone back to Jimmie Carl. We were both smiling. "Sounds like Carl may not be in the best of moods," I said.

"No, sir," Jimmie Carl replied as he put the receiver back into the cradle. His relationship with Carl is complicated, and the older he gets, the more the distance between them grows. "You always seem to catch him that way."

"How about that? That's a funny thing, isn't it?"

He started to answer, but he caught sight of Carl Trimble emerging from the door at the bottom of the stair. His smile disappeared, and he nodded in Carl's direction. "He looks some mad. Already."

I looked over at the approaching Carl Trimble. Even when he was young, Carl tended to be fleshy, with the muscle tone of a ripe persimmon, but now he was simply overweight, and whether it was due to the exertion of coming down the stairs in a hurry, or the exasperation of having to answer my summons, he was red faced and clearly not at all happy. His expression was calculated to show his disdain. Had he not been in his own store and in front of a dozen or so spectators, he'd have approached me differently, he'd back it off a notch, but in front of his customers, he had to appear to be the barking dog. "Yes he does," I replied. "And I've hardly said anythin' to him yet." I rapped on the glass counter with my knuckles. "You watch yourself around him, later. You hear me?"

"Don't worry about me, Big Ray," Jimmie Carl replied.

"I don't. Not really," I said. "Still, watch yourself." There was a time when Carl took out his inadequacies on Jimmie Carl with some regularity. That's partly what led to me breaking Carl's jaw the first time. I don't think he's touched the boy since then, and the fact that Jimmie Carl has grown bigger and stronger than Carl doesn't hurt either.

Carl Trimble was about to the counter and cussing at me like we were the only two sets of ears in the store. "What the hell you want, Elmore? Unless you're buyin' somethin', you ain't welcome in my store, and even then, you ain't welcome." He brushed back his hair, which is normally oiled and combed straight back to cover the thinning crown of his head, but which had come unglued in his agitation and was draped over his face like a thin shower curtain.

I'd remained leaning against the counter, and I stood up when he got within a few feet of me. Carl Trimble's probably five six, five seven, depending on the shoes he's wearing, and I'm probably nine or ten inches taller. I hadn't intended to do it, but standing up like that when he was approaching made him stop and take a half-step back, almost like he'd walked into a cement wall. "You ought to watch your language in public," I said. "Women and children in this store. Aside from bein' offensive and a public nuisance, it's probably not good for business."

"My damn store; my goddamn language. You let me worry about my business. Now, what the hel— what is it you want, Elmore?" He paused and looked at Jimmie Carl. "Boy, find yourself somethin' useful to do. I don't pay you to gawk, or hang around entertainin' white trash like this neither."

We both waited while Jimmie Carl grabbed an auto parts catalogue from under the counter and walked away to take a break; happy to put some distance between him and us.

I opened the envelope and pulled the two photographs out and tossed them onto the glass counter in front of Carl Trimble. "Name John Christian mean anythin' to you?"

He didn't look at the photos, and it took a second or two for my words to get past his anger and into his brain. "Yeah. He was an army buddy of my brother. What's it to you?"

"He's dead."

Carl Trimble seemed confused for a moment; unsure if I was commenting on his dead brother or making a statement about John Christian. Once he realized it was the latter, he took another half-step backward and glanced at the photos and then back at me. If he recognized either of them, it didn't show.

"I take it, you hadn't heard that," I said.

He shook his head, but slowly regained his anger. "Why should I? I hardly knew him. Shit to be him, but what's that got to do with me? Or you, for that matter?"

"Someone killed him last week. Caved his head in. Right in the front room of his own house. Takes vinegar to kill a man like that, in his own place." I got the sense that Trimble started to say something, but I headed him off. "Name Gervais mean anythin'? Gilbert Gervais? Or Lidia Fernandez?"

That registered. His shoulders and chest tightened. "What's this all about?" he asked.

I reached out and shoved the photos closer to him. "You and your brave buddies worked that little gal over a few years back. Cut off her ear with a straight razor, didn't you? I'm sure you remember. And Gervais took the head off of one of your buddies for it. I know you remember that."

"What's this all about? That Gervais son-of-a-bitch was convicted. He's on death row. About to get hisself fried any day now."

"He was," I replied. "It seems he managed to break out of Tucker. State police think he's the one that killed your friend John Christian a week ago. He's on the loose now, and nobody seems to know where he is, but some folks think he might be headed this way." I paused and then nodded at the photographs. "If I was you, I'd want to know who's huntin' me. I'm sure you remember what they look like just fine, but I'd still study up on those."

Carl Trimble glanced again at the photos and then back at me. "What do you mean broke out? What do you mean *huntin' me*? Gervais is loose?"

"That's what I hear."

Carl Trimble worked his mouth like he was trying to prime an old pump, but no sound came out at first. Finally he managed to sputter, "Why's he comin' here?"

I shrugged, as if I had no interest in the matter whatsoever. "I'd think that'd be obvious even to you. I may be wrong, but he's lookin' to settle up a debt, would be my guess."

He glanced around the store, and then looked back at me. "If he's comin' this way, then I want some protection, you hear me? I demand some protection."

"*Demand*, do you? Well, that's why I'm tellin' you. You've been warned. I figure that's protection enough."

"Ain't enough. I demand some protection. What are you goin' to do?"

"You ordered me to leave your store, and now that I've warned you, that's what I aim to do." I nodded my head in the direction of the rifles and shotguns on the shelves behind us. "If you're worried, I'd get myself a gun. You might even consider givin' yourself a discount."

"Fuck that, Elmore. You're chief of police. I pay your salary, and I want some protection. I want a guard outside my house; 'round the clock."

"That so? Now, let's do some math. You're head of the town council. How many policemen do we have employed here again? Three? And you want someone stationed outside your house, do you? Around the clock on top of it all? That puts a mighty big strain on my budget." I took out my Lucky Strikes and lit one up before I continued. I blew the first lungful of smoke out of the side of my mouth as I looked down at Carl Trimble. "But I suppose I can spare Charley Dunn for a few days; how'd that be? Your cousin can watch over you. I'd think that'd make you feel secure."

"I don't want Charley Dunn. If this Gervais fella is comin' after me, then it needs to be—" he stopped short.

"*Me*? I think you were just about to say you want *me*?"

It only took a moment to work that option through his head. He probably was trying to figure out which of us, Gervais or me, would be the greater threat to his wellbeing. "No. No, it needs to be that Forrest boy. Ricky Forrest. I want him. I expect him here, right here at the store durin' the day. He can follow me home and then park out front of my house at night, park right out front so the police car is visible in case Gervais is watchin' the place."

"That right? All day and night?" I said. "Can't argue with your choice. Officer Forrest is a helluva man; one of the best I've ever been around, but he has his limits. You goin' let him sleep or eat? And how about while he's here watchin' you durin' the day? Who's watchin' your wife and son? Or don't they matter?"

"Don't give me that crap, Elmore. It's me he's after; you know that. Besides, I'm sure you'll look after my loving wife."

I should have hurt him on the spot, instead I just smiled.

"It's me that I'm worried about," he continued. "It's me he wants to hurt."

I nodded slowly in agreement. "Probably so. I suspect he might want to do you some harm. Tell me, Carl, you ever ask yourself why it is that so many people can't help but to want to stomp the livin' shit out of you?"

CHAPTER 17

Split Tree, Arkansas
Saturday, November 16, 1963

I told Carl Trimble that he had my word that the Split Tree Police Department, all three of us, would double-up on patrols past his house for the next few days. I told him we'd also leave one of the police cruisers parked on his street when it wasn't in use. I told him that was the best I could do given the uncertainty of Gervais's motives and the limited size of our department. I didn't tell him that anything we did was for Grace and Jimmie Carl's safety and not his. He wasn't happy about it, but despite all the cussing he could muster up, he didn't have much of a response except to loudly tell me that he was going to have me fired, presumably after Gervais was caught. He says that on a regular basis, but the truth is, he couldn't manage to get me canned after I busted his jaw the last time, in his own living room no less, so I doubted he'd have much more luck convincing the town council this time around. I resolved not to lose any sleep over it.

After repeating his threat to fire me, the second time calculated to be loud enough for most of the customers in the store to overhear, just in case anyone doubted that Carl had a spine, he proceeded to tell me to get out of his store. He then started to turn and walk away, but I grabbed his arm. "I'm not finished with you," I said, calculated to be loud enough for most of the customers in the store to overhear, just in case anyone was starting to think that Carl had a spine. He tried to spin loose, but he didn't have the strength, and I held on long enough to make that point obvious before letting go. "I still got a couple-three questions I want to ask you," I continued. "And I'm sure you don't want me to have to come back here and root you out of your hole a second time any more than I do."

Carl Trimble clearly wanted to say something meaningful, but he stopped himself. "The fuck sort of questions?" he finally spit out. Quietly.

"About Ring Johnson. I know you've heard."

"I don't know shit about Ring Johnson, other than he killed hisself. I'll be sure to send some flowers over to Donnie's, other than that, I don't give two flyin' fucks for the man, so don't come in here askin' me questions. Are we finished?"

"That's not what Charley Dunn has to say."

"If Charley Dunn's tellin' you anythin' then he's got shit for brains. I'm startin' to be sorry I ever got him that job."

I smiled despite myself. That was perhaps the first thing that Carl Trimble and I have ever fully agreed on. "He tells me you know somethin' about Ring hirin' in some temporary farm help. He says you told him that. I want to know what you know, or at least what you think you know."

Carl Trimble stepped a foot or so back; far enough that I couldn't grab his arm so easily if he decided to try walking away again. "I told you I don't know nothin'."

"Why's Charley Dunn think you do?"

"Ask him."

"Askin' you. And I'm runnin' out of patience doin' it."

"Don't have nothin' more to say. Now, why don't you get your ass out of my store and start doin' the goddamn job we pay you for. Stop threatenin' me and go look for that killer Gervais before he hurts someone. Or worse."

"Charley Dunn Skinner tells me that you're familiar with the man Ring hired. That he isn't from around here. He says Jo Johnson told you all about him. Why would she tell you that?"

Trimble looked at me and then looked away and then back at me. "Can't account for what he told you. Boy talks too much."

"From what I've seen, that boy doesn't have much imagination, and that seems like a funny detail for him to make up if it's not true." I dropped my smoke to the floor and slowly rubbed it out with the toe of my boot, letting Carl wait before I continued. "When was the last time you saw Ring?"

He shrugged. "Can't recall. I hardly know him to recognize him, leave alone keep track of him."

"That right? You two both belong to some of the same groups, or do I have that wrong? Didn't you two form that John Birch chapter a couple of years ago? Seems you might have some other groups in common as well."

"I'm civic minded. Maybe you should be."

"Not the sort of groups you join."

"Is that a crime?"

I shrugged. "I don't know, is it? All I'm sayin' is that it's a bit late to be claimin' you don't know each other, and if I can believe the officer you hired for me, you also seem to know somethin' about who works for him. And now, here you are, tellin' me you don't know anythin'. I'm tryin' to sort this out, but I get the feelin' that you're shinin' me on."

"Why's any of this your business? Johnsons live out in the county. You can't handle what you're paid good tax money to do. Why you so anxious to take on Ben Cooper's job?"

"You let me worry about what my business is, and what I take on or don't take on," I said. To be honest, I didn't have a good answer to that, other than the fact that if it were left to Ben Cooper, the case wouldn't get solved, and that didn't seem right. "Any idea where Jo Johnson might be? Places she might have gone to? Places where she might have taken their boy?"

"Why would I know?" Carl Trimble bowed up like a rooster. In any other man, it might have indicated that he was preparing to take a swing at me; with Carl it was an empty gesture. "Why would I? I don't know nothin' about her. Her boy neither."

"That right? That's not what Charley Dunn says, and now that I think about it, Jo's father worked for you." I gestured out at the store floor. "Twenty years probably. Right here. Right behind one of these counters, wasn't it?"

He didn't respond.

I continued. "In fact, you watched her grow up, didn't you? From when she was little. She worked here herself a few summers, as I recall. I'd think you know her pretty well." I glanced up to the window of his office. "And you always seem to take a personal interest in the welfare of the young girls you hire."

"I'm a good boss. What else can I say?"

"You could try answerin' my question. You know Ring; you know his wife." I paused. It was calculated to keep Carl Trimble on edge. "Now one of them's dead and the other's missin'. I want to find her before anythin' bad happens to her, and I thought maybe you could help me out."

"We're finished here, Elmore. Get out of my store," he said, and he turned on his heel and walked away.

I let him this time.

CHAPTER 18

Split Tree, Arkansas
Saturday, November 16, 1963

C arl Trimble didn't take the photographs of Gervais and Fernandez with him, and I wasn't much inclined to chase after him. I guess if I'm honest, I wouldn't lose any sleep if Gervais put that dog down, but I didn't want any harm coming to Grace or Jimmie Carl in the process. I put the photos back in the envelope, and as I started for the door, I heard Jimmie Carl call my name. He'd been standing off to the side, leaning on a counter in front of a rack of cowboy hats, reading his auto parts catalogue and watching us. I stopped, and he walked up to me, still wearing my brother's wide grin.

"Well, at least Dad got out of that meetin' without a black eye or a broken jaw this time," he said.

"Barely. It was touch and go for a while. Good thing for him our conversation didn't last another two minutes."

He laughed. Jimmie Carl has come to understand what Carl Trimble is. I suppose there's some feeling there, Jimmie Carl is too good a young man for there not to be, but there isn't the sort of feelings that you'd expect between a boy and the man who raised him. He's seen how Carl treats Grace and knows how he gets treated himself. He loves his mother unconditionally, but Carl's a different thing altogether; even as a young boy, Jimmie Carl preferred to spend most of his time with Ellen Mae and me and our sons. That was all right with Grace. I think it was all right with Carl too, but for different reasons. Grace was the trophy that Carl Trimble wanted; Jimmie Carl was the price he had to pay to hang her on his wall.

"Can I ask a favor? You goin' home?" Jimmie Carl asked.

I looked at my watch. "Not directly. What do you need?"

He shrugged. "Nothin', really. I was goin' to ask you to tell Ray Junior and W.R. that I'll be over by twelve thirty; just as soon as I get off here and change clothes." Jimmie Carl had recently gotten himself a 1951 Bel Air that requires more work than I suspect it's worth, but for him and my two, God couldn't have made a more perfect automobile if he'd done it on the last day of creation with the extra time he had on his hands, and the three of them spend most free weekends busting their knuckles and seeing who can come up with the most colorful cuss words.

"Tell you what, if I see them I will." I pulled the photos from the envelope and handed them to him. "Now, you can do me a favor. Look these over."

He took them and studied them both closely, unsure what he was supposed to be seeing.

"You remember that killin' over in Little Rock a few years back? That army friend of your uncle?" I asked.

"The man who lost his head? Sure."

"That's the one." I nodded at the photographs. "And that's who did it. The other is his . . . I guess I don't know what to call her; his girlfriend maybe."

Jimmie Carl nodded as he studied the photos. "She's pretty." He looked up at me. "Ray Junior and W.R. told me he broke out of Tucker Prison. Where's he now?"

"Well, that's the question, but I don't have the answer. Seems no one knows for sure where he is, but you're right, he broke out a few months back. Looks like she helped him."

"And they ain't been caught?"

"Not yet. That's why I'm showin' you the photos. State police just sent them. They think he might be headed this way, and they think he may have a score to settle with all of the men who were involved. That includes Carl."

"Dang."

"I'm just sayin' *might*."

He looked in the direction of his father's office and then back at me. "That's what you had to tell him?"

"Mostly."

He shook his head. "Stupid son of a . . . you'd think he'd be grateful."

"You know him better than that."

"Yeah. Maybe. But I do know one thing about Dad, if this here man comes lookin' for him, he'll want you around to protect him."

"Between you and me, I'm more worried about protectin' your mother. And you. Mostly your mother. I really don't think this man—his name's Gervais, Gilbert Gervais, if you don't remember—I don't think he'll come here. He got away from Tucker Prison once; if he's smart, he's long gone; he doesn't need to draw more heat than he's already doin'." I paused. "Still, until he's located, it doesn't hurt to be careful. He isn't comin' after your mother, but men like him carry trouble around like you and me carry spare change, and I don't want her around if he decides to show up. I'll keep my eyes open, but I can't be watchin' over your mother all the time. I need you to keep on the lookout as well."

He looked again at the photos and then started to hand them back to me.

"Keep them," I said. "I got more. I need you to study these and show them to Grace. Tape them to the fridge if it helps. I'll tell her personally, but until I can, you make sure she takes care of herself."

"Thinkin' I ought to hang around home; look after Mom."

I shook my head. "You can't spend all your time watchin' her either. He could be on the run for a week, or a year, or we may never catch him. I suspect that's the case, but until we know where he is, I'd rather you be around the house more at night. Ricky and I will be drivin' by durin' the day, but we can't do that all night long."

"Got it."

"You understand me?"

"Think so, Big Ray."

"Not sure you do. Listen, you see anythin', anythin' at all, you call me. Understand? You hear me now, I don't want you to try to deal with this man by yourself." I realized the tone of my voice was not what I wanted it to be, and I softened it. "Like I said, this man likely is headed elsewhere, just as fast as he can go, but—"

"Got it. I do."

"If he does show up, I have all the confidence in the world that you could handle it, but—"

He smiled and held up a hand to stop me. "Got it, Big Ray. Call you if we see anythin'."

I looked at him, he was wearing my brother's grin. "You got it, son," I said. "I know you do."

CHAPTER 19

Split Tree, Arkansas
Saturday, November 16, 1963

I left the store and started back to my office, but I decided to go into the courthouse and check to see if Ben Cooper was around. He normally doesn't work the weekends, but I thought maybe with Ring dead, and Jo missing, that maybe he was. His office is on the second floor. He wasn't in, but Pinto Bean and a couple other deputies were there, shooting rubber bands at each other and listening to the radio. The Razorbacks were getting ready to kick-off to SMU. We all talked for a few minutes, and I determined from them that Ben hadn't learned anything new about Jo and her boy, or, if he had, he hadn't shared it with any of his deputies.

I borrowed the phone and called Ben's house. His wife told me that he was out fishing and that she didn't know when he'd be back, but probably not until closer to dark. We talked a while, and it was clear that if Ben had learned anything new, he hadn't shared it with her either. I couldn't help but think that if a friend of mine had come up dead, and his wife and child were still missing, that I might let the fish go uncaught for another weekend. But then I'm not Cecil Ben Cooper. Maybe that was his way of dealing with it.

I hung up and went back to my office. Charley Dunn was out. It was almost noon, and I guessed that he'd gone after some lunch, or maybe he was parked under a tree somewhere taking a nap. I was just glad to not have to see him; I wasn't in the mood. There was a stack of photographs on my desk, still smelling of developer, copies of the same ones that I'd given to Jimmie Carl. I suspect that Ricky had come in long enough to pick them up from the drug store; for damn sure Charley Dunn hadn't shown that level of initiative. I put a few in the envelope I was carrying, locked the office, and drove home.

My two boys had already left by the time I got there, Jimmie Carl apparently had gotten *Maggie Jean* started, which I think is something he can't take for granted, and like he'd told me he would, he'd come by and gotten them. They'd be at the gas station; Jim Bevins lets some of the local teenage boys work on their cars there on weekends. They'd be gone until the sunlight gave out. Ellen Mae was happy that I was home, and she fixed the two of us some cold meatloaf sandwiches, and we had lunch sitting on the front porch. Afterwards I helped her get the dishes cleared, and then I told her that I was headed out to Ring's place. I asked if she wanted to go with me, and she didn't have anything more pressing to get accomplished, so she agreed. I was glad for her company, and we loaded up the two dogs and drove out there.

I parked in Ring's driveway, almost at the same spot where Ben Cooper and I had stood around the day before. I let the two dogs out, and they began nosing around and tending to bushes and tree trunks with some precision, but they stayed close. We walked around to the back of the house, passing the tool shed as we did. I was a bit concerned at first; I was afraid that the smell might still be strong, and I didn't want Ellen Mae to have to experience that, but I was surprised when I couldn't smell anything but dead leaves and the normal odors of fall and maybe a whiff of bleach and pine cleaner. It dawned on me later that Donnie Junior must have finally come out and mopped the place down like his father had told him to do.

I planned to walk around inside the house again, but my main intention was to talk with the neighbors and see if they knew anything that might be of help. Ring had some small acreage to the west side of his house, but most of it, the part planted in cotton, was to the north across the county road. There are two adjoining farms at the rear of the Johnson property, the Cowans to the west and the Broussards to the east, and because the roads outside of town mostly follow the range and township lines, I figured it might be easier to cut across Ring's back pasture on foot than to loop all the way around the fields, especially this time of year when the grasses are mown and there isn't much concern for ticks and chiggers.

As Ellen Mae and I started across the back lot, and angled west to the Cowan's farm, Todd, who'd stayed fairly close to Ellen Mae's side, broke into a run and made a beeline for their house, about two football fields away. Our dog, Trip, though I'm sure he had no idea why he was doing it, other than there might be some new bushes to pee on, joined him. Ellen Mae and I didn't break into a run, and it took us another six or seven minutes to get there, having a barbed wire fence to negotiate, and when we emerged into the Cowan's back yard, Ken and Susan were standing on their back porch.

"Big Ray. Ellen Mae. Can't say I'm much surprised," Ken Cowan greeted us as we walked up to their back door. Ken was bent over giving Todd a good ear scratch. Trip waited in line. "I see you found Todd. We were wonderin' what happened to him."

"Ken. Susan," I responded. "I guess that answers one of my questions."

The women greeted each other.

"That's some news about Ring," Ken answered. He shook my hand and then turned his attention to Trip's ears.

"Just terrible," Susan added.

"It is," I replied.

"Just terrible," Ellen Mae said.

"I suppose that's why you're here," Ken said.

"I suppose it is."

Ken turned to his wife. "Mother, we got us any coffee?"

They did, and we went inside and sat at the kitchen table. The house still smelled of lunch; fried potatoes and ham. Susan poured four cups of black coffee and put a platter of pound-cake slices in the middle of the table, while the dogs sat at the back step and looked in through the screen door, taking in all the smells, and growing long ropes of slobber. Ken lit up a smoke and offered me one. I joined him, and we all spent a few minutes rehashing how terrible it was what happened to Ring.

"Right now, I'm more concerned about Jo," I finally said.

"Amen," Susan said.

"Y'all have any idea where she is; where she and Joe Dennis might have gone off to?" I asked.

"No," she replied. "When we saw you two comin' from their way, I was hopin' you had some news about her."

"I wish I did," I answered.

Susan shook her head slowly. "You know her folks are dead."

"Yeah."

"I think any family she has are all up in Crittenden County," she continued. "But I don't think she's really very close to any of them anymore."

"So I've heard." I paused and formulated what I was going to say. "Let me ask y'all, how have she and Ring been gettin' along recently? Things all right between them?"

Ken and Susan looked at each other. Finally, Ken spoke. "Ain't our place, Big Ray."

"Noted," I said. "I think we're past that though. Tell me what you know. Any reason to think he might have hurt her?"

"What? No. No," Ken replied quietly. "No. None whatsoever."

"I don't think so," Susan added more slowly. "Not like you're thinkin'."

"Not sure what I'm thinkin', but okay. Still, you didn't answer me on how things are goin'."

Ken shrugged. Susan watched him. He didn't answer.

"Things haven't been good there for a while," Susan said, when it was clear that her husband wasn't going to speak up. "Just sour."

"Sue—" Ken started to say.

She cut him off with a look. "No. Now, that's right. They haven't been. Ain't no secret that Ring's been drinkin' lately. Way too much."

"Sue—"

Susan made a point of looking at Ellen Mae rather than me or her husband. "Jo says it's been gettin' worse, too. You know. The drinkin'. You know they're havin' money troubles? That's what it is. That's the root. She says Ring invested in a used car dealership up in Forrest City; some man he knew from the army or somethin'. Then this partner of his went and ran off with all the money. Just took it all, and left Ring with a bunch of old cars that don't run and nobody wants to buy. That's what started it."

"Susan—" Ken tried again.

"She says the bank's losin' patience. They still have a sizable mortgage from when they rebuilt their house a few years back. After the tornado. I hear he put most of this year's crop and some of his property up for collateral with a bank up there."

I looked at Ken Cowan. He was nodding, reluctantly. "And cotton looks to be down this year as is," he added. "Makes it worse."

Being foreclosed on can be a powerful incentive to kill yourself, I thought; except I knew that Ring hadn't pulled the trigger on his own. "Looks to me that the cotton he's got is about to be spoilt if he doesn't get it in soon," I said.

"Got that right," Ken agreed.

"Speakin' of which, what can you tell me about Ring bringin' in some hired man? Any truth to that?" I asked.

Ken looked at his wife, and then nodded some more. "I know probably about as much as you do, Big Ray. I don't really know anythin' about him, to be honest. That's the fact. You know, Big Ray, we just don't socialize with them all that much. We wave in passin', but they tend to keep private. And we try to mind our own business."

"But you know somethin'. And right now, I can use any help I can get," I said. It's always struck me how different people react to news of trouble. Some folks cozy up to it and make themselves a part of the story; others put as much distance between it and themselves as they can.

He shrugged again. "I know there's been a man in his fields occasionally. Can't say that he gets much done, but I've seen him out there."

"What's he look like? You describe him?"

Ken took a deep breath and let it out slowly. "Big ol' cuss, but I can't say I've gotten that good a look at him. He's kind of raw boned, I guess. You know, he just looks like a hired hand, except . . ."

"Except what?"

"Except he drives a nicer car than you'd expect, and he doesn't look all that motivated to work. Like I say, I haven't seen him much, but he seems to be takin' a break, smokin' a cigarette every time I do."

"And when was that? The last you saw him?"

"A week. Maybe. Maybe a bit more; bit less. Can't say I made much of a note of it."

I thought again about the state of Ring Johnson's crops. "Don't guess you have any idea where Ring found this fella?"

Ken looked at Susan again before answering. "No. He's not from around here, I know that," he said.

Susan nodded and fidgeted with her coffee mug. "Jo says he just showed up one day lookin' for work, and Ring hired him. She . . ."

"Go on," I prompted.

Susan shrugged. "There was somethin'. . . like maybe she didn't want to talk about it. You know? I just assumed she was embarrassed about everythin'; the money problems and needin' to hire in some help, and the drinkin' and all."

"No idea where I can find this hired hand now?"

Ken shook his head. "Like I said, last I seen him was more than a week or so ago. Not since."

"I think Jo said he was stayin' at some campground or motor lodge," Susan answered.

"Motor lodge?"

"Maybe. I think that's right," she said.

"Funny place for a seasonal field hand," I said. "Don't know that I've ever heard of a day laborer who could afford to stay at a motor lodge."

"I may be makin' that up. Maybe it was a campground. I don't remember exactly what she said," Susan replied. "But I thought it was a motor lodge."

I shifted in the chair and adjusted the weight off of my bad leg. "I don't guess you recall if she happen to mention which one? Does the General Fagan sound familiar? Could she have said that?"

Ken and Susan both squinted at the name and looked at each other blankly.

"I don't think she said," Susan replied. "I'm sure she didn't. Why?"

I started to mention the matchbook that Ricky had found in the tool shed, but decided against it. The fewer details that I introduce into the conversation, the fewer of those details I'll hear echo back as God's truth later on. "Let's get back to Jo. Neither of you believe that Ring would've hurt her?" I asked instead.

They both shook their heads in unison. "No, not really, " Susan replied. "Not that we've ever seen."

"And you have no idea where she might be?" I continued. "Any ideas at all?"

"Sorry, Big Ray," Ken said.

"Wish we could help, Big Ray. We haven't seen her or little Joe Dennis at all," Susan added.

I glanced at Ellen Mae, who smiled and winked at me. She knows how much I hate being called *Big Ray*. She enjoys teasing me, and I'd hear about it later.

Susan caught the look and the wink. She must have thought that I was questioning her response, because she glanced at Ellen Mae as if she needed an ally. "Sometime I see her out back. You know, from a distance, hangin' out laundry or workin' in her vegetable garden. We wave mostly, occasionally one of us will walk over and talk a little, but I can't say I've seen her in a good week or two."

I looked at Ken. "How about Ring? Tell me again, when was the last you saw him?"

"About the same. Maybe a week or more. Maybe a bit less. Like I said, we're not that close, and this time of year, you're workin' in the fields until dark most days. You know how it is; unless you just happen to run into someone . . ."

"When'd Todd show up? I assume you're the ones been feedin' him."

"Yeah," Ken replied. He glanced at the dogs sitting at the back door, and then looked at his wife again. "I guess about the same time. He's over here off and on. He's a real mooch. We see him often enough that we didn't think much about it at first, but after a couple of days it was plain as day that no one was feedin' him. So we started."

"You didn't think that was odd?"

Ken shrugged and deferred to his wife.

"Of course. Sort of," Susan replied. "But, you know how it is. We knew that they were havin' some trouble. Ring was drivin' up and down to Forrest City every few days, messin' with all those old cars and the bank up there. Dealin' with the foreclosure. Sometimes I think Jo and the boy would go with him. At first, we just figured maybe they got hung up and couldn't get home. You know how it is; you help out neighbors; don't always wait to be asked."

"Of course. How about lights? You notice any lights on over there?" I asked. I needed to remember to check on how long the power had been off.

Ken and Susan looked at each other and then both shook their heads. "Can't say I noticed," Susan responded.

"I stopped by there a couple-three times. Knocked on the door. No one ever answered," Ken volunteered. "I didn't push it. You know, we're just not that close."

"When was that? The last time?"

"I don't know. Like I say, maybe a week ago Thursday. Somethin' like that. Early in the mornin'. His car was there, in the garage, and you know, lookin' back on it, that's kinda odd; lookin' back now."

"Why's that?"

Ken shrugged. "He doesn't park it in the garage too much. Usually he just leaves it in the driveway. Sometimes in the yard. Anyway, like I said, it was early in the mornin', and the car was there, but I didn't see or hear anythin'. Nothin'. They're usually up early, but it was just so quiet. I thought Ring might already be out in the field. Lord knows he needs to be. But I thought Jo would still be around the house, so I tried knockin'. Just checkin' on them. Wonderin' about the dog and all. You know how it is. I'll bet I've gone by there a good dozen times since, but the car hasn't been back as far as I can tell. I didn't think much of it at first," Ken added. "But then the days just kept addin' up . . . I probably should have come see you."

"No reason you should have. Jo doesn't drive. That right?" I asked.

"No," Susan answered. "I mean, you know, she's a farmer's wife. We all can drive in an emergency, but she doesn't like to. Doesn't have a license anyhow."

"You didn't happen to walk past the tool shed when you went over to knock on the door?" I asked Ken.

"Tool shed? No. I was comin' back from town and stopped on the road; walked up their drive," he said. "Why? I heard that's where Jack Tyler found him. That right? In his tool shed the whole time?"

"And you think Todd showed up about a week ago?" I asked.

"About," Ken replied. "Give or take. Ten days tops. Like I say, he isn't a stranger over here, but I think a week or so back we started noticin' him hangin' around here more. Hungrier than normal."

"Maybe," Susan added. "Maybe less. No more than that."

"I guess we probably should have reported it, but you know how it is. And we're not that close to them, and . . ." Ken said. He looked at his wife, and then back at me.

"You had no way of knowin'," I replied. "So the dog shows up about a week or ten days ago, and you haven't seen anyone else over there for about the same amount of time? That right?"

"I'd say that's about right," Ken Cowan said.

CHAPTER 20

Split Tree, Arkansas
Saturday, November 16, 1963

Ellen Mae and I sat and had a slice of pound cake and another cup of coffee with the Cowans. Their daughter had just had a baby, and Susan and Ellen Mae looked at some snapshots while Ken and me talked about the sorry state of bean prices and how quickly our boys are growing up. Their son is a year behind our two, but he plays on the football team with them, and so that's a common thread that requires pulling whenever we're around them. Very little else was spoken about the Johnsons, other than Ken's offer to take Todd. I told them that Ricky Forrest had a mind to keep him until Jo Johnson showed up. If she showed up.

After a while, the conversation finally bottomed out, and we all went quiet. I looked at Ellen Mae. She nodded and then stood up and carried our empty coffee cups to the sink and then grabbed her pocketbook. I stood up as well. So did Ken and Susan.

"Thank you both," I said. "We've bothered y'all enough. I think we'll head on over to the Broussard's place now, and see if they've seen or heard anythin'."

"You may have to wait on that, Big Ray," Ken said. "I think they're up in Paragould this weekend."

"Julie's niece is gettin' married. Again. Third time's the charm," Susan explained. She looked at the clock on the wall. "Just about now, actually."

I nodded. "That right? Well, I appreciate you tellin' us. Saves us a drive over there. I guess I'll have to check with them later." I looked at Ellen Mae. I was going to give her a chance to ask about Julie Broussard's niece and the wedding if she was inclined, but she smiled at me and signaled that we could go. "Well, I thank you both," I said again. "For the coffee and the information."

"And the delicious pound cake," Ellen Mae added.

"You're welcome," Susan replied. "But I don't think we helped you all that much, Big Ray."

"Is it true what they say, Big Ray?" Ken asked. "About Ring, I mean?"

"Depends what they say."

"You know. That he blew his head off with that old Mossberg of his?"

"Ken—" Susan said.

"Ain't askin' nothin' that Big Ray hasn't already heard; or seen," he replied. "We danced all around it for the last thirty minutes."

Ellen Mae took my arm, and we turned toward the door.

"If I knew what happened, I wouldn't be askin' so many questions," I said, as I pushed the screen door open for Ellen Mae. "Thank y'all again for the coffee and the hospitality. You think of anythin', you'll let me know?"

They both nodded.

We left about two thirty and walked back to the Johnsons' house. I wanted to poke around the inside again, and I thought that maybe Ellen Mae would see something through a fresh set of eyes. We started in the living room and dining room, but soon worked our way to the kitchen. Ellen Mae made note of the dirty dishes and the stale bread on the table, and came to the same conclusion that I had, that Jo Johnson wouldn't have left it that way, and that she'd be mortified beyond words that we were seeing it like it was. She noted all of the candles, and I explained to her that I thought the power had been out for a while.

We went upstairs and started with the boy's bedroom. She looked in the closet and the dresser and at the toys on the floor. Soon we made our way to the main bedroom, and I stood back and leaned against the door frame and watched her walk around the room, touching things lightly with her fingertips and cocking her head from time to time as she pondered what she was seeing, or not seeing; looking for all the world like a chief petty officer inspecting a barracks. She looked at Jo's vanity and shifted her purse to her left arm so that she could pick up a small framed picture of Ring and Jo and their boy, all smiling like a happy family. It was maybe a year old; not much more than that. She looked at it for a minute before putting it back and picking up a bottle or two of perfume or lotion; looking at them and smelling each one. She opened and closed a jewelry box, and picked up a metal hairbrush and replaced it gently. She smoothed out a wrinkle on Jo's side of the bedspread. She also checked the closet, paying more attention to the clothes than I had; she looked at the few items on the shelves, paying less attention to the shotgun shells than I had. She disappeared into the bathroom, and I heard her looking through the medicine cabinet. Finally, I heard her make a sound of disgust, followed by the sound of the toilet flushing.

"Men are pigs," she said as she emerged. "Just pigs. Maybe worse."

"No argument," I replied.

"Jo hasn't been here for a while," she continued.

"No argument."

We stood and looked at each other briefly, and then we walked down the hallway.

"I'm interested in what you have to say, but I want you to look at somethin' else first," I said as we got to the guest room. I pulled the bedspread back and pointed at the soiled pillow on the bed. "Ricky and I noticed that. He says it smells kinda sweet; he was thinkin' maybe hair spray."

She picked up the pillow and looked at it and then held it closer to her nose. She shook her head. "I don't think so," she said. "Not hair spray anyhow. And not any of Jo's perfume either. I wouldn't call it sweet smellin', but I see what he means."

"So you don't know?"

She smiled and put the pillow down and redid the bedspread; smoothing out the wrinkles the way that she was sure Jo would want. "Sorry. What do you think it is?"

I shrugged. I didn't want to say that all I could smell, even a day later, was Ring Johnson. "You know, my sense of smell isn't the best."

She seemed to accept that as a good enough reason for my lack of an answer.

"Well, I reckon I've seen as much as I'm goin' to see. You?" I asked.

"I guess."

I stepped back from the doorway to allow her to pass, but she didn't move. Instead, she squinted and cocked her head to the side and looked at me. "Jo left on her own, or at least she had a say in the matter," she said. "Is that what you think too?"

I squinted back at her. "How do you know that? You got that from smellin' a pillow?" I asked.

Ellen Mae shook her head, as if the answer was obvious, and it was a trick question. "There's no purse."

"What?"

"No purse." She raised her arm to use her own pocketbook for reference. "You noticed that, didn't you? Wasn't downstairs. Not anywhere up here. No. She has it with her."

I took that in. "Can't say I noticed." I thought about it for a minute. "There's a whole lot we don't know yet. Maybe somebody else was here. Maybe someone was here and stole it for all we know."

She nodded as she considered that explanation. "I don't think so. Anythin' else of value missin'?"

"How would I know?"

She chewed on that briefly. "Well, his stupid old guns are in the closet, and her jewelry's still here, and there's a silver-plated hairbrush on the vanity back there. It looks like a family piece; I'd guess it was her mother's, maybe. None of it may be all that valuable, but I suspect it's still worth more than anythin' she might have in her pocketbook. And even if she did have some money in it, which it doesn't sound like from what Ken and Susan told us, wouldn't you just take the money? Why take the whole pocketbook? Lord knows, I wouldn't carry one if I didn't have to."

I didn't really have a good response.

She smiled as she brushed past me and stepped into the hallway. "You're losin' your touch." She poked me in the stomach. "Nossir, *Big Ray*." She drew it out like a long pull of taffy. "Her handbag is gone, and I'd guess she took it."

CHAPTER 21

Split Tree, Arkansas
Saturday, November 16, 1963

Truth be told, I'm not a very good cop, maybe average, maybe a little above average for around here, but I'm definitely not much of a detective. Ellen Mae is a lot more observant than I am, and I learned a good deal from watching her walk around the Johnsons' house. Before we left, I went back to the master bedroom and took the framed photo from Jo's vanity. "You up for another road trip?" I asked Ellen Mae.

She smiled and took my arm. "This is turnin' into quite a date. You buy me a milkshake later?"

"Deal," I replied. We rounded up the dogs and got back into the car headed north, as if we were headed for Marianna.

There were no other cars on the road, and we got there in less than an hour. Ricky Forrest had been right; the General Fagan motor lodge is on the west side of Highway One, a few miles after you cross into Lee County. It was a stretch of about a dozen separate bungalows made out of flagstone and clapboards, clustered around a small swimming pool, which had about two feet of stagnant green water with leaves and trash floating in it. There was a small playground to the side, with a swing and a teeter-totter and some knee-high weeds. Three or four cars were in the parking lot when we pulled in, but no sign of people. I shut off the car, and Ellen Mae and I went inside one of the bungalows that looked like it was the office.

There was no one at the front counter when we first walked in. We stood there and waited for a minute or two. The room smelled of cigarette smoke and mildew and canned soup. There was a mug of coffee on the desk behind the counter, half full, and somewhere further in the back, around a corner formed by a paneled wall, there was a radio that we couldn't see; the volume was low, but we could make out the voice of an announcer calling the Razorback football game, so we knew whoever was working the desk likely hadn't gone far. I called out but got no answer. I called out again, and I was about to slap the bell on the counter when a spare little man emerged from a door at the back of the office. He was carrying a rolled-up magazine, and didn't seem to be overly surprised or concerned to see two customers waiting for him in front of the counter, and certainly didn't seem to be in any hurry to find out what we wanted. He was short-to-medium tall, likely not more than 150 pounds, but he moved like he could take care of himself if the need arose; one of those men who had endured being short and picked-on his entire life and had developed a thick callous of resentment as his armor. He had short, thin, grey-brown hair the color of a cotton rat, cut into a thinning flattop, and it made his head resemble a cement block except for the protrusion of a large nose that looked as if it had been sharpened on a whetstone. He also had one of those lopsided smiles that almost begged to be slapped off of his face, if you were man enough.

"Room?" he asked as he tossed his magazine onto the desk and took a swallow of coffee. Only then did he step behind the counter and really pay any attention to us. He looked at me first and then smiled as he took in Ellen Mae, his pale brown eyes working her up and down more than would prove healthy for him if it continued much longer. "Four dollars. Per room. Per person. Per night. No hourly rate, so get your money's worth. I would." He took his eyes off of Ellen Mae long enough to look at me. "You two married, I can put you in one room. Otherwise, two rooms. That's the law." He smiled again and returned his look to Ellen Mae. "I don't ask to see marriage licenses. So, you people tell me you're married, I have to take your word for it."

"I don't need a room," I said.

"Too bad for you," he answered, his eyes still on Ellen Mae. He wasn't from around here. He sounded Yankee, though I'm not good with accents, and I couldn't tell you exactly where. I had a friend in the navy, up until I watched him die. He was from Teaneck, New Jersey, and he had a similar accent. Ugly sounding thing. This man's wasn't quit the same, but it was similar.

I stepped closer to the counter, partially putting myself in front of Ellen Mae. "You have a name?"

He looked up at me. "Matter of fact, I do. They were handing them out when I was born. How about you?"

"My name's Ray. You own this place?"

"Probably do. Maybe don't."

"I want some information."

"That right? Well, *Ray*, I rent rooms, not information. The people who come here aren't interested in information." He tilted his head to the side just far enough to look past me at Ellen Mae.

"Make an exception," I said. I leaned on the counter and pushed the photo of the Johnsons in front of him. "You ever see this man here?"

"No."

"Mind lookin' at it before you answer?"

He did, reluctantly taking his eyes off of Ellen Mae for a minute. "No," he said again as he pushed the photo back at me. "Eyesight ain't so good. Besides, I don't get paid to remember people."

"Your eyesight seems plenty good."

"Depends on what I'm looking at, I guess."

"Try the photo. You ever seen that man?"

"No."

"You sure?"

He looked at my wife again, and then at me. "You sure you don't want a room, Ace?"

"No."

"Pity."

"I want an answer," I said.

"Who're they to you anyway?"

"I asked you if you were sure. You've never seen him?"

He stepped a couple of feet back and squared up to the counter. "Look, *Ray*, I rent rooms to people who need rooms. Looks like you could make use of one to me. You got the money, I got a vacancy. Otherwise, I'm sorta busy." He returned his look, and his lopsided smile, to Ellen Mae. "*If Ray here doesn't want a room, I can rent one to you. Give you a good deal,*" he said to her.

"I'm sort of runnin' out of patience," I said. "And I'm talkin' to you. If I were you, I'd look at me. It may not be as pleasant, but in your case, it'll be healthier."

That seemed to get his attention. "Look, Ace, I don't want no trouble." He adjusted the distance between his feet so that he was well balanced, the way a boxer does.

"You got a funny way of avoidin' it."

"Ray," Ellen Mae said, taking my arm. "Ray. Let's go."

The clerk's eyes darted back to Ellen Mae and then to me. I think her tone of voice, and her taking my arm, alarmed him. "What is it you want?" he asked. "I told you, I ain't looking for trouble."

"I don't want trouble either. I asked a simple question, and all I want from you is a simple answer. Have you seen this man before? Nothin' more complicated than that. I just want you to give me a straight answer. And I want to believe you when you do," I said. I didn't pull my arm away from Ellen Mae, but I didn't let her pull me back from the counter either. "As soon as I get that, we'll be on our way, and you can get back to all your important business."

The clerk looked at me for a long moment, probably gauging where the conversation would end. Once he'd run the calculations, he picked up the frame and looked closely at the photo. He shook his head and cleared his throat. "No," he said. He cleared his throat again. "No. I ain't never seen this man. Satisfied now?"

"Honest?"

He nodded. "No reason not to be, Ace. Honest."

I figured that he was telling the truth, and while I had him talking, I asked, "You have anyone registered here that might be day labor? Someone that might be a seasonal field hand?"

He was a man who rationed his answers, and I was getting close to the limit. He looked at me like I was crazy, and he sort of laughed. "Look around, boss. This look like the sort of joint that caters to farm workers?"

"I take that as a *no*. And I reckon you're still bein' honest."

"Take it any way friggin' way you want. I'm telling you we don't have people like that staying here."

"Fair enough," I said. I took the frame back from him. "That's all I needed to know. Thank you."

The clerk took another half step back from the counter and watched as Ellen Mae and I turned, and I opened the door and held it for her. As I stepped outside, I stopped and turned. "One more question," I said. "You have any gofer matches?"

The clerk tilted his head in confusion. I realized he probably didn't know what I was referring to, and I started to explain before I got another smart-aleck answer. "Paper matches," I said. "Book matches."

He nodded slowly. "I know what goddamn gofer matches are." He hesitated and then reached under the counter and produced a handful of paper matchbooks. "How many you need?"

I walked back to the counter. "One would be fine," I replied.

He put the handful of matchbooks on the counter. "You look like a jarhead." he said. "You serve?"

Now it was my turn to cock my head. "Corpsman. You?"

He nodded. "*Semper fi*," he said. "Okinawa for a year; Korea for two."

I looked at the matchbook in my hand. It was a dull cherry-red with black text and a drawing of a bearded Confederate general beside the silhouette of a cannon. "How long you printed these in red?" I asked.

He looked at me and then at the matchbook. The question clearly didn't make much sense to him.

"I've got an old one that's green," I continued. "This one's red. When'd you change colors?"

Why in the world someone might be interested in that sort of thing, he couldn't have guessed, let alone cared, but we'd both served, and that seemed to buy me a little more of his patience. He shrugged. "Just did. Got these in last Monday, I think. Probably still got some green ones in the back if you want."

"How long did you print them in green?"

"How the hell should I know? They're goddamn matches."

"You're the owner here. If you don't, who would?"

He shrugged. "Five years. Four years. Six years. Ten years. I don't know. Just what the hell you after mister?"

"Thank you," I said. "That's all I need." I turned and left.

CHAPTER 22

Split Tree, Arkansas
Saturday, November 16, 1963

We drove back to town. Along the way, I apologized to Ellen Mae for starting to lose my patience with the motel clerk. I'm prone to impatience, and it often doesn't end well. She responded by laughing and telling me that she'd let it slide just this once, mainly because the motel clerk had made her skin crawl. She said she'd considered getting a room just to take a shower and rinse off his leer. I told her that if we could convince the clerk we were married, that we could get a single room, and I'd be happy to help wash her back. She laughed again and slid across the seat and leaned into me. "Maybe later," she said. "After the milkshake you promised me."

We stopped first at our house and put the dogs in the back yard and then Ellen Mae and I went to Jim Harland's Drive-In, and I bought her a chocolate shake; like I'd promised. I got a Coke, and we sat in the car and listened to the end of the Razorback game on the radio. They lost to the Mustangs, fourteen to seven. They're pretty poor this year. Mostly, we talked while we finished our drinks, and eventually we circled back around to our examination of the Johnsons' house. Ellen Mae picked through her logic, looking for flaws in her thinking. She was right, of course. She's a smart woman. A whole lot smarter than me. Jo Johnson's pocketbook was nowhere to be found in the house and that meant more than likely that she took it with her. Once Ellen Mae said it, it made sense. Ellen Mae may not always have her pocketbook close by, but when she doesn't, you can damn sure figure it's in one of three places: on the kitchen counter near the toaster, on the floor beside the secretary to the right of our front door, or in our bedroom to the left of her dressing table. If it's not one of those places, then it's hooked on her forearm. And when the boys were little, Joe Dennis's age, it stayed even closer to her than it does now. My mother was the same way, in fact just about every woman I've ever known is the same, and I have no reason to think that Jo Johnson is any different.

We got home a little before five thirty, and Ellen Mae got started on dinner, and I tended to a few chores around the house that I'd been avoiding. Despite it being the middle of November, the yard needed mowing, and the boys had found one excuse after another to put it off. I worked until it was too dark to see and then went in and cleaned up. The boys blew in long enough to eat, and then Jimmie Carl showed up, and they all blew out again. Normally, they have a basketball game on Saturday evenings in November, but there was a county-wide tournament coming up in a few days, and there was no game scheduled. They took advantage of the night off to meet friends at the drive-in and then head off to a dance at the Canefield High School. They'd likely end up going to someone's garage and working late on that old car of Jimmie Carl's.

After we got the dinner dishes cleared, I went and sat on the front porch swing and smoked some cigarettes and tried to sort through all of the puzzle pieces that I was collecting. The evening was warm for November, and with a light sweater, it was pleasant. The air had taken on a crispness over the last week, and that helped to flush the smell of Ring Johnson out of my nose. Ellen Mae took a bath and then joined me. She curled up in the swing beside me and adjusted her bathrobe to cover her knees and put her head on my shoulder. I could feel her damp hair on my neck, and she smelled of Ivory soap and talcum powder.

"I really enjoyed today," she said. She let out a contented sigh.

"You did?" I responded. "I'm glad. Me too. I should take you to investigate crime scenes more often."

"That's not . . . I mean . . . you know . . . what happened to Ring is tragic . . . but . . ."

I laughed and leaned over and kissed the top of her head. "I know what you mean. I enjoyed it too. It's a good thing, I guess. Soon enough, it'll just be the two of us."

She was quiet for a long time after I said that, but I could feel her nodding her head in silent agreement. I hadn't meant to sober the moment, but I had. If you need someone to say the wrong thing at the wrong time, you can generally count on me. "You suppose they'll come back?" she said quietly, almost to herself.

"Of course," I said with all the assurance I could. "They'll go, for a few years, but they'll come back. I did."

She shook her head. "You had reasons to come home. People."

She was right. My father and sister were dead, and we lost my younger brother Reuel in the war, but my mother was still alive when I finally got out of the hospital, and she needed help with the farm, and that drew me home, but I felt that Ellen Mae was referring more to the hold that Grace has over me. "Ellen—"

"Don't Ray," she stopped me; she'd read my mind. "I know what you're thinkin'. I didn't mean it that way. Honestly. Not this time. I meant . . . yes, Grace was here, and your mother, but I guess what I really meant was that you had *people* here. The people of Split Tree. It's in your blood, Ray. More than me. More than anyone else I know really. You could no more leave this place than I could fly to the moon and back. Your roots are too deep in this soil."

"So are the boys'."

She straightened up and looked at me. "No, not like you. This is their home, yes, but with you . . . it's more; it's almost like you were put here to watch over us all."

I laughed, but not in a funny way. "Ellen—"

"It's true."

"Stop. Just stop." I know it came out harsher than I intended, but I had no desire to let the conversation head in that direction.

We sat quietly for a long spell before Ellen Mae spoke again. "I heard you and Ricky the other night. The other night when the two of you were out here. I wasn't eavesdroppin', at least not the way you think. I was bringin' y'all a couple of beers, but when I got to the door . . . I heard you two talkin'. All quiet like. At first, I thought it was man stuff. You know, *man stuff,* but then I heard you mention the boys. I didn't mean to listen. Honest Ray. But I did. All the talk of Vietnam and what's happenin' in the world. I worry about them. I worry about our little town. We're such a small part of the great big world, and our sons have to live in that world."

"And they'll find their way in it. They're good boys. They'll be good men. You've raised them well."

"But will they be able to find their way back here? Will they even want to?"

"Their mother's here."

"I'm serious, Ray."

I put my arm around her and pulled her against me. "I am too. You're a powerful draw. You underestimate how much they love you."

She put her head back on my shoulder and worked it around until she found a comfortable fit. "What you and Ricky were sayin' worries me. It isn't true is it? We just finished a war. Two wars. The president wouldn't get us into another one, would he? So soon?"

"Kennedy's a jackass," I replied too quickly. That wasn't the answer Ellen Mae asked for. "No," I continued. "I don't think we have to worry about him gettin' us involved in another war. I hope not anyway. Not really."

"Why do you dislike him so much?"

"Never met him."

"Doesn't stop you from dislikin' him."

I got my smokes out of my pocket and managed to get one into my mouth and lit without taking my arm from around Ellen Mae. I thought about it as I blew the first lungful of smoke out into the night. "Maybe because he was a navy officer, and that's all I need to know," I answered.

When she decided I wasn't going to continue, she said, "You were in the navy."

"That's my point."

"You should have been an officer. You'd have been good at it."

"I never met one worth a damn. Officers are good at dumpin' young boys off on godforsaken islands to get killed; not sure they're much suited for anythin' else. But from what I read, Kennedy may not be around much longer. I guess it's whoever comes next that we really have to worry about gettin' us into another war."

"You don't think he'll get re-elected?"

I shrugged. "Who knows? The paper says it's not a sure thing. Even the Democrats aren't happy with him. He's goin' to Texas this weekend to campaign, and we're a whole year away from the election."

"Well, I think he'll be re-elected," Ellen Mae said with the confidence necessary to reassure herself. "And he won't let us get into another war. Even if he was a navy officer."

I took another long drag on my smoke and pulled her in closer.

CHAPTER 23

Split Tree, Arkansas
Saturday, November 16, 1963

We sat quietly on the porch, and I think that Ellen Mae may have actually dozed off a couple of times. I badly needed to adjust the weight on my leg, but I didn't want to disturb her or disturb what we had together, and I sat in the same position way too long. I'd pay for it later when I tried to sleep. Granville gave me a bottle of pills a few months ago, to take the edge off when the pain gets too bad, but I try to avoid them. My leg hurts all the time, and I can't take pills all the time.

About ten o'clock, she got up and kissed me, and told me to not stay up too late, and went off to bed. I got up and paced around the porch, stretching my leg as much as my head. I smoked a couple more cigarettes, and about ten thirty I started walking down the street.

I suspect that if you'd asked me at the time, I couldn't have told you what I was going to do when I got there. I was headed to the Trimble house. I could have told you that, but I wasn't going to see Grace. She'd be awake, I'm sure; she was always a bit of a night owl, and it was too early for her to have turned in. There was a time when I think she stayed up late to avoid getting into Carl Trimble's bed; at least, I like to imagine that's why she did. The thought of her with that man still eats away at something inside me, but for the last several years they've slept apart. I know that as a fact. I had something to do with it. Something awful happened to Grace a few years back, something that I can hardly bring myself to think about, let alone talk about even now. It involved her husband, Carl, and his brother, Jay. I beat Carl badly for it. I killed Jay Trimble for it. Probably should have killed Carl as well. I don't know to this day if Carl's aware that I ended his brother, or even if he suspects it, or if his ego would let him acknowledge it if he did. I don't sleep well at night for a lot of reasons, but I haven't lost a minute of sleep for killing Jay Trimble. I also know his body has never been found, and isn't likely to be now, so unless I decide to unburden myself with a confession, there isn't much in the way of proof that I did it. I carry a fair burden for a lot of wrongs I've committed in this life, but that isn't one of the rocks in my load. Grace and her husband now live separate lives; same house, but separate lives, and I'm glad for that. Still, it's also sad in a way. Grace deserves love; she deserves a husband to grow into old age with, to sit on the porch swing with and drink milkshakes with at the drive-in. I have Ellen Mae. Grace has her son, but she deserves more. But that isn't the hand she was dealt, and I reckon, given the options, living a life pretty much separate from Carl Trimble is as good as it's going to get for her. Still, I can't help be feel sad about it.

It took me fifteen minutes, no more than that, to get to West Road. I could see Grace's house when I turned the corner. The street was well lit, but the streetlight directly in front of her place was broken. A couple of weeks ago, some kids, I suspect the three youngest Hudson brothers, had gone on a fall vandalism spree, taking baseball bats to a score of mailboxes and pellet guns to streetlights and car windows. Given Split Tree's budget, it'll be a while before we get everything repaired. *Of all the time for the light to be broken*, I thought. I'd check about getting someone out to fix it in the morning.

I could also see Carl's black Buick parked in his driveway. He keeps it cleaned and waxed, or at least some of his employees at the store keep it washed and waxed, and even in the shadows cast across his property, the car shown like a mirror in the dim light. He was home.

I continued up the block. As I got closer, I could see a faint glow coming from the living room. Everything else was dark, and I wondered if Carl was asleep. I stopped a few houses away and lit a smoke and leaned on a mailbox while I watched the house and the street; listening to the quiet. I heard an eastern whippoorwill working away, but other than that, it was quiet. I needed to talk to Grace. I needed to warn her to be watching for Gervais, and I couldn't trust Carl Trimble to tell her. But tonight wasn't the time. Tomorrow.

I turned and started up the block when a car parked on the other side of the street, past Grace's house near the broken streetlamp, flashed its lights. I almost didn't catch it, but I stopped and watched. It flashed them a second time, and I crossed the street and headed toward it. I'd thought earlier, when I was on the porch swing with Ellen Mae, that I should go to the office and get my pistol. The town issued me a four-inch Colt Commando revolver when I was hired. It probably isn't worth much as a weapon, but it's small and easy to carry, but I never do. It stays in my desk drawer; I've only gotten it out two or three times in the seventeen or so years I've been Chief. Whoever was in the car with the flashing lights, it wasn't Gervais; he wouldn't have any reason to draw attention to himself. Still, it made me think twice about the need to get my gun.

When I got within thirty or forty feet of the car, I recognized it easily; it was a Ford Galaxie station wagon, grey in the night, but I knew it was beige in the daylight. I opened the passenger door and got in.

"Guess I can't say I'm surprised," I said. I shut the door quickly to kill the dome light.

"Chief," Ricky Forrest said. "I can't say I am either. I knew you'd show up sooner or later."

"Should have come earlier."

"It's harder for you to get away. I know that."

"You're the one with the young wife and a new baby."

He laughed. "Right. And that new baby wears that young wife out so bad that she's in bed by eight o'clock every night. I can sit out here by myself just as well as I can sit alone in my den."

"How long you been here?"

"A few hours." He picked up a thermos bottle next to him and held it out for me. "Coffee? You're welcome to it. I'm trying to not drink any more of it; if I do, I'll have to make a pit stop in someone's rose bushes."

"No thanks. Been quiet?"

"Nothing," he replied. "Carl got home a couple of hours ago. No movement in the house; no cars driving down the street," he said, and then he pointed at the broken streetlight. "I'll see if someone can get that fixed tomorrow. Or Monday. Though it's kinda nice to be able to park here and not be seen, but that cuts both ways, I guess."

"I was thinkin' the same thing. It's dark all right. I could barely see your car from up the street."

"It's not parked here by accident," he laughed.

"Guess the army taught you somethin'."

He laughed again. "Not sure the army taught me much, but a couple thousand screaming Chinese trying to kill me sure as shit did."

"I'll bet."

"By the way, I came by your house earlier today to get the dog. You weren't home. I saw him in the back yard, but I didn't want to take him without letting you know. I guess I could have left a note, but . . ."

"No problem. He and Trip have come to an agreement. Todd's as ugly as a three-eyed cow, but he seems like he's a good dog." I paused. "No, we were gone most of the afternoon. Ellen Mae and I went up to the General Fagan. Had me a talk with the owner."

"How'd that go? Productive?"

"Depends on which one of us you ask. He didn't get his ass kicked. I wouldn't have given you odds on that five minutes into the conversation."

"Well, that's productive, but did he know anything useful?"

"He knows a handsome woman when he leers at one, but other than that, it's hard to tell. I don't think he'd ever seen Ring before. I'm pretty sure he was tellin' the truth about that much. I stopped at the Johnsons' house and took a photo of the family so he had somethin' to look at. He didn't have any reaction when he saw it; I really don't think he'd seen him before. I also asked about the matchbook you found. They've got news ones that're red, but that doesn't tell us much. He said they changed colors recently. That one you found could be from last week, or last year."

"It was a long shot."

"I guess."

"Needed doing," he said.

"I reckon, but we also stopped and talked to Ken and Susan Cowan. You were right, they were feedin' Todd."

"Someone had to be."

"Well, it was them."

"How long?"

"They weren't sure, but they don't think that they've seen anyone around the Johnsons' place for a week or more."

"That goes with the condition of the body."

"It does. And accordin' to them, Ring was in over his head with a bank up in Forrest City. Got himself into a bad business deal. I guess he mortgaged everythin' he could lay his hands on, and his house and farm are about to be foreclosed on."

"Good reason to kill yourself."

"Would be, except we know he didn't."

"True. But it's also a good way to get yourself killed. You get desperate enough, you make poor decisions, and maybe start looking for help in the wrong places. Ask the wrong people for money, you find out pretty quick that banks aren't always the worst creditors you can have. I guess the Cowans haven't also been feeding Missus Johnson?"

"No, but Ellen Mae made a good observation. I had her look around the Johnsons' house before we left. Woman's perspective."

"And?"

"And she noticed right off that Jo Johnson's handbag was missin'."

Ricky nodded slowly as he worked that puzzle piece into the picture that he was constructing. "I should have thought of that," he said. "Makes sense when you hear it, doesn't it? I know Kitty doesn't ever stray far from hers, especially now that we have a baby. I don't know which is attached to her arm tighter, Eddie or her pocketbook."

"That's exactly what Ellen Mae said. She noticed it right off."

"More evidence that Missus Johnson left on her own accord . . . or at least left with someone she was comfortable being around. That what you're thinking?" He paused, and then continued. "Damn. I should have noticed that."

"No. Don't hold that one against yourself. I think you'd have to be a woman to pick up on that. That's what I'm tellin' myself anyhow."

We continued talking about the Johnson case but got that moved no further down the field. Then we shifted back to the issue of Gervais being on the loose and ran that into the ground. Finally we ended up talking about children and family, and we smoked some cigarettes, and I drank some coffee. I enjoy talking with Ricky, and I wasn't paying much attention to the time, but after a while I needed to stretch my leg, and I looked at my watch. It was a little after midnight. "Dang, son, we've been here the whole night. At least you have. You need to get on home." I looked at the darkened Trimble house. "Seems quiet; I think we're okay for the night."

"Until we're not."

"Until we're not. You're right about that, still, you've been here long enough. You need to go on home."

He looked at his own watch and nodded. "In a little bit. You know, the Chinese taught me more than just how to make myself hard to be seen. You developed a good sense of when something was about to happen. If you didn't, you were dead."

I nodded. "And what's your gut tellin' you now?"

"Probably the same as yours; that nothing is going to happen anymore tonight, but I still think I'll sit here a little longer."

I looked out the window at the quiet street. "You know, if I were Gervais, I think I'd be willin' to let old scores go unsettled."

He laughed. "You? Ray Elmore? Letting an old score go unsettled? I'm not sure I believe that, boss."

I smiled. "Okay. In that case, let's hope he's not like me. Let's assume he actually has a brain in his head, and if he does, then he's long gone from here. Let's hope he's sittin' on a porch somewhere down in Louisiana with his Cuban girlfriend; countin' his blessin's' that he's not strapped to an electric chair at Tucker."

"Well, my gut doesn't tell me that much, but it does tell me that we're probably okay for tonight."

We'd come to the same conclusion, though I couldn't thank the Chinese for it. "I'll take the watch tomorrow," I said. "Go on."

"Roger. Soon. I'll sit here a bit longer, maybe give it another hour or so, and then I'll pack it in."

"Well, I'm not goin' to pretend to order you," I said. "I know you won't leave until you're ready to go, no matter what I tell you. You're a good man. Get on home soon though."

"I will," he responded. "And I'll be by to pick up Todd tomorrow afternoon."

"Better bring your wife and baby or Ellen Mae will take a big stick to you, and neither Gilbert Gervais or me will be able to protect you," I said.

He laughed and assured me that he would, and with that I got out of the car and closed the door. I leaned on the roof for a minute and looked at the darkened Trimble house. The light that had shown dimly from the living room was now out. The house was quiet.

I thought of Grace. I thought of her and fall nights that seemed a thousand years ago.

And then I walked home and undressed and got into bed. Ellen Mae roused and pushed her body into mine. She was warm and soft and more than I deserved.

CHAPTER 24

Split Tree, Arkansas
Sunday, November 17, 1963

Ellen Mae and I went to church. The boys didn't. They'd worked on Jimmie Carl's car most of the night and ended up sleeping over at a friend's house, and they didn't manage to get home in time to go with us. They generally do, but more and more frequently they seem to find creative ways to avoid it. I don't blame them. I made a real effort to go to church for the first fifteen years of our marriage, for Ellen Mae's sake; she's a believer, but even more than that, she wants the boys to be. I know they aren't, and I can't blame them, but I also thought that going to church wouldn't hurt any of us, and so, I made the effort to go, and I made them go as well.

And then a few years ago, I stopped. Something happened to Grace, something awful, and I just couldn't reconcile how a just and merciful God could have allowed it, and so He and I came to an agreement: He stopped believing in me, and I stopped believing in Him. There were no hard feelings; we just understand that it's best for both of us to stay out of each other's way. And that's pretty much how it was for a year or so, until Ellen Mae had a particularly bad spell. It started a week after Christmas a year ago, and I have no idea what brought it on. Sometimes, it seems to be a lot like getting down in the back. Sometimes you throw your back out lifting something heavy; sometimes it happens because you stepped over a crack in the sidewalk. Her *spells* are like that. Sometimes you can see one coming on, and you know what triggered it; sometimes you can't. This one showed up out of the blue. She'd spent a couple of days running at sixty miles an hour and then crashed like she'd hit a wall head first. It may be the worst one she's ever had, and it lasted almost two months. Honestly, I wasn't sure she was going to be able to crawl out of that hole; it was that deep. I thought for a while that we'd lost her for good, but for all her fragileness, she's a remarkably strong woman, in her own way. I'm not sure how she did it, but she clawed her way back out. Of course, it took another month or so for her to fully recover, and during that time our pastor and his wife were good to us. Not in a religious way, but in a genuine good-person sort of way. They checked on her and visited her and brought meals for me and the boys, and never said a word about it; never tried to turn it into a lecture or a lesson in faith. The pastor's wife would come over and sit with her during the day when I couldn't be around. Mainly, they brought Ellen Mae some light when everything about her was dark. I guess it shouldn't have come as a surprise, but when she'd recovered, the first thing she wanted to do was go to church, and she wanted me to go with her. I might have an understanding with God, but saying no to Ellen Mae is another thing, and so I started going again for her, and I've continued, for her sake, ever since, but I'm no longer committed to forcing the boys.

We attend the same church that Ellen Mae and I grew up in. In fact, after we married, we starting sitting in the exact same spot where she had as a child, on the right side, midway back, next to a stained-glass window of the Pentecost. For a number of years, I used to sit there and watch the back of Grace's head; the shine of her hair; the curve of her neck. Carl Trimble always sits in the first pew, centered square in front of the pulpit, visible to all. He sings loudly and always makes a show of getting out his wallet and depositing something noisily into the collection plate. He used to make Grace and Jimmie Carl sit at his side, also visible to all, and I'd grit my teeth with anger every Sunday. More than anyone else, I knew how embarrassed Grace was, and yet she would sit quietly, her head up, her dignity intact, abiding it all.

Growing up, Grace's father, Judge Davis, always sat in the back of the church, his wife and Grace by his side. That's where I best remember her, and if I close my eyes I can still see them all sitting there now. The Judge always sang quietly and prayed quietly and was never seen putting anything in the collection plate, though everyone knew that he'd carried the church on his back financially through the Depression and during the war, up until he died. For the last couple of years, now that Grace and Carl live their separate lives, she's started sitting in the back of the chapel, very near where her father used to seat his family. Jimmie Carl sits with her, when he attends, which is becoming more and more sporadic. For a while people talked and whispered about it, that's what we do in Split Tree, we talk about other people's problems, but compared to what happened to Grace, and the disappearance of Jay Trimble, and me busting up Carl with my fists, her sitting apart from her husband at church didn't really hold the town's interest for very long. I'm sure every person in the congregation over the age of twelve, if you asked them, could tell you why the Trimbles sat apart, or at least why everyone thinks they sit apart, but nowadays, no one cares to, or thinks to, talk about it. Carl still sits on the front row, Grace sits in the back, and no one notices. Except maybe me.

This time I sat and stared at the back of Carl Trimble's head and thought about Gilbert Gervais and what he might be doing on this Sunday morning. I thought about what I should be doing. I didn't know what it was, but I knew for sure that whatever it was, it wasn't sitting in church. Instead, I adjusted the weight on my hip and looked at my watch. It was almost noon, and the pew seemed particularly hard and the church particularly hot, and Pastor Webb was particularly feeling the spirit and seemed in no hurry to let his lambs loose to stray.

At one point he actually took to pounding the pulpit like he was nailing down a loose floorboard while he waded thigh deep into Romans. *There are vile creatures walking the earth,* he told us. *Low sinful beings that the Lord endures with His long-suffering patience; these vessels of wrath fitted for His destruction.* The vile creature part of the message may be the first thing that God and I have agreed on in a long time, except in my experience, He shows way too much patience, and if you want my opinion, He doesn't dispense near enough destruction.

Despite needing a smoke bad, and needing to walk some feeling back into my leg, I resisted the urge to jump up and leave in the middle of communion, and I endured the remainder of the service with my own long-suffering patience. We finally worked our way through the closing hymn, *Ye Servants of God,* and got sent forth, as sheep among wolves. Not a minute too soon either. There was a time, when I was young, when you got to the end of the service, you'd stand in line with your family to shake the pastor's hand and tell him what a good sermon he'd delivered and how you'd take it to heart, and then you could head on home and slip back into your mortal sins, but nowadays, the sermon is just the beginning of the ordeal. Now we have to mill about afterwards engaging in *fellowship,* which involves eating a cookie and drinking some weak tea and talking to the same people that you've been talking to all week, or worse, avoiding talking to all week. Normally, I pace around in the parking lot like a caged housecat and smoke a cigarette and wait for Ellen Mae to finish serving cookies or pouring tea into little Dixie cups.

But today I had an interest in the fellowship that followed the service. As I came down the steps of the chapel, I saw Carl Trimble in his usual spot, holding court under a small elm tree near the front corner of the parking lot with a bunch of men of similar values and qualities. He seems to value fellowship about as much as I do. But I wanted an opportunity to talk to Grace, and this offered me the best chance to see her without running into Carl. I needed to warn her about Gilbert Gervais. I'm sure that Jimmie Carl had told his mother, like I'd asked him to, and probably showed her the photographs that I'd given him. I was also sure that Carl likely hadn't warned her. In either case, I needed to do it, it was my responsibility.

The weather was still warm enough to congregate outside, and we all began working our way out the front of the church and around to the side of the sanctuary where some card tables had been set up in the grass, and the women were setting out the pitchers of tea and the platters of cookies and slices of angel food cake. During the service I'd seen Mike Taylor sitting on the other side of the chapel, and as soon as I was outside, I hunted him down first. Mike is the director of the town's public works department.

"Big Ray," he said as I walked up to him. He was lighting a smoke and offered me one. "Good to be out in the fresh air. I didn't think Pastor Webb was ever goin' get to the end of that one. Was it as hot over where y'all were as it was on our side?"

"Mike. It was hot all right. Too many sinners in the pews, I guess. Hey, you got a minute?" I took one of his cigarettes, and we both paused while I got mine lit and going.

"What's up?" he asked.

"I need you to get a streetlight fixed. As quick as you can."

He laughed. "Okay. Mind me askin'?"

"The one directly across from Carl Trimble's house is busted out."

"Damn Hudson boys."

"Yep. It's busted, and it's dark as the inside of cow there at night."

He looked at me funny. "Probably not my business, but you got reasons to hang around the Trimbles' house at night?" My past history with Grace Trimble is no secret. Mike Taylor isn't from Split Tree originally, but he's lived here long enough to have heard all the relevant gossip. You more or less get it all when you move to town; sort of like an instruction manual for living here. I'm not sure he meant anything by what he said, but it stung me a bit anyhow.

"Nothin' that I can go into right now. Can you do it?"

He nodded. That explanation was sufficient. "I'm sure it's on the list, but I can see that it gets moved to the top. It'll probably still be a few weeks though. We don't keep many replacement lights, and those dang kids busted out a good two-years' worth. I've got some on order, but it'll be a while before we get them." He paused. "Carl ask you to do this?"

"What do you think?"

He laughed. "Sorry. Heat got to me. Yeah. Give me a couple weeks."

"That's too long. Can't you do somethin' sooner?"

"How important—" he started to ask but caught himself. "Never mind. Big Ray wants it, that's good enough." He took a slow drag on his cigarette and looked down at the grass for a long time. "I guess we could take one from a workin' light somewhere else and swap it out. It'll take some work."

I slapped him on the back. "Tell you what, you can take the one at the corner by my house. Damn thing shines in my eyes when I sit on the porch at night anyways."

He shrugged. "I'll get someone on it tomorrow. That soon enough?"

"I'll owe you."

"You don't owe me nothin'," he said, and then he smiled. "Though I can't wait to hear what this is all about."

"Like I said, I'll owe you. Thanks." Before he could reply, I walked away.

The women had gotten the serving lines going, and Ellen Mae was at one end of the row of tables, standing over a dozen plates of cookies, talking to the pastor's wife. Grace was fifteen feet away at another table, filling paper cups from pitchers of tea and lemonade. I walked over to Ellen Mae and greeted the pastor's wife. I smiled and listened to the exciting news that some of the men in the flock were starting a Bible study group. and there was still time for me to join. I ate a cookie and said that I'd see if my schedule was free. I also told Ellen Mae that I was ready to go whenever she was, but that I needed to speak with Grace for a minute first. "Remember that thing you suggested I talk to her about," I added.

It took Ellen Mae a second to figure out what I was talking about, and then she nodded and touched my arm, as much to reassure herself as to respond to me. She smiled, or tried to. As I've said, normally the thought of Grace and me occupying Ellen Mae's brain at the same time is a source of some serious irrational concern. I wish it wasn't so, but it is, and I also can't blame her. I love Ellen Mae with all my heart, but that doesn't change the past. The problem is that I also love Grace; always have; since we were little kids growing up. Time, and the paths that our three lives have taken hasn't changed that, and I can't pretend that it has or will. Grace has this uncanny ability to wall-off that part of her life better than I can; to put our past in a box and look at it occasionally and keep it closed up tight the rest of the time. I can't, and Ellen Mae can't; at least not for very long at a stretch. For all of our sakes, I've learned to avoid interacting with Grace, as much as I can, as much as it hurts to do so, but sometimes, like now, it can't be avoided. I hoped that by telling Ellen Mae what I was doing, by reminding her that she'd told me that I needed to warn Grace, and by doing it in public, at church, not hiding anything, it would minimize the sting for her. I smiled and touched her arm in return, and then I asked the pastor's wife to excuse me, and I turned and walked over to where Grace was standing.

Grace looked at me as I walked up. I got the impression that she'd been watching me, and she cast a quick look at Ellen Mae, whose eyes were still on me as well, and waved to her, and then crossed her arms, as if to put a barrier in place between us. She knows how Ellen Mae feels, and she goes out of her way to avoid causing her any distress. The two of them get along, and like each other, and can talk pleasantly when they find themselves in the same company, particularly if I'm not around to remind everyone of what they're trying hard not to be reminded of, but the details of our past are never far from the surface. Grace turned her green eyes back on me and smiled, and it felt as if I'd been touched with a live wire.

"Raymond," she said. Her voice had that soft drawl of warm, light syrup. "Pastor Webb must have made quite an impact on you today if you're joinin' us in fellowship."

"Grace," I greeted her. I laughed. "He had an impact all right; like a bullet in the head. I wasn't sure I was goin' to make it to the end."

She laughed. "Oh, I know. I didn't think you would either. I spent a good amount of time watchin' you squirm. Just like when you were a little boy."

I didn't need to hear that. The idea that she was now watching me, like I'd used to watch her, wasn't healthy for me. We both went quiet, and she looked at the row of tea-filled Dixie cups on the table and adjusted the alignment of a couple of them.

"Would you like some tea?" she finally asked. "It's pretty weak, but it's wet."

"No," I answered. "Ah, Grace, I . . ." I took a deep breath. "I need to tell you about somethin' that's come up. Warn you."

She looked at me. We'd skidded over the slickest patch of ice, and we were now back on firm asphalt. She'd walled the past off. "I'm not surprised. Is this about that couple that broke out of jail? Jimmie Carl showed me the photos you gave him."

"It is. His name's Gilbert Gervais. He's with a woman named Lidia Fernandez. She's his . . . partner, I'd guess you'd say. You remember who they are; what they did."

"Of course, but you don't really think they're comin' this way, do you? Would they?"

I shook my head. "I don't know, Grace. I wish I did. Part of me says that Gervais is a long ways away from here. I wish I could say that for sure. I know that if he's smart he is. But . . ."

"But maybe he's not. Maybe he's headed this way. That's what you're sayin'. Maybe he's comin' after Carl."

"Would that be such a bad thing?" It came out too quickly, and I was sorry I said it. Almost.

"Ray." She shook her head.

"Sorry."

"Ray, you don't really mean that. I know you don't."

"All I know is that if Gervais does come this way, I don't want you or Jimmie Carl gettin' between him and Carl. You got to promise me that you'll stay alert. No, he's not after you, or Jimmie Carl, so don't let Carl pull you into this. I'd like you to get away. Is there somewhere you can go for a few days? Just until we know where this guy is, and what he's up to."

"I can't leave, Ray. This is my home. Where would I go?"

"Anywhere."

"No."

"I need you to."

"No."

"Grace. Jimmie Carl can stay with us. You find somewhere. Stay with a friend."

"No." She set her jaw. I'd seen her do it a thousand times. The matter was settled.

"Damn it, Grace. You're too stubborn for your own good."

"And are you the pot or the kettle?" she laughed.

"I'm serious Grace."

"I know you are. And so am I."

"Then promise me this, you see anythin', anythin' at all that looks out of place, you call me; you call Ricky Forrest. You call someone," I said.

She nodded slowly, her eyes never leaving mine.

I wanted to grab her and shake her. I wanted to make her understand what I was feeling. I wanted to hold her. "Ricky was parked outside your house last night," I said. "And I'll be there tonight. One of us will be there every night until he's caught."

"Ray . . ."

"No. Grace. Listen. For once in our lives, listen to me. You have to promise me. Anythin' out of the ordinary, anythin' doesn't look right, smell right, you call. Promise me."

"I promise," she said. She started to reach out and touch me, but stopped herself. "I do. And now, you have to promise me one thing."

"Anythin'," I said.

"You won't let that man harm Carl either."

"Grace—"

"No. Promise me now."

"Why do you care about him? How can you? You don't love him. We both know that. How can you even care? After everythin' he's done. To you. To Jimmie Carl. To . . ."

"To us?"

"How can you?"

She smiled and squinted at me like she was trying to see if I had anything inside my head. "After all these years, how little you know about me."

"I know everythin' about you."

"No, Ray. No. If you did, you'd know it isn't about me. Don't you see, Ray? It's not me; it's because of everythin' he's done to you. That's why. Because I do care . . . I care about *you*. Because of what it'll do to you."

"Don't worry about me."

She laughed. "Too late for that, mister."

I didn't laugh. "It's a good time to start."

She shook her head. "My sweet, sweet, Ray. No. Deep down, I know you won't let that man hurt Carl. Deep down I know that. You're not like that. You're not. You're Raymond Sallis Elmore. You're one of the good guys; one of the last ones. That's the man I fell in love with as a girl. Ray Elmore isn't like that."

"Ray Elmore bled out somewhere in the Pacific. He didn't make it back. Remember? You don't know who I am." *Ask Carl's brother. If you can find his body,* I thought.

"That's not true," she said.

"If you're so sure, then why make me promise?"

She cocked her head. "Because you need to hear yourself do it. Remind yourself who you are." This time she didn't stop herself. She reached out and grabbed my forearm. "I know you better than you know yourself. I always have. I know you've witnessed things no human being should ever have to. And I know what it did to you, because I know you better than anyone else. And I know you've had to do terrible things, but always for good reasons. I know that. Because I know you better than anyone else. I also know that a better man never walked this earth. Don't let Carl Trimble make you into someone like him. He's done enough damage to both of us; don't let him ruin what little we have left. Be the Ray Elmore I love." She paused and looked deeply into my eyes. "What did the pastor say this mornin'? *God shows patience to even the most vile creatures.*"

"I'm not God."

She laughed. "Oh, I know. Believe me. God can remember his girlfriend's birthday."

I smiled. "January fourteenth."

She laughed again. "That figures. Now you remember. Too bad I'm not your girl anymore."

I had no comment.

She closed her eyes and took a deep breath, and when she opened them, she brought us back to what I was trying to avoid. "Promise me Ray."

"I promise," I replied. Even as I said it, I didn't believe myself.

CHAPTER 25

Split Tree, Arkansas
Sunday, November 17, 1963

W e left church, and I took Ellen Mae to the Albert Pike Café for lunch. There weren't many people there when we first sat down, but the church crowd caught up with us, and pretty soon the tables surrounding us were filled with the same people we'd just endured fellowship with. We ate, and nodded and smiled at people as they came and went, and as quickly as we could, we finished our lunch, and I drove us home. Our boys had finally showed up while we were out, but they were both sound asleep upstairs, I suspect they hadn't slept much the night before, and we didn't even try to wake them. Instead, we changed clothes and took to our separate chores. I went back to mowing the yard, and Ellen Mae worked in her flower garden, thinning out some dead azaleas and planting some winter violas.

About two thirty, I finished the yard and decided to take a break, and I went and fetched the two dogs from the back yard, and the three of us sat on the porch and watched Ellen Mae working in her flower bed. She's a handsome woman, and I could watch her all day long, and after a few minutes, she looked up and saw me, and when it was clear I was going to continue watching her, she got self-conscious and got up and went into the house. She came back a few minutes later with two glasses of tea and joined me on the porch swing, and we sat together and sipped our drinks while we swung and talked some more.

We were still doing that when Ricky Forrest's Ford Galaxie pulled up in front of our house. Ellen Mae stood and moved to the top of the porch steps, and the dogs and I got up and joined her, and we all watched as Ricky got out and opened the door for his wife, Kitty, who was holding their baby boy on her lap.

"I told Ricky the other night that he better not even thick about comin' by here again without that baby," Ellen Mae called out to Kitty Forrest as they came up the sidewalk.

Kitty laughed and shifted her son to her left hip so that Ellen Mae could better see his face. "He told me that," she responded. "And I wasn't goin' to let him anyhow."

I couldn't help but notice that despite carrying her son, she had her handbag looped over her forearm.

Ellen Mae stepped off of the porch and met them midway on the sidewalk so that she could take the baby from Kitty. And then we all stood around in the front yard and discussed Eddie, and how fast he was growing up, and how he'd turn two in less than a month, and how he was chewing on everything that he could fit into his mouth. After a few minutes Ellen Mae and Kitty decided that it was too cool outside for the baby, and they went inside, leaving Ricky and me and the dogs on the porch to talk.

Ricky and I both lit up smokes, and I sat back down while he leaned on the porch railing, and the dogs took advantage of Ellen Mae being inside to go piss on her new violas.

"We were just over to Kitty's folks and I thought I'd be a good time to swing by and take Todd off your hands," Ricky said. He nodded at the dog, who was finished with the flower bed and was now sitting in the middle of the front yard staring into the street as if he was waiting for a parade. "Kitty's actually excited about having a pet. She thinks it'll be good for Eddie as he grows up."

"Good dog, from what I can tell. He'll be a good one."

"Yeah, though I still hope Missus Johnson turns up safe and sound."

"Of course."

"But until then . . ."

"Of course."

"Thanks for taking him."

"Of course."

"Speaking of the dog, I guess you've heard the news. I tried calling here a couple times," he said. "No answer."

I shook my head. "Church ran extra-long this mornin', and then Ellen Mae and me went out to lunch. Just got back a little while ago, but I've been mowin' the yard, and I guess I didn't hear the phone." I nodded at the house. "The boys are here, but they're both takin' a nap, and you couldn't wake them if you put a jackhammer to the side of their heads. What news?"

He laughed. "Wonder when it changes. You can't rouse teenage boys to save your life, but if you so much as try to put a two-year-old to bed and then try to tiptoe out of the room, he'll wake up like you'd shot a gun off."

"I remember. Try havin' two at once. About age three or four, I think. Definitely by the time they start school and you have to try to get them up in the mornin'. Hang in there; you don't have long now. What news?"

"Sorry. I assumed you'd heard. They found Mister Johnson's car."

I stopped swinging and sat forward. "Ring's? When? Where? But no sign of Jo Johnson?"

"No sign of her, but it's their car all right. I really thought that you'd have heard by now. Sorry. Yeah, you're not going to believe it. It was in the parking lot to the side of the General Fagan motor lodge. Couple of Lee County Sheriff's deputies happened to drive by it this morning. They recognized it from the BOLO that Ben Cooper put out. But no, Missus Johnson wasn't registered there. I asked specifically. No sign of her."

"Unless she's usin' another name."

"That could be."

"But we're sure it's his car?" I asked.

"Yes sir. Right make and model. Plates are still on it. It's his."

"But nothin' of her?"

"Not yet."

"The damn motor lodge. And I was just up there yesterday."

"I know, but they said it was parked around to the side. From what Ben tells me, it sounds like unless you were looking for it, or were turning around in the side lot, there'd be no way to see it. The deputies just got lucky."

"Their luck is no excuse for me missin' it."

"You're too hard on yourself, Ray."

"Where is it now? Anythin' in it?"

"You mean like blood?"

"Or a body. Or anythin' else that'll help us figure this out."

"Not that I've heard," Ricky replied. "Ben called me late this morning, when he couldn't get hold of you. Probably while you were at lunch."

"I need to go up to Lee County," I said. "Damn. The car still up there? At the motel?"

"No sir. Ben sent Pinto Bean and another deputy up there to get it. They got back a little while ago. It's parked in front of the courthouse now, right across from our office. Locked up. Ben's got the keys."

"I don't suppose anyone thought to check the inside of it before Pinto got in and drove it?"

"Actually they did. That was the first thing I thought of when Ben told me that he had someone driving it back down here. I'm not sure he would have, but someone at the Lee County Sheriff's office thought to photograph the inside. They also dusted it for prints. I guess they pulled quite a few."

"Pleasant surprise."

"Yes sir. Ben says they've already sent them over to Little Rock. He's going to have the state police run them."

I flicked my cigarette out in the yard and exhaled the last lungful of smoke. "I want to take a look in it. You say Ben's got the keys?"

"Up in his office."

I glanced at my watch. "I also need to pay another visit to that motel."

"I figured. Want me to go with you?"

I looked at the front door. I could hear Ellen Mae and Kitty and the baby. "It's Sunday afternoon; what's left of it. You need to spend time with your family," I said.

"Want me to go with you?" he repeated. He flicked his own cigarette butt into the azalea bed.

I let out a long sigh. "I admit I could use a back-up," I said.

"Not sure I believe that, but I'm game."

"No. I do. I need someone to make sure I don't kill that goddamn motel clerk."

CHAPTER 26

Split Tree, Arkansas
Sunday, November 17, 1963

I was anxious to get going, but I didn't want to rush the Forrests into leaving before they were ready, or before Ellen Mae was ready for them to go. We didn't have to wait too long; Eddie was starting to get irritable and soon enough Kitty decided that he needed a nap. I told Ricky that if he was serious about his offer of help, that he could meet me at the office in an hour after he took his family home. I suggested that he put his uniform on if he planned on going to the General Fagan motor lodge with me, because I planned to cinch the knot up a little tighter.

With that he rounded up Todd and his family and they left, and I went upstairs and showered and changed into my uniform. It was almost five thirty, and I told Ellen Mae that I'd be late for dinner, and then I drove to the office. Ricky arrived ten minutes later, and we went across the street to Ring's parked car, a four-door Dodge sedan. I walked around it and examined the exterior of it, while Ricky, I suspect to save me from having to negotiate the stairs with my bad leg, ran up to the second floor of the courthouse building to get the keys from Ben Cooper's office.

We opened all four doors and the trunk and looked at it from different angles. Ricky was on the passenger side, and I was on the driver's side. The dashboard and seat were blackened and smudged with fingerprint powder, but otherwise the car was remarkably clean. There was no trash in it, and the trunk was largely empty aside from a jack and a worn spare and an unopened can of oil. The round knob on one of the rear window handles was missing, but the upholstery was in good shape and the trim, and the whole car, looked well maintained.

Ricky kneeled down and looked up under the dash, and opened the glovebox, finding nothing of interest. There was some dried grass straw on the floor mats, probably from the underside of someone's shoes, but it didn't appear all that interesting. All in all, Ring's car was cleaner than any one that I've ever driven. Except for the ashtray. It was filled with a dozen stubbed-out cigarette butts.

"What do you make of that?" I asked Ricky, pointing to the ashtray.

"Someone's a smoker."

"Can't argue with that logic."

"What can I say? I went to college. I'm a licensed thinking machine now."

I laughed. "We still don't know if Ring smoked."

"Ben would know."

"Yeah. I hoped to ask him yesterday, but he was out fishin'. Can you tell what brand?"

Ricky leaned into the car and pulled the ashtray out an inch more. He poked at the jumble of butts and picked out a few, placing them in his palm. He turned them over and looked closer. "Unfiltered. Camels maybe." He held one out for me to take.

I took it. "Maybe. Smoked down to a nubbin'. Same way Granville does."

He laughed. "You want me to pull Doc Begley in for questioning?"

"If we can't get another suspect, maybe we'll have to," I replied.

Ricky was continuing to poke around in the ashtray. "There's another type in here. Not as many. Filtered. I can't tell the brand."

"So, we got two people. Doesn't help much," I responded.

"Probably not," Ricky said. He was holding one of the butts closer to his eyes. It was starting to get dark, and he turned his body to the west to better catch some additional light. "Can't tell for sure, but it sure looks like one of them wore lipstick."

CHAPTER 27

Split Tree, Arkansas
Sunday, November 17, 1963

W e locked the car, and Ricky ran the keys back up to Ben Cooper's office while I took some of the cigarette butts to my office and bagged them as possible evidence. Just in case. Charley Dunn was sitting at his desk playing solitaire, and I told him to fill a thermos with coffee and then get his ass over to West Road and park his car in front of the Trimbles and keep an eye out for Gilbert Gervais. I told him that he'd better take a piss before he left, because I didn't want him to budge from that spot until I relieved him. He grumbled but did as he was told.

As soon as Ricky rejoined me, we got into my cruiser and started up Highway One. It took about forty minutes to get there, and it was dark when we pulled into the parking lot, a new moon casting very little light despite an absence of clouds. The motor lodge looked about the same as it had the day before, there were three cars in the lot and two of the bungalows had dim lights behind the drawn curtains, but there was no other sign of activity. What little illumination there was came from a flood lamp aimed at the motel's sign by the highway, and a small orange neon light that flickered that there was a *VAC- -CY*.

We entered the office bungalow. The clerk, the same one I'd talked to before, was at his desk, his feet propped on an open drawer, reading a *Stag* magazine, and he briefly looked up when Ricky and I walked in. If the fact that the two of us were wearing uniforms concerned him, he didn't let it show, and he struck me as a man who'd had his share of experience with policemen, and had learned that showing respect or deference had gotten him nowhere.

He went back to looking at his magazine but said, "You back? Ray, isn't it? I'm guessing you still don't want a room?"

"No room, but I still want information, and I'm not lookin' to make a third trip." I stepped up to the counter. Ricky stayed a couple of feet back, closer to the door, but where he had a clear view of the clerk.

"That right? I thought we covered that before. I rent rooms. Not information." He closed his magazine and tossed it onto the desk with a backhanded flip and slowly stood up. He looked at Ricky and then at me. "If you two tell me you're married, I'll have to take your word for it."

I didn't take the bait. I put the framed photograph of the Johnson family on the counter. "Asked you yesterday if you'd seen this man."

"That right? I don't remember so good. What'd I tell you?" He walked slowly to the counter and stopped a couple of feet away, squaring and balancing his stance. He cut another look at Ricky Forrest. "Although I do remember asking you who this man is to you, but I don't recall you answering."

"Murder victim. That's who he is, and now I'd like some straight answers."

"To what?" If the fact that I was asking about a murder victim concerned him, he didn't let that show either. He definitely was a man who'd had his share of experience with the police, and volunteering information didn't seem to have developed into a strong habit.

"You said you hadn't seen him. Take a closer look. You still say that?" I asked.

He looked down at the photo, but not with any apparent interest. "Answer's the same. Never saw him."

"So why was his car found parked outside?"

He began nodding slowly as he stepped closer to the counter. Dots were starting to connect-up in his mind. "So that's what this is about. I ain't never seen that car before this morning, when a couple of Lee County's finest came in here asking about it."

"No idea how it got here?"

"Nope. Do you?"

"Murdered man's car shows up in your parking lot," I looked out the window and gestured with a nod of my head. "You don't look to do that much business. Hard to believe that a car shows up and you don't know about it." I tapped the photo on the counter. "You still say you never saw these people?"

The man squinted and looked at me and then at Ricky and then back at me. I suspect he'd been boxed in a few times in his life, and he'd learned to be wary when he saw walls starting to go up. "Now, you're putting words in my mouth, Ace."

"How's that?"

"I never said that I hadn't seen *them*."

I turned and looked at Ricky. He shrugged slightly. I turned back to the clerk. "I'm about wore out by your bullshit. I'd advise you to stop shinin' me on. Simple enough question; you seen this man or not?"

He took a half step backward and rebalanced his stance. He went up on the balls of his feet, and he looked like he expected me to come across the counter, and he was ready for it. "I said I ain't never seen that man, and I ain't. But that ain't what you just asked; you just now asked me if I'd seen *them*. Yeah, I seen *her*; not him."

CHAPTER 28

Split Tree, Arkansas
Sunday, November 17, 1963

That was about as close to the last thing I expected the clerk to say. "Say again. What do you mean, *her*?" I asked. I pushed the photograph closer to him. "You haven't seen the man, but you've seen her?"

The clerk looked quickly at Ricky and then back at me. His shoulders dropped slightly, as if he'd relaxed, convinced that no one was coming over the counter in the next thirty seconds. "Yeah. I seen her. That's what I just said."

I tapped the framed photo again. "You're sure? This woman? Her name is Jo Johnson. She's been here?"

"Don't know her name, but she's been here. I don't get paid to ask names."

"She here now?"

"No."

"But she has been?"

"That's what I said."

"But not him?"

"What's the matter, Ace? You the type that takes quite a few repeatings?" He smiled, that same lopsided smile that begged to be slapped off of his face. I was tempted to now. "Like I said, people tell me they're married, I have to take their word for it," he replied. "I don't ask to see marriage licenses."

I had to think about that for a moment. "You're tellin' me she was here with another man? Not this one?" I tapped the photo again.

He shrugged, as if it was obvious.

I sensed Ricky Forrest stepping up behind me. Maybe he was interested in hearing better; maybe he was genuinely concerned that I might jump the counter and kill the clerk. I took a deep breath and let it out slowly. "I stood here yesterday, and I asked you if you'd seen him. Maybe you hadn't, but goddammit you'd seen her," I paused and took another deep breath. "Didn't dawn on you to maybe offer that detail up?"

"And who the fuck are you?" His shoulders tensed again. "Huh? Don't know you from Adam."

"I'm a goddamn police officer, and I'm losin' patience."

"Yeah? So, maybe you're a police officer, but I didn't know that then, and I don't know it now. I've seen guys like you my whole friggin' life. You just look like trouble to me, and I don't ask for trouble. Understand? What am I supposed to think? You want to know about a man in a photo, and he's posing there next to a woman that sure as shit looks like she should be his wife, except I know that she's been coming here with some other Joe. You don't say who you are; how do I know you're not looking to settle a score with this guy? That's your business, not mine. Maybe you're another jealous boyfriend. Maybe you're her protective brother. Maybe you're a private dick. Hell, maybe you're just a dick. All I know, you asked me a question, and I gave you an honest answer. So, don't come in here and blame me if you don't ask the right questions. It don't pay me to inquire too much into the people who frequent this joint, or give out too many answers to people like you. You follow me Ace? They pay their money, they buy their privacy. Just like that dish you came in here with yesterday. I didn't ask you who she was."

"Fair enough," I said. "Let's back up. You say you recognize her; has she been here recently?"

He shrugged. "Not for a while. Maybe a month."

"A month. You sure of that?"

"I said *maybe*. That word mean something different down here, or you got chewing gum in your ears?"

"And the man that was with her," I nodded at the photo. It was clear that I had to be specific with my questions. "You're sure it wasn't him."

"Sure," he said.

"You know who it was? Describe him. What name did he use?"

"I don't recall."

"You keep a register?"

"Of course. It's the law. But," he smiled, like he was talking to a child. "If he was here with someone that he shouldn't have been, I doubt the name is going to help you people much."

"I reckon you're right," I said. I got my Lucky Strikes out and offered him one. He hesitated and then took it, tentatively, and we both lit up. "I think we got off on the wrong foot. So, help me out. How about a description? You recall what he looks like? Anythin' about him?"

He shook his head. He relaxed his stance and moved forward and leaned on the counter. He took a long drag of his smoke and blew it out slowly. "Look, *Ray*, to be honest, I can't. And I'm being honest with you people." He tapped the photograph. "Wasn't him, I know that," he said.

"Young? Old? Anythin'?"

"You're age. Maybe. White. A bit fat. A lot fat."

"Doesn't help much."

He shrugged. "Usually he had on a coat and tie. Hell, I don't know. I tend to remember the women better than the men."

So I noticed, I thought. "But you're sure it was her? This woman," I pointed again at the photo.

"Yeah. Nice ass on her. Real nice. Good set of pins, too. Saw her up close a few times. She came in here once or twice to get some ice out of the machine, otherwise she waited in the car while he checked them in." He looked out of the window into the parking lot. "But I'd see her walking from the car to the room. Yes, sir. I distinctly remember thinking, nice ass, real nice ass, especially for a mother."

"Couple times? How often they come here? Was she always with the same man?"

He nodded. "Maybe a dozen times, give or take a few. I don't think she's a working girl. Always the same man."

"The one you can't remember?"

"What can I say? He didn't have a nice ass."

"You said *for a mother*. How'd you know she was a mother?"

He screwed up his forehead as if he hadn't seen the question coming, and then he nodded at the frame. "I assume the kid in that picture is hers."

"You assume right, but you just saw the photo yesterday. And you said you thought it when you saw her walkin' to the room. Why'd you think it before?"

He smiled as if I'd caught him at something. "Maybe I saw her with the kid a couple of times. Sometimes he'd sit in the car; sometimes she'd have him play on the swing while his *parents* were busy inside."

"The boy was with her?"

He shrugged. "I think I just said that."

"Back up. How often were they here?" I asked. "You said a dozen times. Weekends? Durin' the weekday? Days or nights?"

"Different times. Weekdays most often. I think. Doubt they ever spent the night. They never stayed that long. Couple hours usually. He tried to jew me down. Wanted an hourly rate in the beginning."

"You don't think a look in your guest register would help jog your memory?"

He smiled again and started to give me a flippant answer, but he stopped himself. He seemed to have decided that cooperating with me would cause him the least amount of headache later, and he shrugged again and parked his cigarette in the corner of his mouth and opened his guest register. He flipped backward a couple of pages. There weren't that many entries, and he used his finger to scan them quickly. "Lots of *Smiths* and *Jones* and *Greens* and *Browns*. Funny how that is. Must be common names around here. Could be any one of them." He closed the book and took his cigarette and flicked the ash onto the floor.

"Nothin' else that you can think of?"

"Nope."

"And the car that was found around back, how long you think it could have been there?"

"Not more than a couple of days; maybe a few more. I don't walk around that side too often, but I was over there a few days ago, and I know it wasn't there. So, not more than three or four. Five."

"And you're sure that when this woman and . . . the man she was with, you're sure they weren't drivin' that car any of the dozen or so times they were here? It's not theirs?"

"I don't know whose it is. I told you, I never saw it before. Positive."

I smiled. "Positive? For a man with a bad memory, that sounds pretty sure."

He took a final puff on his smoke and then dropped it to the floor and stepped on it with some precision, like he was squashing a big bug. "What can I say? I like good asses and good cars. They weren't driving that piece-of-shit Dodge. I know that."

"That right? Any idea what they were drivin'?"

He pushed the framed photo back across the counter toward me. "Sure I do. I just said that I like good asses and good cars. Black Buick Riviera. Shined up like a freakin' mirror."

CHAPTER 29

Split Tree, Arkansas
Sunday, November 17, 1963

Ricky Forrest didn't say anything as we walked out to the car, but once we were on the road headed back to Split Tree, he spoke up. "What do you make of all that, boss?" he asked. I was driving, and he was staring out the window at the darkened floodplain.

"Dumb son-of-a -bitch," I responded.

Ricky laughed. "Been waiting for that. I'm a mind reader. Like Mandrake the Magician."

"That son-of-a-bitch," I repeated. I adjusted my vent window so that the wind was directed at my face.

"I hear you, Chief, but we don't know for sure it's him."

"Like hell. You know of any other shiny black Buick Rivieras in this county? Driven by a fat man?"

"No, sir, but for the record, we're in Lee County right now."

"Barely. And I'm not sure that doesn't point to him even more. Makes sense, right? You goin' have an affair, would you do it in town? Not the way our town gossips. Everyone would know in the first thirty minutes and be talkin' about it even sooner. Look, we know that son-of-a-bitch Carl Trimble doesn't mind takin' some of the young girls he hires up to his office, that ain't no secret and never has been, but foolin' around with a married woman is somethin' else. That'll get you shot; or worse. No, I'd figure him to take her somewhere."

Ricky nodded. "Like a motor lodge two counties away."

"That's right. Like a run-down motor lodge operated by a man with a poor memory."

He laughed. "Except for cars. And women's asses."

"That son-of-a-bitch," I repeated.

"Which one?"

"Both, but I meant Carl Trimble."

"So now what?"

I looked at my watch, turning my wrist to catch some light from the dashboard instruments. It'd be well after seven thirty by the time we got back to Split Tree. "Not sure," I responded. "What in the hell would a woman like Jo Johnson see in a pig like Trimble? What the hell was she thinkin'?" I looked at my watch again. "I need to talk to that son-of-a-bitch Trimble. But not tonight. He ain't goin' anywhere. I tell you what though, I feel a whole sight better about Jo Johnson. We may not know where she is, but I'm startin' to think that wherever it is, that it's her idea to be there. What she knows about her husband's death, we'll still have to figure that out, but for now I'm less concerned about her safety."

"Where do you plan on talkin' to Carl?"

"Where or when?"

"Where."

I shook my head. "Not sure. Haven't had time to think about it. Probably his office would be best." I paused. "The truth is, I'd like to go to his house right now and drag him into the front yard and whup his goddamn ass. Nothin' would give me more pleasure."

Ricky laughed again. "Can I advise against that? Your call, and you know I'll back you up either way, but maybe his office would be better. After you calm down."

"I know. If nothin' else, Grace doesn't need to witness all that." I looked at my watch again. "For now, I'll get you home to your family.

I'll stop by my house and grab somethin' to eat with Ellen Mae, and then I'll head over to the Trimbles' to relieve Charley Dunn."

"But you'll stay in the car?" Ricky asked after a short pause. He wanted some reassurance that I wasn't going to follow through with my desire to drag Carl into the front yard.

"That son-of-a-bitch," I replied.

"I swear, I'm better than Mandrake the Magician."

We got back into town about 7:40, and I dropped Ricky Forrest off at his house, and then I went home. Ellen Mae had already fed the boys, and they were out on the town somewhere. She and I had a light dinner of scrambled eggs and fried potatoes, and we sat in the den and watched a little television afterwards. *Bonanza* was on, but I had no interest in the Cartwrights and their problems, but I did want to spend some time with Ellen Mae, and so I endured it. When it was over, I told her that I needed to relieve Charley Dunn in front of the Trimbles' house, and that I'd be late coming home and that she shouldn't wait up for me. I'm sure she wasn't thrilled by the idea, but the fact that Ricky had been there the night before and Charley Dunn was there now, seemed to reassure her that it was more about catching Gilbert Gervais and less about Grace Trimble and me. She made me a thermos of black coffee and put an apple and a candy bar in a paper sack for me to take. I kissed her, and she went upstairs to take a bath, and I drove to my office and got my service revolver from my desk drawer, and then I headed over to West Road and relieved Charley Dunn.

I spent the night parked in front of the Trimbles' house, occasionally getting out of the car to stretch the kink out of my leg and water some rose bushes. I smoked some cigarettes and drank my coffee and ate my apple. And I thought.

CHAPTER 30

Split Tree, Arkansas
Monday, November 18, 1963

When I dropped him off the night before, I'd told Ricky that I'd probably be a few minutes late the next morning. I'd ended up staying out in front of Trimbles' house until almost four a.m., before I finally decided that Grace was safe for the night, and then I went on home and crawled into bed next to Ellen Mae and slept soundly for a few hours.

I pulled into my parking spot around eight thirty, but before going into the office, I had someone I wanted to talk to, and I was starting across the street, headed for the Farmers Bank, when I saw Ben Cooper standing on the sidewalk, hands on his hips, looking at Ring Johnson's car as if it had just landed from Mars.

"Ben. How you doin'?" I asked him. I stood next to him.

He looked at me briefly, and then back at the car. "Good as a yeller tom cat with two hairy peckers, I reckon," he replied automatically, without much enthusiasm. "How you doin', Big Ray?" He asked with even less enthusiasm.

"Fair to middlin'. What you thinkin'?"

"I'm thinkin' that for the life of me, I can't figure out why Ring's car would be at that motor lodge up in Lee County. How you explain that? Don't make no sense. Must have been stolen, I guess."

I didn't answer directly. "When do you suppose you'll hear about the fingerprints?" I got my cigarettes out and offered him one.

"No idea. How long do you think it should take?" He looked at me and nodded his thanks and took one of my smokes.

I lit my own and then handed him my lighter and waited for him to get his going. "Depends on the priority they gave it when they sent it in. The state lab can turn it around pretty quick if they need to." I'd already decided to call Art Hennig when I got to my office and see if he could juice the process, but I didn't offer that to Ben.

"You think the prints will tell us somethin'?"

"I'm thinkin' you don't have much else at this point. Maybe."

He nodded as he thought about that. "You don't think they'll just be Ring's?"

"I guess we'll see. His and Jo's, but someone drove that car up there, and we know it wasn't Ring."

"But Jo don't drive."

"That's what I hear."

A picture started to firm up in Ben Cooper's head as he connected the dots, and it didn't look like he was happy with what he was seeing. "We still don't know where Jo is . . . you think she was up there? At that motel?"

"Do you?"

"Maybe . . . but that'd mean . . . you think she might have been with somebody else? I've been hearin' stories . . ."

"I don't know what I think, Cecil Ben. Maybe the car was stolen, just like you said." I knew she'd been up there and that she'd been there with somebody else, and that somebody else was Carl Trimble, but I also knew that they hadn't been driving Ring's car.

"But if that's the case, we still don't know where Jo is now. Where can she be?"

"Wish I knew."

He looked at me with a newfound look of worry. "I'm startin' to think maybe we need to . . . you know . . . maybe we need to search their farm. What do you think, Big Ray? You know, maybe look for a ... search for her body. You think?"

I shook my head. "I don't, Ben. You want me to be honest with you? I really don't, but I can't tell you not to worry, and if doin' somethin' like that helps you, then maybe you should do it."

"Ain't about helpin' me. It's just . . ." his thought trailed off and died.

I pointed at the car. "Ashtray's full of butts. I guess you saw that." I doubt he had, but he wasn't going to admit to it either way. "I've been meanin' to ask you; you knew him pretty well. Did Ring smoke?"

Ben Cooper shook his head and looked at the cigarette he was working on. "Naw. Not really. I think he did some when we were boys. We all did. He chews plug some now, but he isn't much of a smoker. He'll still do it sometimes, if you offer him one, especially if he's around other folks who are, to be social, but he doesn't normally. Never known him to carry a pack of his own anyhow."

"How about Jo?"

He smiled and almost laughed. For a minute, his worst fears were pushed to the side. "Well, she wasn't raised to, that's for sure. Her daddy wouldn't have put up with that. Her momma neither. They were pretty strict."

"But?"

"But, yeah. We're not all that close, you understand, but the last few years, I've seen her take a puff or two. On occasion. She's kinda like Ring, if you offer, she'll accept. I think just to spite her daddy's memory. Hell, I've even seen her take a drink once and a while. Why?"

I thought the question was obvious, but I didn't want to say too much. I still had a lot to sort out before I started telling people what I thought. "Just tryin' to make sense of all the butts in that ashtray."

He accepted that and didn't pursue it. We talked a few more minutes, and then I told him I had to see someone at the bank, and I left him standing on the sidewalk, still looking at Ring's car as if it were going to speak to him. A whole new host of fears were working their way into his brain.

The Farmers Bank is located on the western side of the town square, opposite the courthouse from my office. It was a little before nine, and the bank hadn't opened for business, but I'd called Nick Mitchell from my house before I left, and he told me that he'd be in his office and that I should just knock on the door when I got there. Nick is the bank president. Actually, his father is the president, and Nick is the vice-president, but his father's in bad shape and can hardly count to ten anymore, and Nick has run the place the last five or six years. Nick is a good man. He was in the army and lost six toes to frostbite in Belgium in late 1944, and he wears shoes with metal plates in them to help him balance, and he uses a cane most days. He limps like it hurts him, but I don't think it does.

I knocked on the glass door of the bank; Nick was standing at a counter talking to one of the tellers and looked up and walked over and opened it.

"Get on in here. What can I do for Big Ray Elmore this mornin'?" he greeted me. He led the way, and I followed him into his office off the main lobby. "Take a seat," he said. "Want some coffee?"

"No thanks. I appreciate this Nick. I know you're busy. I won't take much of your time."

He smiled and nodded in the direction of the lobby. "The girls do most of the work around here. I'm not so busy that I can't ever meet with you. What can I do you for? How's Ellen Mae and the boys? I saw Ray Junior scored eighteen points the other night. I tell you what, the Razorbacks will be makin' a mistake if they don't put him on scholarship."

"Thanks, Nick. Yeah, they're all fine. Boys are a big and dumb as boys that age can be, and Ellen Mae is as pretty and smart as ever. I told her I was goin' to see you this mornin' and she said to tell you hey for her." I took a deep breath and let it out slowly. "Nick, I need a favor, and I understand it may put you in a difficult position."

He adjusted his weight in his chair and leaned forward, putting his elbows on his desk. "Shoot."

"You heard about Ring."

"Of course. Terrible. Any word yet on Jo? I heard she and the boy are still missin'. That true?"

"Afraid it is. I don't a clue where she is yet."

"Damn. I sure hope she's okay. So, this about him?"

"Sort of. I need to know, did Ring come to you about money?"

He nodded and hesitated. "You know, that's not the sort of thing I normally discuss. You know that, right?"

"I do."

He nodded some more. "I don't normally talk about people's affairs, but . . . he's dead, so, I guess I can tell you. Anybody but you, I wouldn't, but . . . yes. About a month ago."

"I hear he was havin' money troubles. You give him a loan?"

"No. No." He shook his head and hesitated some more. "You're right about the money troubles, but, no. I just couldn't even if I'd been willin' to. We already hold the mortgage on his farm and the title on his tractor, and just about every other piece of equipment he owns, and he's behind on all those as is. And damn if it don't look like cotton's goin' to be down this year. Again. No. I'll be honest, I hate to speak ill of the dead, but he's gone and put himself and this bank in somethin' of a pickle."

"How so?"

"You know, I never did think much of Ring Johnson; I didn't actually dislike him, but I never particularly cared for him either. I don't approve loans on the basis of my personal likes and dislikes for people, you understand, but I also don't have to bend the rules for people I don't like. Fact of the matter, he's lucky we haven't called in the loans he's got." He made a palms-out gesture with his hands to indicate that his patience with Ring was about gone. "I should have. I really should have, and now I'm not sure what's goin' to happen. I need to have a long talk with Jo."

"You know that he took out another mortgage with a bank up in Forrest City?"

"What? You're shittin' me? You serious? On the farm?" He sat back quickly in his chair and threw his arms up in frustration. "Shittin' me? You sure?"

"Afraid so."

"Goddammit. Goddammit. Now what bank is that goddamn stupid? Forrest City? That sounds about right. I'll bet I know which bank too. Goddamn. I don't suppose they ever heard of doin' somethin' called a title search? God damn it to hell, if that doesn't complicate it all to shit."

"Sorry, Nick. But right now, I'm tryin' to sort out my own end of this problem. I need to know about Jo Johnson. Has she been in to ask you for money?"

He was still shaking his head at the prospect of a protracted legal fight to get control of Ring's farm, but he looked up and squinted as if my question didn't make much sense. "What? Jo Johnson? Jo Johnson? No. Apart from Ring, you mean? No. Why would she?"

"Here's the part that puts you in a bind, and I'm sorry. I need to know if Carl Trimble has written any checks to her; transferred any money to her; anythin' like that. Recently. What can you tell me?"

"Whoa, whoa, whoa," he said, pushing back from his desk, as if putting more distance between the two of us also put distance between him and the thought of exposing Carl Trimble's bank records to me. "Goddamn, Big Ray . . ."

I held up my palm, as if I was stopping traffic. "I wouldn't ask without a reason."

He got up and closed his office door and limped back to his desk. He dropped his voice, almost to a whisper. "Goddamn, Ray. You know damn well that Carl Trimble's my biggest customer, not to mention the biggest merchant in the town. You know what kind of shit he could cause me? What the hell?"

"I hate to ask you this, but I need to know."

"You got a warrant?"

"You know I don't. And I don't want to have to get one either. This may lead nowhere, in which case this conversation never took place, but if it does lead somewhere . . ."

"Lead where? What are you sayin'? What's Carl got to do with anythin'?"

"I just need to know if he's given Jo Johnson any money in the last month or so. That's all."

Nick Mitchell closed his eyes and sat quietly for a long minute. Finally, he said, "Carl doesn't write many checks. He deals in cash, and I'd have no way of knowin' who he gives cash to. Most of his checks get written on his company account. You'd need to talk to his accountant about those."

I shook my head. "No, I think he'd want this quiet. I don't think he'd do this on his store account."

"Do what? I'm still not followin' you."

"Write her any checks. If he did, it'd be on his personal account."

"I don't understand, but like I told you, it don't matter; he don't write many personal checks."

"All right. How about cash? You say you don't know who he gives cash to, but has he been withdrawing unusual sums of money recently?"

Nick shrugged. "Hell, I don't know, Ray. Carl's pretty frugal mostly. Tight. You know that. I think he gives Grace a small allowance."

I nodded. "That'd be pretty uniform, I'd think. How about somethin' unusual. I mean, have his expenses been pretty much the same amount every month?"

"I guess. He operates on a budget. Like most of us."

"So, if he was withdrawin' more than usual in the last month or so, it'd stand out?"

He closed his eyes again and shook his head slowly. "I don't know. Maybe. I don't know." He opened his eyes and looked at me. "What's this really about, Ray? Really."

I was putting Nick Mitchell in a bad spot, and I owed him an explanation. "I don't think Ring killed himself," I said.

"Holy . . . holy shit. Holy shit. Holy . . ." He dropped his voice to a whisper. "What are you sayin'? Ben Cooper says he shot his head off. Shotgun. Ain't that right? In his tool shed. What are you sayin'? *Holy shit.*"

"I'm sayin' that somethin' isn't right; that's all I'm sayin' right now. Somethin' ain't right, and Jo Johnson is missin', and I need all the help I can get figurin' it out. Findin' her. And before I can start puttin' the picture together, I need to get all the puzzle pieces turned face up on the table. I'm also sayin' that I haven't told anyone else this. I need you to keep it between us for now." I had, of course, discussed it with Granville Begley, and Ricky, and Ellen Mae, but I needed Nick to understand that I was placing my confidence in him and that I hoped that he'd do the same.

"You really need this?"

"I do."

"If it was anyone but you . . ."

"Thanks."

"Anyone else . . . I'd shove that question right up their ass. Sideways."

"Wouldn't blame you if you did now. You also know I wouldn't ask if I didn't think I needed it."

He nodded and got up and limped to the door of his office and opened it and stepped out. He was gone for about five minutes and then returned with a ledger book. He sat down and began flipping pages back and forth, occasionally writing some figures on a legal pad. Ten minutes later, he closed the ledger and sighed. "Damn, Ray. How'd you know?"

"What?"

"Carl's pretty consistent in his deposits and withdrawals; just like we figured. At least goin' back to January. I suspect if I checked, last year would be about the same."

"But?"

"But seven weeks ago he withdrew a hundred dollars. Nothin' anythin' like that sort of withdrawal prior to that."

"Interestin', but I guess it doesn't prove much," I replied. Maybe this line wasn't going to pan out.

"No, it doesn't. Except," he looked at the numbers on his legal pad. "A week later, another hundred. Six days after that, fifty. Week after that, ninety. Two days later, another fifty. All totaled, almost four-hundred dollars."

"Damn, that's a sizable sum. And no explanation why?"

"We don't ask why. His money, he can do with it like he wants. He might have told one of the tellers, but I'd be surprised."

"What days of the week? Any pattern?"

"No. Not really. Mondays; Tuesdays. Looks like maybe a Friday."

"When was the last withdrawal?"

"Two weeks ago. Thirteen days to be exact. Tuesday." He looked at me. "I don't follow where you're headed with this. You think he gave money to Jo Johnson? Jo Johnson? For Christsakes, why?"

"Maybe."

He shook his head. "I don't follow. I don't. I don't know where you're headed with this, but I can tell you that the Johnsons were way over their heads in debt. Shit, and that's not countin' a goddamn second mortgage; with a bank in Forrest City that ought to have its charter pulled. Four hundred dollars wouldn't start to cover what the Johnsons needed."

He was right, of course, but I didn't think Jo Johnson was looking to bail out her husband.

CHAPTER 31

Split Tree, Arkansas
Monday, November 18, 1963

I walked back to my office. Ben Cooper had apparently wrung whatever answers he could get out of Ring Johnson's car, and he was gone. I seriously doubt it held much more for him than it did for me.

"Oh, Chief, thank God you're here," Jewell Faye said as I opened the door. All five-foot-two of her jumped up from her desk like she'd been kicked in the rear with a pointed boot. Under normal conditions, she has a voice that resembles a seldom-used hinge, and when she gets excited, which admittedly isn't too often, it makes you want to find a quick means to oil it. She was really squeaking now.

"Mornin' Miss Jewell. What's up?" I asked.

She looked at me and then nervously at the door to my office. "Chief, some men are here. They're lookin' for you."

"That right? What kind of men?"

She shook her head and looked again at the door. "New York lawyers," she said. "They're here to see you. From New York."

I smiled to try to calm her down. "Is that right? Can't be much," I said. "Can't imagine what a lawyer would want with me; let alone one from New York." I winked at her. "Don't worry. Whatever it is, we'll deal with it. You seen Ricky?"

She pointed at my office. "He's in there with them. Stallin' them until you got here."

"Then I'm sure everythin' is already under control." And, partly to give her something to do to distract her from her concern, I asked, "Coffee made? I could use some."

Her eyes were still on the door, but she nodded. "Just made some fresh. I'll get you a cup."

"I'd appreciate it," I said, and I turned and opened the door to my office.

"*. . . I'll tell you again, that isn't what happened,*" I heard Ricky Forrest patiently talking to someone.

I stepped inside. Ricky was seated at my desk, leaning forward on his elbows, shaking his head slowly. Three strangers in dark suits were sitting on the other side; two of them were white men, the other was a light-skin black. To their right were Ben Cooper and Joe Irwin, our mayor; and Powder Graham, the town's attorney; on the other side was Carl Trimble, who was looking particularly pleased with himself. Ricky stood up when I entered; the others stayed where they were, but almost on cue they all swiveled their heads to look at me.

"About fuckin' time, Elmore," Carl Trimble said, almost under his breath. He was wearing a brown suit and leaning back in his chair, his arms folded across his chest, and he resembled a fat cow tick. "Town doesn't pay you to show up for work at ten o'clock. Ought to fire you for that alone."

"Joe. Pow. Ben. Gentlemen." I nodded at each of them in turn, ignoring Carl Trimble. It was easier for me to stomach it that way, and safer for him if I pretended he wasn't there.

Ricky got up and stepped away from my desk to open up my chair for me. "Chief, these men are lawyers from the ACLU," he said. "They're here to talk to you."

The three strange men finally stood up. One of them, he looked to be the eldest and the one in charge, extended his hand. "Chief Elmore, my name is James Allen."

I shook his hand. "Mister Allen. Good to meet you. I'm Ray Elmore," I said by way of introduction.

He nodded at his two companions. "Let me introduce my associates. This is Mister Abrams," he said, referring to the other white man. "Mister Abrams and I are out of the New York office. And this is Mister Moore. Mister Moore has joined us from our Saint Louis office."

I nodded at the other two lawyers. Neither had extended his hand, so no handshakes were in order. "Gentlemen. Sounds like y'all have come a long ways. I hope we can help you with whatever it is you're after." The four of us sat down, and Ricky moved to his desk and sat on the corner edge.

Before anyone could respond, there was a light rap on the door, and it opened; Jewell Faye stepped in, carrying a cup of coffee that she put in front of me. It looked like she was starting to calm down some, but she was still upset.

"Can I offer you gentlemen some coffee?" I asked as I winked a *thank you* at Jewell Faye.

Mr. Allen spoke. "Chief Elmore, this isn't a social call. I wish it were."

"Didn't think for a minute that it was, but then I was offerin' you coffee, not askin' you home for Thanksgivin'," I replied. I looked at Ben Cooper, who shrugged. He didn't seem to have much more understanding of what was going on than I did, which made me feel better, because I'd seen him less than an hour ago, and it would have put me out more than a little if he knew something about all of this and hadn't given me a heads-up. I nodded at Jewell Faye that she could go, and then I returned my attention to men in front of me.

"We don't have to be here at all," the lawyer who'd been introduced as Mr. Abrams said impatiently. "Like Jim has already said, we're here as a courtesy." He had the look of a man whose underwear didn't fit well and was looking to take it out on someone.

"A courtesy? Well then, I suppose I should thank you," I said. "And as soon as I know what I'm thankin' you for, I'll get after it." I lit up a cigarette and sat up straight in my chair and blew the first lungful of smoke in the direction of the ceiling. Some of the others had been smoking prior to me showing up, and there was already a thin lens of blue smoke undulating at head height in the room. It was almost hypnotic to watch. "Now, since we've established that this isn't a social call, why don't we get to whatever it is that you gentlemen have come all this way for?"

Mr. Allen reached into a briefcase and removed some papers that were held together with a large black metal paperclip. He placed the papers in his lap but didn't look at them. "Chief Elmore, as we were explaining to your assistant here, we have—"

I held up my hand to stop him. "I don't have assistants. I have people that I work with, and if you're referring to this man," I nodded at Ricky Forrest, "then he's a sworn police officer. Now, you're welcome to call me *Ray*, I actually prefer that, but I'd appreciate you callin' him Officer Forrest. He's earned it." I looked at Mr. Abrams, to make sure that he understood my message. "Since we're not bein' social."

The three men looked at each other and then Mr. Abrams leaned forward and adopted a tone that might have sounded menacing if it came from someone who looked like they could back it up. "You have no idea what kind of trouble you're in," he said. "Do you?"

"That's right. You stepped in it deep this time, Elmore. Real deep," Carl Trimble added.

"Carl, please," Powder Graham said. "You need to just not say anythin'."

I continued to ignore Carl Trimble, but I responded to Mr. Abrams. "You're right about that, I don't," I said. I was quickly getting a case of the ass for these three lawyers; Abrams in particular. "So maybe one of y'all could start tellin' me, because as much as I'd like to spend the day talkin' to you, I've got work to do."

Mr. Abrams laughed derisively. "I'll bet," he mumbled.

I looked at Mr. Allen. If he was the leader of the three, then I expected him to keep his people in line. The way I was raised, I was taught that it's rude to be rude. I had no idea why these men were here, but they were in my office, and I expected some civility. He seemed to read my thoughts, because he put a hand on Mr. Abrams' forearm. "Chief Elmore, as we've already told Officer Forrest and Mr. Graham, we're here partly to gather some facts, partly to give notice."

"As a courtesy," I said.

He smiled and took his hand off Abrams' arm. "Yes. You see, some rather disturbing facts have come to light."

"Facts?"

"Yes. Perhaps I should have said *alleged* facts. The American Civil Liberties Union has requested that the Department of Justice open a criminal investigation into what appears to be your department's gross violations of civil rights. We are informed that DoJ will in fact initiate such action; we expect within the week. We also are pursuing a possible separate and collateral civil suit and will seek substantial monetary damages against the city of Split Tree should the findings show merit."

I looked at Ricky, but he didn't look at me. He was staring at the three strangers with an intensity that I imagine he'd sighted down the length of a gun barrel in North Korea; right before he'd squeezed the trigger and ended some unlucky Chinaman's day. I looked at Ben Cooper, who did look at me; he still had the same blank look on his face that'd he'd had when I first walked in. I looked at Powder Graham, who responded with a small shake of his head, to indicate that I shouldn't say much. I didn't look at Carl Trimble.

"Well," I said after a pause, "Thank you for that clarification, but I'm not sure I know much more now than I did five minutes ago. Mind tellin' me, just who is the Department of Justice goin' to be investigatin'?"

Carl Trimble laughed. "How damn stupid can you be, Elmore? They're comin' for you, you damn stupid hick. I hope you go to jail this time. About damn time. Jail."

CHAPTER 32

Split Tree, Arkansas
Monday, November 18, 1963

P owder Graham leaned forward in his chair and looked past the three lawyers. Powder's a small man, prone to civility, but he had a look on his face that suggested he'd like to strangle Carl Trimble. "Carl, as the town's attorney, I'm askin' you to please stop talkin'. In fact, I'm tellin' you. Just stop. Let these men speak their piece, and then let me handle this. Will you? You're here only because you're the head of the town council."

Carl Trimble folded his arms and made a protesting noise, but he sat back in his chair and closed his mouth.

"Mister Allen, I'm afraid you've sort of sprung this on Big—on Chief Elmore here; on all of us, really," Powder Graham continued, his attention now focused on the three lawyers sitting next to him. "I think we all owe it to him to back up a bit and let him hear all of this from the start. Could you repeat what you were tellin' us before the chief walked in? If you don't mind."

Mr. Allen nodded and adjusted the papers in his lap. "Of course. Chief Elmore, on August sixteen last, a sworn officer under your supervision did cause the unlawful arrest and detention on Leonidas Jackson. Is this correct?"

Powder Graham leaned forward and started to say something, but I held up my hand to stop him. "Is that what this is all about?" I asked Mr. Allen. "That black preacher?"

"Mister Jackson is a Negro, that's correct. Do you contest these facts as I've presented them?" Allen asked.

"Not sure I *contest* anythin', but I can say that if that's what this is all about, then y'all made a long trip for nothin'. That whole thing was a misunderstandin'. Nothin' more than that."

"So, you will attest to that fact?" Allen asked again. He read from the paper on his lap. "Specifically, that on August sixteenth last, a sworn police officer under your immediate and direct control and supervision did cause the unlawful and illegal arrest of Leonidas Jackson in violation of his federal constitutional rights, that you were on constructive notice of that act, and that you did then knowingly and willfully conspire to commit the subsequent wrongful and false imprisonment and detention of the same?" He looked up and glanced at Ricky and then turned back to me. "And please let me caution you, before you answer, you should know that Mister Young, the jailer, is prepared to give us a written statement attesting to the facts as I have described them."

I looked at Ricky and then at Powder and then at Allen. I wanted to respond, *before you say any more you should know that Johnnie Young can barely write his own name.* Instead, I said, "That certainly was a mouthful, Mister Allen, but as I told you a minute ago, that whole thing was unfortunate and a complete misunderstandin'. Yes, one of my men brought him in, you got that part right, but as soon as I heard about it, I directed that Mister Jackson be—"

"Reverend Jackson," Mr. Abrams said. It was clear that he didn't think much of me. If he'd been a foot or two closer, I think he might have actually tried to spit on me.

"Of course. As soon as I heard about it, I called Mister Young and directed that *Reverend Jackson* be released immediately. I also went directly to the jail, where I apologized to him in person. I also made sure that the officer involved, who is relatively new to the job, won't make that sort of mistake again."

Mr. Allen nodded slowly. "I'm sure we can all agree that when a man is imprisoned unjustly, the amount of time hardly matters; be it a minute or a month."

"That may be true, Mister Allen, but tell me, when y'all were talkin' to Mister Young, or Reverend Jackson for that matter, did either of them happen to mention that he wouldn't leave the jail even after he was told he was free to go? He didn't seem to be feelin' the injustice quite as much as you and Mister Abrams are right now. Did they tell you that every time the cell door was opened, he'd close it on himself? They tell you that I had to finally lock the door open with a pair of handcuffs?"

The lawyer nodded some more and paged through the papers on his lap until he found what he was after. He continued as if I hadn't said a word. "I believe that Reverend Jackson was also denied access to a phone. Despite clear and repeated requests on his part. As you are aware—"

"As I'm aware," I interrupted him; I probably shouldn't have, but I did, "I told Jackson that he wasn't under arrest, that he had my apology, and that he was free to go. And, as I'm sure you're aware, you bein' the lawyer, the purpose of the phone call is to seek legal assistance when you've been arrested. In this case, because he wasn't under arrest, and wasn't bein' detained, there was no need to make a call, and he damn well knew that. I'm also aware that he didn't want to leave until he'd made a long-distance call, to New York as I recall. Didn't make much sense at the time; now I reckon I know who he wanted to get hold of so bad."

"As was his right."

"I'll leave that for you lawyers to work out, but I suspect there's way more to it than that, and you know it as well as I do. I'll say it again, the man wasn't under arrest. We couldn't get him to leave the cell short of draggin' him out of there, and I'm sure that Johnnie Young will give you a written statement *attesting* to that. And I'll *attest* to the fact that my young officer is likely a dumbass, but from where I'm sittin', it sure looks like Mister Jackson—*Reverend* Jackson—how would you say it? That he *willfully and with notice* cooked this whole goddamn thing up, and damn if y'all aren't conspirin' with him to do it. That's what I can *attest* to." I looked at Powder Graham for some help.

"Gentlemen," Powder said. "This little room seems to be gettin' a tad warm, and I don't think it's just on account of this new holiday sweater I'm wearin'. Now, I'm not sure that much more is goin' to be gained here. Not right now." He leaned forward in his chair. "As is often the case in matters like these, there seems to be two versions of this particular fish story. I tend to lean toward Ray here, and not just because he works for the town, but because I know the man. I believe that this is all just one big misunderstandin', that's all it is, and Ray here has said he apologized. He said there was no harm intended, or caused. And if Ray says it, you can damn well take that to the bank." He stood up and clapped his hands together. "So, what do you say; why don't we go on over to the diner, and I'll buy everyone here a thick slice of nut pie. We can have us some pie and get this all worked out, and you boys can be headed on for home before suppertime. What do you say? Jean over at the Albert Pike makes the best pecan pie in the whole state. Uses so much Karo syrup that it'll make your dental fillings ache for a doggone week. Wins more than her share of awards every year. So unless you have any other questions for Ray— for Chief Elmore—then I'd say maybe—"

"We didn't travel all this way to eat pie," Mr. Abrams interrupted.

I stood up, so did everyone else.

"Maybe not," Powder Graham replied patiently. "But then you haven't tasted Jean's pecan pie."

CHAPTER 33

Split Tree, Arkansas
Monday, November 18, 1963

I didn't go with them. I like a slice of nut pie as much as the next southern boy, but I wasn't in much mood to be around those lawyers more than I already had been, and I expect the feeling was somewhat mutual, so I let Powder Graham coax the three of them into going over to the Albert Pike Café without me. Powder's a good lawyer, and a better person, and I figured that if anyone could make sense out of what was going on, it'd be him, and I also figured that he didn't need whatever help, or hindrance, I might be. I watched him pull Ben Cooper and Carl Trimble aside as they were walking out of my office, and he made it clear that he'd get more accomplished if they didn't tag along either. Ben looked happy to get cut loose; he never did seem to understand why he was there, and to be honest, neither did I, except for the fact that the jail is technically under his control; the town just rents some cell space when we need it. Carl Trimble didn't have any more business being there either, except that I'm sure that once he heard about it, he saw it as an opportunity to watch someone taking a stick to me, and he wasn't about to let himself get disinvited from a front-row seat to that show. I saw Powder try to talk him out of going with them, but it didn't work.

As they walked out, Powder turned back to look at me, and he nodded and winked, as if to tell me that everything was going to be okay. I suppose that would've been comforting if I'd understood what the problem really was. From where I was sitting, all I could see was that thanks to Carl Trimble, I'd been forced to hire a dumb-ass employee by the name of Charley Dunn Skinner. And from my experience, when you hire dumb-ass people, dumb-assed things tend to follow.

Ricky Forrest stayed behind, and as soon as Powder and the others had left, Jewell Faye came into my office and joined us. She still seemed as skittery as an old barn cat in a dog run.

"What the hell was that all about?" I said. I caught myself. "Back up, first, sorry that y'all two had to deal with that; whatever *that* was. I was over at the bank talkin' to Nick Mitchell. My apology. Now, *what the hell was that all about?*"

"Are you in trouble?" Jewell Faye asked. "They're from *New York*." She glanced quickly at the door, as if those strange lawyers might be sneaking up on her from behind. "*New York*, Ray."

I laughed. "I can't believe that I am, but I have to confess, this was about the last thing I expected to be dealin' with on a Monday mornin'." I looked at Ricky Forrest. "What do you make of all that?"

Ricky moved around behind his desk and sat down, shaking his head the whole time. "I'm not so sure, Chief. I'm not sure that it's just nothing. Before you got here, they were reeling off a laundry list of charges. Sounded serious to me. Mr. Graham regained his feet, but even he looked a little shell-shocked at first."

"What kind of charges? I'm still not quite clear on what I was supposed to have done."

"They say that you, and maybe me—I'm not entirely clear if I'm involved or not—conspired to deprive Mister Jackson of his constitutional rights. They want to make this a federal charge."

I laughed again. "I got all that, but I thought maybe I was misunderstandin' what I'd heard. I figured there had to be more. Hard for us to conspire when neither of us knew anythin' about it."

Ricky wasn't laughing. "Maybe so, but they're saying that you're liable for it nonetheless. They cited the—wait a minute, I learned a new expression; wrote it down." He fished his small notebook out of his shirt pocket and flipped it open and read from it. "You're liable for Charley Dunn's actions under the doctrine of *Respondeat Superior*. Mister Graham seemed to understand that."

"Damn. Is that right? Well, I guess if a New York lawyer says it in Latin, it must be true. I'll bet I can probably guess, but why don't you tell me what it means."

"Well, if I understand it correctly, it means that you're the boss, and in situations like this, the crap rolls uphill. Whatever Charley Dunn did while wearing a badge, you're responsible for it."

"Oh, Lord," Jewell Faye said. She turned in a couple of complete circles, as if she were an old dog getting ready to lay down. "Oh, Lord. Oh, Lord. Oh, my dear Lord."

"Oh, Lord, is right," I said. I took a deep breath and closed my eyes and let it all sink in. After a minute, I asked, "And just what rights did I conspire to deprive him of?"

Ricky Forrest flipped back a page. "I wrote some of this down. They say that Jackson was here, legally trying to register black voters, and that you had him arrested and detained in violation of his Fourth and Fifth Amendment rights. Also his First. Fifteenth was thrown around. Maybe his Sixth as well, though that one is a little more obscure for me, but Mister Graham nodded when they read it off. There were also six of seven federal and state statutes."

"But he wasn't held more than a half hour," I said. "It took longer to get rid of him."

Ricky shook his head. "I know. I was there when you tried to get him to leave his cell. But like that one lawyer, Mister Allen, said earlier, in their eyes, it doesn't matter if it's one minute or one month."

"Goddamn it," I said. I realized Jewell Faye was still standing there. "Sorry, Jewell Faye. I cuss too much."

"Heard worse," she said. "I'm married to Clement, remember?"

"No excuse." I took a deep breath and let it out slowly. "I don't get it. Hell, they're killin' men over in Mississippi for the same thing. Shootin' them down in their own homes not a hundred miles from here, and these damn New York yahoos have got nothin' better to do than come after our little town because some stupid cracker-assed police officer, who had no business being hired in the first place, went and accidentally locked a man up for all of maybe thirty minutes. Really? I've waited my turn at the barbershop for longer than that."

Ricky and Jewell Faye both looked at me but didn't respond; no response was required.

I opened the window behind me and then lit up a cigarette and let a wave of nicotine clear my head. "Well, if anyone can get this sorted out, my money's on Powder Graham. In the meantime, we just need to stay focused on what we're paid to do. Right now, I'm more interested in figurin' out where Jo Johnson is and makin' sure that her little boy is safe."

"Oh," Jewell Faye said. It sort of erupted from her like she'd just backed herself into a hot stove. "Oh, oh, I almost forgot, with those lawyers bein' here and all. I got myself so rattled. Your friend from Little Rock called. The one from the state police. He wants you to call him back."

CHAPTER 34

Split Tree, Arkansas
Monday, November 18, 1963

T he telephone rang a good five or six times before Art Hennig's secretary picked up, and it took a couple of minutes for her to run him down. "Doc Elmore, what are you up to bubba?" he asked when he finally got to the phone.

"Art. You tell me. I heard you called," I responded.

"I did. I did at that. I got some good news for you, Doc."

"I could use it." I started to tell him about the ACLU lawyers, but decided that it was a ball of yarn that I didn't have the energy or patience to untangle. Besides, Powder Graham was cleaning that mess up as we spoke. I hoped.

"Well, it's about that Gervais fella and that little Cuban firecracker of his."

Ricky had stepped into the outer office to talk with Jewell Faye, and he walked back in and sat on the edge of his desk again. I held the receiver away from my ear so that he could hear the conversation.

"Hey, Art, Ricky Forrest just walked in," I said. "Can you speak up so he can hear?"

"Of course; *hey there, Ricky,*" Art boomed. "*How you doin', boy? Ready to move to the big city and do some real police work?*"

"Good morning, Sergeant Hennig. Fine. How you doing?" Ricky replied, loudly enough that Art could hear.

"Better than I probably deserve, at least to hear my mother-in-law talk anyhow. Hey, listen, I was just tellin' your boss here that I have some good news for y'all about Gervais and his girlfriend."

"You goin' tell me you caught them?" I asked.

"Next best thing," Art replied. "Next best thing, if you follow. We have an unconfirmed sightin' of them just this side of Shreveport. Unconfirmed, but still pretty reliable. The sheriff down there saw them at a gas station. Green Chevy Impala with Arkansas tags. A big raw-boned guy and a pretty little dark-haired gal. Report came in yesterday evenin', but I just now saw it."

"You say Shreveport?"

"I did. Shreveport, Louisiana. Gateway to the Fisherman's Paradise. And the last time I checked, that's out of our fair state, and that means he's out of our fair hair. Mine and yours. If you follow."

"I guess I'm not a bit surprised," I answered. "Makes sense. I've thought all along that if I were him, I'd make a beeline for Louisiana. My father used to always say, don't borrow trouble. I'd think if you're lucky enough to get out of Tucker Prison one time, don't push your luck, and there ain't a better place to get lost in than Louisiana."

"Except he couldn't keep from knockin' off that fella in Magnolia."

"No, but then it's on the way to Shreveport. How far away is it?"

"Magnolia? Funny you should ask; I just looked that up myself. It's eighty miles from Magnolia to Shreveport; give or take."

"Kind of makes my point. Well, good riddance," I replied.

"Told you it was good news."

"So you can take a breath now."

Art Hennig laughed. "I wish. No, if it's not one thing, it's another. If you follow. Gervais may be gone, but we got us a memo this mornin' from our director. The dang president is headed down to Dallas this Friday on a campaign trip."

"So I've heard. The president's activities affect you now, do they?"

"Not directly, but there's talk he may stop by here in Little Rock on his way back to Washington. I guess he wants to glad-hand the few democrats that'll still vote for him. All three or four of them. The head shed's got us jumpin' through hoops like it's really goin' to happen. Which it won't. Never does. He don't give two shits for Arkansas. Except in election years, and we're still a dang year out."

"Sorry to hear you have to deal with all that. Can't say I give two shits for him either."

"Yeah. Well, I have to admit I voted for him, but I held my nose all the while I did; if you follow. Damn navy officer. Just couldn't bring myself to vote for that Nixon fella. My daddy would come out of his grave and whup my ass red raw if I voted for a Republican."

"Sounds like we may have had the same father."

He laughed. "No, I guarantee you don't want my father. My old man was as mean as cat shit. Anyhow, about this stop in Little Rock, we have to prepare for it like it might actually happen. I guess it's what we get paid for. If you follow."

I laughed. "You mean, it's what you get paid overtime for."

Art laughed as well. "Well, you got that right; still, I'm not sure it's worth the headache, even with overtime."

"So I guess that means our fingerprint case gets put on the backburner for a few days."

There was a momentary silence on his end. "What fingerprint case?"

"Came in from Lee County. Car found at a motor lodge up there," I said. "Likely stolen. I'm told they sent it to y'all."

"Lee County? What the hell does it got to do with you? Or have I gotten my geography all cattywampus?"

"Not completely sure, except that the car belongs to a local case that Ricky and me are workin' on. The owner lives here in Locust County. *Lived.* We found him couple days ago with his head blown off; looks like maybe he had some help doin' it."

"Dang, son. Dang. Sorry. I wasn't trackin' that. If I'd known we had a case from Doc Elmore, I'd have the boys workin' on it around the clock. When'd it come in? Just recent?"

"I'm not sure. Lee County Sheriff would have sent it in; that's my understandin' anyhow. Car was found yesterday, so you may not even have them yet."

"Well, thanks for the heads-up. I'll make sure to fast-track it. So, these latents, you think they might just belong to your killer, do you?"

"I doubt it, I really do, but we don't have much else to work with right now."

"Well, I'll go check with the evidence room as soon as we hang up. If it's here, I'll light a fire under the right dang asses and get you an answer, *chop chop*; if not, I'll keep an eye out and get my best examiner on it as soon as it arrives. One way or the other, we'll get to it and get you an answer, and I'll give you a call when we do."

"Thanks. I'll owe you."

"Like hell, Doc. I wouldn't be here breathin' if it weren't for you."

I didn't want to get into that. "Listen, Art, thanks for the good news about Gervais. I'll let you go now," I said. "And good luck with the president."

"If he comes."

"Yeah."

CHAPTER 35

Split Tree, Arkansas
Monday, November 18, 1963

I hung up the phone and leaned back in my chair. "I reckon you heard all that?" I asked Ricky. "With Gervais and that woman of his in Louisiana, maybe we can focus on sortin' out this mess with Ring. If nothin' else, we can get some sleep anyways."

"I heard enough of it." He stood up and walked behind his desk and sat in his chair. "You think Gervais is really gone?"

"Don't know. I know I want to. What do you think? It makes sense. As much as I'd like to kill Carl Trimble myself some days . . . most days actually . . . I don't see riskin' goin' back to death row for it. If I were Gervais, I'd find me a little shack tucked away in some back bayou and spend the rest of my days layin' low with that girl of his. Countin' my lucky stars. Carl Trimble isn't worth it."

Ricky Forrest leaned forward. "So, what do you want to do about watching Missus Trimble? Continue doing it?"

I thought about that. "I don't want you to do anythin'," I answered. "You've done plenty. I'm fixin' to be out there tonight, maybe tomorrow too. We'll see how it goes, but unless we hear anythin' else, I think we can probably cut and dry this one in a couple-three more days."

"We can split time. Alternate if you want."

I nodded. "We'll see. Like I said, I've got the next night or two. If it looks like we need to go beyond that, maybe I'll let you spell me. Give it a day, and maybe Art can verify that Gervais is actually a long ways from here."

"Roger." He paused and shifted gears. "Doesn't sound like we'll have those fingerprint results anytime soon."

I bowed a kink out of my back before I responded. "No, probably not. Sounds like Art'll get a rush job on it when he can, but I guess it'll depend on how much they get tied up providin' security for Kennedy. You heard all that too, I guess."

"Yes, sir. Makes me glad I'm not working for the state police."

"You and me both."

"You know, it dawned on me while you two were talking that I should call up to Lee County and make sure they sent the prints over to Little Rock like we were told. I should have checked yesterday. I'd hate to wait around for a week and then discover that they're still sitting on someone's desk up there."

I nodded. "Good idea." I swiveled in my chair and looked out of the window while I stretched my bad leg out straight and shifted the weight off of my hip. We were both quiet for a minute or so, and then I said, "I got thinkin' last night about Ring's car. Been tryin' to figure out how it got up to that motor lodge. Doesn't make sense." I laughed. "Hell, like any of the rest of it does."

"What'd you come up with?"

I looked out of the window for a moment. I could see Ring's car parked across the street in front of the courthouse. "Not much. I finally got to ask Ben Cooper about it this mornin', and he says Ring didn't smoke. At least not regular enough to fill that car's ashtray the way it was. He said Jo will light up sometimes, if someone offers her one, and she wants to kick up her heels, but neither of them make it a habit."

"Some of the butts had lipstick smudges," he said.

"True. But a lot of women wear lipstick, and even if those are her smokes, that still leaves us with explainin' the other ones."

"We know that she's having an affair."

"We know she's havin' sex with a pig. Not sure it counts as an affair, but I get your point."

"Okay. We know Missus Johnson is going to that motel with Carl Trimble. I think he smokes some."

"We do, but the clerk identified Carl's Buick. We got no reason to think they ever went up there in Ring's car. Besides, I'll admit that it's been a long time since I paid any attention to what Carl smokes, but I don't think they're Camels. Cigars mostly. I guess I can ask Grace about it; Carl sure as shit won't tell me." I took a deep breath, and let it out slowly as I looked out the window again, before I continued. "I was goin' to talk to that fat prick about what the hell he's been doin' with Jo Johnson and how long it's been goin' on. I intended to do it this mornin' until those damn lawyers went and got me sidetracked."

"You think he'll honestly tell you?"

"Who knows? Probably not. Especially now. With them lawyers pissin' on my leg, he's feelin' pretty superior to me, and that gives him more backbone than he normally has."

"Maybe you should wait a little while then."

I nodded. "Probably right. Don't want to put it off too long though, but you're right about waitin' a bit. In the meantime, let's get back to Ring's car. So, if neither Ring or Jo drove it up there, just how'd it get there? Cars don't drive themselves."

"Could have been stolen. Sounds maybe like you're leaning in that direction."

I shook my head. "No, not necessarily. You're right, that's what I told Art, but I'm not sure how I'm leanin' really, but that makes some sense, doesn't it? It fits. Ring didn't drive it there, neither did Jo. But still . . ."

"What's bothering you about it?"

"Aside from havin' no evidence it was stolen? Well, a bunch of things, but mainly it just seems like one hell of a coincidence that Jo

210|T H O M A S   H O L L A N D

Johnson is havin' an affair at the same rat-hole motor lodge that her husband's stolen car gets abandoned at. Forty miles up the road from their farm. Hundred places you could dump a car. Hell of a coincidence."

"And you don't like coincidences."

"No, sir, I don't," I responded. "Coincidence is a crutch for lazy thinkin'."

"So what's next?"

"Well, aside from us waitin' on the fingerprints to come back, that's a damn good question. That's what I spent most of last night thinkin' about. We know that someone had to drive that car up there, and like I said, we know it wasn't Ring. Unlikely anyhow. And if it was, that'd just leave us with explainin' how he got himself home. Plus that'd mean their car was up at the motel longer than we think it was. Nossir, Ring didn't drive it up there."

"And probably not Missus Johnson."

"Probably not. Unless she recently learned how," I said.

"And you don't think it was Carl Trimble."

"Not from what the clerk told us. Carl drove his own."

"If the clerk's telling the truth about the car being a black Buick."

"I suspect he is," I answered. "About that part, anyhow. He might not have paid attention to Ring's old Dodge, but we know for sure that he paid attention to Jo Johnson, and he says he only saw her in Carl's Buick."

"So we're back to thinking it was stolen."

I nodded. "Maybe. As I was sayin', I gave it some serious thought last night. So, let's start with what we know, or can assume. Ring's car got abandoned there, or left there, we know that, and let's assume that neither Ring or Jo or Carl drove it up there; let's start with that too. So, stolen or not, someone else drove that Dodge up there and abandoned it. Okay, now, if that's true, and let's assume it is, then how'd they leave? We know they're not stayin' at that motel, and there's not much else around there. So, where'd they go, and how did they go? Another car? Someone followed the first driver? That means another person. Two cars, two drivers."

Ricky chewed on that for a minute. "Here's somethin' else I don't understand; let's assume the Johnson car was stolen, okay, what I don't figure is, why steal the car in the first place if you're just going to abandon it?" he asked. "Stealing it for money is one thing, but then why abandon it there? No money in that. Maybe we're overthinking this, Ray. It could be something as simple as just some dumb kids out joyriding."

"I doubt it. I really do. I thought about that, but there's still the coincidence part of it to explain. No, kids would have just left it where they got tired of it, or where it ran out of gas; that's been my experience. When we looked in the car yesterday, there was almost three-quarters of a tank. Did Ben or Pinto say anythin' about fillin' it up before they brought it down here?"

"No."

"Wouldn't think so. I doubt they did. Wouldn't have spent the county's money to fill it up anyhow. No, I don't think it was joyridin'. I think if someone stole Ring's car, then you have to assume it's probably the same person who blew his head all over the shed wall. We know Ring's been dead for a week or more; right? But the car hasn't been at the motel that long. So, maybe whoever's been usin', drivin' it around, maybe he's also smart enough to know that sooner or later it'll get too hot. At least in Locust County, where folks would start lookin' for it, or might recognize it. When that happens, what do you do?"

"Steal another one?"

"Makes sense. That's as good an explanation as any. Changin' cars like that buys you a couple more days. Especially if you do it in another county. You count on the police not talkin' to each another."

Ricky nodded and let the information sift itself out in his head. He was warming to the idea. He leaned forward in his chair. "Like you said, not much around that motor lodge for several miles in any direction."

"Go on."

He nodded some more. "If you dump it off along the roadside, or in a field, it'd be found quickly. Quicker anyhow."

"And you don't want that. You want as much time as you can get. Go on."

"So you leave it where strange cars don't look strange. Maybe behind a motor lodge. It looks like it's just parked there. Cars come and go. Doesn't raise any suspicions. It may be a week or more before it's found."

"Which it was. Except?"

"Except, like you say, you'd need another car to leave with. Unless you were hitchhiking."

"That's right; that's what I'm thinkin'. Now, if someone was hitchhiking, there's no way we'll ever know it, but if someone swapped it for another car, another stolen car, well, then, that's a horse of a different color. We got a chance at that. Where'd that second car come from, and where is it now?"

"That still leaves us with the fact that the Johnsons' car got dumped off at the same place that Missus Johnson is going with Carl Trimble," Ricky said. "That sounds like a coincidence, and you don't like coincidences."

"It does, and that still bothers me, but I'm not sure we'll figure that out until we sort out the other part of it. As I said, whoever it was that abandoned it there, and let's assume that's what happened, they'd have to leave somehow, and I doubt they walked. So, our best bet is to figure out where that second car came from. See where that leads."

"No stolen cars in this county recently," he said.

"Only Ring's."

"Only his," he repeated, as he began thumbing through an address book on his desk. He reached for his phone. "While I'm asking Lee County if they sent the fingerprints to Little Rock, I'll check to see if there are any cars reported stolen about a week ago."

CHAPTER 36

Split Tree, Arkansas
Monday, November 18, 1963

I smoked a cigarette and looked out the window while I listened to Ricky Forrest talk to a deputy up in Lee County. I heard him confirm that the prints from Ring's car had already been sent to Little Rock like they should have been. Art Hennig had already promised me that he'd check with the lab and get someone working on them when they arrived, so I knew that there wasn't anything else for me to do about that but wait. Checking on stolen cars reported in Lee County was taking longer, and I could tell that Ricky was being passed around to different people and finally was put on hold.

While I waited on him I made a phone call myself. I'd tried Granville Begley a few times over the weekend but never caught him; I wanted to ask him about what he'd determined from examining Ring's body. This time, I finally got hold of Anne, his wife. She told me that he was out at Boy Crawford's place, but that she expected him back any minute, and that he didn't have any patients waiting for him and now was a good time to come over. I told her I'd be there in five minutes.

Ricky was still drumming his fingers on his desk, waiting for the next person on the phone to ask him the same questions that the previous two or three had already asked him, when I grabbed my hat and stepped into the outer office. I sat for a couple of minutes and talked to Jewell Faye, who had calmed down some from her earlier upset. She'd finished a couple pots of coffee in the last hour, and unlike the way that'd affect most people, with her it seemed to have a soothing effect. She apologized for getting worked up, but said that she was worried about me, and I told her I appreciated it, but that I was sure that the whole thing would turn out to be a fairly small rock in my shoe and not to worry any more about it. I told her that Powder Graham would have it all worked out by the second slice of pie. I also told her that I was going to run over to Granville's place, and that I'd be back in thirty minutes.

Granville lives on Main Street, a couple of blocks north of the center of town. There are some nice houses up that way, built by a few of the richer planters a hundred years ago and now occupied by some of the more prominent of our town's inhabitants. Big houses. Powder Graham lives up that way, as does Nick Mitchell's father. Granville's is not an overly big house, but it's nice, even if it's showing its age. Much like its owner. He used to maintain an office downtown, but he's slowing down some, and he gave that up about a year or so ago; he now sees patients in a couple of rooms off of the side of his house, and Ann serves as his nurse and receptionist.

I went around to the side entrance and knocked on the door and walked into what had once been a summer parlor, but which now served as a small waiting room. Anne Begley was sitting at a tidy desk to the right of the door, drinking from a teacup and looking through a *Life* magazine, which had a picture of Richard Burton and Liz Taylor on the cover. I remember a time when she used to wear a starched white nurse's uniform, and a folded white cap, but with the decline of Granville's practice, I see her more and more dressed just in everyday clothes, looking like someone's grandmother. Today she had on a pink dress and a green-and-white apron, which was dusted with what I took to be flour. I could smell cinnamon and butter and baking cookies.

"My word, has it been five minutes already," she greeted me. She smiled big, and stood up and walked around the desk to give me a hug and a quick kiss on the cheek, careful to not get any flour on me. "Seems like we were just on the phone a second ago."

"Been closer to ten," I said. "Got hung up leavin' the office. How have you been, Anne?"

She laughed. "Now, Ray, you should know better than to ask an old woman how she's been. We've got nothin' better to do than tell you, and if you're not careful, you're just liable to spend the next hour hearin' about it, but I'm fine; thank you for askin'. How are Ellen and the boys?"

"Now Anne, I'm not sure who you're referrin' to; I don't see any old women around here, but I'll remember that advice for the next time I meet one," I said. "Ellen Mae is fine, just fine. So are the boys; I think anyhow. They're at that age where they're never at home, but I also don't see them when I stop by the jail, so I'll assume everythin' is good." I hung my hat on the rack. "Where's the old man? He back yet?"

She started to answer, but Granville cut her off by walking into the room, drying his hands on a towel. "Well, Raymond, I thought I heard you out here. Annie told me you were headed this way. Glad to see you."

"Granville," I greeted him. "I've been tryin' to touch base with you all weekend, but I never could seem to be in the same place at the same time. You got a minute? It's about Ring Johnson."

He handed the towel to his wife and motioned for me to follow him to a small office that opened off of the reception room. In contrast to the rest of the house, it smelled of phenol and green soap and cigarette smoke and old books. "I have nothing but time these days, my friend," he said as he took a seat behind his desk and moved some stacks of paper to one side.

"I don't know about that; you seem to keep pretty busy for a man who claims to be slowin' down," I said, as I sat on a small couch positioned along the side wall. It was old, and the springs were shot, and I sank deeply into it.

He laughed. "Well, I may not have many patients anymore, but the few that I still see manage to keep me busy; that's true enough. A couple of them, anyway."

"Anne said you were out at Boy Crawford's. I haven't seen him for a while. How's he doin'?"

"I was. Oh, you know Boy. Nothing wrong with him except the rather painful need for some human attention; a great many strange aches and pains that defy diagnosis and which all seem to disappear as soon as you sit down and have a cup of coffee with him. Effective medicine, even if it doesn't pay well." He made a dismissive gesture and sighed. "So, our late Mister Reginald Johnson. You talk to Donnie yet?"

"I did. He showed me the body. He had it floatin' in the bathtub. I was surprised to see that it's not as far gone as we thought when we first saw him. Donnie says he's startin' to think maybe Ring hasn't been dead as long as we initially figured."

Granville got out his Camels and offered me one. I declined, but he lit up. "I think Donnie's probably correct on that account. The head's a mess, of course, so are the thoracic and abdominal regions, but the rest of that old boy isn't too far gone."

"What do you make of that?"

"Well, I'm—"

We were interrupted by Anne Begley who brought in a small plate of large sugar cookies. We stopped our discussion of Ring Johnson long enough to sample a couple and to tell Anne that she still made the best sugar cookies in the state. Which she arguably does. She smiled at the compliment and left, and we returned to our conversation.

"What'd you ask?" Granville tried to pick up the thread. "Oh, yes, what do I make of the pattern of decomposition? Wasn't that it? Well, now, the head we understand. As best as I can tell, there was a single shotgun blast to the face. Intermediate distance. Some gunpowder tattooing on the more intact tissue, which would suggest that the muzzle was closer than three or four feet, but not in contact either. I found pellets embedded in the roof of the mouth and the malars—the cheek bones—and the frontal bone." He parked his cigarette on the lip of a glass ashtray and touched his forehead and cheek. "Here and here."

I nodded. "We more or less knew that."

"We did." He took another cookie. "As I was saying, we understand the condition of the head. It's about what I'd expect." He finished the cookie in two bites and swallowed and then picked up his cigarette and took a long drag on it and exhaled before continuing. "Now, what bothers me, Raymond, is the midsection. The old boy's belly. The *breadbasket*, as my father would say. You saw it. It was about gone from all the insect mischief. That bothered me last Friday when we were out at his place, and I've continued to wonder about it."

"As warm as it's been, I'm not sure that I'm trackin' what the problem is. I saw bodies in the Pacific that'd be rendered down to bone in just a couple-three days."

"I'm sure you did. I can't much imagine, but this isn't the battlefield, nor some island in the Pacific. That's the point."

"I'm still not trackin'. What is the point?"

"What do you know about blowflies, my learned friend?"

I laughed. "Not as much as I think I'm fixin' to learn," I said. I got out my Lucky Strikes and lit one up and adjusted my weight on the couch. I sank deeper.

He leaned back in his chair and folded his hands into his lap. "Blowflies. Family *Calliphoridae*, or some such thing as that. I believe that's right; been sixty years since I took biology. Order *Diptera*. I remember that. It's Greek for two wings. It includes the familiar green and blue bottleflies, not to mention that old bastard, the screwworm fly. Voracious eaters in their larval stage. I believe we encountered some of them dining on our friend Reginald."

"I believe we did."

"Now, here's the interesting thing about them." Granville paused while he chain-lit another Camel and got the old one stubbed out. "It seems that momma blowfly is unusually attracted to dead things. To a female blowfly, there is nothing in this world so enticing as a decomposing corpse on which to lay her brood, be it a dead bovine or canine or in this case, our late friend, Reginald. But as enticing as a dead body can be, the momma fly can't pierce the tough hide of a human with her little ovipositor, her egg-laying apparatus; at least not without some help. The eyes, nose, the mouth, now those are all good natural openings, you see, but aside from those, she needs some assistance; a break in the skin."

"Like a head blown open with a shotgun."

"Precisely. As I said, I'm comfortable with the pattern that we saw with his head; in fact, I would expect nothing else than what we observed."

I was starting to understand where he was headed. "But there's no natural opening to the belly. Is that what you're sayin'?"

"Precisely. That's what bothered me last Friday, and it still bothers me today. I don't have a ready explanation."

"And your autopsy didn't help?"

He laughed and leaned forward in his chair. "I make no claim that what I performed was an autopsy. Far from it. Donnie and I rinsed the maggots off, and I probed around a bit, but his entire midsection was eaten out. There wasn't anything left to examine."

"What'd Donnie think about it?" I asked. "He's seen more dead bodies than both of us combined. He think it was unusual at all?"

Granville shrugged and took a long draw on his smoke. "No offense to our mutual friend Donnie, but I'm not sure that it dawned on him to think much of anything. No reason to, really. No, he didn't say anything about it, and I didn't bring it up. I certainly trust Donnie's discretion, but I wanted to think about it some more, and I wanted to talk with you first before I opined openly. You and I suspect foul play, but I wasn't sure how widely you wanted that known at this point."

"Ricky Forrest came to the same conclusion. He knows."

"Smart boy. Well, as far as Donnie is concerned, Reginald Johnson removed his own head with his own shotgun. Case closed. That's what Cecil Ben says happened, and Donnie doesn't have any reason to question it. I haven't filled out the death certificate yet, and I can sit on that for a few more days. I don't plan to say any more about it until you're ready for me to do so."

"Thanks," I replied. I leaned forward. "Buy me a few more days if you can."

"I can do that. Until we find his next of kin, there's really no sense of urgency to that end of the business." He paused. "Still no sign of Josephine?"

"Not yet. Still workin' it, but let's get back to Ring. Maybe I'm still not trackin' fully. So what are you sayin', Granville? Spell it out. How do you explain all those maggots in his belly?"

He looked down at his desk blotter for a long moment, and then up at me. "I've been trying to rationalize another explanation, but I haven't been able to do so. I guess what I'm saying is that he wasn't just shot in the head. No, Raymond, something else opened up that man's midsection."

CHAPTER 37

Split Tree, Arkansas
Monday, November 18, 1963

I sat and looked at Granville for a moment. I'd heard him, but I was slow to appreciate what he'd just said. "Somethin' like what? I'm sorry to be so dense here, but what are you sayin'? You think he was shot in the belly as well?" I asked. "Two shots?"

He shook his head. "No, I'm not saying that, exactly. There's really no way of telling at this point. I know that I didn't find any shotgun pellets in the region when I was probing about."

"You said it. His gut was pretty eaten up; maybe they weren't there anymore."

"No. Maggots are voracious eaters, but they prefer decomposing tissue, not lead pellets. If he was shot in the abdomen, then I'd expect the pellets to still be present. They weren't."

"Then what? Did you look at his clothes? Maybe his shirt shows somethin'."

He shook his head. "I'm sorry Raymond. I'm a bit embarrassed in that regard. I was summoned out to the Dumas place to deal with one of their boys. I've never seen such a bunch of—"

"Granville. Don't go runnin' off on me. Finish tellin' me about Ring's clothes."

"Of course. Umm, no, I'm sorry about that Raymond. Perhaps I am getting too old for this job, but the truth is that I didn't think about it in time. Because I didn't share our suspicions with Donnie, he didn't think there was anything unusual about the case; I'm afraid he didn't save the clothing. As you saw, they were covered in blood and maggots. Donnie burned them in a drum out back while I was away tending to the Dumas boy. I'm so sorry."

"Don't kick yourself," I said. "They probably wouldn't have told us much."

"Perhaps. Still, an unfortunate lapse of judgment on my part. Very unprofessional."

"Don't kick yourself. So, forget the clothes. You didn't answer me. What do you think happened?"

Before he could respond, we were interrupted by the sound of Anne Begley's voice. She was talking to someone in the reception room, but the creak of floorboards indicated that they were headed our way.

". . . *nonsense, I'm sure they won't mind. How's Kitty?*" we heard her say. "*More importantly, how's that baby boy of yours?*"

"*Growing up fast,*" we heard Ricky Forrest reply. "*Kitty's fine; she's worn out and tired all the time, but fine. Everyone's well.*"

Anne laughed in response and then knocked on the door frame and addressed us. "Boys, look who's here. You have a guest. I assured him that whatever it was that you two were talkin' about, that it couldn't be so important that he couldn't interrupt you." She stepped to the side so Ricky could pass. "*Make sure they save you a cookie or two. Granville's had enough as is,*" she said to Ricky. She winked at him and patted his arm and then went back to her magazine.

"Richard," Granville greeted him. "Come on in. Have yourself a seat, young man. And partake of a cookie while they last. Annie makes the best sugar cookies in the South. I've always said that."

"Doc. Chief. I'm sorry to interrupt," Ricky said.

"Not interruptin' nothin'," I replied. "Come on in. We were just talkin' about Ring Johnson. You better take a seat though; Granville's about to tell you way more about blowflies than you care to learn."

Ricky Forrest didn't step into the room but remained standing in the doorway. He had his hat in his hands, and he looked nervous. I've known that boy for several years; he's not the type to get nervous.

"Ray . . . I . . . we need to talk," he said. "Do you mind? Maybe outside?"

"Outside? Somethin' that can't be talked about in front of Granville? Not sure what that'd be," I responded.

"Want me to step out?" Granville offered.

"Hell no, Granville. It's your office. If anyone steps out, it'll be us," I replied. I looked back to Ricky. "What is it? It's all right. You okay?"

Ricky took a deep breath. "Powder Graham stopped by the office a few minutes ago. He was looking for you."

I turned to Granville. "I started to tell you, but we got onto other things. You heard about that black preacher that was through here a few months back?"

Granville nodded. "I remember that Charley Dunn arrested a Negro back in August. That the one? He was registering voters or something, wasn't he? Out in the county mostly?"

"Yeah. I'm not sure how much he was actually gettin' done, but it was all perfectly legal. As far as I can tell, the man wasn't doin' a thing wrong, and Charley Dunn had no business arrestin' him, none whatsoever, but he ended up spendin' fifteen minutes in jail. The minute I heard about it, I called Johnnie Young and had him released, but damn if he didn't go runnin' off and call the ACLU. Couple of their lawyers from New York showed up this mornin', in their expensive suits, if you can believe that. Came all this way. They're after me apparently. They say—" I stopped and looked back at Ricky. *"What's that term they used? I'll bet Granville knows it."*

"Respondeat Superior," Ricky answered. He didn't have to look in his notebook this time.

"That's it," I replied. I looked back at Granville. "You familiar with it?"

"No. Not exactly," Granville said. He leaned forward in his chair. "But my Latin is good enough that I believe I can decipher it. Let's see, *Respondeat Superior;* that would be *the Master must answer.* Something like that. Is that correct? I'm a country doctor, not a New York City lawyer, but I'd say that it means that they aim to hold you responsible for the wayward actions of young Charley Dunn."

"That's exactly what it means," I said. "They're tryin' real hard to spin this thing up into a problem. They claim they got the whole Department of Justice involved. Kennedy brothers are probably just salivatin' to do it too. Fortunately, Powder's handlin' it, so it won't go anywhere, but not for their lack of tryin'. Powder took them over to the Albert Pike for pie and discussion." I turned back to Ricky. *"So, what'd he have to say? How much do I owe him for the pie?"*

Ricky Forrest looked at Granville and then back at me. "Chief, you've been suspended. Effective twenty minutes ago."

CHAPTER 38

Split Tree, Arkansas
Monday, November 18, 1963

I never wanted to be a police officer, let alone the chief of police, and if I'm honest, I can't really say that I much want to be one now. Growing up, all I ever expected to be doing with my life was working the farm, growing old with my brother Reuel, taking care of Grace and our half-dozen or so children. That was all I wanted, that was all I needed, and I didn't set my sights much beyond that target. The war changed that, of course. I wasn't in any shape to work a farm full time when I first returned. Reuel didn't make it home to grow old. And Grace and I never had our family together.

In 1946, Jim Bailey took a single-blade axe to his wife. Don't know why; never had a good chance to ask him. Jim was a little younger than me; he'd gone to school with my brother, and I knew him well enough to wave to in passing. I don't recall him as anything special, but I guess he was a good enough man, at least until he came home from Italy in 1944 with a two-inch metal plate in his head and a different way of seeing things, including his wife. Up until the war intervened, I'll bet that he had no greater aspirations than I did: raise his family; work his farm; grow old. That all changed for him when a one-inch piece of mortar shrapnel caved in the side of his head. Jim's wife, Louise, was cooking dinner one evening, frying some potatoes, when Jim got up from the couch and went to his barn and came back with an axe and proceeded to split her head open like it was a stick of kindling. He then went to his refrigerator, got a glass of buttermilk, and sat back on his couch and turned on the television. His five-year-old son was taking a nap in the back of the house, and his ten-year-old daughter was playing with her dolls in the next room. She's the one who wandered into the kitchen when she smelled the potatoes burning and discovered her mother on the linoleum.

Our police chief at the time was a man named Dave Sanderson. Sandy had been chief since the early thirties, and was maybe adequate on his good days, and less so most of the time; especially when he'd been drinking, which he'd taken up with some enthusiasm by then. Unfortunately, the day Jim Bailey took an axe to his wife wasn't one of his good days. I got the call from Granville. Jim Bailey's daughter had run to the neighbor's house and reported what happened, and when the neighbors, who half thought that the little girl must be making the whole thing up, got to Jim's house, he met them at the kitchen door with a twelve-gauge shotgun in his hands and a strange look in his eyes. The neighbor backed off and called Granville. He also called the police, but Sandy was nowhere to be found. Neither was the sheriff. Granville called me instead.

I really had no business going out to the Bailey place that day. I think I knew it then, and I know it for sure now. Jim met me at the same kitchen door with the same shotgun and the same strange look that the neighbors had seen. I like to tell myself that I did it because Granville asked me to, or because there was a little boy in that house, or because in some strange way I thought maybe I could help Jim Bailey deal with his demons, but I tend to suspect that maybe I just didn't care if he blew me in half. If I'm being honest with myself again, maybe that's why I went; if I'm being honest, maybe I was hoping that Jim Bailey would turn that gun on me.

Jim never said a word. When I got to the door of his house, he stepped aside and let me in as if I'd come over to fix a leaky sink. When I asked where his son was, he nodded toward the bedroom at the end of the hall. He never said a word when I carried that boy out and across the field to the house next door. He didn't say a word when I returned five minutes later with two red apples that I got from the neighbors. We sat down at the kitchen table, on opposite sides, and we each quietly ate our apples. Jim Bailey finished his, and then he slowly twisted the stem off of its core, counting each rotation like he was a hopeful schoolgirl. He briefly looked at me, and wiped his mouth, and then he set the butt of the twelve-gauge on the floor between his feet, placed his chin over the muzzle, and reached down and pushed the trigger, all in one quick movement. Never said a word. I still think about that day a great deal. Jim Bailey doesn't get in line to visit me in my sleep like the others do, but I wouldn't blame him one bit if he did.

I suspect I might have been able to handle it better.

The next week the town council gave Sandy Sanderson a new casting rod and some fishing tackle as a retirement gift, and they hired me. I didn't want the job, but I selfishly let them give it to me. I'd already proposed to Ellen Mae, and I knew that I'd be needing a paycheck soon, but I never thought I'd do it for long. Maybe a year. Eighteen months. That was seventeen years ago last summer. I didn't want it when I got it, and I don't guess I can really say that I'll regret losing it now; I just figured that when the time came, that I'd end it on my own terms.

I had to laugh. "Well, I never saw that comin'," I responded to Ricky Forrest. "Suspended? Damn. For how long?"

"Indefinitely. Pending an investigation," he replied.

"That's just nonsense," Granville said. "Who suspended him? With pay I hope."

"The town council," Ricky replied. "Without pay."

"You mean Carl Trimble," I said. "That's his doin'. Town council didn't do that."

Ricky nodded. "Yes, sir. Carl wanted you fired outright."

"I'm sure he did," I responded. "He's wanted that for years."

"And Powder Graham agreed to it?" Granville asked. "Suspended? Has that boy lost his mind?"

"I'm not sure he had much choice," Ricky replied. "Sorry, Chief. Mister Graham wants you to call him as soon as you can. He's pretty upset about it himself. He wanted to tell you in person, but I told him it might be better if he let me break the news."

"Thanks. You're right. It is," I said. I leaned back into the couch and sank deeper.

"Damn. That's about the dumbest thing I've seen this town do in fifty years, and I've seen it do some damn stupid things. Indefinitely? Of all the stupid damn things . . ." Granville's thought trailed off and he paused and looked at me. "I don't mean to be indelicate, Raymond, but we're friends, so take this in the spirit intended; you need some money to hold you over until this damn craziness has run its course?"

"What?" I responded. It was starting to sink in, and I was thinking of Chief Sanderson, and Jim Bailey; remembering him twisting off that apple stem. I was only half listening. "Oh. No. I'm fine. Thank you, Granville. No. We'll be fine."

"This could last a while," he said. "You sure?"

I shook my head. "Yeah, I'm sure. Thank you, though." I stood up. My leg had gone numb, and I was a bit unsteady until I could bend it and flex it some. "I guess I need to go find Pow Graham and get some details."

"What do you want me to do?" Ricky asked.

I was still only half listening. "What? Oh. Sorry. Well . . . anythin' you want, I guess. You're actin' police chief now, Ricky. But if I were you, I guess I'd start by callin' Charley Dunn to tell him to not bother comin' in tomorrow." Charley Dunn had worked the weekend, and he had the day off and was probably at home.

"Ah, Chief . . ." Ricky started to respond, but stopped himself.

"Go on," I said. "He needs to be told, and I sure don't want to talk with him. Better for all of us if you give him the bad news. And tell him it'll be healthier for him if he stays away from me for a while."

"You may want to sit down again, Chief," Ricky responded. "They didn't suspend Charley Dunn. They just suspended you."

CHAPTER 39

Split Tree, Arkansas
Monday, November 18, 1963

Ricky and I left Granville's house. Ricky was headed back to the police station, and I told him I'd be along shortly, but first I needed to stop by Powder Graham's office and sort things out. Hear it all from him. Powder was at his desk, waiting for me, when I got there. He was looking a bit overcome. We talked a little, and he apologized a lot, and as I suspected, it was Carl Trimble that offered me up on a platter. Powder said it had been going good, and he'd even gotten that one lawyer, the disagreeable one—Abrams—to admit that the nut pie was pretty damn good. That was the first step in getting to a workable solution. That's when Carl got involved; it was Carl who jumped in and told the ACLU lawyers that he'd fire me, that they shouldn't settle for anything less, and that he'd do it immediately if they agreed to drop the whole thing, that maybe he'd do it even if they didn't drop the lawsuit. Powder told me, and I believe him, that he was able to wedge back in at that point and get the lawyers to understand that firing me, at least immediately like Carl had promised, was unrealistic, and probably unlawful from the town's standpoint. Instead, he convinced them to settle for my suspension. Powder told me, and I believe him, that that was the best damage control he could manage under the circumstances. It seems that once Carl had offered them my immediate dismissal, there was no backing up and starting over no matter how many slices of pie got served up. He said those lawyers smelled blood like pigs on stink bait, though he did manage to wring a concession out of them: I get turned out onto the streets immediately, even if it was just suspension, and they'd drop the civil suit against the town. He was confident that we could win if we chose to fight it; like me, he couldn't see much to their complaint, but he also said that fighting a civil suit would cost way more than our town has to spend. Powder told me, and I believe him, that the ACLU has what they call *deep pockets* and could drag it out for months, or years, and that the cost of fighting it would bankrupt the town; so, getting them to drop the civil suit is a big win for us.

He wasn't as sure about a criminal investigation. He knew I hadn't done anything wrong, but he said there was some merit to that *Respondeat Superior* thing they were tossing about, and that if the Justice Department was looking to nail someone's hide to a tree, that was the closest hammer to grab. That's also why Charley Dunn wasn't suspended. Carl told them that Charley Dunn was just a young man, new to the job, who was just following my orders. I'm not so sure that that's been much of a defense since the Nazis tried it, but Powder says that those lawyers seemed happy enough to accept it. They were after the biggest fish they could hook, and Carl made it plain that they could have me free and clear for the cost of throwing Charley Dunn back into the pond.

As bad as all that sounded, Powder told me to try and not worry about it anymore than I had to; he said he was working on it and that he'd handle it as best he could. No promises, but he said he has a good friend who works in the Justice Department, a classmate from Ole Miss, who he hoped might be able to help, and that he'd already tried calling him and would keep trying until he got hold of him. He said in the meantime, I should enjoy spending more time with my family. Maybe go fishing. I thought about Chief Sanderson. The town at least gave him a new rod and some tackle.

I went to my office. Jewell Faye met me at the door with a hug. She'd heard, of course, I suspect most of the town had by then, and she'd been crying, and the trash can looked like a small snowdrift of balled-up tissues. She was still teetering on the edge, and it was all I could do to get her settled down again. In all the years that I've known her, I'd never seen her so much as moisten up a tissue before, not even when her husband, Clement, had his heart attack a few years ago, and we weren't sure he was going to pull through. I sat beside her desk and told her not to worry, that I had all the faith in the world in Powder Graham, and I even joked that the very worst that would happen is that Ricky Forrest would be made police chief, which in my estimation would be an improvement, so maybe I wasn't joking. She hadn't eaten her lunch, and after I got her calmed down, I told her to take her sack, with her pimento-cheese sandwich and her yellow apple and that bottle of Tab that's she taken to drinking, and go find a sunny spot to sit and eat and then to go on home for the day. I told her that there wasn't a thing in the world that she was working on that couldn't wait until Wednesday when she was due back in the office. She was reluctant, but finally agreed.

After I got her shooed out the door, I went and sat down at my desk and lit up a smoke. Ricky had been sitting quietly at his desk, giving me a chance to talk with Jewell Faye, and we both continued in silence for a few minutes. "Just realized I don't have the authority to tell Jewell Faye to go home," I finally said.

"You have all the authority you need. Now what?" he asked.

I shrugged. "I'm not sure I rightly know. I'm at a bit of a loss, to be honest. Powder told me that I'm allowed to clean out my desk." I laughed. "I can probably stretch that out for a good two minutes." Even after seventeen years on the job, I don't have much in the way of my own personal property in my desk.

"He give you any idea how long this will last? He didn't volunteer much to me, and I didn't think it was my place to ask until you had a chance to talk with him. I figured you should hear it all first."

"No. Not really. He's callin' it indefinite. What that means is anyone's guess, but he said it could drag on for months. He was pretty blunt, really. This can still take a turn for the worse. Just the times we're livin' in. He said someone, I'm not sure just who, will do an investigation."

"Months? For what? What's there to investigate?"

I shrugged again. "No idea. You get in touch with Charley Dunn?"

"Tomorrow will be soon enough. I'd really rather not see or hear from him today."

There was a glass ashtray on the corner of my desk. It has a photograph of my boys glued to the bottom so that their smiling faces show through. W.R. made it in grade school or Cub Scouts. I leaned forward and pulled it toward me. It was about all that I wanted to take home.

"Did he really say this might go on for months?" Ricky continued.

"He did. He thinks that the Kennedys are embarrassed by what's happenin' over in Mississippi and Alabama, and they want to crack down. Election is comin' up in less than a year, and the ACLU is goin' to be holdin' their feet to the fire. They need to look like they're doin' somethin'."

"We're not anything like Mississippi. Or Alabama."

I shrugged. "I guess I've lived here too long; there are times that I'm not so sure about that, Ricky. I reckon you're right. We aren't gunnin' men down in their driveways or blowin' up children in churches, but I'm not sure that lets us cast any stones."

"That's a mighty low bar," he replied.

I opened the center desk drawer. There wasn't much in it: a half-pack of stale cigarettes, box of matches, some pencils and paperclips, a ruler, some rubber bands, a couple of thumbtacks. I closed it. "Maybe that's the point," I said. "Tacklin' a mess like they have over in Mississippi is a tall order; Split Tree is another matter entirely. Kennedys can come in here and throw their weight around on somethin' stupid like this Jackson fella bein' detained for a half hour, and then go home and feel good about themselves. They can feel like they're nippin' a problem in the bud. Makin' the South a safer place for black voters."

"So what do you want me to do?"

"Not for me to say. Like I told you, you're chief now. Likely for some time," I replied. I opened another desk drawer. It was full of road maps from around the state. I closed it and opened another. It had a couple pads of yellow lined-paper, the top sheets covered with circles and boxes and arrows. Sometimes when I get stumped on something, I tend to try to work it out on paper. I think better that way; not in words so much as drawings and lines connecting things. Circles and squares. I was never much good in school. I was smart enough, but I had trouble with reading and writing; getting the words and letters to line up like they do for other people was always a problem. Still is. Same for my father, and my son Ray Junior takes after me in that regard. My mother and my sister, Sally, and Grace, helped me work through it, but even today, I still think better with pictures. I closed the desk drawer and looked at Ricky. "You better cinch up your britches, partner; I'm not sure I'm goin' to be back. Powder didn't say so directly, but he also didn't sugar-coat it. There's only so much he can do. Not really how I expected to leave this job, but maybe this is a good thing. Maybe this is a good time. You'll be a good chief; damn sight better than I ever could hope to be. I've known that since the first day I hired you. No, you better get used to it; I may not be back."

"Not going to listen to that. You're the chief; I'll just be keeping your chair warm."

"Well, you'll do fine. And in the meantime, you know where to find me if I can help. And you can always call Art Hennig if you do get in a real bind. I expect he'd do about anythin' for you if you ask. Speakin' of which, what'd you find out about stolen cars in Lee County. They able to tell you anythin'?"

"Damn, Ray. Sorry. I meant to tell you, and then Mister Graham caught me and gave me the news about you getting suspended, and it just completely slipped my mind."

"Yeah. Slipped my mind as well. So, what'd you learn?"

Ricky picked up a pad of paper from the corner of his desk; unlike me, he makes notes. "You might have been right about whoever dropped off the Johnson car; about them needing another ride. Sheriff says that they've had four cars reported stolen in Lee County in the last three weeks. They say that's a bit more than average for them." He read from the paper. "Two were in the north, one truck, one car, way up near the border with St. Francis County; both were almost two weeks ago. Haven't been recovered. A third was reported missing six days ago, but it was found the next day on the outskirts of Marianna; out of gas. Like you were saying, the sheriff thinks it was some joyriding kids who drove it until it ran empty."

"Good to know kids will be kids, no matter what county they're in."

Ricky nodded and looked back at his notes. "But the fourth one is a bit more interesting. Pontiac Bonneville. Two-door. Silver. Nineteen fifty-nine. Stolen from downtown Lagrange. They say you can almost throw a rock and hit the motor lodge from there. No leads as of yet."

"You ever been to Lagrange?"

"No."

"If it has a downtown, I'm not sure they know about it."

"That small?"

"Smaller. When?"

"Reported missing last Friday."

"Friday. That'd make it . . . two days before the Johnsons' Dodge was found abandoned."

Ricky nodded. "Maybe we'll get lucky after all."

"We could do with some luck. Get on the horn. Put the word out that I want to know the minute anyone so much as thinks that they see that car. And don't—" I stopped short. I laughed. "Sorry. I don't give the orders anymore, do I?"

"You give them, and I'll follow them."

"No sir. Get used to it, *Chief Forrest*. But my suggestion is to get the word out on that car. That's what I'd do anyhow."

Ricky smiled. "Already did, but only because I knew that's what you'd want me to do."

"There you go. Always a step ahead of me. Like I said, you'll be a damn sight better in this chair than I ever was."

"I'll keep you posted if we hear anything about the car." He paused and allowed the conversation to downshift. "So what are you going to do now? I mean, just until they clear you to come back?"

I flicked my cigarette butt out of the half-opened window and leaned back in my chair, adjusting the weight off of my bad leg. "Chores, I reckon. Lord knows I've got a slew of damn things to do around the house. For every one that I put off doin', Ellen Mae adds two more to the list. I was never good with math, but the numbers don't seem to be workin' in my favor. Maybe this will be a blessin' in disguise; allow me to get caught up."

"What about watching the Trimbles' place tonight? You still want to continue that?"

I nodded. "Don't see that this changes that much. We're probably in the clear, but until Art confirms that Gervais is down in Louisiana, it's smart to keep an eye on the place for another day or two. Just to be on the safe side. You keep patrollin' by there in the daytime, and I'll sit out there at night. Lord knows I've got the time now. I'll plan on bein' there by around seven thirty, if you can cover until then."

"I was going to call Sergeant Hennig this afternoon to check on how those fingerprints are coming; I'll ask about any update he has on Gervais. Unless you want to call him."

"No. You do it." I smiled at him. "That sounds a lot like police business; I'm just a civilian here. You might also check with the power company; find out when they cut the juice to Ring Johnson's place. I keep meanin' to do that, and now I don't have the authority."

"Roger. I'll let you know what I hear."

"Thanks." I opened the last desk drawer. My Colt Thirty-eight Special was in it. I took it out and set it next to my son's ashtray. It was probably the one thing in the desk that I didn't have a right to take with me, but I was going to anyway

CHAPTER 40

Split Tree, Arkansas
Monday, November 18, 1963

I had Ricky drive me over to Donnie Hawk's place. In addition to suddenly having no job, I also realized that for the first time in almost seventeen years, I had no vehicle of my own. Since I was always on duty, I'd always used one of the department's cruisers as my personal car. I couldn't really justify doing that now. Donnie loaned me his old truck, it was either that or his hearse, and I figured that Ellen Mae would rather be seen driving to church and the grocery store in the truck.

Then I went home. Ellen Mae was surprised to see me. When I hadn't shown up for lunch, she assumed that I was busy and wouldn't be home until the end of the day. She was working in the yard and stopped what she was doing to sit with me on the porch. She didn't ask directly, but she knew something was wrong, not just because I was driving Donnie's old truck, or because it was an odd time of day to be home, but because I was carrying the ashtray that W.R. had made. I had to tell her what had happened, and I couldn't help but feel a bit embarrassed to say that I'd been suspended indefinitely. That there was going to be an investigation. That I wasn't going to be bringing home a paycheck. That for the first time in my life I wasn't working. That I'd somehow let her and the boys down. I'd told

Granville that we'd be all right with money, but the truth is that being chief of police for Split Tree is not a high-paying job, and I didn't have much in the way of savings. I had enough for a couple of weeks tucked away, but then I'd have to figure out what I was going to do for income.

Ellen Mae took the news well. I almost could have predicted her immediate response: she said that the town didn't deserve me, and how she'd always felt that way, and that this just proved it once and for all. She said that I shouldn't go back even if the whole town council came crawling on their knees and begged me to. For good measure, she said that someone needed to punch Carl Trimble in his fat belly, and she wanted to be first in line. Once all that was out of the way, she took a deep breath and told me that I could feel sorry for myself for the rest of the day, but after that, there was a whole list of chores that she needed me to tackle, and that maybe this was a blessing in disguise; maybe I could get caught up. I disagreed with the first part, but didn't argue it, and I agreed with the last part, and I told her I'd get to the chores first thing in the morning. Her reaction would change later; I was equally sure of that. Once it settled in, she'd start to worry and get anxious about our financial security. I hoped it wouldn't trigger another one of her spells, but for now the momma bear was bristling in defense of her family, and that was foremost in her brain.

I went upstairs and changed clothes and hung my uniform in the closet, maybe for the last time, and then I got back into Donnie's truck and drove to the Western Auto. I might not be the police chief anymore, but I still had some business to attend to.

I saw Carl Trimble's Buick Riviera parked in front of the store, so I knew he was in. I could imagine him gloating to anyone who'd stop and listen to him about how he'd fired me, or at least how he'd had me suspended. That was okay. He could gloat all he wanted, as long as he answered my questions.

A few people stared when they saw me driving Donnie's truck, and a few stopped me on the sidewalk and a couple more once I got inside the store. Everyone had heard the news, and they all wanted to tell me how sorry they were and to tell me that they were sure everything would shake out in the end. I politely thanked them all and made a beeline for the stairway door leading to Trimble's office. I saw Jimmie Carl at the gun counter, talking to a customer, and I returned his wave but kept going.

At the top of the stairs, I opened the door to Carl's office, not stopping, or even slowing, to knock. Carl was laying down on a couch near the window that looked out onto the sales floor below. He had his shirt unbuttoned and his shoes were off, and he was smoking a cigar and looking as if he'd just undertaken something strenuous. Ten feet away, twirling around in an office chair like it was the circus Tilt-a-Whirl, was Tim Beauchamp's daughter, Tammy. All seventeen or eighteen years of her. She was wearing a simple yellow dress and no shoes and a blank expression. He father, Tim, is a farmer from south county. He's a widower, and he now spends more time drinking than he does farming, and what little time he has left he spends slapping his daughter around. Ben Cooper's been called out there on more than one occasion, and one time, after Granville had to stitch the girl up after a particularly bad episode, I paid Tim a visit. I like to think that put a stop to it, the physical part anyway, but that didn't make him a better father. I guess I really wasn't that surprised to see Tammy in Carl's office. She's just the sort of broke-wing sparrow that animals like Carl prey upon.

The girl jumped up from the chair when I walked in. She looked embarrassed and a bit frightened, and she began smoothing her hair as if she had done something wrong. Carl would have jumped up as well had he been able to, but he was sunk too far down into the couch cushions, and was too overweight, to manage much more than a loud bellow. "The fuck is goin' on, Elmore? Who the hell do you think you are bargin' in here like this?"

I looked at Tammy Beauchamp and motioned to the door. "Go on," I said.

She glanced quickly at Carl Trimble and then back at me, and then she grabbed her shoes from under the desk well and quickly went past me and out into the stairway. I closed the door behind her.

Carl was struggling to stand up and had managed to get both feet onto the floor and was starting to rise by the time I'd closed the distance. I pushed him in the chest, and he toppled back into the depths of the couch cushions. "Sit down and shut up," I said. "And button up your damn shirt. I don't have much patience left in me today, so you need to listen to my questions and then give me answers. Nothin' else."

"You go to hell, Elmore," he replied.

Leave it to Carl to screw up the simplest instructions, I thought, although he did button up his shirt.

"Who you think you are?" Carl continued. "Ain't you heard? You ain't a cop no more."

"Haven't you heard? I'm not a cop anymore," I said. "And that means I can stomp the livin' shit out of you and even a bunch of ACLU lawyers comin' all the way from New York can't stop me. If I were you, I'd do as I was told. Shut your goddamn mouth unless you're answerin' a direct question, and maybe you'll be able to chew your food tonight."

He started to respond, but caught himself. Instead he glared at me, as if that would substitute for grit. He also kept shooting quick glances toward the closed door, and I suspect he was hoping that Tammy Beauchamp had thought to call for help, though I can't image who he thought that help was going to be.

"Tell me about Jo Johnson. Tell me what's goin' on with the two of you and for how long," I said.

He still didn't respond, and he was still glancing at the closed door.

"That was a question, Carl. And now you can answer. What's goin' on with you two and for how long? Do you know where she is now?"

"Screw you. Why's that any of your business?" He smelled of sweat and sour mash.

"You seem to be full of wrong answers today." I spoke slowly and firmly, like you do with a small child or a distracted bird dog. "I want to know what's goin' on with you two and for how long. Mostly, I want to know where she is now. And her boy."

"People saw you come up here. You're in enough trouble. People know you're here," he responded.

"Good. Then they'll know that in about ten minutes, they can send someone up here with a couple of mop buckets. Because if you try my patience any more than you do by just breathin' the same air, I swear to God, Carl, I'll do more than break your jaw this time."

He looked at the door again, and then back at me. "Why would I have any business with Ring Johnson's wife? I'm married."

Don't remind me, I thought. "You tell me," I said. "I didn't say I wanted to know *why* you were doin' it; I think I've got that figured out. I said, I want to know what the extent of it is and how long it's been goin' on. Mainly, I want to know where she is now."

"Don't know nothin'."

"You're tryin' me, Carl. And I'm warnin' you. Don't. I already know you've been takin' her up to a motor lodge in Lee County. The clerk at the General Fagan remembers you. And her. I know about Joe Dennis playin' by himself on that overgrown swing set while you rutted on his mother like the pig you are. I know it's been goin' on for more than a month. I even know the weeks and the days. I know what rooms you stayed in. I know how many towels you soiled." I didn't, not exactly, but I also knew that Carl didn't know that.

He shrugged in what he hoped would convey some small level of defiance. "If you know all that, then why're you askin' me all these questions? We're finished here, Elmore."

"I'm not jokin', Carl. I'm so close to layin' hands on you right now, it's not funny." As much as I would have liked to break his jaw again, I wanted answers even more. I grabbed a chair and placed it directly in front of him and then I sat down. "Let's try this; maybe this will be easier for you to handle. Here's the way I see it. You tell me if I'm wrong. I think Jo Johnson came to you for money. That right?

Maybe Ring did as well, but Jo came to you privately. Separately. On her own. She'd worked for you as a girl. I suspect you took advantage of her then, and now you saw another chance. Am I right?" I didn't wait for a response. "She's needin' money. Ring's in over his head, and there's no way out, and she needs money, and she knows you have it. She also knows exactly what she needs to do to convince you. And maybe to someone who's desperate enough, like she is, maybe it's worth it."

"So what if she did? What's it to you?"

"Her husband is dead, and I think someone murdered him. In fact, I know it. And I aim to figure out who did it."

That news shook Carl. He sat up straighter, and the look of surprise crowded out some of the smugness on his face. "Ring killed hisself. That's what everyone's sayin'. He killed hisself."

"No, he didn't," I said. "Someone blew his damn head off, and now his wife and boy are missin', and I have a witness up in Lee County that says you were havin' an affair with her for at least a month beforehand. I'm startin' to connect enough dots that I can see a picture emergin', and that picture is lookin' a whole lot like you."

"Bullshit, Elmore. That's bullshit. You know I didn't kill nobody."

"Is that right? I know that, do I? What I know is that I'm askin' you questions, and you're shinin' me on. And that makes you look plenty damn guilty. So, don't be tellin' me what I know and don't know."

Carl Trimble began shaking his head. "I was screwin' her. So what? She wanted it. She begged me for it. She came to me, just like you said. I didn't ask for it, but I wasn't goin' turn it down. That's all there is to it."

"All there is, huh? She wanted it, did she? I think we both know that what she wanted was money, Carl. How much did you give her?" I knew how much, almost to the penny, but I didn't want to betray Nick Mitchell's confidence in sharing Carl's bank records.

He shrugged and tried to look matter-of-fact. "Couple hundred maybe. Not for sex though; like I said, she wanted that. I don't have to pay for trim. Never have."

"Just the goodness of your Christian heart."

"Screw you. She needed some money; maybe I gave her a loan."

"A loan? So she was goin' to repay it?"

"Different ways of makin' payments. We worked somethin' out."

"Couple hundred? Sure it wasn't more?" I knew it was, but I couldn't tell him how I knew.

He shrugged again. "Maybe. Sure."

"What'd she need it for? She say? From what I hear, Ring was in some serious debt. A few hundred wasn't goin' to help."

"Maybe she was goin' away," he answered. "Without her damn drunk husband."

Maybe she was, I thought.

CHAPTER 41

Split Tree, Arkansas
Monday, November 18, 1963

I didn't get much more out of Carl Trimble. With every minute that passed without me laying hands on him, his confidence that he wasn't in immediate physical danger grew, and he clammed up tight. A couple of times I almost called his bluff and took to stomping on him just for good measure, but as much satisfaction as that would have brought me, it would have resulted in even more headache for Ricky Forrest, and I didn't want that.

I left Carl sunk into his couch, and I went home and loaded up Trip, our dog, and then I drove up north, to Lee County. I needed to get Carl Trimble out of my system the way you sweat out a bad hangover. I drove past the General Fagan motor lodge, and I drove through what passes for downtown Lagrange, where the silver Pontiac Bonneville had been reported stolen. I detoured by Ring Johnson's farm on my way back. Mainly I just drove and thought; drawing circles and squares in my head, trying to connect them with lines and arrows.

And then I went home.

Ellen Mae and I had an early dinner. Our boys had been in and were out again; basketball practice and then out carousing with some of the seniors; it was becoming the usual routine for all of us. After we got the kitchen cleaned up, we watched the Huntley-Brinkley

Report on television, and then I did a couple of small chores before I ended up on the porch. I smoked and thought, and Ellen Mae baked some pies for one of the church groups she's in. Thanksgiving was falling late this year, and was still better than a week away, but the church was putting together some food for some of the older folks and the widows and widowers around town and she was getting a head start. In between back-and-forth trips to check the oven, she joined me on the porch swing.

About seven thirty I told Ellen Mae that I needed to go sit outside the Trimbles' house. She started to remind me, as if I needed reminding, that I wasn't on the police force any longer, but she caught herself. She knew that wasn't going to make a difference, and it didn't need saying. I suspect she also wanted to say something about me and Grace, but she knew that didn't need saying either, and instead, she smiled and stood up and went inside. I wasn't sure if she was mad at me or what to make of it, but a few minutes later she returned with a paper sack and a thermos of coffee. The sack had an apple and a small ball of tin foil holding a handful of sugared pecans that she'd been roasting in preparation for Thanksgiving. She gave me a kiss on the cheek and told me to be safe. I kissed her back and told her I would, and then I took the coffee and the sack and drove Donnie's noisy truck over to West Road.

Mike Taylor had done like he said he'd do and gotten the streetlight in front of Grace's fixed. I'm not sure where he got the light from, but I noticed that the one in front of my house was starting to buzz and come on when I left the house, so I know it wasn't from my street. I was glad; the repaired light lit up the Trimbles' driveway and front yard like an aerial flare, and it'd make it hard for Gilbert Gervais to get close to the house without being spotted, but it also made it hard for me to find a good place to park if I wanted to remain unseen. I drove past their house once, slowly, and did a U-turn in the intersection and came part way back up the street and parked on the opposite side from the house, far enough away from the streetlight that the shadows were the darkest. I killed the engine and cracked the window and lit up a smoke and settled in for the night.

There were a few cars that came and went down the street, but for the most part everything was quiet. A couple of times I got out to stretch my leg and wake myself up. The first time went fine, but the second time, probably around nine thirty, I managed to get a half-dozen neighborhood dogs barking, so I got back into the truck and resigned to stay put as long as my bladder held out, though I did find it somewhat reassuring that if Gervais decided to make an appearance, in addition to the bright streetlight, he'd probably cause a similar ruckus.

From where I sat, I could see the windows in the front and to one side of the Trimbles' house. Over several hours, I watched different lights come on and go off, and a couple of times I saw a shadow move past the curtains. I imagined Grace going about her evening, working in the kitchen, getting ready for bed.

About nine thirty a car turned onto West Road and slowly drove down the street, as if the driver was looking for something in particular. I hadn't seen one in over an hour, and I watched it out of my rearview mirror as it pulled up behind my truck. Once the driver killed the lights, I relaxed; I could see the silhouette of the gumball on the roof; a minute later Ricky Forrest opened the passenger door of my truck and got in. "Chief," he said. "Everything quiet?"

"*Chief Forrest*," I replied. "Yeah. So far. You've had a long day. Shouldn't you be home?"

"Went home for dinner and then had to go back to the office for a couple of things. In case you haven't heard, the police department is a little short-handed right now."

"That so? I guess maybe I heard that."

He laughed. "I'm headed to the house now, but I thought I'd check on you first. You need anything?"

I held up the paper sack. "I'm good. Ellen Mae packed me somethin' to eat if I get hungry. Got some coffee."

He looked across the street. "I assume everything is quiet?"

"So far. Carl hasn't come home yet, neither has Jimmie Carl. I expect them before too long. In the meantime, I've had plenty of time to think."

"Come up with anything?"

"Not much, but I was workin' on somethin' right before you showed up. Maybe you could run it down for me tomorrow? Probably nothin'."

"Shoot."

I paused. I'd had plenty of time to think, but not much time to organize my thinking, and I wasn't sure how to make sense of it to anyone else. "You ever do the laundry around the house?"

Ricky laughed. "Kitty put you up to that?"

I laughed as well. "No. Honest. No. I was just thinkin' that this sort of reminds me of when you do the laundry and you find that one damn sock."

"I don't necessarily disagree, but what are we talking about?"

"Sorry. I'm so used to you bein' two steps ahead of me, I'm surprised you're not there yet. I've been thinkin' about Ring's car, and that Pontiac Bonneville that's missin' from up in Lagrange. I drove through there earlier today; it's even smaller than I remembered. Hard to do much there without bein' watched. I'll bet that Bonneville was reported stolen within a couple minutes of it bein' gone, if not sooner. That's part of what's been eatin' at me all evenin'. Ring's car was abandoned, and we think that they, whoever they are, may have taken that Pontiac in Lagrange to get away in."

"Well, we don't know that for sure, but I'm still waiting to see what this has got to do with my socks."

"No," I acknowledged. "You're right, we don't know that for sure. We don't know much at all to be honest, but let's work on the assumption that they're connected; the two cars."

"Sorry to be so slow on the draw here, Ray. It's been a long day for both of us."

I nodded. "No apology necessary. You've been busy, and I've had plenty of time to think. Too much time, probably; I tend to go down rabbit holes if there's no one there to stop me. No, what I mean is it's like that one damn sock that you find in the washin' machine. Right? You know that there has to be another one around somewhere. Under the bed or on the floor of the closet. Socks tend to run in pairs."

"You're saying stolen cars come in pairs?"

"Not exactly, but it's like the socks in that they're connected; we think these two are anyhow. Someone was drivin' around in Ring's car and needed to ditch it. Okay, but if you abandon Ring's car, you have to steal another one to get away in. Okay, we're good with that too. That explains the Pontiac. Okay. But what we didn't ask was the next question: what was he drivin' before he stole Ring's old Dodge in the first place? How'd he get here to Split Tree? I'm assumin' that whoever he is, he's not from around here, it's not someone local; if he was local he wouldn't need to be drivin' around in stolen cars, not one taken from Lagrange anyhow. I'm thinkin' it was someone who blew in here. Probably recently."

Ricky nodded and thought about it. "Could be someone who jumped the train, or came in on a bus; could have hitchhiked."

"Maybe, but I don't think so. This doesn't feel like a damn hobo; not to me anyhow. You steal two cars, my guess is you're not the type to jump trains; my guess is that these weren't the first cars he's taken." I looked at Ricky. "Am I crazy? What do you think?"

"I think maybe Kitty's right; I need to start doing the laundry more."

CHAPTER 42

Split Tree, Arkansas
Tuesday, November 19, 1963

T
he remainder of the night was as quiet as the first part had been. Jimmie Carl came home around ten thirty; Carl never did. I assume he spent the night on the couch in his office. Maybe alone; probably not. As long as he wasn't sleeping in Grace's bed, I really didn't care where he was, or who he was with. I got home about four fifteen in the morning. I slept until almost seven thirty and then got up and showered, a little uncertain what to do with my day.

My sons were in the kitchen when I got downstairs, finishing breakfast and getting ready for school. Ellen Mae was doing some laundry, but she stopped long enough to sit with me while I had a couple cups of coffee. I hadn't seen my sons the night before, and they were anxious to know about my suspension and what was going to happen. I didn't have that many details, nor was I interested in speculating about what I didn't know, but I told them about what Powder Graham was doing and explained that Ricky Forrest was going to be filling in for me until things got sorted out. I also explained how we might need to tighten our family belt for a few weeks, and then I shrugged it off as best I could. "How's Jimmie Carl gettin' on with that old car of his?" I asked, hoping to change the subject.

"Needs a new dang water pump," Ray Junior replied as he carried his breakfast plate to the sink.

"I doubt that's all it needs," I laughed.

"Keeps overheatin' somethin' awful," W.R. said.

"Sounds like a water pump," I said. "Could be the thermostat. Could just be that it's an old car. Y'all think of that? That's what old cars do. But I guess with the weather coolin' off like it is, that's not so big a concern; less of a rush to get it fixed." I stood up and refilled my coffee cup.

"No, sir," W.R. replied. "We need to get it done. Pronto. Jimmie Carl thinks he can sell it."

"Sell it?" I laughed again as I sat back down. "I hope not to one of you two knuckleheads."

"No, sir. Man from up in Helena says he's interested," W.R. said. "He says we did such a good job gettin' it runnin' like we did that he wants to buy it."

"Let's go," Ray Junior impatiently prompted his brother. "We're goin' be late."

"Someone wants to buy that old Bel Air? A grown man?" I asked.

"Yes, sir. He says he'll pay cash money for it just as soon as we replace the water pump," W.R. continued.

"Is that right?" I replied. "A grown man?"

W.R. stood up and carried his plate to the sink and rinsed it off. "Yes, sir. Even with the cost of the water pump, Jimmie Carl figures he'll make a least a hundred more than he paid for it."

I laughed again. "A hundred dollars? Well, good for him. But then what'll you three do with your time? If you're not careful, y'all might actually have to spend your afternoons doin' homework. Or maybe chores."

"Heaven forbid that," Ellen Mae laughed.

"Time to go," Ray Junior said again as he left the room. A few seconds later we heard the front door open and heard him call from the other room. "Ride's here," he yelled. Jimmie Carl picks the boys up each morning and gives them a ride to school.

"We're lookin' at a nineteen fifty-four Corvette for sale over in Canefield. We're thinkin' we can go in on it together. It needs a lot of work, but it's a super sweet car," W.R. answered me as he dried his hands on a dish towel and started for the front door. "But first we got to swap out that old water pump on the Bel Air."

I didn't respond. Boys need goals, even when they're stupid ones.

"But first you need to kiss your mother goodbye," Ellen Mae said.

W.R. rolled his eyes and reversed course. He kissed his mother on her cheek. "See ya," he said.

"Not so fast; since your brother ran off, you have to kiss me twice," she said.

W.R. rolled his eyes again and reversed course again. He kissed her a second time and then hurried off. We could hear a car horn honking out at the street.

Ellen Mae stood up and starting clearing off the kitchen table. "If I live to be a hundred, I'll never understand boys. When do the finally grow brains?" she said, more to herself than to me.

"Gasoline and perfume. Turns a boy's brain off."

"You're assumin' they have brains," She said, turning to face me. "You want anythin' more than coffee?"

"I'm good."

"So, speakin' of doin' chores, what do you have planned for the day?"

"Not sure. Haven't given it that much thought; although, I have to say, sittin' here watchin' your rear end might just be the best thing I can think of doin'. You've got a fine-lookin' rear end, Missus Elmore."

"So, speakin' of chores, what are you plannin' to do today?" she repeated.

I think I heard a smile in her voice, and I think I saw her wiggle her hips a touch more. "Haven't fully sorted that out," I replied.

She turned to face me and stood with her hands on her hips. "Well, Mister Elmore, *Big Ray*, that's unacceptable. The town may have just suspended you, but I haven't. There are plenty of things to do around this house. Productive things. Do I need to start listin' them for you?"

I held up my hands in surrender. "You're worse than them New York lawyers. Let me rephrase my answer, counselor. What I meant to say is that I haven't fully sorted out which one of my many chores I plan to start with this mornin'."

She smiled. "That's better. Let me give you a little help. There's the hinge on the back door; there's the drippy faucet in the tub; I know, how about fixin' the roof? That'd be a good place to start; before it rains again and ruins the carpet." A leak had shown up near the fireplace chimney around midsummer. It wasn't too bad, but there was a stain the color of strong tea, and about the size and shape of a small pie pan, that had been growing on the ceiling plaster over the front door.

That more or less decided it, or Ellen Mae more or less decided it, and thirty minutes later I was on the roof installing some new flashing. That's where I was when Ricky Forrest drove up and got out of my old police cruiser, the one with the bent bumper.

I stopped and watched him come up the sidewalk. "See you're drivin' the *Old Horseshoe*. I would have thought you'd take the good car and let Charley Dunn have that one," I said.

"Morning, Chief," he greeted me. He turned and looked quickly at his car and then back up at me and smiled. "Yeah, well, if it's good enough for Ray Elmore; good enough for me. I told you, I'm just keeping your chair warm; the same goes for your car."

I had a cigar box with some roofing nails in it, and I tucked it behind the chimney, to keep it from sliding off of the roof, while I shifted my weight to my other hip. "I got a little more to do up here. You got time to stay? Is it worth me climbin' down from here?"

"You may want to stay where you are; at least you're seated," he replied. He was standing about midway up the walkway, his hands on his hips. "Got some news I think you need to hear."

"Aw crap. That right? Not sure I like the sound of that; I think the last time you said that, I got fired. They gettin' ready to tar-and-feather me next? This have more to do with those New York lawyers?"

He smiled. "For the record, boss, you're suspended, not fired, but, no, sir, I haven't heard any more about them. I suspect we will, but that's not why I'm here. I got two pieces of news, actually. First, I checked with Delta Gas and Electric. The Johnsons' power was shut off last month. They were ninety days overdue in their payments."

"Ninety days? Well, I guess that tracks with what we know about his money troubles. It also explains all the damn candles. And the empty refrigerator."

"It does, but it doesn't really help pin down when anyone was there last."

"Guess not. Good work anyhow. What's the other piece of news?"

"Well, here's the one you need to sit down for," he said. "I did like you asked me and spent the morning checking on any stolen cars in the area."

"Did you? Any luck, or am I completely off base? Again."

"What do you think, Ray? One of us never doubted you. You really need a lesson in seeing the glass as half full. I called Phillips County, Lee, down to Desha County, even over to some places in Mississippi. Tunica, Coahoma, and Bolivar County. A half-dozen more."

"Jewell Faye will throw a fit when she sees the phone bill."

"Yeah, well, I'm counting on you being back to work by then."

"Don't bet on it. That may just be the incentive I need to go into the handyman business. So, you called all those places?"

"Yes, sir."

"And?"

"Nothing."

I shrugged. "We always knew it was a long shot."

"And a good one as it turns out. Glass half full, remember? After I spent two hours on the phone striking out with just about everyone wearing a badge within a hundred miles of here, I took a break, and I was headed out to the car when I ran into Pinto Bean. We got talking, and he asked about you and how you were taking this whole thing; said to send his regards by the way. Anyhow, I ended up telling him about the Easter egg hunt I was on for you, and that's when he up and tells me that there's an abandoned car over near Canefield."

"Canefield?"

"Yeah. Goes to figure. I got so busy worrying about whether there were any strange cars up in Lee County, and everywhere else, that it didn't dawn on me to ask Sheriff Cooper if there'd been any turn up here in Locust County."

"We haven't seen any flyers on a stolen car."

"No sir, we haven't."

"What kind is it? When was it found?"

"It was first reported about two weeks ago. Abandoned near the edge of a field about midway between Canefield and the old Bell Brothers gin. Up on County Road Fifty-three; east side. It's just a burned-out shell. After Pinto told me about it, I went up to see Ben Cooper, and he confirmed it, but he says no one's given it much thought. They never opened a file on it; that's why he can't tell me exactly when it was found."

"Why no file?"

"He says no one in the county has reported a car like that missing, so he hasn't paid it much attention. That's why we didn't see a bulletin. There're also a couple of old washing machines and a bunch of mattresses dumped in the same field. It's been fallow for a few years."

"I think I know where you're talkin' about. You mean the old Davenport place. That's got to be thirty, thirty-five acres. I'll bet that land hasn't been seriously farmed since the war, at least since the midfifties. I was by there a month or so back, and I remember thinkin' then that it was startin' to become a damn eyesore."

"Yes, sir. All sorts of garbage. That's why no one took notice of an old car; just one more piece of trash. Ben says they figured it was an old junker that got abandoned, and then some kids came along and torched it. No tag on it."

"Burned? How bad? Can you get the make and model? How about color?"

He smiled again. "I told you that you better stay seated. Sheriff Cooper says it looks like it was a four-door Chevy Impala. Might have even been seafoam green at one time."

CHAPTER 43

Split Tree, Arkansas
Tuesday, November 19, 1963

I tossed my hammer to the ground and grabbed my cigar box of nails. Something was telling me that I wasn't going to be checking anything else off of my to-do list today. "Impala? Green? How sure?" I asked.

"Sheriff Cooper says it's pretty burned out, but Pinto saw it, and he thinks there's some green paint on the frame."

"Shit. That'd be one hell of a coincidence if it is. So, you haven't been out there yet?" I asked Ricky.

"I came straight here," he replied. "I thought you'd want to know."

"Thanks. Call Art Hennig yet?"

"I was going to swing back by the station before I head out to see the car. I didn't know if you wanted to call him."

"You're the chief."

"I'm sure he'd rather hear from you."

"I'm not sure about that, but I'll come with you, if you don't mind."

It took me a few minutes to climb down from the roof and a couple more for us to drive to the office. When we got there, Ricky made a point of sitting at his desk, rather than mine, while he put the call through to Little Rock. Art Hennig wasn't at his desk, but whoever

Ricky talked to promised to hunt him down and have him call us back in a few minutes. Ricky gave him our office number, and the two of us sat and smoked cigarettes while we waited.

Ricky picked up our conversation about the abandoned car. "I know that Ben Cooper says there isn't much to see, but I'd feel better if I checked it out myself. Unless you tell me otherwise, I'll head out there as soon as Sergeant Hennig calls back. You still want to go with?"

"I do," I answered. "Probably won't be of much help, but—" I was cut off by the phone ringing. I pushed the lit button and picked up the extension on my desk. "Police department. Ray Elmore," I said into the receiver.

"Doc? That you? I heard you called," Art Hennig answered.

"Hey, Art. Thanks for callin' us back. I know you're busy."

"Don't be silly; of course I called you back. I was plannin' on it anyhow; just haven't had a spare minute to even take a whizz. How you holdin' up, bubba?"

"Fair to middlin'. You?"

"Well, now, that depends. Things are goddamn crazy here, that's a fact, but what I want to know about is you. I really was just about to call you. I'm hopin' you can make sense out of what I'm hearin', because it don't make any sort of sense."

"Speak up," I said. "I'm tryin' to let Ricky listen in on this." Ricky got up from his desk and sat on the corner of mine. I held the phone away from my ear so that the sound would carry better.

Art Hennig increased his volume. "*Hey, Ricky.* Yeah, what I said was, I was plannin' on givin' you two peckerwoods a call, but you went and beat me to it. I need someone to tell me what the hell is goin' on over there. It sounds slam crazy to me."

"Not sure what you're referrin' to," I responded. "I was callin' because Ricky and me need to tell you somethin'."

"What I'm referrin' to is that someone's drawn a damn bead on you, son, got you in their damn crosshairs, and I want to know what the hell is goin' on. I come in this mornin', expectin' to spend the whole friggin' day in plannin' meetings for the president's visit, and damn if there isn't a memorandum from my Colonel sittin' in the middle of my desk like a steamin' fresh cow pie. Accordin' to what I'm readin', the damn state attorney general has directed that we coordinate an investigation into . . . hold one," he paused. The sound of papers rustling came over the phone. "Here. Let me read this crap to you, and I'll skip to the meat. It says here that we are *hereby directed, pursuant to state law* . . . blah, blah, blah, here it is, *directed to assist the Federal Bureau of Investigation in conducting an official inquiry into potential professional malfeasance*—like any of us shit-kickers know what the hell that word means—*and alleged criminal wrongdoin' on the part of the Split Tree police department; specifically, to ascertain and document alleged criminal violations of civil and constitutional rights by its chief of police, Raymond S. Elmore, upon the person of one Leonidas S. Jackson, a Negro.* Whoo." He paused briefly and then continued. "And it goes on like that for a friggin' half page or more. Lots more *pursuants* and a few *to-wits*. And I'm thinkin', *to-what the fuck?* Wrongdoin' and Doc Elmore? In the same sentence? Now, that just don't make no sense."

"FBI? Crap. Just keeps gettin' better," I said. I looked up at Ricky, who simply shook his head in response. "Yeah, Art, I'm sorry to hear that you're gettin' drug into this. I really am. It's unbelievable, that's what it is."

"Unbelievable doesn't start to describe it. Wrongdoin'? Criminal violations? *Pursuants?* What the hell is goin' on over there?" Art Hennig asked.

"Long story, and not an interestin' one, I'm afraid. But right now there are other things more important."

"I can't imagine what they'd be. This sounds pretty damn important to me. Did I tell you this is filled with a dozen or more *pursuants? Pursuants and to-wits.* What the hell is goin' on? The FBI, Doc? Are you really in trouble with the feds? Criminal violations? What the hell d'you do?"

"Later. Like I said, Ricky and I need to tell you about somethin' else. This may be more important. We got a report this mornin' of an abandoned car here in Locust County. It's been here maybe a couple-three weeks, but no one paid any attention to it. From what we've been told, and we're headed out there now to check on it, but from what we've heard, it matches the description of the car Gervais was drivin'."

"What? *Gervais*? Shit. Gervais? *Shit*. You serious?"

"Afraid so. Same make and model; maybe same color. If it's not his, it's a hulluva coincidence, don't you think?"

"But that ol' boy was seen down in Louisiana."

"If it was him. You ever able to confirm that?" I asked. "That's kinda why I'm callin'; you were goin' to try to run that down."

"No. To tell the truth, we got so wrapped around the axle with the prospect of the president comin' through here, that I didn't follow through on it. Damn. I've been hopin' that ol' boy was long gone."

"Well, we might know more in an hour, once we've laid eyes on it ourselves, but if it is his car, then I don't need to spell out what that means. I'm not tryin' to tell you how to do your job, but we may have lost too much time on this."

There was a long silence on the phone before Art Hennig responded. "Let me know what you find ASAP. So where is this car anyway? How close to y'all?"

"It's here in Split Tree. West and north of town, in an abandoned cotton field. It's south of Canefield about five miles," I looked at Ricky for confirmation, and he nodded. "Yeah. Five miles. No more than that."

"Dang. Okay. You're in Troop D's area. Let me make some calls here, run it upstairs, and see if we can't get someone headed down to Split Tree. Better safe than sorry. If it is Gervais's car, then what the hell's he up to?"

"I think we know," I said.

"I guess we do, and if it is his car, then you're right, that ol' boy's got a significant head start on us. Damn. I'll get someone down there

PDQ, and I think we need to get someone watchin' that guy's house—what's his name?"

"Carl Trimble."

"Right. Trimble. I've got his address here somewhere. Damn, I just put that file away yesterday. Damn. Figured we were done with that boy. Damn." Art Hennig went silent for a second or two and then continued. "I think we probably also want to start checkin' roads in and out of there, but that'll take a decision above my rank, but I can arrange to get someone to sit outside his house for now. May just be a false alarm, but false alarms we can justify; dead tax-payin' citizens are a helluva lot more paperwork. Believe me."

"That's why we called you first," I replied. "We're headed out to check on this abandoned car right now. We'll let you know what we find. Like you say, it may be a false alarm, but we didn't think we could risk losing another minute if it isn't. One of us will call you back in a bit."

"Do that. Damn."

"Will do," I said. I started to hang up.

"Hey, wait," Art Hennig said quickly. "Not so fast there, Lone Ranger; you ain't gettin' off the hook that easy. Thanks for the intel on Gervais, but let's back this whole shebang up, okay? One of you two needs to tell old Art what the good-goddamn-hell is goin' on with this memo from my boss—the one with all the *pursuants*. Let's get back to that. An FBI investigation? Of Doc Elmore? Do I need to come over there and knock some sense into some people? What is this shit anyway?"

It may not have been the last thing that I wanted to discuss, but it was close to the bottom of the list. I also had to figure it was about the last thing Art Hennig needed to have heaped on his plate right now, and so I owed him an apology as much as an explanation.

I proceeded to tell him what I knew, including how I was suspended indefinitely and how Ricky was the acting chief, and he listened for a couple of minutes and then responded with a snort. "Sounds like bullshit, if you ask me."

"Can't say I disagree with you, Art, but no one seems to be askin' either one of us for our opinion. All I can say is that I'm really sorry to drag you into this. You and Ricky both. Every time I tell myself that'll it'll all work out, I learn somethin' new; like the fact that the damn FBI is investigatin' me now. It's like chewin' on a knot of gristle. The damn thing just keeps gettin' bigger the more you work on it."

"Bullshit is what it is. Did I say that before? That's what it is. Do you suppose the Department of Justice has ever looked at a map?" he asked. "Suppose they know where Arkansas is? Because I hate to break it to Mister Kennedy's boys, but our fine up-standing neighbors to the east are killin' folks in their own driveways, and the FBI is worried that one of Doc Elmore's deputies may have locked up a Colored boy for ten minutes. Dang."

I sighed. "I hear you, Art. Like I said, I'm truly sorry for you to get pulled into this."

"Hey, don't sweat that part; it's you I'm worried about. I've seen how these fed investigations can spin out of control. I'm not really involved all that much, but now I wish was. The memo went out to all the department heads. When these things happen, I get notified just in case we've done any lab work for you that might be involved. You know the drill, we're told to hold all evidence and correspondence from the previous six months in the event it becomes relevant, etcetera, etcetera. But in your case, I don't think we've done anythin' for you in a couple of years."

"Except for the fingerprints from that car that got sent over last week."

"Yeah, dang. Thanks for remindin' me. I still owe you some results on that, don't I? Lee County, right? Yeah, they sent those in, so technically that's not your evidence, but I still owe you an answer. I dropped the ball."

"I know you're busy," I replied. "Thanks."

"Don't thank me yet; you ain't got nothin' yet." Art Hennig paused and then said, in a lower voice, "Hey, Doc, gettin' back to this . . .

thing, this FBI investigation, I'm serious as a heart attack here; don't drop your guard. Tell you what, I'm not technically involved, like I said, but let me ask around a bit; see what I can nose up. If I can find out who's headin' up this bullshit investigation, maybe I can do somethin'. Maybe I can make sure that it goes in the right direction; if you follow; make sure it flows downhill properly. I know some of the FBI guys in the field office here; served with a couple of them in the Corps. Let me see if one of them may have gotten assigned as the main head buster. If so, maybe I can take care of it for you. If you follow."

"Art—"

"No. Don't even start to *Art* me. Ricky and me have got your back. You know that, right?" He raised his voice so that it carried into the room. *"Ain't that right, Ricky? We got Doc's back. You with me here, son?"*

"Roger," Ricky replied. Loudly enough for Art Hennig to hear. "Five by five, Sergeant."

"I'm not askin' you to do that, Art," I said. "Neither one of you. If it's like you say, y'all need to stay clear of this tar baby." I looked at Ricky and shook my head. I really didn't want him to get splattered by any more of this than he'd already caught.

"I know you're not," Art Hennig replied. "Dang, you're probably the only man I know who wouldn't ask. That's why I'm willin' to do it. Besides, I need to work off my debt to you."

"You don't owe me anythin'."

"Like hell. I'm breathin', ain't I? I owe that to you, and Art Hennig pays his debts."

CHAPTER 44

Split Tree, Arkansas
Tuesday, November 19, 1963

A fter we got off of the phone, Ricky locked up the office, and we got into his car and headed west on Tupelo Street until it intersected with County Road 53, then we turned north for a few miles until we got to the old Davenport farm. As we got close, we could see the blackened and burned-out shell of the car sitting in the field less than fifty feet from the road; its top visible over the waist-high jimsonweed and cockleburs and occasional scraggly cotton volunteer. As Ricky had said, there were mattresses and washing machines and all types of household junk dumped in the same area, the field having not been worked for cotton or beans in well over a decade, and the shell of the car blended in with the general scatter of trash and overgrowth.

We parked in the road. Ricky opened the trunk and got the lug wrench, and then we walked over to the field, approaching the abandoned car from its front, hoping to not disturb any tire tracks or footprints that might still be visible. It was a wasted hope. The area immediately around the car was a patch of scorched floodplain clay turned black and bright orange by the heat, but it had been walked over and driven over, either by Ben Cooper and his deputies, or by people dropping off more junk. In either case, while we could still make out the tire tracks of the car, any hope of associating specific footprints with it was gone.

The fire had been a hot one, and the tires and upholstery had been completely consumed by the heat. The little paint remaining on the metal frame was blackened and blistered.

"Would have been nice to have seen this a week ago," Ricky said. "Might have still been able to tell something about it. How long you think it's been here?"

"Pretty walked over," I replied. "Hard to tell. I don't think long. No weeds growin' close around it."

"Looks like it was pretty hot. I wouldn't expect any, would you? I'd think the fire would have killed them."

I laughed. "For the only son of a farmer, you don't seem to know much about farms."

"Dad raised livestock." Ricky's father had raised pigs and chickens, but never put much into cultivation.

"Well, take it from me, damn weeds will grow anywhere and anytime they have a mind to. Never known cockleburs or hedge-parsley to be put off by a little fire."

Ricky glanced down at his ankles. "You're right about that," he said. "I've already got a million stick-tights on my socks. I'll be picking them out all evening."

"No, I'd say this hasn't been here very long," I said, nodding at the car body. "What'd Ben tell you? They found this two weeks ago?"

"About. Maybe. No one remembers exactly."

I nodded. "Well, then my guess is it hasn't been here much longer than that." We walked around it, and I ran my fingers over the charred and blistered paint. "Hasn't started to rust yet."

"Hasn't rained much recently," Ricky said.

"No, but this close to the river, I'd still expect some if it's been here a while. Bunch of damn bullet holes in the rear quarter panel, but that doesn't mean much. There isn't a square foot of scrap metal within a hundred miles of here that someone hasn't used for target practice. If I had to wager money, I'd say this hasn't been here more than a month; probably less."

The front passenger door was open, but the one on the driver's side was closed and stuck shut. Ricky wedged the tire iron between the door and the frame and worked it back and forth until it sprang open. "Pinto was right," he said. He nodded at the left door jamb where the paint had been partially protected from the heat and the original color was still visible. "Looks light green. I guess if I were a Detroit ad-man, I'd call that seafoam green."

I walked around to the driver's side and looked over his shoulder. "Maybe if you grew up in Detroit. I saw more sea foam than I like to remember, and none of it looked like that, but I suspect you're right," I said.

Ricky got his notebook out of his shirt pocket, and then he knelt down and used his thumb to brush away some soot from the stainless-steel VIN tag spot-welded beneath the hinge. "Here we go. One, one, eight, sixty-nine, S, twenty-six, fifty-six, six, last one's maybe six. Eight maybe." He licked his thumb and rubbed the tag again. "Yeah. I think six." He wrote the numbers into his book and then stood up.

"That first number, that's the year of manufacture. Nineteen and sixty-one. What year car was Gervais drivin'? The one that's supposed to be down in Louisiana right now."

"Nineteen sixty-one."

"Damn. Fits. Almost wish it didn't." I pointed at his notebook. "I don't recall exactly what the next four or five numbers mean. I know they tell you the make and model, but we can see it's a four-door Chevy Impala. It's the last half-dozen numbers that will tell us for sure if it's the same car."

"Sergeant Hennig should be able to run them."

I walked a few feet away from the car and stood in the field and turned in a slow circle. There was nothing but farmland for several miles in each direction. Most of this part of the county is planted in either cotton or beans, but harvests were about over, and the adjoining fields were largely bare or ready to be disked for the winter.

"What are you thinking?" Ricky Forrest asked. He walked up beside me and offered me a smoke. We both lit up.

I completed another circle. "Not sure. I guess I'm thinkin' I don't understand any of this. If this is Gervais' car, then he's been here for a couple of weeks. So, where is he? What's he been up to?"

"We don't know for sure it's his, and we probably shouldn't jump to too many conclusions until we do. You're usually the one telling me that. I'll call the VIN into Little Rock as soon as we get back to town. It shouldn't take Sergeant Hennig but a minute to confirm it if it is."

I shook my head. "I hear you, but it's just too big a coincidence for it not to be. I'm worried that I've been asleep at the switch, Ricky. I've dropped the ball on this one, and that could get someone hurt." I turned to him and smiled. "Tell you what, they probably should have suspended me just for gettin' too damn old. Chief Sanderson at least got a new fishing rod when they put him out to pasture."

"Let's get back to town," Ricky replied. "The sooner I call this in, the sooner we know for sure what we're dealing with. I've still got my fingers crossed that this is a false alarm."

I turned in another circle, hoping that the view across the fields would prompt some insight, and when it didn't, we started making our way back toward our car; taking a more direct route now that we weren't concerned with walking over any footprints. As we did, a state police cruiser drove past, headed east, toward Split Tree.

"You don't normally see troopers on these back roads," Ricky said. "Looks like Sergeant Hennig made those calls like he said he was going to do."

"Yeah, it does. I hope for everyone's sake you're right, that it's a false alarm, but I'm glad to see him. I'll feel a damn sight better with one of those shiny state police cars parked out in front of Grace's house. If Gervais's in the area, that should give him somethin' to think about."

CHAPTER 45

Split Tree, Arkansas
Tuesday, November 19, 1963

W e went back to the station, and I waited while Ricky called Art Hennig. The trooper that he talked to said that Art was in another meeting, something to do with the president's visit, and he wasn't sure how long it'd last. Ricky gave the trooper the VIN from the abandoned car and asked that he pass it along to his boss.

We sat and talked for a few minutes after he got off of the phone, but when it became clear that Art wasn't going to call back anytime too soon, I had Ricky run me home. He needed to cruise around town, just as a matter of routine, and I thought once about riding along with him, but I also realized that being suspended meant being suspended. I hoped the ACLU lawyers had left town, but I wasn't sure, and it wouldn't be good for Ricky to be seen driving around with me in his squad car. Instead, I had him drop me off at the house, and I got back up onto the roof.

As it turned out, my interest in patching shingles wasn't as strong as my interest in Gilbert Gervais, and I caught myself several times, just sitting, staring out over the rooftops of the neighborhood houses, drawing circles and boxes and arrows in my head, trying to make sense of what I knew and didn't know. After about twenty minutes, I gave up on the roof and climbed down again. Ellen Mae was getting ready to fix us some lunch, but I told her that I needed to run an errand. I told her that I'd be as fast as I could, and I got into Donnie's truck and drove back to the office. Ricky was gone, I figured he was likely still out patrolling the town, but I still had my keys, and I let myself in. Ricky is very organized, and it didn't take long to find what I was after; the brown envelope was in the file cabinet behind his desk. I grabbed it, locked the office up, and got back into the truck and headed north.

Forty-five minutes later I pulled into the General Fagan motor lodge. It was a little after one o'clock, and there was a single car in the lot. I walked into the office. The manager was at his desk, his feet propped on an overturned waste basket, eating a baloney sandwich and paging through the same *Stag* magazine that he'd been working on a couple of days earlier when I'd last talked to him. He looked over the top of it briefly and then returned his attention to whatever story he'd been reading.

"You're like a damn bad penny . . . *Ray*," he said. "You keep turning up."

"Need you to answer a few more questions," I said. I walked up to the counter and waited.

The manager slowly dropped his feet to the floor and slowly closed his magazine. He swallowed a bite of his sandwich and chased it with something from a dirty coffee mug and then wiped his mouth on his dirty shirt sleeve. Only then did he stand and deliberately bow a kink out of his back, probably as much to keep me waiting at the counter than to actually stretch a muscle. "Is that right? I thought I made it clear enough the last time; I don't get paid to answer questions."

"And I thought I made it even more clear last time that I'm gettin' a might tired of your shit. How about we cut it?"

He ignored my response. "You can't seem to make up your mind whether to wear a badge or not. Which is it this time? You here as a cop or not, *Ray gun*? Hard to keep track," he said.

"I'm here with a couple-three questions. That's all."

"Yeah? You said that the first time you were here. Or was it the second? Or the third? I'm losing count. You by yourself today? You know what, *Ray*? That nice little gal you had with you the other day; now, she's a looker. You bring her back here, and it might just help loosen up my tongue. I'll bet money she's got ways to get answers out of me."

"So do I," I said. "We'll see if it comes to that."

He ignored me again and looked out the window into the parking lot. "I thought maybe you left her in the car this time." Then he made a face. "What the hell is that? That your piece of shit truck? Ray, Ray, Ray; hell, no wonder she's not with you."

"The quicker you answer my questions, the quicker you can get back to your important business," I replied. The man was goading me, and it was close to working. We were both going to regret it, but only one of us seemed to know it.

He slowly walked to the counter. "Tell me—*Sting Ray*—all these questions; what's in it for me? Huh? Anything? You come in here, time and time again, and you ask all your questions: have I seen this man? Seen that woman? When? How often? What color friggin' matches I use? What room? You always seem to get something out of it. What's in it for me?"

"How about doin' your civic duty?" I said. *How about not gettin' your ass kicked?* I thought.

He must have read my mind, because he squared his stance once again. "You know, you resemble a man I was just reading about in the newspaper. There was a story yesterday about a police chief down in Split Tree. I think that's where it was. Is that where you're from? Seems this policeman got suspended for mistreating a nigger. Now, would that be you? Is that what you do? Not that I got anything against you mistreating niggers, mind you, but . . ." he smiled. "I ain't one; so don't try it with me."

"You enjoy jerkin' my chain? You get some kick out of bein' a jackass? Fine. Let's both agree, you're good at it." I opened the envelope that I'd brought from the office and pulled out the mug shot of Gilbert Gervais. I put it onto the counter and pushed it toward the manager. "Now, how about cuttin' the crap and helpin' me out? You seen this man?"

The manager cocked his head and looked at me for a few seconds, and then he looked down at the photograph on the counter. He nodded and smiled. "Hard to forget them," he answered.

"Them? Only one photo here."

He smiled bigger and gestured at the envelope in my hand. "Like I told you the other day, *Sting Ray*, I like good asses. I hope you got a picture of her in there."

I reached in and pulled out the mug shot of Lidia Fernandez.

He stepped closer to the counter and picked up the photograph. "That's her," he said. "Yes, sir. Uh, uh, uh. What a piece of ass; ought to be a crime against parading around with tail like that."

"So they were here?"

He was still looking at the photograph and shaking his head slowly in appreciation. "I don't normally go for the browner ones. You understand? Nothing personal against them, but I normally like white meat. I'm old fashioned that way. The whiter the better—I guess you know what I mean." He looked up at me. "Like that young gal you had with you the other day."

I let it slide. "So they were here?" I repeated.

He looked back at the photo. "But this one, now I'll make an exception for her. Hot little tamale like that. Talked like a Spick. Mex, I think. Yes, sir; the caboose on that train makes you want to buy a round-trip ticket. Nice rack, too, for her size." He laughed. "Something funny going on with her ear, though; not that I care much about ears. Who really looks at them anyway?"

"She's Cuban."

"No shit. Maybe she knows Desi Arnaz. What do you think?"

"When were they here?"

"Can I keep this?" he asked. "Don't guess you got any more? Maybe one from the neck on down? They missed the best parts. Fucking cops."

"How about answerin' my question?"

He stepped back slightly from the counter; just far enough that I couldn't easily reach out and grab the photograph away from him. "A couple weeks back," he replied. "Maybe."

I tapped my finger on the picture of Gilbert Gervais. "When I was here before, I asked you if anyone had checked in that looked like a farm laborer. You said no. How about this guy?"

He was still looking at the picture of Lidia Fernandez. "Did I? I'm not sure that's what I said, but even if I did," he looked up at me and then down at the mug shot of Gervais on the counter, "You asked about farmers. That man isn't a farmer. I'm not sure what he is, but it sure as shit isn't a farmer. Wait; take that back, I do know what he is; he's not someone that you want to ask many questions about, that's what he is. And he sure isn't a man I want to be *answering* questions about."

"Tell me about him."

He shrugged. "You're kind of hard of hearing, aren't you, *Sting Ray*? Nothing to tell. I think I just said that."

I ignored him. "He say what he was doin' here?"

"Can't say it came up. Also can't say I asked."

"Take it you didn't talk much with him?"

The manager turned and dropped the photograph of Lidia Fernandez onto his desk, next to the *Stag* magazine. "You got wax in your ears, *Ray boy*? I just told you, he's not the type of man you pass the time with."

"If I didn't know better, I'd say you sound scared. I was startin' to think you weren't the sort of man who gets scared. Maybe I was wrong."

"Who said I am?" He started to bow up in response, but caught himself and let it go, realizing that I was trying to rattle him. He shrugged again. "Besides, I hardly saw the man. That little lump of brown sugar of his was the one that came in here, and that was just fine with me. Real easy on the eye. But he stayed out in the car; when he wasn't in one of the bungalows with her, taking care of business."

He paused and then finished his thought. "But I saw enough of him to know all I needed to know. I've seen men like him my whole life."

"What kind of man is that?" I asked.

"Like I said, Ray boy, the kind that I don't want to be asked questions about."

CHAPTER 46

Split Tree, Arkansas
Tuesday, November 19, 1963

My patience with the clerk was about to run out, but I also didn't need to be borrowing more trouble. "You say he was here a couple of weeks back, any chance you can fatten that hog up?" I asked. "I need to know when. Your desk register any help with that?"

"Not if I don't remember his name," the manager replied.

"And I reckon you don't remember his name," I said.

His eyes flicked to the photograph of Gilbert Gervais still on the counter and then back to me. "I'd say he looks like a Mister Jones. What do you think? Maybe a Mister Smith. Hard to tell. I told you, my memory's not so good anymore."

"Except for women and cars. So you told me. What about her? I don't suppose you have any call to remember her name."

He smiled. "Maybe. Yeah, I believe her name was . . . Missus Jones. Or maybe Missus Smith."

Go to hell, I thought.

He must have read my mind, or saw the look on my face. He smiled with some satisfaction. "Anything else I can help you with, this time, *Police Officer Ray?*"

"No, I think I've had about all the help out of you that I need."

He smiled again. "Always glad to help the police. Next time, bring that little gal back with you; the one that was here last Saturday. If you tell me you're married, I can rent you a room."

I put the mug shot of Gervais back into the envelope and turned to leave.

"Hey. *Sting Ray.*"

I stopped and looked back at him. For a man who couldn't remember names, he was wearing mine out.

"What'd they do?" he asked. "Them two?"

I started to laugh. "You want to ask me questions now?"

"Seems only fair."

"Does it?" I asked. "All right. His name's Gervais. Gilbert Gervais, and he killed a man over in Little Rock a while back. Didn't just kill him, he drug that man behind a car until his head came off. That's what he did. He's been waitin' in line for a seat in the electric chair." I nodded at the photograph of Lidia Fernandez on the desk. "And she broke him out of Tucker about three months ago." I paused. "And you're right, I'd say neither one of them is someone you want to mess with."

He turned and looked at the photograph. Most people would be taken aback by the details. He wasn't. "Damn," he said. "Ass and attitude. A woman of my dreams."

"So I answered your question; now how about a favor? You got a phone book?"

"I look like I have a phone book, *Ray Gun?*"

I nodded at the telephone on his desk. "I don't know what you look like to me, but I can see you got a phone. How about lettin' me use it?"

"Sure. That one is the office phone; it's for office business. Phones here are for paying guests. Every room's got one; you rent a room, you can use the phone. Local is a quarter; long distance is a dollar-fifty plus the cost of the call."

I didn't hurt the man, though I strongly recommend it to the next person that has to deal with him. Instead, I drove down the road a couple of miles. When I'd been up this way the day before, I'd noticed a small gas station and diner about midway between the motor lodge and the town of Lagrange. I pulled into it and asked the waitress for a dollar's worth of change, and I had directory assistance connect me through to Little Rock. Art Hennig was away from his desk again, and I explained to the woman who answered that I was calling long distance on a pay phone and needed Art to call me back as soon as possible. I said it was urgent and that he'd know my name. I said I'd stay put for thirty minutes. Then I gave her the pay phone's number, and I used the rest of my change to order a cup of coffee, while I sat at a table near the back and thought and waited for him to call me.

It took about ten minutes. I got to the phone on the second ring.

"This is Sergeant Hennig of the Arkansas State Police," Art said. "This is official business. I'm tryin' to reach Chief Ray Elmore. Who am I talkin' to?"

"Thanks for callin' back, Art. I know how busy you are," I replied.

"Doc? Damn bubba, didn't sound like you. Connection's shit. What number is this anyway?"

"Callin' from a pay phone. I'm at a diner outside Lagrange."

"Lagrange? Where the hell is that?"

"Lee County."

"You do get around. Tell me later. I got some hot news for you. I just came from the lab. We got a match to those prints from that car."

"It's Gervais."

"Damn. Right. Gervais and that girl of his. Fernandez. Lidia Fernandez. You don't sound surprised. How'd you know?"

"You run that VIN that Ricky called in a couple hours ago?"

"No. Not yet. I got a note here on my desk, but I've been in one meetin' after another. That the VIN for the Impala you were tellin' me about?"

"Yeah. I'm sure it'll match to the one Gervais was seen drivin'."

Art laughed. "Well, damn. I guess we can safely assume he's not in Shreveport like that dumb-assed peckerwood sheriff down there thought; not if you got his fingerprints from another car showin' up in

Lee County. Damn dumb Cajuns. Never met one that could piss and hold his dick at the same time. You say you're in Lee County now? I assume it's got somethin' to do with all this."

"I found where they've been hold up. At least where they were. It's a motor lodge in Lee County; they were stayin' here a few weeks back. No surprise, it's the same motor lodge where they found that stolen car with their prints. Manager confirmed it was them."

"You think they're there now?"

"No. I doubt it. Pretty sure not. The manager isn't much help, but I doubt they're here. If nothin' else, the local sheriff findin' that stolen car in the motel parkin' lot would have scared them off."

"So, no idea where they are now?"

"No."

"Too bad."

"Yeah."

"Worries me that he's got that much of a head start on us. What's he been up to all this time?"

"Don't know, but you can bet he didn't come here to vacation. They're still close, though. I just got a feelin'."

Art went quiet for a few seconds. "The guy that Gervais is huntin' down there . . ."

"Carl Trimble," I answered.

"Right. Trimble. Didn't you say his brother lived up in Blytheville or somewhere like that?"

"Yeah, he did. I told you, he's dead."

"Yeah, so you said, but listen to me, Doc, you know he's dead, and now I know he'd dead, but does Gervais? You reckon he knows it? If you follow. I can't say I'm familiar with the ugly-ass half of the state where you live like I should be. How far is Blytheville from this Lagrange?"

"Couple hours, maybe. Longer if you get behind a truck up near Memphis."

"And how far is it from Split Tree?" Art asked. "About the same?"

"Lagrange? No. Forty-five minutes. What are you thinkin'?"

"Not sure. I guess I'm thinkin' that maybe Gervais parked hisself on a wide spot in the road, midway between the Trimble brothers. One up in Blytheville; one in Split Tree. He could go either direction from that motel you found. Right? You haven't seen him around your town; so I'm wonderin' if he might just be up in Blytheville right now. You and me know that's a dry hole, but it might be takin' him some time to figure that out. That's a bigger place; maybe he's up there wanderin' around, tryin' to get the lay of the battlefield. It could take a while to reconnoiter, especially if you're tryin' to lay low at the same time. If you follow."

"Maybe. I reckon he could be, but I'm more concerned that he's in Split Tree now."

"Hear ya, Doc. Not disagreein' with you at all; just thinkin' on my feet here, if you follow. We got to figure out how best to deploy our forces. We got every trooper in the central part of the state chasin' his own tail with this Kennedy trip, and we just don't have folks to spare. I just heard that the order went out to check all roads in and out of Locust County, that's good, but I'm not sure for how long we can keep it up. I'm guessin' someone upstairs has stuck their neck out about as far as they're willin' to. We can't sustain that without some proof that he's in the area. If I were a bettin' man, I'd say that we've got forty-eight hours, but after that . . ."

"We found the car he was usin', and we got his fingerprints on a second stolen car. He was here. Probably still is. So is the man he's aimin' to kill. What more proof do you need?"

"Ain't me. I got all I need. You asked for it, that's good enough, but last time I checked, I'm a sergeant; I'm a lab rat in the basement; I don't get to make decisions, I get to follow orders. I've got some pull around here, but I'm already messin' in stuff I got no authority over. I'm fine with that, but I'm goin' to have to convince the brass on the third floor that this is a bigger priority than the president. That ain't an easy sell, and I tell you what, Doc, that FBI investigation into you isn't helpin' neither. Other than me, nobody in this buildin' had ever heard of Split Tree before this mornin', and now it's a headache comin' at the worst time. I tell you, you're not high on anyone's list right now, not in a good way anyhow. But I'll deal with that; for now, the real problem, as I see it, is that all your intel is a couple weeks old. That makes for a harder sell, if you follow. We may know Gervais was there two weeks ago, but we don't know where he is now. That's the problem. It costs money to maintain roadblocks."

"Costs more to bury innocent people. If Gervais takes out Carl Trimble, I won't lose any sleep, but if anyone else gets hurt, that's another matter."

"I hear you. Thank God, that hasn't happened. Yet."

"Maybe." *Ring Johnson didn't blow his own head off*, I thought. "But I'm worried," I said.

"Look, Doc, I run the lab; I don't run field operations, but you got my word that I'll pass all this up the chain, you know that, I'll do what I can, but I'm just tellin' you the realities here. Welcome to the big-badge police. It's all about *overtime*. End of the day, that's what it all comes down to. People are money, and money is money."

"Thanks, Art. I know, and I know you'll do what you can."

"Hey, don't need to thank me. Hell, you just said you were worried. And you know what? If Doc Elmore says he's worried, well, that should scare the rest of us shitless."

CHAPTER 47

Split Tree, Arkansas
Tuesday, November 19, 1963

A state trooper stopped me at a roadblock shortly after I crossed back into Locust County. I got out of the truck and talked to him for a few minutes. He had photos of both Gervais and Lidia Fernandez on his car seat, and he knew who he was looking for and why. He was a young kid, but seemed sharp enough. I told him who I was and that I'd just come from the General Fagan motor lodge up in Lee County, and that I'd confirmed that Gervais had been staying there. He nodded at that and adjusted his stance and hooked his thumbs into his belt and looked intently up the road, like he expected to see Bonnie and Clyde come driving his way any minute and was determined to be ready for them. I told him to watch himself when he pulled folks over, that Gervais wasn't someone to take lightly. He was a young kid and took my recommendation the way young men tend to take suggestions from old men; he was convinced that he was more than a match for whatever came his way and that the best thing I could do was stay out of the line of fire.

I got back to Split Tree around two thirty and stopped by the police station first. Ricky had just gotten back from an extended patrol through town, and we sat in the office for a while, and I brought him up to speed on what I'd learned and what Art Hennig had said on the phone. I also told him that the state police were stopping traffic in and out of the county, and he told me that he'd just talked on the phone with a major out of Troop D up in Forrest City and had been told the same thing. He said that the current plan for the state boys was to maintain the roadblocks for forty-eight hours and then reassess based on the threat and their available manpower. I wasn't sure forty-eight hours was going to be enough, and I told Ricky that it sounded to me like a plan to get someone killed before it was all over. He didn't disagree.

I swung by Jim Bevins' gas station next on my way home, hoping to see Jimmie Carl out back working on his old Bel Air. I wanted to reiterate my warning about Gervais to him, but he wasn't there. Jim said that he'd been around over lunch, putting in a rebuilt water pump, but that he'd left about two and headed back to work. Jim and I talked briefly, and he expressed his unvarnished feelings about New York lawyers and how the town was treating me, and I thanked him. He also gave me his unvarnished opinion of black preachers stirring up trouble, and I let it slide.

I went by Grace Trimble's house last. I wanted to tell her what I learned about Gervais and to make sure that she was extra careful, and that she'd do as she promised and call me if she saw anything that looked out of place. We stood on her porch and talked, in sight of the state police car parked in front of her house, and she reminded me that I'd promised to not let Gervais hurt Carl. As I was leaving, I stopped and talked to the trooper watching her house for a few minutes and told him what I knew. He said that they were on six-hour rotations, and that there'd be someone coming in to relieve him around eight or nine. He said they were instructed to continue doing that until further notice. He said that he was there to make sure Gervais didn't get to Carl Trimble. I told him that he'd better make sure that Gervais didn't get to Grace.

Ellen Mae was working in the yard when I finally got home, and I told her about where I'd been and what I'd found out. I told her that she'd made quite an impression on the motel manager and that he'd asked me to pass along his compliments, which made her shudder and throw a dirt clod at me. Afterwards, we discussed whether or not it was too late in the year to put in some azalea bushes, and how the yard would probably need mowing one last time before winter set in. Then she observed that from what she could tell, the roof wasn't making much progress on patching itself. I reluctantly acknowledged the fact and got the ladder out and climbed back up onto the house.

Our sons came home around four o'clock, long enough to change clothes and grab a sandwich before heading back to school for a late afternoon basketball practice. That'd be the last we'd see of them until bedtime. Ellen Mae and I finished our chores and had a light dinner together, and then we got cleaned up, and I took her to the movies. We saw a damn stupid Hitchcock film about a bunch of birds attacking people in California. Ellen Mae liked it and said it was filled with all sorts of symbolism, but I just kept thinking that a damn shotgun and a good birddog would have fixed their problem. Afterwards we drove the truck over to Jim Harland's Drive-In, and I bought her another milkshake, and we talked some more. We got home around eight fifteen, and I went out to the porch and sat and smoked some cigarettes and thought. Ellen Mae still had some pies to bake, and she went straight to the kitchen.

Ricky Forrest showed up a few minutes later.

"Chief," he said as he stepped up onto the porch. He was still wearing his uniform, and it was still creased and sharp. "I figured I could catch you sitting out here."

"Ricky," I greeted him. "You're keepin' late nights. I'm guessin' you haven't been home yet."

He sat on the railing and lit a smoke. "No, sir. Too much work. Headed that way now, though. I just came from the Trimbles'. I went by there to check on things, and I thought I'd bring you up to speed."

"Thanks. You're a good man. I hope the state police are still there. I dropped by earlier this afternoon, and the trooper I spoke to said they were on six-hour shifts. I've been thinkin' about drivin' back over there myself, but with the state police all on alert the way they are, I'm thinkin' it might just complicate things. It's not like I can do anythin' that they aren't already doin' except get in their way."

"May be right about that. They're stopping every car in and out of Locust County, and that's on top of the cruiser they're keeping out in front of the Trimble house around the clock."

"Nothin' at Carl's store? He isn't home all that much. Not that I'm complainin'; I'd just as soon he stay as far away from Grace as we can get him. I'm fine lettin' the state boys keep an eye on her, but if they're lookin' to protect Carl, they're at the wrong spot."

"No, sir. They're stretched thin as it is. As I understand it, they're watching the roads and his house. That's it. They figure that where he chooses to spend his time is his problem."

"But they'll be at his house around the clock? We're sure about that?"

"Yeah, they're on a six-hour rotation, like you heard. They just switched out. I talked to the trooper who just came on duty before I drove over here. He's sitting out in front of the Trimble house right now, and said he'll be there until he's relieved around two, two thirty." He laughed. "I showed him the best yards and bushes to piss in if he has to."

"He seem okay to you?"

"He does. Seems solid. He was in Korea about the same time as I was. He was in an arty unit, you know how those cannon cockers are, but he seems like he knows his business."

"Well, then I guess he knows how to sit and wait and watch."

"I guess you're right; he came home alive, didn't he? You didn't get to do that if you didn't learn pretty fast how to watch and listen." He adjusted his position so that his back was leaning against the porch column and he could look out at the street. "Speaking of sitting and watching, here comes some trouble for sure," he said. His tone indicated that we weren't talking about Gilbert Gervais any longer.

I looked toward the street, following Ricky's eyes. I saw my two sons walking up the driveway.

"Hey, Ricky," my son W.R. called out when he was close enough to see Ricky sitting on the porch railing. "Hey dad."

"Hay's for horses," I replied automatically. My mother would always correct my brother and me when we said *hey*. It bothered her something awful. Her correcting never stopped us, but until the day she died, she kept trying, and I can still hear her saying it. "I see Larry and Moe. Where's Shemp?' I asked when they got to the steps.

Ray Junior dropped into the rocking chair. W.R. stayed standing. He was carrying a basketball and tossed it back and forth between his hands. "Jimmie Carl didn't get us," he said.

"So I see. Y'all walk all the way from the high school? I'm so used to seein' you in his car, I wasn't sure your feet worked anymore."

"No, sir," W.R. responded. "Billy Hudson gave us a ride most of the way."

"Billy Hudson," Ricky laughed. "Oh boy. I hope you didn't stop off along the way and shoot out any streetlights."

"That's his younger brothers did that," Ray Junior said.

"Town's still payin' for it," I said. "So, what happened to the third stooge? He get a better offer?"

"Didn't show," Ray Junior answered.

"Let me guess; car trouble?" I asked.

"No, sir. He got the water pump swapped out," W.R. said.

"So I heard. I was by Jim Bevins' place earlier. He told me."

"You know that fifty-four Corvette I was tellin' you about?" W.R. asked.

"I know you mentioned it. You said it was over in Canefield. That right?"

"Was," Ray Junior said.

"Dang thing sold. Told you it was a sweet machine," W.R. finished the explanation. "Someone else bought it before we could."

"Corvette?" Ricky got back into the conversation. "What in the world were you two, you three, going to do with a hot rod like that? That's a lot of car."

"*Spend all their money fixin' it; that's what they'd be doin'*," I said to Ricky. "Sorry to hear that," I said to my son. "Probably for the best. Y'all haven't quite come to realize that you're goin' to need every penny you got for college. Jimmie Carl too. Not to mention, a fast car like that, if you did manage to get it runnin', you'd worry your mother sick every time you started it up." I nodded in the direction of the house. "Speakin' of worryin', you best check in with your momma. Let her know you're home, safe and sound. You in for the night?"

"Yes, sir," W.R. replied.

"Guess so," Ray Junior added. He clearly wasn't happy about it.

"Early for you two, isn't it? I understand you didn't get that fast Corvette, but don't you still have an old car to mess around with?" I asked. For the last couple of months, the routine had been for them to find someone's garage to work in until around midnight.

"Not tonight," Ray Junior said.

"Don't know where Jimmie Carl got to," W.R. explained.

"Well, nice to have you home for once," I said. "Your mother will be glad."

They talked to Ricky for a couple of minutes, passing the basketball around between the three of them, and got off onto the sorry state of Razorback football this year. They'd lost to SMU the previous Saturday and needed to beat Texas Tech to finish out the year at five and five, and neither of my boys gave them much of a chance. They could have continued on that topic all evening, but I reminded them that they needed to check in with Ellen Mae. They closed out their conversation with Ricky, and then they went inside and I heard them announce that they were home. Then I heard them in the kitchen. Then I heard their mother fixing them some pie. Then I heard them finish up and go upstairs.

Ricky and I continued talking for another thirty minutes; mostly small talk. He's a lot like my brother Reuel, or at least what I imagine my brother would have grown into if he'd made it back from the war. Ricky's a good man, and I enjoy his company, and while I don't want to sound presumptuous, I suspect that maybe I've stepped into the shoes of his late father a bit.

I finally convinced him to get on home to his real family, and he left a little before nine thirty or so. I continued sitting on the porch after he left, trying to recapture my train of thought about Ring Johnson, but the temperature had started to drop and before too long it got unpleasant enough that I moved inside. I wasn't sleepy, having spent the last couple of nights in a car outside the Trimble house had reset my clock, and my brain was still buzzing with all that was happening, and so I got a pad of paper out of my desk, and a handful of sharpened pencils, and I sat at the kitchen table and drank some coffee and drew some circles and squares and arrows. And thought.

Progress was slow, and I dulled a good half-dozen pencils and balled up a dozen sheets of paper in the process of getting nowhere.

I was in the middle of redrawing a short arrow between a large box labeled *motor lodge* and a small circle labeled *matchbook* when I felt a soft kiss on the back of my neck. It startled me. I'd heard Ellen Mae's footsteps on the stairway, and I'd heard the soft sticky sound of her bare feet on the kitchen linoleum, but I hadn't really tracked where she was or what she was doing. I realized all of a sudden how quiet the house had become.

"Ray, come to bed," she said. She stroked my hair and rubbed my back. "The doodles will wait."

I straightened up and leaned slightly into her. "Soon," I answered. "Pretty soon. You about ready for bed?"

She laughed. "I've been in bed for almost two hours now. And I'm here to tell you that I'm gettin' lonely."

"Two hours? What time is it?"

"Almost midnight."

"You're kiddin' me," I said. "Twelve? Damn. I'm sorry, Ella. I must have gotten . . ."

She leaned her hip into me and pulled the side of my face into her stomach and held me close. I could smell her bath soap and feel the warmth of her skin through the thin material of her nightgown. "Oh, I know. You got sidetracked. I know. But, *Big Ray*, I also know that the boys are sound asleep, and I've got somethin' a whole lot more interestin' for you to work on than some old doodles."

CHAPTER 48

Split Tree, Arkansas
Wednesday, November 20, 1963

That kid, the young one from Wisconsin or Ohio, Dolski, was staring at me. He's always staring at me. Every night just about. There were others with him, thirteen others, but he's there, in front, as he always is. He wasn't smiling. He never is anymore. He said he was cold. He always says that. He's always cold, and he wants to know why I'd failed him. Why I always fail him. He was holding his severed arm and showed me his infected seahorse tattoo and told me he was cold. *Ray*, he said.

Ray. Ray. Ray!

"Ray. Honey." It was Ellen Mae. She was shaking my arm. "Ray. The phone."

"What?" I said. "What?"

She shook me some more. "Ray. Wake up. The phone."

The phone was ringing downstairs. It was dark. I blinked and freed my arm from the covers and tried to focus on my watch, but it was too dark to see. I reached up and fumbled and found the switch on the lamp beside the bed and turned the knob and blinked against the light. The clock showed 1:24.

"Ray," Ellen Mae said. "Wake up. Honey. Wake up."

I worked free from the blanket. My head was full of molasses and my leg was stiff and numb and slow to respond, but I got to my feet and stumbled my way downstairs.

"Ray Elmore," I croaked into the phone. I had no idea how long it had been ringing, but I counted seven and I suspect I'd slept through at least that many.

"Ray. Oh, thank God," Grace Trimble replied. She sounded scared, and Grace doesn't scare lightly. "Are your boys home? I'm so sorry to call."

"Grace," I said. "The boys? Yeah. Yes. They're asleep. In bed. I don't . . . Grace, what's wrong?" I looked at my watch, to double-check the time. Ellen Mae had followed me downstairs and was standing on the bottom step, watching me.

"Ray, is Jimmie Carl there? Please tell me he is," Grace said. "Please tell me."

"Jimmie Carl? No, I don't . . . no, I don't think he's here. We haven't seen him at all this evenin'." I looked at Ellen Mae.

She shook her head, confirming it.

"No, Grace. He's not here, unless . . . no. Let me double check," I said. I nodded to the top of the stairs. Ellen Mae understood and went to look in the boys' rooms. "Talk to me, Grace."

"He hasn't come home," she said. "I don't know where he is. Ray, I'm worried; he never stays out this late unless he's with your two. I was hopin' maybe he was there; I know it's a school night for them, but I was . . ."

"Okay. It's okay, Grace."

"No! It isn't. No, it isn't, Ray. I'm used to him bein' out until midnight. Always workin' on that old car with your boys, but when it got to twelve thirty . . . I started to worry. And then past one. I wanted to call you, but I didn't want to bother you and Ellen Mae; I know I should have, I know, but it's so late, and I knew he'd be home any minute, and I didn't want to embarrass him, you know, his mother checkin' on him, and I thought maybe he just lost track of time, and he'd be home any minute now, and . . ."

"It's okay. Slow down. Calm down. I'm sure it's okay. He's not here, but he's got a good head on him." I looked at my watch again. "I'm sure he's out with some friends. You're right, he's probably in someone's garage, workin' on that old car of his. You're right, he just lost track of the time. When did you talk with him last?"

"Dinner. We had dinner together, and then he went out. I don't know; maybe . . . seven. Ray, he doesn't have that many friends that he'd be out with, not this late anyhow, not unless Ray Junior and W. R. are with him; if they were with him, sure, but . . . where could he be? He's got to be there. Tell me he is. Maybe he's there and you don't know it. Maybe he showed up, and you don't know it."

Ellen Mae had returned. She shook her head. Jimmie Carl wasn't upstairs.

"Grace, he's not here. Our two had basketball practice and walked home. They hadn't seen Jimmie Carl this evenin'," I said. I shook my head and blinked hard to work the remaining cobwebs free. "Okay. Talk to me. Slowly. You saw him at dinner, and then he went out. Did he say where he was goin'?" I looked at Ellen Mae again and made a drinking motion with my free hand. I wasn't sure what was happening, but it looked like it was going to be a long night, and I needed to clear my head. She nodded and went to the kitchen, and I heard her making a pot of coffee.

"Helena. Or West Helena," Grace Trimble said. "I think that's what he said. Yes, West Helena. But that was hours ago."

"West Helena?" I said. "What in the world is he doin' up in West Helena?"

"Somebody wanted to see that old car of his. I think someone wants to buy it. He was goin' to meet a man there to look at it. I thought Ray Junior and W.R. were . . . I just assumed your boys were goin' with him, and I just assumed . . . Ray, that was hours ago. I thought Ray Junior and W.R. were with him. They always are."

"No, I . . . no, they had ball practice." I repeated. I tried to lighten my voice. "But that makes sense. It does. It's startin' to make sense. Yeah. Now that you say that, W.R. told me that someone was interested in that old Bel Air. That explains it." I looked at my watch again. I gave a little laugh to break the tension. "My guess is he's probably stuck on the side of the road. Cussin' like a hungover sailor right now. They told me this mornin' that his old car was overheatin' pretty bad, and I saw Jim Bevins this afternoon and he told me that Jimmie Carl had spent the afternoon puttin' in a rebuilt water pump. My guess is that the new pump didn't fix the problem like he'd hoped. I'll bet his damn radiator boiled over. That's probably all there is to it. Somethin' simple like that. Boiled over and he's stuck on the side of the road. It probably got him far enough before it conked out that he can't just walk home, and there's not enough traffic this time of night to hitch a ride."

"But Ray, it's past one. Past one-thirty. Ray—"

"I know, Grace. I know. It's late, but it's probably just somethin' dumb like that. Old cars will do that to you. Always at the worst place and worst time. You know that. Let me get dressed, and I'll drive up that way. West Helena? You don't know where in West Helena do you?"

"No, I'm . . ."

"That's okay," I said quickly. "That's okay. Ain't but one good road to take, and there'd be no reason for him to try a back way. I'll head on up there. I'll probably catch him walkin' back to town; embarrassed and mad as a wet tomcat. It's not that cold, though, so he'll be all right." I looked at my watch again. "Half hour up there; another half back. Even if I have to go all the way to West Helena, it shouldn't be much more than an hour. I'll call you when—" I stopped myself. "What am I sayin'? I won't need to call you; I'll see you when I drop him off at your house. Safe and sound. I know it's a waste of time to say this, but try and not worry."

"Ray . . ."

"Try not to worry, Grace. Where's Carl? Have you called him?" As soon as I asked, I knew it was a stupid question. Carl wouldn't be of any help in a situation like this.

She was quiet and then answered slowly. "Who knows? Still at his office probably. I called him earlier, and that's where he was. He's taken to sleepin' there some nights. I tried callin' him again a few minutes ago, but he's not answerin' this time."

"Tell me, is the state trooper still out in front of your house?"

"Yes. Why? Oh, Ray . . . you don't . . . you don't think this has anythin' to do . . ."

"No," I said quickly. "No, Grace, I don't. Okay . . . ahh . . . Okay. I'll get . . . let me get on the road. Would you like Ellen Mae to come over? I can drop her off on my way out of town. Would that help? She could sit with you."

"Ray . . . our boy."

"Grace. Grace, it's goin' to be all right."

CHAPTER 49

Split Tree, Arkansas
Wednesday, November 20, 1963

I hung up the phone. Ellen Mae was still in the kitchen, and I went upstairs and got dressed. I probably shouldn't have, but I put my uniform on, and I got my service revolver out of the nightstand and put it in my pants pocket, and then I went back downstairs.

Ellen Mae was waiting for me by the front door. She was holding my jacket and a thermos of coffee. "Be careful," she said. "You awake enough?"

"Yeah. I'm fine. I will." I took the thermos from her and set it on the end table and tossed my jacket onto the couch. I put my arms around her. "I guess you heard enough."

"You told Grace everythin' was goin' to be all right."

"I did."

"I saw your face. You told her that, but you don't believe it. Do you?"

I pulled her closer. "I may be gone a couple hours."

"What can I do?"

"Be here when I get back."

"Always. That's not what I mean. What can I do? I want to help."

"As much as I hate to, I need you to go wake up W.R. Ask him if he can think of anythin'; see if he knows somethin'. I'm goin' to run by Ricky's place and let him know what's goin' on. I'll probably be there a few minutes before I head out. If W.R. tells you anythin' that you think I need to know, call Ricky. You can catch me there."

She nodded, and I kissed her and picked up my jacket and thermos, and then I opened the door.

"Ray," she said, as I stepped onto the porch.

I stopped and turned to face her.

"You didn't answer my question. Is everythin' goin' to be all right?"

I shook my head. "I don't know, Ellen. I don't."

CHAPTER 50

Split Tree, Arkansas
Wednesday, November 20, 1963

In the still night air, the belch and grind of Donnie's old truck sounded like a Sherman tank rumbling through the street. Ricky Forrest lives in a quiet neighborhood just to the south and west of the center of town, the opposite of where I was headed, but I needed to talk to him.

His house was dark, as I'd expect given the hour, and I seriously thought twice about the need to bother him. With me being suspended, he'd be shouldering a lot of the town's burden and might be doing that for a while, and I thought he was already looking tired when I'd seen him earlier. I was on his front porch, about to knock, thinking it over, when the door opened.

"Heard you coming a block away," Ricky whispered. He was standing in the open doorway in a t-shirt and his shorts, holding his sleeping son against his shoulder and swaying back and forth slowly. "What's happened?"

"Hate to bother you, but we need to talk. I need to tell you somethin'." I dropped my voice to the same low whisper.

He unlatched the screen door and stood aside so that I could step in. "Eddie's been having some trouble with these teeth coming in," Ricky explained. "Kitty's been up most of the night with him; I'm spelling her so she can get a little sleep." He nodded at a rocking chair. "I was sitting here looking out the window when I heard the truck. Must have gooks in the wire, or you wouldn't be here at this hour. What happened?"

"Maybe," I said. "Grace called me about fifteen minutes ago. Jimmie Carl's missin'. Or at least he hasn't come home."

"Shit." Ricky adjusted his sleeping child on his hip and looked at his watch, trying to read it in the little illumination that the streetlight cast through the window into his living room.

"It's past one thirty," I told him.

"And your boys don't know where he is?"

"I didn't take time to ask them after she called. Ellen Mae's checkin' with W.R. right now; she'll call here if she finds out anythin', but you were there when they came home. It didn't sound to me like they knew anythin'."

"Gervais?"

"That's what's worryin' me. Seems mighty unlikely, but . . ."

"But it seems unlikely to be just a coincidence. That trooper still in front of her house?"

"Yeah. I think she's okay; it's Jimmie Carl we need to worry about now. It's probably nothin', but we need to play it safe. I don't know, Ricky, I don't, but somethin' here doesn't make sense. Not Jimmie Carl anyhow. I don't make Gervais to be the sort that'd come after a man's family. Do you? I understand goin' after Carl, that makes sense, but you don't go after a man's wife and kids."

"How much do we really know about Gervais? We know he decapitated a man in a public street and beat another to death in his own house. A man like that sounds like he could be capable of a lot of things."

"Yeah, you're right, he might be, but both of those men had it comin', at least in his mind. Jimmie Carl's another story. I really don't see him goin' after an innocent kid."

"But you're not sure. If you didn't think he'd target Carl's family, you wouldn't be so worried about Missus Trimble. You're afraid he might come after her."

"I'm only worried because she might get caught between Carl and Gervais, not because I see him comin' after her."

"So what's the play?" he nodded at my uniform. "I see you suited up."

"Don't mean to step on your toes," I replied.

"Don't give me that shit, Ray. Not me, of all people. You know how I feel about that. You should never have taken your badge off in the first place. You're still the boss." He walked over to the sofa and gently laid his son down, careful not to wake him. He stood up and turned back to me. "Sorry I'm not dressed. Give me a minute to get some pants on and tell Kitty."

"You don't need to do that. Not yet. Grace says that Jimmie Carl was goin' to meet someone up near West Helena. She doesn't know who or where, other than West Helena. Some man who wants to buy that old car of his, that's all she knows. W.R. told me the same thing. He thought it was Helena, but Grace says West Helena. Same as far as I'm concerned. I'm headed up there now. I'm hopin' that he's just broke down on the side of the road between here and there. I'm hopin' it's nothin' more than that; a dumb kid and an old car."

"Pretty late for it to be just that. When'd she see him last?"

I nodded. "You're right, it is late. He left sometime after dinner. Seven, maybe. Yeah, I know. It's late, and I told Grace not to worry, but that explanation's pretty poor, and she knows it. If he made it all the way there and broke down, he'd be able to get to a phone. No, the only way it makes sense is if he got stranded halfway between there and back; far enough that he can't walk it easily."

"There's always your thumb."

"There is, but there's not much traffic out that way this time of night. Thumb doesn't do you much good if there's no one to see it. I hope he's just sittin' in his car right now, waitin' for the trucks and the farmers to hit the road at sunup so he can hitch a ride. I gotta hope for that. In any case, I figure I can be up there and back in an hour. Hopefully, with Jimmie Carl."

"And if he isn't by the side of the road?"

"Don't want to think about it."

"I should come with you."

"No. I'm good. If this does involve Gervais somehow, Split Tree's a whole lot better off with you here rather than runnin' up and down the highway in the dark."

Ricky pointed at a small table near the front door. "Keys to the Horseshoe are right there. At least take it. From the sound of your truck, we don't want both of you broke down out there. It'll also help you get through the roadblocks faster. Plus, it's got the radio; if I hear something, I can go to the office and get a hold of you."

I shook my head. "No. I know that old truck sounds like a wreck waitin' to happen, but Donnie assures me it's reliable enough; I think it'll get me up there and back. Besides, you're goin' to need the car. I hate to ask you this, Ricky, but the state boys should be swapping out shifts pretty soon. I need you to go by Grace's in a little while and just double check on her; make sure that everyone's on their toes. Just in case. Maybe you can ask them to radio the state cars watchin' the roads up toward West Helena; ask if anyone's reported a stalled Bel Air; maybe they can keep their eyes open for him. But mainly check on Grace. That's the most important thing you can do for me right now. I'll be a lot more effective if I don't have to worry about her."

"Roger. Copy. Before you showed up, I was actually sitting here thinking I should go check on Missus Trimble anyhow." He looked at his son sleeping on the sofa. "I was just waiting for him to go down for the count. Looks like he is. For a while anyway."

"And as much as I can't believe I'm sayin' this, I think someone should check on Carl Trimble as well. Grace said she's tried callin' him at the office, but no answer. I'm sure he's holed up there, but someone should check. If Gervais's on the move . . ."

"You're right. I can't believe you're saying it."

CHAPTER 51

Split Tree, Arkansas
Wednesday, November 20, 1963

I was right about one thing; there was no traffic out in the direction of West Helena at two in the morning. The state trooper who stopped me just this side of the county line was the only car I saw the whole way up there and back. Unfortunately, that didn't include a 1951 Chevy Bel Air with a rebuilt water pump.

I went to Grace's house as soon as I got back to town; I was hoping that maybe Jimmie Carl had shown up, and I could put my growing fear to rest. She was standing on her porch, at the top of the steps, looking up and down the street. The temperature had continued to drop and there was a wet fog trying hard to roll in from the direction of the river. Grace didn't have a sweater, and she had her arms wrapped around herself, but I don't think it was in response to the falling temperature.

The state police cruiser was sitting directly in front of the Trimbles' house, and unlike the shadows that Ricky and I had sought out, it was intentionally parked in the bright yellow glow of the newly repaired streetlight. His job was to keep Gervais away, not catch him, and it was safer for all concerned if he was clearly visible. I pulled up behind him and turned off the truck engine; it continued to turnover and cough a few times before going quiet. I could see the trooper looking closely at me in his rearview mirror, glancing down several times at his seat and then back to the mirror. I suspect he was comparing me to a mugshot of Gervais. I got out and slowly closed the truck door; the trooper started to do the same. I don't know if he finally saw my uniform, or if it was Grace running out to meet me, but he decided that I wasn't the threat he was there to prevent, and he settled back into his seat. I waved to him in his mirror, and he waved back.

"Where's Jimmie Carl?" Grace called to me. She was looking at the empty cab of the truck and starting running toward it. "Where is he, Ray? Where is he?"

I sped up and caught hold of her as she got to the end of her walkway. She tried to pull away, but I kept my grip. I saw the trooper start to get out again, confused by Grace's response to me, but by then I'd put my arms around her and waved to the trooper again, and Grace let me lead her back up to her house.

"Where is he, Ray? Where is he?" she kept repeating. "You said you'd find him. You promised."

"I don't know, Grace. There was nothin' on the road. I went all the way into West Helena and then came back on some of the county roads. I didn't see him, Grace." I guided her up the steps onto the porch. "Let's go inside. It's cold. Your arms are like ice."

"To hell with my arms," Grace responded. She tried to pull free from me again and turned back toward the street. "Where is he, Ray? Goddamn you, Ray. You promised. How could you let this happen?"

I grabbed hold of her and pulled her toward the door. I opened it and got her inside. "Grace," I said sharply. "Grace. Grace. Grace Louise."

I finally got her attention.

"Grace, I didn't find him, but I haven't given up. You know I won't. Now, I need you to calm down and help me out. We need to think. His car wasn't broken down along the side of the road. I was hopin' it was, but it wasn't. So, I'm goin' to keep lookin'. I'll find him."

"Why did you let this happen? Why, Ray? You promised you'd never let him get hurt."

"And I aim to keep that, but I need some help. I'm goin' to keep lookin'."

"Where? Where are you goin' to look? Where, Ray? All I know is he said he was meetin' someone in West Helena to look at his car. How could you let this happen? You promised me, Ray; you promised. How could you let this happen? Where were you?"

"I'll find him. He told you West Helena, and maybe that's where he is. Maybe he's there, or even Helena. I was able to check the roads up there and back, but the towns are just too big for me to search on my own. I'm goin' to go get Ricky Forrest; get him to start lookin' with me. I'll have him call the police department in West Helena; get them out. We'll get the Phillips County Sheriff out too, and I asked the state trooper watchin' the roads out that way to keep an eye open. He's already radioed it in to his boss. We'll soon have every cop on this side of the state lookin' for him. We'll find him. Just like I promised. He'll be embarrassed all to hell when we do, but we'll find him."

She closed her eyes and went quiet. I pulled her to me and wrapped my arms around her. "I'm also goin' to wake up Ben Cooper and have him flush all his deputies out onto the roads. Maybe he had some reason to go somewhere else. Just because he didn't break down on his way to West Helena doesn't mean that he didn't boil over on some other back road here in the county. We'll find him. I promise."

She remained quiet for a moment and then took a deep shuddering breath and let it out slowly. She kept her face buried in my chest. "I've been tryin' not to think . . . I've been tryin' hard not to think that this is . . . part of all that nightmare with Carl and that man from the prison. I've been tryin' to . . ."

"Grace," I interrupted her. "I don't know if it is, but let's not imagine the worst. I don't know where Jimmie Carl is, but Gervais wants Carl. It's Carl he has a score to settle up with. I don't think he wants to involve Jimmie Carl. Or you."

"He can have me; just don't let him hurt Jimmie Carl. Promise me that."

"I'm not goin' to let him hurt either one of you. You know that." I took her by the arms and made her look at me. "Did you ever get hold of Carl? You said you'd tried, but he didn't answer. You ever get him? Any chance he knows somethin'?"

She shook her head. "I tried callin' him just a few minutes ago. I can try again."

"No. I'm headed that way. I'll check with him. Does he usually answer when you call? Is it normal for him not to pick up?"

She shook her head again. "I don't call him that often. The last few years, we sort of go our own ways, but yes, he normally answers. If he knew it was me he probably wouldn't, but he doesn't know."

"But you're sure he was at the store earlier this evenin'?"

She nodded. "He answered. I called him around ten. Nine. No, ten maybe. I don't know. He answered. He was there." She went quiet and focused her eyes on the middle of my chest without blinking.

"Grace?"

"Ray. Oh, Ray." She looked up at me. "I didn't think it was important . . . someone called for him earlier. For Carl. Twice. A man."

"Okay. Is that unusual? Who was it? You know who it was?"

She shook her head. "No. I know most of the people who call for him. He's got a small circle of his . . . his buddies, but they all know now to call him at the store."

"What'd this man want? What'd he sound like? Did he say it was business? Leave a name?"

"Deep voice. Funny accent. I didn't . . . I don't know what he wanted. It didn't sound like a business call, but I don't know. He didn't say all that much. No name. He asked for Carl Trimble; that's all." She returned her look to the middle of my chest and blinked quickly, trying to recall the conversation. "He asked for Carl Trimble. Carl Trimble. Not just Carl. He used his full name, like he didn't really know him."

"What'd you tell him?"

"I just said that he wasn't home, and I wasn't sure when he'd be back. He thanked me quickly and hung up. I didn't have a chance to ask what he wanted. Or get a name." She looked up at me again. "You don't think . . ."

"You said he called twice. Same man?"

She nodded and she replayed the call in her head. "The second call was maybe a half-hour later. I don't think it was a full hour. Same man. He wanted to know if Carl Trimble was home yet; he said it was important, and that he needed to talk with him."

"Go on. What'd you tell him? He hang up again?"

"No. He said it was important, so I said he was at work, and I gave him the number of the phone in Carl's office."

"When was this again? Did you already tell me?"

"It would have been right before I called Carl. Whenever that was. Nine or ten. That's why I called him; I wanted to tell him that someone was tryin' to reach him, and it was important."

"And that's when you say Carl answered? What'd he say to you? Did he seem to know who the man was?"

She shrugged. "I don't know. He was . . . he'd been drinkin'. He does that a lot now days. A lot of nights he never makes it home. There was a time when he stayed at work late because of some poor girl who needed a paycheck more than her pride. He used to do that, but now I think he just sits up there alone and drinks until he passes out."

"But he didn't give you any indication that he knew who might be lookin' for him at that hour?"

"No. He'd already been drinkin' for a while. That's why I'm not surprised that he isn't answerin' now. I assumed he was already passed out, but he wasn't." She paused. "Ray, do you think that's who called here? That Gervais man?"

"I can't believe Gervais would call to make an appointment," I replied, but I'm not sure I believed it even as I said it.

"But if it was that man . . . then he's here . . . and Jimmie Carl . . ." she didn't need to finish her sentence. Instead, she put her arms around me and buried her face in my chest again.

I looked out the front window. With the inside lights on, all I saw was our reflection in the dark glass. I saw Ray and Grace, standing in the living room, holding one another, just like it was supposed to be, just like it used to be. I was tempted to close the door and turn off the light and hope that the sun never rose, and the moment went on forever.

But that wasn't going to find Jimmie Carl.

CHAPTER 52

Split Tree, Arkansas
Wednesday, November 20, 1963

I needed to check in with Ricky Forrest, and the most direct route from Grace's house to his took me through the center of town. When I turned west onto Tupelo, I saw a sheriff's car parked in front of the Western Auto, and what looked to be two deputies sitting on the hood; Carl's black Buick was next to it. I went on up to the next intersection and did a U-turn and was headed back to talk with them when I saw my old car parked in front of the police station across the street from the courthouse. That meant Ricky was around, though there was no light showing in our office. I pulled in beside it and killed the engine. As soon as I opened the truck door, I heard a low, quick whistle, and I looked up to see Ricky emerging from the shadows in the courthouse lawn, walking across the street toward me.

"Tell me you found him," he said.

"I wish I could," I replied.

"Damn. That's not good."

"No. It's not. What are you doin' here?"

"Watching."

I gestured toward the Western Auto and the two deputies. "What's goin' on?"

He offered me a cigarette, and we both lit up before he responded. "Not sure. I'm still trying to sort it all out. That's Pinto and Lee Malone. Ben Cooper was here until about five minutes ago; you probably passed him coming into town."

"I've been over at Grace's."

"Roger. How's she holding up?"

"About like you'd expect."

He looked at his watch. "I was headed over to check on her shortly. Had the state troopers changed shifts yet?"

"Not yet. So, what's goin' on here?" I asked.

"Yeah. Well, from what I can tell, what Sheriff Cooper told me, it seems that Carl Trimble called him earlier in the evening and demanded some police protection. As in immediately. Pinto and Lee were working the night shift anyhow, and the sheriff figured they could grab-ass out here as well as in the office, so he sent them over to babysit."

"Why didn't Carl call you? We're in the town limits."

Ricky laughed. "I'll let you ask him that. No, I somehow get the impression he doesn't have much confidence in the Split Tree police department."

"He could have called his cousin, Charley Dunn."

He laughed again. "Like I said, he doesn't seem to have much confidence in our department."

"So why does he need protection all of a sudden?"

"Your guess is as good as mine. He told the sheriff that the state police were wasting their time out in front of his house, and he wanted someone to watch over him personally."

"And next year's an election year. Poor Ben."

"Yes, sir. He didn't feel like he could tell him to pound sand." He shifted gears. "So, no sign of Jimmie Carl. Damn. What do we do now?"

"Wish I had a good answer. I need you to call the police in Helena and West Helena and get them on the lookout; that's one thing we can do."

"Roger. Copy all. I went and told Sheriff Cooper about Jimmie Carl when he was here. Hope that was okay?"

"Of course. You're always a step ahead of me. I was goin' to ask you to do that too. I was thinkin' maybe Phillips County sheriff as well."

"Sheriff Cooper thought of that on his own. He said he'd take care of it. He's also going to get more of his people out looking for Jimmie Carl at first light, as soon as the morning shift comes on. There's got to be something else we can do until then."

"I want to talk to Carl Trimble."

"You think he knows something?"

"I don't know, but I think somethin' isn't quite right." I nodded at the Western Auto. "Looks dark. Are we sure he's inside?"

"Yes, sir. His car's there, and the hood's cold. I've been sitting on a bench across the street, watching the building. You're right, it's dark, I haven't seen any lights inside yet, but there's movement upstairs. If you watch closely, you'll see the shadows shift around. Not much, but you can see it. There's a bit of a pattern to it too, like someone keeps coming to the window to check on something."

"But no one's talked to him?"

"To Carl? No, sir. I asked Pinto a while ago, but he says they haven't seen him either, and I don't think Ben spoke to him face to face. I tried. I knocked on the door to his store and called up to him; I thought maybe I could get him to come to the window. Nothing."

"When'd Ben get the call? He say?"

"A few hours ago. What are you thinking?"

"Don't know that I know, but I'm gettin' a funny feelin' about this. You know what I mean when I say that?"

"Yes, sir. I think I do. In Korea, you always knew when the Chinese were going to attack. Even before they started blowing those damn bugles, you could feel it. Couldn't hear it; couldn't see it. But you damn sure felt it. You felt it in your chest; you felt it in your balls; they'd cinch up on you. That sort of feeling?"

"Yeah. It was the same with the Japs." I leaned my hip against the side of the truck. I'd been standing still too long and my leg was starting to go numb. "Grace said someone called for Carl last night. Someone she didn't know."

"Is that unusual? I wonder how often he gets phone calls at night"

"I asked her that. Not very often. She said most people who'd be callin' Carl at that hour know to call him at the store. She also didn't get the feelin' that whoever it was knew Carl. He wouldn't leave a name, or say what it was; just said it was important. I guess he called twice; the second time she gave him the office number and told him to try there."

"But she doesn't know if this guy ever called Carl?" he asked.

"Well, now that's the thing. She says she called Carl right after she got off the phone with the strange man the first time. She said Carl answered, and she told him someone was tryin' to reach him, and it was important. But later, when Jimmie Carl hadn't come home, she tried callin' him again. And again. She says she's tried numerous times. He wouldn't pick up on any of them."

"Does she know what time it was when she called him the first time? When he answered."

"Nine or ten," I replied. "She couldn't remember for sure. The later calls were closer to midnight. She said she didn't think that much about it; him not answerin'. I think she was even a bit surprised when he picked up the first time. She didn't even think to tell me about it at first. She said Carl's taken to drinkin' himself stupid every night, and she said he sounded like he'd already gotten a good start on it when she talked to him the first time. So, she figured he was just too passed out to hear the phone."

"Sheriff Cooper says Carl called him at a quarter-to-ten."

"Did he now? There sure seems to be a lot of phone calls comin' and goin' at the same time. Funny that Carl should pick that time, out of the blue, to decide he needed some immediate protection."

"And Grace says that he hasn't answered since?"

"Not since. And she tried again just a few minutes before I got over there. He's not pickin' up for some reason."

Ricky looked at his watch. "I've been staring at that window for the last forty-five minutes. Someone's up there, walking around. If it's Carl, he isn't passed out drunk."

"Then we need to figure out why he isn't answerin' the phone."

Ricky looked at the Western Auto for a moment before replying. "You know boss, I'm starting to get that same feeling you have. What if it isn't Carl up there?"

CHAPTER 53

Split Tree, Arkansas
Wednesday, November 20, 1963

W e both continued watching the store window for a few minutes. Ricky was right, it was subtle, but you could see faint changes in the shadows, as if someone periodically walked to the window and looked out and then retreated. "I need to talk to Carl Trimble," I said.

Ricky nodded. "Roger. But what if that isn't Carl moving around up there?"

"Gervais?"

He shrugged. "That's what we're talking about, isn't it? We're out here now because we're worried that Gervais might be here. Carl was worried about it enough to call the sheriff at home. What if Gervais got to him? What if he got up there but didn't get away before Pinto arrived? And now he's trapped."

"You really think that?"

He shrugged again, "I don't know, Chief. I told you, someone's pacing around up there, checking the window frequently. Maybe Gervais is hoping the coast will clear. He's thinking those two will leave soon."

I thought about it. Not a great deal, but I thought about it. I value Ricky's opinion too much to not give it some consideration. I shook my head. "I hear you, but I don't see it that way, Ricky. Maybe he did get to Carl, but even if we work with that, I just don't see it. Gervais isn't someone to mess with. He's got nothin', absolutely nothin' to lose, and he's got a pair of balls on him that you and me can only wish for. I just don't see it. No way that Pinto Bean, sittin' outside on the hood of his car, is goin' to spook a man like that. If he wanted to leave, he'd leave."

"You always tell me, there's no need to borrow trouble if you don't have to. Maybe he figures he can sit tight and wait Pinto out."

"They don't look like they're goin' anywhere to me. If that's Gervais up there, he's got to know by now that they're here to watch the place, and he'd know he doesn't have all day to wait either. The sun will be up in a few hours, and gettin' away then won't be easier. Plus, he'd know that employees will be showin' up soon, and then what? If you're lookin' to make a break, now's the best time. No, it's not Gervais up there. I'd bet on it."

You willing to bet your life?"

"I don't think it'll come to that. Not here anyhow."

"Okay. So, it's not Gervais, it's Carl Trimble up there; you think he's going to talk to you? He's not answering his phone. Ben Cooper couldn't get him to respond. When I first got here, I tried to check on him myself; I stood outside and called up to the window, I thought maybe he'd answer me from there. Nothing. Doors locked, lights out. If it's him, he's hunkered down, and in case you haven't noticed, he doesn't like talking to you under the best of circumstances."

"No, he doesn't. But I aim to talk to him whether he likes it or not."

"Roger. Give the order. What do you want me to do?"

"What you do best, Ricky. Keep your eyes open."

Pinto Bean and the other deputy, Lee Don Malone, were sitting on the hood of their cruiser when Ricky and I walked up to it. I'm not sure what they were doing, but it involved the two of them trading punches on each other's upper arms and laughing and cussing like they were in gym class.

"Boys," I greeted them. "All quiet?"

"Evenin' Chief Ray," Pinto Bean answered. The sight of me back in a uniform didn't seem to trigger any more curiosity in him than did the fact that I was standing in the middle of the street at two o'clock.

"Mornin' Chief Elmore," Lee Malone said. Pinto had just popped him in the arm, and he was rubbing it and coming off a prolonged string of swear words.

"As quiet as a sinner on the front pew," Pinto continued, as he stood up and adjusted his gun belt.

"How long you boys been out here?" I asked.

Pinto looked at his watch and knotted up his face as he struggled with the arithmetic in his head. "I'd say . . . about four-and-a-half hours. Sheriff Ben called right at ten. Lee Don and me was working the night shift, and we came straight over from the office."

"So you were here by what? Ten ten? Ten fifteen?"

"Ten fifteen at the latest," Lee Malone contributed to the answer.

"Ten fifteen," I repeated to myself. That made sense. Probably no more than thirty minutes after the stranger called Grace looking for Carl. "And it's been quiet since you got here? Either of you two actually seen Carl? Talk to him?"

They looked at each other, and then back at me, and they both shook their heads.

"What do y'all know about all this? What'd Cecil Ben tell you? You know why you're here?"

Lee Malone spoke up. "All I know is Sheriff Ben says that Mister Trimble called, like we told you. He said that he wanted some extra protection. That guy from prison might be after him."

"Nothin' specific? Ben say anythin' about Carl gettin' a phone call? A threat?"

"No, sir, Big Ray," Pinto Bean answered.

"Thanks, boys. I'm sure Carl appreciates your diligence. I'll tell Ben what a good job y'all are doin' when I see him," I said. I stepped up onto the sidewalk in front of the Western Auto and tried the door. It was locked, and I stepped back and looked up and to the left of the main entrance, at the dark window of Carl's office. I glanced back at Ricky. He was standing next to Pinto, and the two deputies were talking to him. He smiled and said something to them in response, but his eyes never left the window.

"Carl Trimble," I called up. "Carl. I know you're up there. I want to talk to you. Come open up."

No answer.

"Carl Trimble. It's Ray Elmore. Come open up, now. I'm here to talk with you. It's about Jimmie Carl. Open up."

No answer. I looked back at Ricky. His eyes were on the window, and he gave me a quick nod. He'd seen some movement among the shadows. I walked back to the curb.

"Maybe he's asleep, Big Ray," Pinto Bean said. "I know I wish I was."

"I guess so. You're probably right. I reckon it's nothin' that can't wait until mornin'; sun'll be up soon enough," I replied. "Well, you boys keep at it. I know Carl can sleep better knowin' you're out here." I nodded at Ricky and we walked back across the street to Donnie's truck.

"What are we doing?" Ricky asked. "He heard you, or whoever's up there heard you. Someone came closer to the window when you called out to him."

"Yeah, he heard me. If he's scared enough to call Ben Cooper, he isn't takin' a nap. I still need to talk with him, and I'm not sure we have a lot of options here. If he won't come down, I don't have much choice but to go up. I goin' to need you to keep Pinto and Lee out here. I may have to convince Carl he wants to talk with me, and it'll be better if those two don't learn any bad habits."

"Copy. How are you getting in?"

I stood there for a minute, looking at the front of the Western Auto. "No one's watchin' the back are they?" I finally asked. "I'd be surprised. That wouldn't dawn on Cecil Ben to do. You can get to Carl's stock room from the shoe store next door, or at least you used to. It was all one buildin' at one time, until Carl's father sub-divided it up and leased part of it out. Unless they've boarded it up, I'm thinkin' I might still be able to get in through there."

Ricky nodded. "You'll probably need a key. I think I've got one." He walked to the rear of his squad car and popped the trunk. He retrieved the lug wrench and a flashlight and walked back and handed them to me. "You know, boss, I meant to tell you, I think I got an anonymous phone call earlier this evening. Someone had sprung the back door on the shoe store. I'll have to check it out in the morning."

I took the lug wrench and flashlight. "Yeah, you'll need to do that."

"Watch yourself," he said, and then he walked across the street, headed back to distract the two deputies.

I started up Donnie's truck and drove up a block and turned right, and then right again onto Cypress Street, which took me past the rear of the Western Auto. I parked in the store's loading area and got out. It took less than thirty seconds to pop the rear door of Larson's shoe store, and maybe another minute or so to find the connecting door to the Western Auto. It hadn't been boarded up, but it had some boxes and old shelving in front of it, and I had to move some things around before I could get the door open. Five minutes later, I was into the Western Auto.

The sales floor was dark. There was a little light coming in from the front windows, and a little more was coming from the illuminated Exit signs over several doors. I didn't want to use the flashlight because I didn't want Pinto or Lee Don to see something moving around inside and feel the need to investigate it. I figured I could trust Ricky to keep them occupied, but I also figured I didn't need to make it hard for him.

As I walked past the sporting goods counter at the rear of the store, I paused. The gun area looked to be in disarray. There were boxes of shells spread about. I lit the flashlight, covering the lens with my fingers, and played a narrow beam onto the shelving behind the counter. There were a couple of gaps, and while I couldn't be sure, it looked like several rifles or shotguns were missing. I figured that Carl had armed himself.

I went up the stairs quietly. If Carl did have a loaded gun, I didn't want him deciding to shoot at sounds in the dark, and if it wasn't Carl, then I didn't need to give Gervais more warning than necessary. When I got to the top of the stairs, I stood outside the office and held my breath and listened. I thought I heard someone walking around inside; the wood floor creaking under their weight. I stood to the side of the door and knocked. "Carl. It's me. Ray Elmore. You know my voice. Now, open up."

No answer.

"Goddamn it, Carl. We don't have time for this shit. Open up. I aim to come in there and talk to you, one way of the other." I held my breath again and listened. The walking stopped. I hoped I'd guessed right, but I got my pistol out of my pocket just in case. If we were wrong, if it was Gervais pacing around inside, he was a big boy, and I'd likely need a cannon to stop him, but all I had was a .38 revolver. "Open up Carl. Now."

"Fuck you, Elmore," he replied.

That's progress, I thought. At least I knew it was Carl. I put my gun away. "We can figure out who fucks who later," I said. "Right now, I need to talk with you. It's about Jimmie Carl, and I don't have time. Open the damn door."

"Go away. I'll fuckin' shoot you; I'll kill you. I will. I gotta gun. You're just a prowler."

"You ain't goin' kill anyone, Carl. The most you're goin' to do is piss me off worse than I already am. Don't do that. Now open the goddamn door."

"I've got a gun."

"I know you've got a gun. Probably a couple of them. I also know you don't have the balls or brains to use it. Now, I'm comin' in. Don't make the mistake of tryin' to stop me."

"I'm tellin' you Elmore—"

He was in the middle of whatever he was going to tell me when I put my hip into his door. The building is old, and the wood dry, and the doorframe gave way easily in a spray of splinters; my hip is old too, and something in it gave way as well. I stumbled into the dark room off balance.

Carl was standing in the middle of his office, pointing a pump shotgun at me. "I'll shoot. Damn it to hell, I will," he said. "I'll kill you Elmore. I ought to."

I regained my balance, and squared up in front of him. My leg felt like I'd leaned into an electric fence. "Shut the hell up. I'm tellin' you, shut up and put that goddamn gun down before I really get pissed off. I'm here to talk. That's all."

He raised the gun a couple of inches, pointing it square at the center of my chest. He wasn't going to shoot, but I'm not sure he knew that. In either case, he made the mistake of letting me get too close to him, and I reached out and grabbed the barrel and in one movement jerked it out of his hands. He yelped like a kicked dog. I don't think I broke his finger, but it must have gotten caught up in the trigger guard and twisted backward, because he immediately grabbed it and started hopping around like he was doing a rain dance.

"Damn you, Elmore. God damn it, god damn it. I should have shot you," he said. "Damn it."

I jacked the shotgun and no shell ejected. He hadn't chambered a round. *You goddamn moron*, I thought. "Shut up Carl. Stop your bellyachin'," I said. I went to the window and looked down into the street. Pinto Bean and Lee Don were back on the hood of their car and were completely absorbed with trading punches again; Ricky stood a few feet away, arms crossed, staring at the window. I got close enough that he could make out that it was me and waited for him to give a small nod of his head, and then I backed away and turned to Carl.

"Sit down," I told him. I pointed to his office chair. "We're goin' to talk. I need to know some things, and I don't have all night to get to it."

He was still holding his finger and whining about it, but he sat down. I jacked the shotgun three or four more times until all the shells were ejected and then I tossed it onto Carl's couch. There was a scoped, bolt-action 30.06 Springfield hunting rifle and two large caliber pistols on his desk. Carl was prepared to make this his Alamo. I didn't take the time to unload them, but I did pick them up and put them on the couch outside of his immediate reach, and then I stood in front of him. "Quicker you stop jerkin' me around and answer my questions, the sooner you can get a splint and some ice for that finger. Now, do you know where Jimmie Carl is? I need to know if you do."

"You broke my goddamn finger"

"I doubt it, but don't start givin' me ideas. Do you know where Jimmie Carl is?"

He shook his head.

"Did Gilbert Gervais contact you? Phone you?" I asked. "You didn't just decide to start a huntin' club. Was it him that spooked you so?"

"Why are you in here? You should be out there. You're the police chief; you should be out lookin' for him. I deserve protection."

"Is that a *yes*? Is that who called Grace lookin' for you? Was it Gervais? He called here, didn't he? That's why you called Ben."

"That man's a killer. He's after me. You need to stop him."

"You're right. He is after you. But why'd he call? He didn't call because he's sweet on you, Carl; he doesn't want to just talk with you the way I do. He wants somethin' else, and I want to know what it is?"

"Me. He wants me."

"You're doin' it again, Carl. I don't have time to waste with your bullshit. We know he wants you; I want to know why he called. What'd he want?"

"He said he's comin' to get me. Kill me."

"No he didn't. Try again. He's got no reason to give you fair warnin'. Men like that just want to kill you, not play games with you.

If he called, it's because he wants somethin' else. Now, what is it? Why'd he call? Tell me exactly what he said."

Carl shook his head. "Go find him, Elmore. You're the goddamn police chief."

"Not anymore, Carl. You know that. All I am now is someone with little patience lookin' for a boy that's gone missin'. A boy that means a lot to me, and I aim to find that boy, and I better not decide that you're standin' in my way of doin' it. And right now, it looks a lot like you are. I'm askin', for the last time, what did he say?"

He shook his head again. "He's crazy. He's insane."

"Probably. All the more reason for you to talk to me."

"He said he was goin' to kill me."

"We've chewed that plug; it's time to spit now. What else did he say, and why didn't you tell Ben about it? You didn't tell him that Gervais called; I want to know why? You just said you wanted some protection, but you didn't mention a specific threat." I nodded in the direction of the street. "If Ben had known Gervais had actually called you, he wouldn't have Pinto Bean and Lee Don out there trading licks like schoolboys. He'd have every state trooper and every deputy in the county out there. Why didn't you want Ben to know?"

"He was bluffin'."

"I doubt it," I said. "He intends to kill you. Men like that don't waste time bluffin'."

Carl looked at the window. "He's bluffin'. I'm tellin' you, he's bluffin'. That's all it was."

I looked at him in the dim light. It took me a minute to figure out what he was saying. "What do you mean? Bluffin' about what? About what, Carl?"

Carl continued looking at the window.

"Shit," I said. A box and circle connected in my head. "You sorry goddamn bastard. You sorry sack of shit. It's about Jimmie Carl, isn't it? He told you somethin', didn't he? He's got him. Where is he?"

"It's me he wants," Carl said. "Me. He doesn't want that boy. He's bluffin'."

"Where is he Carl? What did he say?"

"He's bluffin', I tell you. Me. I'm his target. Me. I'm the one who needs protection. Besides, it's way past midnight. He hasn't called back. It's all a bluff."

CHAPTER 54

Split Tree, Arkansas
Wednesday, November 20, 1963

C arl didn't say much more, but he'd said enough. I left him in his office; I didn't reckon that he'd go anywhere, and I knew where to find him later if I needed to. I made my way downstairs through the darkened store and out the back. I left the truck parked in the loading bay; it was too noisy and I didn't want to alert Pinto and Lee Don that I was still in the area, and instead, I ran, as best as I could, up to the intersection and then cut over to the courthouse square. Busting in the door with my hip had done something, and my whole right leg was managing to hurt and go numb at the same time. It felt like someone had driven a roofing nail into my kneecap.

I stayed in the shadows and made my way back to my office, across the street from the Western Auto. I whistled, low and quick, the way Ricky had greeted me earlier. His attention was still focused on Carl's window, and I had to do it three times before he heard. I saw him search out the source, turning his head slowly side to side, using his peripheral vision to spot my movement in the dark. I knew when he finally saw me, because he stepped up and clapped Pinto on the back and said something to the deputies and then turned and casually began walking in my direction as if he was going back to his office.

"What'd he say?" Ricky asked, as he walked up. "Learn anything?"

I motioned to his cruiser, and we both got inside.

"You're limping pretty bad. You okay?" he asked.

"Yeah. Listen, Gervais has Jimmie Carl. Or at least he did," I replied.

"Shit. What do you mean, *did*? Tell me he's okay?"

"Don't know."

"Shit." He looked over at the store window. "And Carl? He still alive?"

"Yeah. For now."

"But he told you Gervais had him?"

"Yes."

"Carl knew about Jimmie Carl and didn't tell anyone?" he asked.

"You surprised?"

"What do we need to do?"

"Get Jimmie Carl."

"Right. He tell you where he is?"

"I don't think he knows." I pointed at the ignition. "Fire this up and take me back to my truck. If I'm right, we're already out of time."

Ricky started the cruiser and put it into gear. "If I'm going to help, you need to talk to me," he said.

"Sorry. I'm still tryin' to sort it out in my head. Okay, we were right; it was Gervais who called Grace. And like we figured, he also called Carl; that's what spooked him into gettin' hold of Ben Cooper. So that was about ten o'clock. Gervais told Carl he had him, he had Jimmie Carl, and he was willing to let him go if Carl agreed to meet him somewhere."

"You think Gervais was the mystery man in Helena that Jimmie Carl was to planning to meet?"

"I assume so. Goes to figure, right? But it doesn't matter anymore how he got hold of him. Gervais told Carl that he's got him, and we have to figure that he does. He also told him that he'd swap Jimmie

Carl for him. He said he'd call back and give him the location. He told him he had until midnight to make up his mind."

Ricky looked at his watch. "Fuck."

"Yeah. I know," I said. "We're way past that deadline."

"Why didn't Carl tell someone? Call Ben? Call you?"

"You gotta ask? Because he's a spineless piece of shit. Because he knew that if Ben or me found out about it, we wouldn't let him hide out in his office. We'd make him go meet Gervais. No, he couldn't tell anyone."

"But you don't think he knows where Jimmie Carl is? Gervais didn't call back?"

"Carl says he didn't, but I don't believe him. He tried to make it sound like it was all a bluff. He said that if Gervais really had Jimmie Carl, he'd have called back, and he didn't. But that's bullshit, and we both know it. We know Grace tried callin' Carl, before and after midnight. Multiple times. Grace says he wouldn't answer. You know as well as I do that Carl ain't no psychic; he doesn't know when the phone rings if it's his wife or his fuckin' nightmare. So, either Grace is lying about him not answerin', or Carl is, and I know where to put my money." We'd gotten to the rear of the Western Auto, and I motioned for Ricky to pull into the loading area and park next to Donnie's truck.

"So what are we doing?" he asked.

"Give me your handcuffs," I said. "I'm goin' back upstairs. I'll need this car in a little bit too."

Ricky turned the ignition off and handed me his cuffs. "Boss, I got your back, you know that. But—"

"Don't worry, Ricky. I'm not lookin' to hurt Carl, but I am takin' him to meet Gervais. If it's not too late. This isn't about revenge. Not yet, anyhow. I still aim to get that boy back to his mother."

Ricky nodded.

"I'll be right back," I said, and I went upstairs.

I found the office door shut. I'd splintered the frame earlier, and the door wouldn't latch, but when I tried it, it also wouldn't budge easily. It felt like Carl had wedged something heavy against it.

"Carl. Goddamn it. Open up," I shouted.

"What do you want now, Elmore? I said all I had to say to you. Go away."

"Open up. Let's not do this again."

"Go away. I'll call the sheriff this time. I can have you arrested."

We didn't have time for Carl's games. We both knew what the outcome was going to be, but for some reason, pride I guess, he wouldn't let us get there easily. "I'm comin' in," I said. "If you've gone and picked up a damn gun again, I'm tellin' you now to put it down carefully. Don't make me take it away a second time." My thigh had tightened up, and I could tell that it was swollen from busting in the door the first time. I have scar tissue, what the doctors call adhesive lesions, associated with the metal plate and screws in my leg, and I'd torn something earlier. This time I put my shoulder to the door. There was definitely something up against the it, but it gave easily enough, and I could hear whatever it was sliding backward on the other side.

The whole time, Carl kept yelling, "Don't you come in! Don't you come in! I'm tellin' you, don't you come in! I mean it Elmore! I'll shoot! I will!"

I pushed the door about halfway open and stepped into the room. I was right, Carl had shoved the couch against it. I guess it never dawned on him that if he could push it all the way across the room on the waxed wooden floor of his office, that I could push it just as easily in the opposite direction.

"I told you not to come in," Carl said. He was again standing in the middle of the room, again leveling the same shotgun toward my chest. "I got my legal rights to shoot you as an intruder. I'll say I mistook you for Gervais. No one will blame me. No jury in the—"

This time, I didn't have the energy to warn him. I grabbed the barrel again, same movement as before, and twisted it up and to the left. Another man might have learned, but not Carl Trimble. He let go and cried out and grabbed the same finger that he'd claimed I'd broken before. I don't think I did the first time, but I was more pissed off the second time around, and maybe I had a bit more enthusiasm.

He bent over and grabbed his right hand with his left, and half bawling, half whimpering, kept saying, "you broke it this time. For sure. Damn you. Fuck you. Damn. Damn. Damn." He varied it some, but he repeated some version of that a half-dozen times.

"We're takin' a ride. One way of the other, you're comin' with me," I said. "I'm askin' nicely."

"Go to hell. My finger. Damn you, Elmore! You broke it, you prick. I ain't goin' nowhere. You broke it. Damn you. I ain't goin'. I'm safe here."

"Like hell," I said. I didn't have time or patience, and I took the barrel of the shotgun in both hands. "Carl, look at me," I said. "Look at me."

He took his eyes off of his injured hand long enough to look up. When he did, I jabbed the gun butt into his nose. I didn't do it hard enough to break any bone; I've done that to him a couple of times, and I've developed a good sense now on what it takes, but that doesn't mean that it didn't hurt like hell. Blood spurted, and he staggered backward and started to fall. Normally, the couch might have caught him, and he would have landed softly, but he'd pushed it up against the door and it was now situated at an angle in the middle of the room; without it as a backstop, he crumpled against the wall and slid to the floor. He was holding his nose and blood was quickly spotting his shirt. He rolled up into a ball like a pill bug and began whimpering.

I reached down and grabbed him by the back of his collar. He's a fat boy, and it wasn't easy, but I'm a big boy and I was motivated, and I jerked him more-or-less to his feet in one movement. "Like I told you, Carl, we're takin' a ride. I tried askin' nicely," I said. I started pulling him toward the door.

It took him a few steps to finally get his feet under him, but soon he began walking under his own power; all I had to do was steer him since he couldn't see; his eyes were filled with smeared blood and he was holding his face with both hands. I got him down the stairs and out through the loading bay with a minimum of barked shins, and then through the connecting door to Larson's shoe store.

Ricky was standing beside the car when we got outside.

"You all right?" he asked, and then he looked at the blood covering Carl's shirt. "I was about to come up. He okay?"

"Yeah," I replied.

Carl started to say something, but then he realized that Ricky wasn't there to save him, and he kept quiet.

"He took more convincin' than he should have," I continued. "You'd think he'd learn." I led Carl to the squad car and put him in the back seat and closed the door.

Ricky watched it all. "You're limping worse."

"I'm okay."

He nodded, and then gestured to Carl, who was bent double, holding his face. We could hear him cussing to himself. "Not about revenge," Ricky said.

"Don't have time for that. It's about tryin' to get Jimmie Carl back alive. I told you that. I'll settle my score with this sorry piece of shit later. I just hope there's still time to make that meetin' with Gervais. We need to go."

"Where?"

"Ring Johnson's place. if I'm right. If I'm wrong . . ."

"We going alone? You want the state police, or are we brassing this out ourselves?"

I shook my head. "No. Ben Cooper neither. We're past that, I'm afraid. If I'm right, I may be able to talk Gervais into lettin' that boy go. I just have to hope that there's still time, but I'm sure this delay isn't puttin' him more at ease. You know as well as I do, Gervais isn't goin' to be taken alive; he's got nothin' to lose. A bunch of cars and men with badges and guns will only jack this up more than it is."

"You think he'll just let you have Jimmie Carl? Don't see it. Makes more sense to just kill all of us."

"He wants Carl, and I'm goin' to deliver him. I gotta believe he doesn't want to hurt that boy."

"So what do we do?"

"I want you to take the truck. It's too noisy, and I want to get close enough to Gervais to see what the hell's goin' on before I spook him into doin' somethin' we all regret."

"Not tracking here, Chief. Why two cars? Why the truck at all? If it's too noisy for you, it's too noisy for me. It's going to be hard to provide much in the way of back-up if he hears me coming."

"Carl and me are headed out there by ourselves. You can follow later. First, I need you to go and get Ellen Mae and take her over to Grace's."

"Boss—"

"Listen, Ricky, I don't have time to argue. This is likely to go south; maybe it already has. If anythin' happens to Jimmie Carl, I want Ellen Mae there when Grace hears about it." I paused as I thought about what I'd said. "And I guess I want Grace there if Ellen Mae hears somethin' about me."

"Watching your back is more important to me."

"It's not for me. I thank you Ricky, but if you want to watch my back, you'll do like I ask. Get Ellen Mae. Then you come on out to the Johnsons' farm. I can handle it until you get there, and if I can't, then it's probably already too late."

Ricky looked at me quietly and then hurried to the cab of the truck. "Wilco, but for the record, boss, I'm not convinced. I think it's a dumb idea."

"For the record, I think you're right."

"Roger. I'll be right behind you."

"I know you will. But do like I ask first, get Ellen Mae over to Grace's, and then get on out there. And let's hope I got this figured right."

"My money's on you, even if it's a dumb idea."

I opened the driver's door of the cruiser and started to get in. "A fool and his money, Ricky. Your father never tell you that?"

"Watch yourself until I get there, Ray."

"Will do, Chief Forrest," I replied, and then, "Listen, there's a Springfield thirty-ought-six in Carl's office. On the couch. It's got a scope. Looks like a good weapon. Might come in handy. Just make sure there's a round in the chamber."

"Roger."

"And Ricky," I said. "Tell Grace that I intend to keep my promise."

CHAPTER 55

Split Tree, Arkansas
Wednesday, November 20, 1963

With the sky clear, the thin sliver of a waxing crescent moon laying low on the horizon made the asphalt road stand out like a pale grey ribbon against the dark harvested fields. That allowed me to kill the headlights a quarter of a mile before we got there, and I shut off the engine when we were still a football field away, letting the car coast on the level road as far as it would. We came to stop within sight of Ring Johnson's mailbox. I sat in the car, watching the house in the distance for a minute, and then, after warning Carl that I'd rip his throat out if he made a sound, I rolled the window down and listened. There was a late season nightjar finishing its evening, and the crickets were chirping slowly in the cool air, but for the most part it was quiet in the way that only harvested fields in the dead of night can be quiet.

I rolled the window back up and then clicked the dome light switch, so it wouldn't come on when I opened the door. I turned to Carl in the back seat. "Reach up here with one of your arms," I said quietly. "I don't care which."

"Go to hell. Why?" he responded, too loudly. "What are we doin' here? You're in enough trouble, Elmore. This is kidnappin'. I'm tellin' you—"

"And I'm tellin' you, lower your damn voice and do like I said."

"Why?"

"Because we're out of time, and I'll hurt you if you don't."

He was still favoring his right hand and its swollen finger, and he stuck out his left hand, and I impatiently grabbed it and pulled him forward as I put the handcuff around his wrist. Before he could pull back and cause me any more trouble, I clicked the other end to the steering wheel. "You'll be all right out here. As long as you keep quiet," I said. He started to say something, but I quickly cut him off. "What don't you understand? Now shut your mouth and listen. I'm goin' in there. You're stayin' here. You make a noise, you do anythin' to screw this up, you do anythin' more that puts that boy at risk, and I'll come back here and kill you. It's that simple. Don't overthink this, Carl. I'll kill you myself, and Gervais will have to get in line to piss on your corpse. You understand me? If you do, you can nod."

He did.

"Good," I said. I patted my pants pocket, with my leg going numb, I couldn't feel my service revolver pressing against my thigh; I was sure it was still there, but I wanted to double-check. Then I grabbed my flashlight, and as quietly as I could, I opened the car door. My leg had stiffened considerably just in the short drive, and it was all I could do to bend it and swing it out of the car. Once I got to my feet, and got my balance, it worked a little better, but the pain had also gotten worse. It made quick movement difficult.

I slowly walked up the road, not because of my leg but because I wanted to make sure I wasn't walking into something. I stayed in the shadows and stopped every few feet to hold my breath and listen. All I could hear was my pulse throbbing in my ears. And then I'd walk a few more steps. I got to the house and went up the driveway, and then worked my way around the front of the house, and one side, and then back to the driveway. It was dark. I knew the power was turned off, and so I looked carefully for even the faintest hint of a candle. If there were people inside, awake, or alive, they were either in the dark or were further back in the house, or upstairs. Or maybe I'd figured it all wrong.

I noticed that the garage door was closed. I'd opened it when Ben and I looked around the day Ring's body was found, and I know we hadn't closed it, but I couldn't remember if it was open when I brought Ellen Mae out. I also knew that I couldn't risk the noise of opening it to check, but then I remembered seeing a small window in the back wall. I walked around to the rear and tried to look in. It was pitch black, but I could make out the dark shape of a car; one that hadn't been there the other day. I covered the lens of the flashlight with my left hand and turned it on, and then I slowly adjusted the spacing of my fingers to control the beam of light. I held it up against the glass window pane and widened my fingers until the chrome grillwork of the car was visible. It was the humped nose of a Chevy Bel Air.

CHAPTER 56

Split Tree, Arkansas
Wednesday, November 20, 1963

As quickly as I could manage, I walked around the house, crouching at each window and trying to look in. Everything was dark, and I didn't see any movement. I made a complete loop and ended back at the driveway, beside the door to the kitchen, and I was standing there, trying to figure out what to do next, trying to calm my breathing and my heartrate, getting ready to try the knob, when I heard someone inside. It sounded like the chain lock on the door being removed. A second later, I heard the doorknob start to turn.

There wasn't anywhere to hide and my leg wouldn't let me respond fast enough to get around the corner, but it was dark, and I took advantage of that as best I could and flattened myself against the side of the house, just to the left of the door. I dropped the flashlight to free up my left hand; in my right I had my service revolver.

The door opened, and then the screen door pushed outward, and in what little moonlight there was, I saw a slender arm emerge, holding a small suitcase. Even in the dim light I could tell that it was Lidia Fernandez. Exposed like I was didn't give me many options, and as soon as she cleared the door, I grabbed her from behind and pulled her tight against my body and pressed the barrel of my .38 hard against the side of her head. She dropped her suitcase and got out a small cry of alarm before I got my hand clamped down over her mouth, but she also quickly realized what was happening and stopped moving and made no effort to pull free.

I expected Gilbert Gervais to be right behind her, alerted by her short cry, and I quickly pulled her backward and moved us a few feet away from the door. As big as he is, I needed the space if he came bulling out behind her. He didn't show.

"Don't move; just listen. I got no intention of hurtin' you, unless you make me. I also won't hesitate if you do," I whispered to her. "I'm not here after you. Or Gervais. You understand?" I waited for her to nod before I continued. "I'm here for the boy. That's all. Is he here?"

I slowly took my hand away from her mouth, but she didn't respond at first, and I motivated her by pushing the barrel of my revolver tighter against the side of her head. The last thing in the world that I'd normally do is hurt a woman, but Jimmie Carl had changed the normal rules.

"Looks like y'all plannin' to leave," I continued. "If that boy's here, that's all I care about. Give him over to me, and y'all can go. You got my word. We go our separate ways. You understand?"

She nodded. "*Sí*. Yes," she responded quietly.

"Where's Gervais?" I asked.

She didn't answer.

I screwed the gun tighter into her head.

"Inside," she said.

"How about bein' more specific. I don't want that boy hurt, and I'm guessin' your man doesn't want you hurt. We do this right, we can all be happy."

She didn't respond until I put more pressure on the gun barrel. "He upstairs."

"And the boy?"

"Upstairs. Both of them."

"And he's all right?"

She nodded.

"Let's keep it that way," I said. "Now, we're goin' to go inside. Slow and quiet. Anythin' happens, and you'll never know it. Understand? You'll be the first one down. But you help me, and no one needs to get hurt. Not you; not your boyfriend. No fast movement; no sounds. *Comprendes?*"

She nodded again.

I grabbed a handful of her hair at the back of her neck, and I repositioned the gun barrel behind her right ear. I pushed her forward, and she opened the door, and we stepped inside.

Once we were in the kitchen, I tugged on her hair, like you'd rein in a horse, and signaled her to stop. We stood still for a few seconds. The house was quiet and dark, but once my ears adjusted to it, I could make out the low sound of someone singing coming from the upstairs. Not loud enough to be heard from the outside, but in the relative quiet of the house, it was clear enough. "Which room are they in?" I whispered to her.

"Bedroom. Big bedroom," she answered.

"Both of them?"

She nodded.

"Good. Now, slow. Let's take it slow. When we get upstairs, I want you to call him out into the hallway. Get him to step out. Tell him you need help with your suitcase or somethin'. Understand? Not a sound until then. I don't want to hurt anyone."

She nodded.

We moved slowly and started up the stairs. The sound of the music grew louder. It was Marty Robbins singing *Sometimes I'm Tempted.* The stairs creaked a few times, and with each one I grabbed Lidia Fernandez's hair tighter, to make sure she understood to not make any more noise than we had to.

At the top of the stairway, I paused us. The music was coming from the main bedroom. It had a tinny sound, like that from a small radio. There was also a faint flickering light coming from the doorway as well.

We stepped forward. My leg wouldn't let me move quickly, and I didn't want the stairs at my back if I had to react to Gervais. I pulled her hair and leaned down and put my mouth close to her ear. "Now," I whispered. "Call him out here. Don't get anyone hurt."

She didn't move.

I tightened the grip on her hair. "Do it," I said. "Be smart."

"Gilberto," she called. "Gil, I need some help, *por favor.*"

I kept my eyes on the open doorway. The light continued to flicker but there was no indication of any movement.

I pressed the gun barrel into her neck.

"Gilberto," she repeated, louder. "*Amorcito.* Can you help me?"

I heard a floor board behind me creak under a shifting weight. "You move an' you da dead man, you," a voice said.

CHAPTER 57

Split Tree, Arkansas
Wednesday, November 20, 1963

Gilbert Gervais was behind me. He'd been in Joe Dennis's room, and he'd been waiting on us. Waiting on me. And now he'd gone and gotten the jump on me. "No reason for anyone to be dead," I replied calmly.

"Let her go," Gilbert Gervais said. "Now."

"Not goin' to happen," I replied.

"You okay, *Cher*? He hurt you?" he asked her. "I was checkin' on da boy. I tink I hear you yell."

"I'm fine, Gilberto. *Bien*," Lidia answered. "Do as the man says."

"You even scratch her, you die painful," he said to me.

"Didn't come here to hurt anyone," I replied. I slowly began to turn us so that I could see him. I kept a good hold of her hair. Once I had eyes on him, I said, "I'm here for the boy. He gets hurt and both of you die painful, right here. Right now."

Gilbert Gervais was standing at the end of the hall, barely visible in the shadows. He was even bigger than I'd pictured him, and I'd pictured him to be plenty big. He was a good couple inches taller than me, which is not something that I'm used to seeing, and he was as wide as a broom handle at the shoulders. I put him at maybe 290, 300, mostly gristle and muscle and concrete. He had an arm, the diameter of a fireplace log, stretched out straight, pointing a large caliber revolver directly at my head.

"You no his papa," Gilbert Gervais said. "Who you den?"

"Doesn't matter," I replied. "Let me have him, and I'll leave. Simple as that."

"Let her go first."

"I'm not stupid."

"You abou' be dead, you."

"Not what I'm aimin' for, but I'll have some company if that's how it goes; startin' with her. Now, we're goin' to step into the bedroom where we can all see each other. It's sort of tight out here, and I don't think that's puttin' either of us at ease." The truth of the matter is that he had the advantage on me; what little light there was in the hallway was to my back, and while Lidia and I were silhouetted, he was barely visible in the shadows. The fact that he hadn't already blown my head off was about the only thing I had going in my favor.

He didn't respond, and I took advantage of that to slowly begin backing into Ring's bedroom at the other end of the hall. I thought if I could get us in there, at least he wouldn't have the advantage of me being backlit. Gilbert Gervais followed; his gun stayed pointed directly at my head.

I got Lidia and me into the bedroom without getting shot between the eyes. There were several candles lit, including a couple on Jo Johnson's vanity beside a small battery-operated radio. The room wasn't bright, but in contrast to the darkness of the hallway, it was like the sun had come up. I looked around but saw no sign of Jimmie Carl. Either they didn't have him, or he was in another room. Or he was already dead. I eased us over to the bathroom door and quickly looked in, making sure no one was there, I'd been caught unaware once and didn't need to make the same mistake again, and then I moved us back toward the center of the room. The bed was messed up, and I suspect that Gervais and Lidia Fernandez had been in it. Otherwise, it looked much like it had when Ellen Mae and I saw it.

"Where is he?" I asked her. "The boy? Where's the boy?"

"The other bedroom," she replied.

"Tell your friend to go get him. Bring him in here," I said. "I want to see him."

"I no goin'," Gervais said in response. "Wha' do now, Lid?"

I pressed the barrel of the gun into her skull as a reminder. "Do it."

"Gilberto, it is okay. Get the boy. It is okay," she said calmly, as if she was trying to sooth a worried child.

Gervais was reluctant, but he did as she instructed him. He backed out of the doorway, keeping his pistol pointed at my head until the last moment, and then he disappeared into the dark hallway. He returned a minute later, with Jimmie Carl in front of him. He had his left hand, which was the size of a catcher's mitt, gripping Jimmie Carl's jaw, and just like I was doing to Lidia Fernandez, he had his revolver pressed tightly into the side of the boy's face. Jimmie Carl's hands were tied with a length of cord.

"You see? I told you, the boy, he is safe," Lidia Fernandez said.

"You all right, boy?" I asked.

Jimmie Carl nodded and started to answer, "Yes, sir, Big Ray, I—"

"Shut up," Gilbert Gervais said to him. He tightened his grip, and it made Jimmie Carl grimace and go quiet. "Who you?" he asked me.

"Nobody. I'm just here for the boy."

Gervais squinted and looked closely at me in the dim light. "You wearin' a damn badge. You a cop. A damn cop. You a dead man comin' here, you."

"I'm just here for the boy. Untie him. Let me have him, and we all go our own ways," I said.

He squeezed Jimmie Carl's head tighter. "I come here for dis boy's papa. I goin' kill him, me. Why ain't he here? Where he? He no answer da phone. Why dat? He call you instead?"

"No."

"Like hell. Where he den? I no leavin' widout killin' him, me."

"Give me the boy, and I'll give you Carl Trimble," I said. "You can do what you want with him."

"Bullshit. You a cop. Wha' you mean? You ain' goin' jus' give him to Gilber'," he said.

"I told you, I don't want either of you. I want this boy. I want him to get home to his mother, and that's all I want, and I'll give you whoever I need to if that's what it takes."

"Leave her go," he said.

"Been over that. Not goin' happen," I said. "Not until that boy is safe."

Gilbert Gervais looked confused. He was a man who could likely tear me in two without even looking for a weak seam, but he also was a man who best followed a plan, and none of this was in his plan. He looked at Lidia Fernandez. "Wha' do now, Lid?" he asked her.

CHAPTER 58

Split Tree, Arkansas
Wednesday, November 20, 1963

Lidia Fernandez shook her head. "There are state police all over. Many. We saw them earlier," she said to me. "If we give you this boy, how do we get away?"

"That's your problem. They're goin' to be lookin' for you no matter what happens here. Killin' this boy isn't goin' help you," I replied. "But, if you let him go, maybe I can. I grew up here. I know every back road in this county. You let the boy go, and maybe I'll tell you how to avoid the roadblocks. That's your best chance of gettin' out of here alive."

"How abou' you tell us anyways," Gilbert Gervais said. He punctuated it by gripping Jimmie Carl's jaw tighter.

Jimmie Carl made a small sound.

"You go easy on that boy," I said. I pulled Lidia's hair until she made a similar sound. "No call for that. You let him go, you got me; as soon as he's safe, I'll let loose of this woman, and I'll put my gun down."

"And you would help us get out of here?" Lidia asked.

"I can."

"Firs', we wan' Carl Trimble," Gervais said. "I goin' kill him."

"I can give him to you," I replied. "In exchange for the boy; one for one."

"You have him?" Lidia Fernandez asked. "Where?"

"I do. I got him handcuffed outside. I came prepared to trade."

Gilbert Gervais took the gun from beside Jimmie Carl's head and pointed it at me again. "You got him, you give him up now. Maybe I no kill you, me."

I pulled Lidia Fernandez's hair again until she winced. I needed to make my point. "Don't be stupid. I'm willin' to give you Trimble, but if you want this girl's brains to decorate the wallpaper, keep pushin' me. There's two ways this can end. Make the right choice."

"Both of you men put your rabos, *your penises away,"* Lidia Fernandez said to us, and then to me, she asked, "You will really give us Carl Trimble?"

"As soon as the boy's safe. My car's outside. He can take it and go. Let him leave. I'll stay, and as soon as he's clear of here, I'll give you Trimble."

"And how do we know this boy will not drive down the road and tell the police?" she asked.

"You're a smart woman, figure it out. I tracked you down. I knew where to find you, if I wanted the police here, I'd have called them before I came."

Lidia Fernandez nodded. "And why you no do that?"

"The more cops, the more guns . . . like you say, lot of dicks swingin' . . . I didn't think that was goin' to help the situation. I just want the boy to get out of here unharmed."

She nodded some more. "And you will let us have Carl Trimble? Maybe that is why you did not call the police. Maybe other policemen would not let you do that, no?"

"I value this boy more than I care for Carl Trimble. It's that simple. I'm willin' to make that trade," I said. "Others may not be. It's good for all of us that I'm the one here."

"Maybe Gilber' jus' shoo' you an' den kill de boy too, an' den I go find Trimble, me," Gervais said.

"Maybe you let her do the thinkin'. She knows that if try anythin', she'll be dead before I hit the floor, and you'll never get Trimble on your own. Where I have him, you can look for the next week and not find him, and you don't have a week. Now, time's wastin'. The sun will be up shortly. If you got any chance of gettin' out here alive, you better make your choice now."

"Maybe I jus'—" Gervais started to say.

"*Maybe you just shut up, Gilberto. Let me think,*" Lidia Fernandez cut him off. "How do we do this? How do you get us this Trimble?"

"You and me will go get him," I said. "We go outside; we walk down the road; we get him; we come back. As soon as we get back, you let the boy go. I stay. You can have me and Trimble."

"And you tell us how to get away? *Sí?*"

"You let the boy go first. *Sí.*"

CHAPTER 59

Split Tree, Arkansas
Wednesday, November 20, 1963

Getting down the stairs was harder than I'd figured it was going to be. My leg would hardly bend, and feeling my way down the steps in the dark, while keeping Lidia Fernandez under control, was a problem. I'd told Gervais that Lidia and I would go down first, and that he and Jimmie Carl should stay in the bedroom until Lidia called for them, and then they could come down. He wasn't happy about letting Lidia out of his sight again, but she told him that it was okay. She also told him that he was to put a bullet through Jimmie Carl's head if I tried anything.

When Lidia Fernandez and I finally got to the bottom of the stairway, I paused while my eyes adjusted to the dark. It also gave me a chance to listen for any sound of Gervais moving around. As big as he was, he couldn't take a step without the floor creaking under the strain. I didn't hear anything, which told me he was doing as Lidia had instructed him to do and was staying put in the bedroom until she called for him. That was a good thing to know.

I let go of her, and we walked across the living room to the kitchen. I remembered from one of my earlier searches of the house that there was a box of candles on the counter by the sink, and we soon got some lit, and I had her carry a couple of them back to the living room. They didn't provide much light, but it was better than stumbling around in the dark. The one thing I knew for sure was that I didn't want to go outside and have to come back into a dark house where I couldn't see 300 pounds of Gilbert Gervais waiting to shoot me or gun slap me.

"You are limping. You are hurt?" Lidia Fernandez asked me as she was trying to get one of the candles to stand up on the fireplace mantle.

"You care?"

She shrugged and moved to the coffee table to put the other candle down. "No."

"War injury. I'm fine," I said. I decided it was to my advantage to get her talking. "Y'all don't have much to lose, I know that. But I also know you don't really want to hurt that boy," I said. "You're not like that. I don't think Gervais is either."

"You know about me and Gilberto?"

"Enough."

She shrugged. "Then you know it all. You are right. Gilberto, he cannot be captured. This you understand?"

"I do. All the more reason to let that boy go and try to get out of here as quickly as you can. The longer that he's missin', the more heat he's goin' to draw. You might be able to get out of here on some of the back roads, if you leave now, but if he doesn't get home to his mother soon, there won't be a cop within a hundred miles of this place that won't be lookin' for you, and they'll shoot on sight. I told you, I figured out you were here, others will to."

"Gil will not go until he kills Trimble. Then we will leave. He has family in . . ." She caught herself and almost smiled. "First he must kill this man Trimble. He must do this."

"Let me take that boy and go. Talk to him. He'll listen to you."

She nodded. "*Sí*. He listens to me. I am the one who told him to kill Trimble."

CHAPTER 60

Split Tree, Arkansas
Wednesday, November 20, 1963

There was a creaking sound of a heavy weight moving around upstairs. "Lidia? Lid? *Cher*? Where you at? You okay?" Gilbert Gervais called out. "Cher? Wha's goin' on? Wha's takin' so long? Talk to Gilber'."

I motioned for Lidia Fernandez to come toward me, and I stood behind her, but I didn't grab her hair this time. "Tell him to come on down. Slowly," I said to her. Calmly.

"Gilberto. I'm fine. Come down," she called out. "Bring the boy."

I kept my gun pressed lightly into the middle of her back, and my left hand on her shoulder, where I could grab her hair quickly if I needed to control her, and we watched Gilbert Gervais and Jimmie Carl come down the stairs. Gervais was an easy target, he was a foot-and-a-half taller than Jimmie Carl, even taller because he was on the stairs behind him, and was easily twice as wide. If it came to it, I was sure I could take out both Gervais and Lidia, but I wasn't sure I could do it without Jimmie Carl getting hurt. If I was planning to shoot it out with them, this was probably going to be my best chance, but I decided to let it play itself out.

Once they got off the stairs, Gervais kept Jimmie Carl in front of him, but he pointed his pistol at me. "What do now?" he asked.

"Now Lidia and I are goin' outside, and you're goin' to stay right where you are," I said. "You don't move. I don't want to come back and not see you right there. I don't see you, I get nervous, and that's not good. We'll be back, and we'll have Trimble with us, and you're goin' to be standin' right there where I can see you." I squeezed Lidia's shoulder. "Let's go."

I backed us into the kitchen and then out the side door. Once I was sure that Gervais wasn't following us, we sped up, as much as my leg would allow, and we walked quickly to the road and then to my car.

When we got there, Lidia Fernandez laughed. "This the secret spot where you keep Trimble? We would have found him."

"Yeah. Well, now you don't have to look," I replied. I positioned her a couple of feet away from the front fender, and I opened the door.

Carl Trimble erupted when he saw Lidia Fernandez standing there. "What the hell? What's she doin' here? How stupid are you, Elmore? Shoot her. Shoot her now, and let's go before—"

"Shut up Carl. I told you to stay quiet," I said. I unlocked the cuff on the steering wheel, and then opened the rear door. "Get out," I told him. "And do it quietly."

He didn't, at least not at first, and I had to reach in and grab him by his shirt collar and pull him out. Once he'd gotten back to his feet, I took hold of his wrist and pulled him to the front of the car and slapped the open cuff on Lidia Fernandez's right arm. "Carl, meet Miss Lidia Fernandez, although I think you've met before," I said.

"What are you doin'? You're goddamn crazy, Elmore; that's what you are. You know who this woman is? Shoot her. You got a gun. She's with him," he said. "Arrest her. You have any idea—"

She slapped him.

"You bitch, I—" Carl started to say.

She slapped him again. Harder.

"Goddamn bitch, I ought—"

She slapped him a third time.

"Shut up, Carl," I said. "I'm tempted to take the cuffs off and let her have a piece of you right here and now, except that's not part of the deal. Jimmie Carl's up there in Ring's house, and I plan to get him out. Listen up, this is the plan, and you're goin' to follow it. We're goin' to walk up there. All three of us. And we're goin' do it without any of your bellyachin'. I've got my gun, and I'll keep it pointed at her, and I'll use it if need be. Now, once we get up there, I'll unlock you two, but I'll still have my gun." I turned to Lidia Fernandez and put the keys to the handcuffs in her jacket pocket. *"You'll need these,"* I said to her.

She looked about as happy being handcuffed to Carl Trimble as he looked to be cuffed to her, but she also knew what the plan was and was willing to be patient. She knew she'd get him soon enough. Carl didn't completely understand what was going on, and he didn't want to cooperate, but I hadn't put it up for a vote. I pushed him and dragged him and got him moving. I told them both to stay quiet and keep to the shadows, just in case Gervais had decided to follow us outside and jump us. Carl started to mouth off a couple of times, but I rapped him hard on the back of his head with my gun barrel when he did, and he soon got the message. When we got close to the kitchen door, I grabbed him by the shirt collar and brought them both to a stop. I needed to make sure that Gervais had stayed put; I didn't want to tangle with him as soon as we stepped inside. I had Lidia Fernandez call out, and he answered; he was still in the living room.

I opened the screen door and pushed Lidia in first, with Carl close behind. Cuffed together, I didn't have to worry about either of them making a quick move. I followed.

Gervais had done like he'd been told, and was still standing at the base of the stairway, Jimmie Carl in front of him. He still had his pistol pressed against Jimmie Carl's head, but when the three of us walked into the living room, he pointed the gun first at me and then at Carl and then back at me, not sure who the better target was. He looked at the blood on Carl's face. "Hoo. You do dat?" he asked me. He laughed. "Looks to Gilber' like da job, it is half done."

"I delivered him," I said.

"Part of him. He hurt as bad as he look?"

"Bloody nose. Plenty of him left for you," I answered.

"Yeah. Da's a good ting. I tell you, Gilber' no tink you'd do it, you bein' a cop." Then he looked at Lidia. *"You okay, Cher?"*

"I am fine, Gilberto," she answered.

Gervais turned his attention back to Carl. *"Mais.* You. Fa' boy. You remember ol' Gilber' Gervais?" he asked. "Long time, no see, *mon ami."*

"Elmore," Carl pleaded with me. "What are you doin'? You can't do this. You got a gun. Shoot them. Both of them. Do it." He tried to get behind Lidia Fernandez, to put her in between Gervais and himself. She pulled free.

"You no answer da phone, fa' boy," Gervais continued. "I tink da's what we goin' call you. *Fa' Boy.* How dat? Tell me, Mister Fa' Boy Carl Trimble, how come you no answer, you? I call you. Many times, I call. You no wan' to talk to Gilber', no?"

"I didn't do anythin'," Carl said. "I didn't hurt anyone. Elmore. *Ray.* You have a gun. You've got to stop them. You're a cop. This is a mistake. It was all my brother. He's the one." He looked at Lidia Fernandez. *"I didn't hurt you. You remember. I tried to stop them."*

She nodded. *"Sí.* I remember. I remember your brother. Very much, I remember. I remember you watched. I remember you laughed," she replied. "I remember all." She reached up with her left hand and pulled back the hair on the right side of her face, looping it behind her ear; she turned her head to catch the light of the candle. Her ear was deformed by scar tissue and the top half of it was missing. "I remember your brother. But I also remember you." Then she spit on him.

Gervais laughed. "Hey, Fa' Boy, you still no told Gilber' why you no answer da phone. You no care for your son? Huh? Dat it? You no care, you?" He nodded. "Or maybe you jus' a damn chicken. *Mais,* I tink da's it. I tink I know you. You jus' like my old man. He was worthless piece da crap too. I tink you no answer da phone 'cause you too damn chicken to try an' save your own boy. Is dat right? Huh? Mister Fa' Boy Chicken Man." He turned Jimmie Carl's head toward him. *"Tell me, boy, what we do wid a papa like dat? Huh? I tink I do you a favor. I tink I goin' kill him for you."* He turned his attention back to Carl Trimble, "I tink I goin' kill you Fa' Boy Carl Trimble," he said. "I tink da's wha' I do."

"Let the boy go first," I said. "Then he's yours."

"Yeah? Why? Maybe dis boy, he wan' see Gilber' kill Fa' Boy Chicken Man," Gervais answered.

"Let him go. That was the deal."

"Or wha'?" Gervais said. "Maybe I kill you too, *Elmore*."

"Shut up, Gilberto," Lidia Fernandez said. "You talk too much."

That stung Gervais. He looked quickly at her. "We need jus' kill him now," he said.

"But I didn't do nothin'," Carl pleaded. He looked at me. "Elmore, tell them."

"You hurt *mon Cher*, an' you no even try your boy to save, no," Gervais said. *"Ça va.* Da's plenty for me. I vote guilty. Guilty as charged, Fa' Boy Chicken Man. An' Gilber' Gervais, he sentence you to da bullet in da ass."

"He ain't mine. That bastard's not mine. Why should I care about him?" Carl said. "And I didn't hurt her. Why are you doin' this?"

Gervais started to say something, but before he could get it out, Carl's words made it into his brain. He knotted his forehead. "Wha' you mean, you?" He looked at Lidia Fernandez for help. *"Wha' he mean?"* he asked.

No one answered.

Gervais pointed the gun at Carl. "Wha' you mean Fa' Boy? Wha' you mean he no your son?" He gripped Jimmie Carl's jaw harder and shook the boy's head. "You no his papa, den why he bring you here, you? Huh?"

"Because he's my son," I said. "And we're wastin' time."

Gervais didn't understand, but Lidia Fernandez did. She looked at me and then began nodding; she looked at Jimmie Carl and back at me. *"Sí.* Yes. I see it." She started laughing. "Oh, Gilberto. We are so stupid," she said. "Yes. Yes."

There wasn't much to be thankful for in that minute, but I will forever be grateful that in the dim candlelight, I couldn't fully see the expression on Jimmie Carl's face.

"We're wastin' time," I said. "You got Trimble. Now let the boy go."

"You firs', *mon ami*," Gervais replied. The look on his face indicated that he still didn't fully understand what was going on, but he understood that he wanted Carl Trimble.

I pointed my pistol at Gervais' head, but I gave Carl Trimble a shove in his direction. He and Lidia Fernandez both stumbled forward. "You got the key," I said to her. "In your pocket. Go ahead and unlock your cuff and fasten it to the table leg, and then step back toward me. Slowly."

I didn't take my eyes off of Gervais, but I could tell that Lidia Fernandez was doing as I'd told her. She unlocked the cuff from her arm and fastened it to the leg of the end table beside the couch, and then she slowly stood up, rubbing her wrist, and took a step backward.

"Okay," I said. "We have a deal. Now let the boy go."

"You said you would tell us how to get away," Lidia said.

"First, the boy goes free. That's the deal. Once he's gone, I'm yours," I answered.

She nodded. "Okay. How do we do this?"

"I give the boy my car keys, and he goes. Your friend keeps a gun on me; I keep a gun on him. Trimble stays cuffed to the table. You stand where I can see you," I said. "We all just sit tight. The boy goes to my car, and he drives back by here." I nodded at the picture window at the front of the room. "As soon as I see the car go by out there, I'll put my gun down. After that, we play by your rules."

"You do dat?" Gervais asked. "Jus' like dat, *Elmore*? I no believe you."

"I'm doin' it." I said.

Lidia Fernandez looked at me for a full minute and then at Gervais. "Let him go, Gilberto, but keep the gun on him."

Gervais did as he was told and let go of Jimmie Carl and shoved him forward. Jimmie Carl took a step and stopped and looked down at Carl Trimble. Maybe he started to say something. I saw Carl reach out toward him.

"Jimmie Carl. Listen to me. Step over to the woman," I told him. And then, to Lidia Fernandez, I said, *"Untie him and step away."*

He slowly moved in front of her and held his arms out, but I don't think he ever looked at her, or me. He kept his eyes on Carl, and I kept my eyes, and the gun, on Gervais.

The cord was tightly knotted, and it took her a minute to get it worked loose, but once his hands were free, she stepped back.

"Now, come on over here, boy," I said. "Come on, son."

Jimmie Carl came over to my side, and I got the keys out of my pocket and held them out so that he could take them. "Now listen to me, son," I said. "Listen carefully. My car's about thirty yards east. You get in it, you drive on past here, and then you hit it and drive like hell out of here. You go home; you go straight to your mother. Understand me?"

"I can't—" he started to protest.

"You go on now," I said sharply. "You go, and I don't want you stoppin' for anythin'. You don't even look in the rearview mirror when you leave here. You understand?"

"I can't—"

"Your mother's waitin' for you. I promised her. Go."

He did.

CHAPTER 61

Split Tree, Arkansas
Wednesday, November 20, 1963

G ervais rolled his shoulder, as if he was trying to work a kink out of it. "Your arm, it get tired, no?" he asked me. He was still standing in front of the stairs, his right arm still extended, the heavy large-caliber revolver still pointed at my head.

"I'm fine, thanks for askin'," I replied. I had my right arm extended; my .38 caliber Colt Commando still pointed at Gervais' head. My arm was about to give out. "But feel free to take a rest if you need. I'll wait."

He laughed. "*Mais*. You funny, you. You know, I no tink you really give us da Fa' Boy. An' you a cop. Wha's dat sayin'? Somethin' abou' da pigs flyin', I tink. You a cop, but you turn him over."

"You drive a hard bargain."

"Yeah? In dat case, how abou' da udder one? Fa' Boy's brudder. Jay Trimble," he said.

"What about him?"

"Can you give him to us too?" Lidia Fernandez asked. "Tell us where to find him."

"I brought you this one."

"We really want da udder one. We spend a week up in Blytheville tryin' to find dat son bitch," Gervais said. "People up dere, dey say he gone disappear. Dey no seen him. Some tink he dead. Dat true?"

"It is."

"Damn," Gervais said. "I wan' dat bastard wors' of all. Really dead? How I know people dey no just say dat? How come you so sure, you?"

"Because I killed him." I wanted to look at Carl Trimble's face when I said that, but I couldn't afford to take my eyes off of Gervais.

Gervais looked at me for a moment. "Damn," he repeated. "Damn, *mon ami*, I tink maybe I start to like you. I hope you made it hurt. Hope you do it slow an' painful. How you do it?"

I shook my head. "I'm not here to discuss my sins."

Gervais laughed again. "Yeah. You an' me, *mon ami*, I tink we are a much alike."

"We're nothin' alike."

Lidia Fernandez slowly stepped next to Gervais and took hold of his left arm. She leaned into him gently and cocked her head and looked at me like she was trying to figure me out. "Tell me, Elmore, how did you find us here? How'd you know we were here?" she asked.

I wasn't inclined to discuss it, but I decided that keeping everyone talking might be the best thing I could do under the circumstances. "Ring Johnson didn't smoke," I said.

"Yeah?" Gervais said. "Dat right? Speak of, I wish you no gone an' say dat, me. Gives me da *envie*." He nudged Lidia Fernandez. *"Hoo, Gilber' could use a smoke right now, me. How abou' it, Cher?"*

Lidia Fernandez reached into his shirt pocket and pulled out a pack of Camels. She put two between her lips and reached down and got one of the candles and used it to light them. When she got them going, she put one in Gervais' mouth.

He took a long drag on the cigarette and exhaled through his nose and then continued. *"Ça c'est bon.* Gilbert, he need dat. So, our old friend Ring, he no smoke, no? I'm no sure I trus' a man who no smoke, but so wha'?"

"When we found his body, it was obvious someone had been stayin' here. Just assumed it was Ring at first, it's his house after all, but there were cigarette butts in the head, and he didn't smoke. His wife neither. That meant someone else was here; probably the same people who left some in the ashtray of his car." I nodded at Gervais. "You also use hair tonic. Sweet smellin' stuff. Ring didn't. It rubs off on the pillows. Didn't take much to figure out you two were stayin' here for a while; it made sense that you'd come back. You'd feel safe here."

Gervais laughed. "Go to bed! How abou' dat? *You hear dat, Lid? Cigarette butts an' da hair awl. Dis man, he gone figure all dat out from some cigarette butts an' my hair awl.*"

I wanted to keep him talking. "I answered your question, now answer one for me. What I don't understand is how you got here in the first place. How'd you came to find the Johnsons?" I prompted him. "I figure it had somethin' to do with the motor lodge. The one up in Lee County. I know you were stayin' there when Trimble and Jo Johnson were there. Is that how it happened?"

He laughed again. "You tell me, Mister Hair Awl Elmore; wha' you tink?"

"Okay. I think she was havin' an affair, and you found out about it. You used that somehow."

"You damn close. You good, Hair Awl Elmore. You know, da funny ting, we pick dat stupid damn motor lodge by chance. By chance. We can flip da coin; we have no idea where to stay when we show up dere; we jus' want a place where people, dey no look for us, an' it look like a place where no one ask too many questions. We been dere but one day when Fa' Boy Trimble, he show up. Of all da places, right? I mean, we look for him, an' he up an' drive into da very place where we stay. How abou' dat? Lidia, she recognize him right off; I did no, but she did. Me, I want to kill him right dere, but he no stay long enough; by da time we sure it was him, dey go. *Mais*, a couple days later, bingo, here dey come again. The manager, he like Lid, he like her a lot; she go to da office, an' he tell her anythin' she ask. He say da Fa' Boy an' Jo come dere regular; couple times a week, he say. We tink we had time, an' we also want to figure out wha' da shit is goin' on wid da Fa' Boy's brudder. So, da next time dey show up, we follow dem when dey go. We see da Fa' Boy drop Jo off here at da house. Lidia tink it up right away. She's a smart one, her. Right away she tinks dis up; I jus' walk right up to da door an' tell Jo dat I was lookin' for some work, me. Of course, she tell Gilber' to get lost, an' den I say, *Hey, don't I recognize you? Sure I do. Ain't you da woman I see wid her husband at da motor lodge?* I say dat. An' den I apologize for botherin' her, an' I say to her dat maybe Gilber', he go to talk to her husband abou' da work. *Mais, I'll jus' go see him,* I say." He chuckled. "Next ting you know, she say she take care of it, an' she convince her husband to hire me. Funny how dat work out."

"And you moved in here?"

He shrugged. "Seem like da ting to do. Ring he could no pay me worth a shit, no, but he offer us da spare bedroom. It was only until he get his crops in."

"And you continued stayin' here; even after you killed Ring Johnson."

Gervais looked genuinely confused. "What da hell you talk abou', Hair Awl Elmore? I no kill him. Now, I'm about to kill da Fa' Boy here, but I no kill no Ring Johnson. Don' blame dat on me."

"Ring didn't blow his own head off," I said. My arm was really beginning to tire. I had to assume that Gervais' arm was as well, but I needed to keep him talking.

"I did no say I no blow his head off," he sort of laughed. "I say I did no kill him."

"Then who did?" I asked. "And where's his wife and boy? You hurt them as well?"

"I tol' you, *mon ami*, I no hurt nobody. Who knows where dey are?" he replied. "Da las' we see dem, dey was gettin' on da

Greyhound bus for Memphis. We take dem to da station. An' dey was jus' fine."

"Memphis?"

He shrugged. "I no tink da's where dey were headed, but da's where da bus was goin'."

I hadn't drawn that box on my yellow pad, but I penciled it in in my head and started connecting it with some of the other boxes that I hadn't been able to make sense of. "She killed her husband," I said. The picture suddenly became clear. "Jo Johnson did, and you helped cover it up."

"*Hey, Lid, dis guy's pretty damn smart for a cop,*" Gervais said to Lidia. "You damn smart, Hair Awl," he said to me. "Although comin' here, dat was pretty dumb. *Couyon, mon ami.* You foolish."

"Why'd she do it?" I asked.

"I was no dere, but I tink maybe da same reason mos' women kill dere husbands; maybe she get tired of gettin' da shit kicked out of her. Dat Ring, dat old boy was one piss-mean drunk. Every night, same ting. We hear dem fight, argue downstairs. Yell. Dey get into it like da cats an' da dogs. An' den, every night, he go slap her around. One night it get so bad dat I almost go downstairs to stop it, but Lid, she say I should tink; tink an' remember what we were dere for, an' mind my own business. It keep gettin' louder an' louder, an' den all of a sudden it get quiet as da graveyard. I tink he kill her, an' me an' Lid go downstairs; we find Jo, she sit at da kitchen table, she covered in blood, her. Ring is on da floor right dere. Damn if she had no gut dat old boy with a kitchen knife. Open him up like a dressed hog."

"And then you made it look like a suicide."

"Yeah. Dat was Lid's idea too. You had to sort of feel sorry for Jo. *Pauvre ti bête.* She no deserve to get boxed around like he do. I hate to see women get hurt. Ain't right. So, she an' Lid work out da plan. She go away, maybe a week, an' den she come back to da sad news dat her husband he kill himself while she gone; no questions dat way. I take him out to da tool shed so he no stink up da house, no, an' den we take her to da bus station da next mornin'. We stay in da house for a few days. We tink for sure she come back by now, but when she no come, Lid, she start to tink maybe Jo was settin' us up, so we go. We go up to Blytheville to look for da Fa' Boy's brudder." He glanced at Lidia Fernandez. *"Ain't dat right, Lid?"*

She'd moved away from him and was looking out the front window. She wasn't listening. "Here comes a car," she said. "It's driving slow."

"As soon as we know it's the boy," I said.

"It is the police car," she said. "It is him. He is speeding up." She stood up and walked back to Gervais' side. "He is gone."

I nodded. I slowly leaned forward and put my revolver on the arm of the couch, and then I stepped back.

CHAPTER 62

Split Tree, Arkansas
Wednesday, November 20, 1963

Gilbert Gervais dropped his arm. "Damn. Damn, dat feel good. I was no so sure I can keep dat up much longer," he said. "I tink maybe I have to go ahead an' shoo' you before my arm he give out." He rolled his shoulder a few times and shifted the gun to his left hand and worked the cramp out of the fingers of his right. He looked at Lidia. *"Wha' do now, Cher? We kill dem? Wha'?"*

"Not yet," Lidia Fernandez said. She turned and looked at me. *"First, how do we get away?"*

"Not sure you do," I answered.

"You said you would tell us how," she responded. "We let the boy go. Now, you tell us. How do we get away? Tell me."

"Can't do that."

"Shit. No time make da *veiller*. I jus' kill dem, me," Gervais said. He pointed his gun at my chest.

"Let me think," Lidia Fernandez said.

"We have no da time," he replied. "As soon as dat boy he get where he go, da cops will swarm out here like da flies on da horseshit. We need go. *Allons.*"

"You will not help us get away?" she asked me again.

I didn't reply.

"What if we don't kill you? What if we let you go?" she asked. "Will you help us then?"

I didn't reply.

"We're not killers," she said. "I think you know that, yes? I don't want to kill you."

I didn't reply.

"Lid," Gervais said. "We have no da time for dis, *Cher*. Hair Awl no goin' talk, no."

She shook her head at me and sighed. She turned to Gervais. "Okay, Gilberto. You can kill them now. Both."

Gervais smiled. "I've been waitin' long long time fo' dis, me. Da Fa' Boy first," he said.

Carl Trimble began pulling frantically at the handcuff. "Elmore, do somethin'. Elmore. You can't let them do this. I didn't hurt no one." He looked at Lidia Fernandez. "*I tried to stop my brother. You remember that. I didn't hurt you. It was them other three. The other ones.*"

Gilbert Gervais stepped forward and looked down at Carl Trimble, who'd crabbed himself backward as far as the handcuff would let him. His body was pressed against the couch, and his face was buried in the seat cushions. Gervais pointed the barrel at the side of Carl's head. "You no idea how many nights I spend tinkin' abou' dis," he said. "*C'est tout*, Fa' Boy Carl Trimble."

I thought about my promise to Grace. I'd gotten Jimmie Carl released, but I'd also promised her that I wouldn't let Gervais hurt Carl. She was worried what it would do to me. It was too late for that.

I never heard the shot. I heard a sharp *pink*; the sound of glass breaking, and I felt something warm and wet splash against my face.

It was blood. And brains.

CHAPTER 63

Split Tree, Arkansas
Wednesday, November 20, 1963

L idia Fernandez turned and screamed; a low, guttural sound of an animal. She seemed to be the one person in the room who understood what was happening. What had just happened,

Gilbert Gervais collapsed on top of Carl Trimble. His head had exploded like a dropped melon, and the couch and carpet and Carl Trimble were already wet with Gervais' blood and tissue.

Carl Trimble went silent; unsure of what had happened and why Gervais had dropped onto him like a bucket of red wet concrete.

Lidia Fernandez went to Gervais, dropping and crawling the last several feet on her knees. She kept calling his name. Over and over.

I stepped forward and picked up my revolver from the arm of the couch, and then I knelt as best as I could and took the revolver from Gervais' hand..

Carl was no longer making sounds or talking, but he was slowly getting his senses back, and he began frantically twisting and pushing, trying to get free of Gervais, trying to get out from under his body.

I stood back and watched. Gervais was dead before he hit the ground. There was nothing for me to do but calm my pulse and wait and get a handle on what was happening.

Trimble finally got the big man's body off of him.

Lidia Fernandez was on her knees, crouched over Gervais, cradling his shattered head in her arms. She was rocking back and forth, crying and softly calling his name.

Ricky Forrest came into the room. He was carrying the scoped 30.06 Springfield from Carl's office, as well as his service revolver. He quickly checked the area, making sure it was secure, before looking directly at me. "You okay, Ray?" he asked.

"Thanks to you," I replied. "Nice shot."

He held up the Springfield. "Good weapon. It's pretty dark in here. Wasn't easy. I didn't think I was going to get a clean look, but he finally moved in front of the window. Good thing he's a big target."

"Wasn't sure you were out there."

"I said I'd be there. I got your back."

"I know. I wish I could say I wasn't worried, but I wasn't sure I could keep them talkin' long enough."

"Wish I could say I wasn't worried either. I can't." Ricky nodded and surveyed the room and looked at Carl. "Everyone okay? Any of that blood his?" Carl still hadn't spoken, and Lidia was still holding Gervais and keening softly.

"No. That's all from Gervais. They didn't have a chance to hurt him," I said.

"Good."

"How about you? You okay?" I asked.

After a long pause, he sighed and said, "Yeah."

"What is it?"

He shook his head. "I don't know. Funny thing, Ray; I killed a lot of men in Korea. Too many. But, you know, the thing is, they were all trying to kill me. It was always them or me. That's an easy decision. I guess I never just bushwhacked a man before. It's different. Not sure how."

"I'm sure it is. Listen, I'm not goin' to tell you it's not, Ricky. I'm the last person to tell you it's okay, but Carl Trimble is alive because of you. So am I. Focus on that."

He nodded some more. "I am, and I'm glad of that; don't get me wrong, but . . ."

I changed the subject. "You see Jimmie Carl?"

"Yes, sir," Ricky responded, glad to refocus his thoughts. "I caught him when he came out of the house. That boy looked shell shocked."

"I don't blame him."

"He said you told him to go straight to his mother's. I told him to do that, but I also told him to tell the trooper out in front of their place what's going on. I told him to make sure the trooper knew where we were and to get out here as quickly as he can. They should be here any minute."

"Not that we need them now," I replied.

"Except to mop up. Literally."

"And to take credit."

"They're welcome to it."

"Agreed," I said.

"What a mess. Oh. Almost forgot. It just came over the radio about twenty minutes ago. Ben called the Phillips County Sheriff and got them looking. They found an abandoned Pontiac Bonneville in West Helena. Looks like the one stolen from Lagrange."

"That right? Makes sense." I gestured at Gervais' body. "They've got Jimmie Carl's Bel Air in the garage outside. They were gettin' ready to leave in it when I got here."

"Good thing you did. I doubt they were planning to take Jimmie Carl with them."

"No. I reckon you're right. We cut that one too close."

"Maybe, but you figured it out."

I pointed at Carl. "No thanks to that son-of-a-bitch."

"Roger. You sure he's okay. He doesn't look so good."

"I suspect he's in shock. Probably will be for a while. I hope not too long. As soon as he recovers, I plan to kick his ass."

Ricky pointed at Lidia Fernandez. "She doesn't look much better."

"No."

"What do you want to do now?"

"You're the chief."

"And you're the first officer on the scene. Your call."

"Well, as much as I'd just as soon leave him chained up like a dog, I reckon we should start by lettin' Carl go. If you can do me another favor, how about unlockin' him? My old leg is makin' it hard to move."

"You okay?"

"Fine. Just a bit gimped up."

"Roger. I can run you past Doc Begley's as soon as the state police get here."

"I'm fine. Just let Carl loose."

"You got my handcuff keys."

I nodded at Lidia Fernandez. "Actually, she does. They're in her jacket pocket."

Ricky holstered his pistol and leaned the rifle against the couch and walked over to Lidia Fernandez. He leaned over and touched her lightly on the shoulder. "Ma'am. I need you to stand up. Please. Slowly," he said.

Lidia Fernandez didn't respond. She just kept rocking back and forth, holding the remains of Gervais' head in her arms.

"Ma'am. Please. I need you to stand up now."

She still didn't respond.

"Ma'am," he said more forcefully. "Miss Fernandez. I'm sorry, but I need you to stand up."

Lidia Fernandez stopped rocking and quietly sat upright. She gently laid Gervais' head down on the carpet. Her eyes were straight forward, not focused on anything in the room.

"Ma'am."

Lidia Fernandez slowly stood up, and Ricky stepped backward to give her room. She turned to him, her eyes still not focusing on anything.

"Ma'am, I need the keys; the handcuff keys."

Lidia Fernandez slowly reached into the pocket of her jacket. She turned her head to look at me, and in that instant, I saw something in her face. I'd seen it before; I knew what it was. I saw her move.

She was fast.

I was slow.

Ricky Forrest turned to me. I saw something in his face. I'd seen it before too. I knew what it was.

"What the hell? Ray—" Ricky said. It was quiet and matter of fact. He looked down at his right breast. Blood was quickly soaking into his shirt like a grotesque sweat stain under his arm.

I looked back at Lidia Fernandez. She looked at me. In the dim light I caught the glint of the straight razor in her hand. She growled and lunged at me.

I raised my pistol and shot her between the eyes.

CHAPTER 64

Split Tree, Arkansas
Wednesday, November 20, 1963

Ricky Forrest looked at me. I can still see it. He looked me right in the eye, and I looked at him. It seemed like an hour. I suspect it was only one or two seconds. Then he blinked a couple of times and dropped to his knees and fell sideways, on top of Lidia Fernandez. Blood was everywhere. She'd sliced through an artery, and he was bleeding out quickly.

I went to him and knelt down. As I did, I felt something in my leg tear away, but it didn't matter. I pulled him off of her body and began looking for the wound. There was a thin, neat slit in his shirt, just under his arm. It was hard to see, the blood was flowing so quickly and there was so much of it, and the cut seemed so small. I tore his shirt off of him, so I could get to the wound. It was just under his arm; it was so small but deep, and the blood was coming out in rhythmic gushes, like water from a well pump.

"Ray," he said to me. "What the—"

"Shut up Ricky. Shut up, damn it. Shit. Let me concentrate," I said. The candles didn't give off much light, and my body cast a dark shadow over him. I leaned to the side and moved his arm to better see where he'd been cut, but that only opened the wound wider; it was the brachial artery, and the blood spurted out, splashing across my chest and into my eyes. I wiped it away with the back of my forearm, as best as I could. I couldn't see, and I needed to get hold of the severed end of the artery. And I couldn't see. It had snapped back into the deep tissue. It was hard to get pressure on it, and I couldn't see it.

"Ray. Kitty," he said

"You're goin' be all right, Ricky. It's okay. Goddamn you Ricky; you're goin' to be okay. Stay with me. Goddamn. Goddammit. Shit. Don't you die on me."

I finally managed to get got hold of the end of it and pinched down hard, but my hands are too old and too big and too stiff. It slipped out of my fingers like a damn watermelon seed. More blood spurted. I got hold of it again. And again. Each time it'd slip away. I put my fingers into the wound and tore his flesh open, ripping the skin and muscle. I needed room to get my fingers deeper inside. Blood was everywhere.

"Ray. Damn—"

"I've got it, Ricky," I said. I didn't, and I needed to open up the wound even more, and I was running out of time. His eyes were wide open, but his focus was going. I leaned heavily onto his arm, putting as much weight on the wound as I could, trying to pinch it off while I looked around. The carpet was soggy with blood. Everything was red, and the candles flickered, and it was hard to see anything. I began slapping the wet carpet in the dark, trying to find it. I finally got the straight razor, and I used it to cut deeper into Ricky's arm, cutting away some of the muscle until I found it. I got hold of the end of the artery and pinched. It slipped away again. I dug after it again.

"Ray. I'm cold. Ray . . ."

"Goddamn you Ricky." I got hold of it again. It slipped again. "I'm here. I'm right here, Ricky."

"Ray. Cold. I'm cold."

"I'm here. I'm with you."

"Ray . . ."

"It's okay, Ricky."

"Kitty."

"You're okay."

"Ray. Don't . . ."

"Ricky? Ricky? Ricky? Aw, goddamn you, Ricky."

CHAPTER 65

Split Tree, Arkansas
Friday, November 22, 1963

I didn't get any sleep on Wednesday, and I was at the hospital until about midnight on Thursday, when Granville gave me some painkillers, stronger ones than he'd given me before, and then he handed me a cane and sent me home with instructions to get myself into bed. He threatened to put me in a wheelchair, but he knew that wasn't going to work, so he settled for telling me to stay off of my leg as best I could and get some rest. It was seriously messed up, and he warned me that if I didn't let it heal up proper, that it'd require surgery, and even then he couldn't guarantee it'd ever work right again. Too much scar tissue.

I slept for a couple of hours when I finally got home, and then I got up around nine and dragged myself into the shower. I'd rinsed most of Ricky's blood off of me at the hospital, but I couldn't get it completely scrubbed away. I'm not sure I'll ever fully get it off. I stood there for a long time, letting the hot water run down my leg and the cold thoughts run around in my head. I'd missed seeing everything until it was too late. It was all there. It was laid out in front of me like a roadmap the whole time. Boxes and circles waiting to be drawn, and lines that I'd failed to connect properly. I got dressed and went downstairs. Ellen Mae had been up for a couple of hours and had spoken to Kitty Forrest on the phone and was anxious to get going. I apologized for sleeping so long, and she said she hadn't wanted to wake me; that Granville had made her promise not to disturb me if I did manage to fall asleep. She stood behind me and stroked my head, and we talked a little while I quickly had a cup of coffee and another handful of pills. If I took enough of them, they numbed my leg enough to let me drive the truck.

The door to the room was ajar when we got there, but it was dark and quiet inside, and we knocked gently and stepped in. Kitty Forrest was standing looking out the window, swaying slowly back and forth, her son, Eddie, sleeping on her hip, when we walked into the room. She turned and smiled, in a way I couldn't have mustered. and we greeted her, and I gave her a quick kiss on the cheek and squeezed her arm. Ellen Mae held out her hands, and Kitty handed the waking baby to her. I leaned onto my cane and looked down at Ricky. "How you doin' boy? You gave us all a scare there for a while," I said.

"He just came around this mornin'. A few hours ago," Kitty said to me. Then she looked at her husband and took his hand and spoke softly to him. *"Chief Elmore was here the last two days. He stayed with me the whole time. Wouldn't leave."*

Ricky nodded weakly.

"So, how are you feelin'? Aside from probably gettin' fed up with stupid questions about how you feel," I asked. "I remember when I was in the hospital, that's what drove me crazy."

"Fine, except I don't remember much," he replied. "I just can't . . . I remember talking to you, and the woman and . . . there's a lot I'm anxious to find out about."

"There's a lot I'm anxious to talk to you about. As soon as you're stronger."

"Yeah . . . I feel like . . . I was run over with a truck."

I laughed. "No. I reckon you'd look better if it had been a truck."

"Just laying here . . . exhausts me," he said. His voice was soft but it got stronger the more he used it. "And Kitty says all I've been doing . . . is sleeping. Two days."

"I don't doubt it. Not many men can lose blood like you did and even be here afterwards to complain about it. I'd have bet money that a man couldn't bleed out like you did."

"I hear you gave me some of yours," he responded. "The doctor told me this morning."

"You looked like you needed it more than I did. Consider it a loan."

"I hope I never have to repay it." He smiled and nodded at my chest, where normally I'd be wearing a badge. "I also hear you owe the town for a replacement badge. That right?"

"Yeah. Good thing I decided to wear it after all," I said. I never could get a good enough hold of Ricky's severed artery to pinch it off, it was too slippery for my fingers, and the way it was buried in the muscle tissue, I never could get enough pressure on it to get it to seal. I thought I was going to lose him for sure, in fact, I thought I had, but I finally pried the pin off the back of my police badge and managed to bend it into sort of a clamp. It worked well enough, I guess. "Just wait until Jewell Faye hears that we have to buy a new one. I have no idea how much a badge costs."

"Doctor Koenig did the surgery on me. He says he couldn't have done a better job than you did, given the circumstances."

"They say he's pretty good," I replied. Doc Koenig is about my age; he'd moved to Split Tree the year before, and people were starting to go to him regularly. He's one of the reasons that Granville has started slowing down his business. I know him well enough to tip my hat to, but I haven't found the time to talk to him at much length. I decided that I needed to hunt him down now and thank him for saving Ricky.

"He was telling us he was a MASH surgeon in Korea," Kitty said. "Lucky for us he specialized in chest wounds."

"That right?" I said.

Ricky smiled. "Yeah, and it turns out we were over there at the same time; we overlapped by about six, seven months." He laughed and coughed and winced at a stab of pain. "*Damn.* Don't let me do that again. Yeah, Doc Koenig . . . it's kind of ironic, don't you think? I spent the better part of two years over there getting shot at eight days a week, and I hardly got a scratch. I have to come all the way home to Split Tree to get cut on by a MASH doc."

"Just be glad," I replied. "Not a knock on Granville, but he'd be the first to tell you that Doc Koenig probably saw more cases like yours in a week than Granville's seen in his lifetime. I'm just glad he's here; he could be makin' a lot more money elsewhere. We got lucky."

We all nodded, and cleared our throats, and went quiet. Ellen Mae bounced Eddie, who was now awake, on her hip and made soft cooing sounds to him, trying to get him to smile.

"*You need to tell the Chief,*" Kitty Forrest said quietly to her husband, after the silence became thick and awkward.

I looked at Ricky. He didn't look like he was anxious to tell me whatever it was. "What is it, son?" I prompted him.

"Art Hennig called me," he said. "A little while ago. You know, to check."

"Not surprised," I replied. "He's been callin' about you a lot the last two days. I talked with him last night. He thinks a lot of you. You had all of us worried."

He started to laugh again but stopped himself. "Yes, sir. Well, you know how he is. He says he and I are now part of the Doc Elmore fan club. That's what he calls it. He says since we both owe you our lives, we're going to start holding regular meetings and charging each other dues."

I sighed and shook my head, but I didn't say anything. All I could do was look at him and think about how slow I'd been to respond. I'd seen the look on Lidia Fernandez's face. I knew what she was going to do, probably before she did, but I couldn't react fast enough, or didn't, and Ricky had almost paid for it with his life. Sometimes I think I poison just about everything that I touch.

"Tell him," Kitty repeated. Quietly.

He cleared the thickness from his throat. "You know the Sergeant. He sort of offered me a job," he said.

"He always offers you a job," I replied. "Lucky for me, y'all don't want to move. Lucky for Split Tree."

Ricky nodded but didn't say anything. He exchanged a look with his wife. She squeezed his hand.

"Go on," I said. "There's somethin' else. What is it?"

"I don't know. I . . . I need to think, Ray. I need to think, and right now I can hardly keep my eyes open, but . . ." He looked again at Kitty and then at the baby in Ellen Mae's arms, and then back at me. "This one was close, Ray. I don't need to tell you that."

"Damn close."

"Roger. And it makes you think; does me anyhow. You know, before . . . I didn't . . . but I have a baby now. A son. A whole family." He smiled like he was apologizing for what he was saying. "I'm not sure I can do this anymore. Not sure I want to do this anymore. This was too close. You understand, don't you? It's important that you understand."

I nodded at him. "I do. Listen to me, Ricky. You don't owe me a thing. Not a damn thing. This town neither. No one would blame you. The town needs you, it damn sure does, but your family needs you more, and that's what's important. Ain't nobody in this town can blame you if you make that choice; leastways me. I'm not sure the state police is any safer; fryin' pan into the fire, but if that's what you decide, you know I'll support you."

He didn't respond.

"You need to tell him, Ricky," his wife said. *"All of it."*

Ricky hesitated and then nodded at his right arm and shoulder, which was heavily bandaged and splinted so he couldn't move it. There were tubes putting liquid in and tubes draining liquid out of him. "The doctor was in here a while ago. Turns out you can't cut through an artery without cutting through a bunch of nerves at the same time." He looked at his wife and smiled. "I tell you what, though, as much as this son-of-a-gun is hurting me right now, I got to believe he got all of those nerves sewed back together."

"Ricky," his wife said. Her tone was getting impatient. "Tell him, or I will."

"Yeah." He looked back at me. "The doctor says a bunch of nerves got cut. I guess those are the hard ones to fix. The muscle will heal back, but he's not so sure about the nerves. Time will tell, but the good news is that he says I get to keep the arm, and believe me, that's good news." He smiled and shrugged and winced again. "It just may not be worth much."

"Aw damn," I said. My stomach turned over. I couldn't help but think about the way I'd ripped at his flesh and then taken the razor to him, trying to open the wound up wider so that I could get hold of the bleeder. What Lidia Fernandez hadn't cut, I had. "Ricky, I—"

He waved me off. "Anyhow, Sergeant Hennig says he can get me into the crime lab. With my college degree, and my experience in the army, and the time here with you, he thinks I could make supervisor pretty quickly. He says that he's about ready to bug out, and he thinks he can have me ready to take over his job." He looked down at his shoulder again. "Turns out you only need one arm to work in the lab. Assuming I can learn to write with my left hand, I ought to make a fine bureaucrat. Don't you think?"

There wasn't much for me to say. I nodded and laughed. "Never saw a man that takes to filling out forms like you. Worst that you'll have to worry about is paper cuts."

He smiled and reached out and patted his wife's hip with his left hand, and looked at her. "But it may not come to that, right Kitty? The doctor says it's still way too early to tell, and he assures me he's a miracle worker. I may just surprise us all and get this old arm working again." He winked at her. "I got a boy that'll need to learn to throw a baseball in a few years, and I've got a hell of a pretty wife to chase around the kitchen for a lot of years to come, and I know I'll want two arms for that. How's that for some motivation?"

I shifted my weight onto my left leg and leaned my cane against the side of the bed, and then I reached out to take Eddie from Ellen Mae. I put him on my hip. He reached out and felt my face, and I held him close and rubbed the stubble on my jaw against his cheek, and he giggled and grinned. "You're right, Ricky. That's about all the motivation a man needs," I said.

Ricky was looking tired, and we said that we needed to go and let him get some rest. We promised to check back in a little while and told Kitty to call us if she needed anything. That's when we heard some commotion in the hallway outside. Not quite a scream really, but certainly raised voices, and the sound of feet running back and forth in a hurry. We all turned and looked at the door, which was standing partially open. We saw a nurse run past. It looked and sounded like she was in tears.

"What do make of that?" Ricky asked.

"Not sure," I replied. I held Eddie out for his mother to take him, and I looked at Ellen Mae and reached for my cane. *"Can you tell what's goin' on?"* I asked her.

Ellen Mae stepped to the door and stuck her head out. She looked up and down the hallway and then looked back at the three of us. She shook her head. "I don't know." She leaned out again. "I'm not sure," she said over her shoulder. "It sounds like somethin' may have happened to the president."

EPILOGUE

Split Tree, Arkansas
Sunday, November 24, 1963

After the state police arrived at Ring's place that night, they got Ricky and Carl Trimble to the hospital. Ricky went straight into surgery; Carl went straight into a bed. He spent a day there. Severe shock, the doctors said. I guess. He was pretty shook up, and for a man of Carl's tenuous fiber, I suspect that what played out there in Ring Johnson's living room could strain his limits. Granville tells me it may be weeks before he completely comes out of it, if he does, but he and every other doc who looked at Carl figured he'd mend up just as well at home as he would in a hospital bed. Carl had a poker buddy of his pick him up the next morning and run him by his house. I'm told he packed up the few clothes he still had hanging in the closet there, and then he moved permanently into his office at the Western Auto. Didn't even say goodbye to Grace or Jimmie Carl. I'm also told he immediately crawled deep into a bottle of sour mash, and no one is completely sure he'll crawl out this time. I'm not losing sleep over it.

The state police talked to me at length last Friday. They sent a captain from their major case squad over from Little Rock to oversee putting it all into a box and nailing it shut, and he seemed satisfied with what happened and how everything turned out. It actually tied up all sorts of loose ends for them with a minimum of paperwork and a maximum of attaboys from the governor. I didn't know it at the time, but the attorney general had approved a shoot-on-sight order for both Gervais and Fernandez, so that worked out nicely, and the fact that I shot Lidia Fernandez rather than a trooper or Ricky, and the fact that I'm not a cop anymore, don't seem to be problems. The state isn't inclined to split hairs when the press is favorable, and the press was very favorable. Especially compared to the shit storm raining down on Dallas.

Cecil Ben Cooper came to the hospital that first night, and I told him what Gervais had to say about Jo Johnson and her involvement in Ring's death. I have no reason to think he wasn't telling me the truth, and I thought Ben should know; what with her being his wife's kin, sort of. Maybe she'll turn up one of these days, and he'll have to deal with it when she does, but until then, I thought maybe it'd help him sleep better at night knowing that she and the boy are okay, wherever they are. I can't say I approve of killing people, but there are times when it's called for, and while I don't condone what Jo Johnson did, I sure don't think much of what Ring was doing to her either. There's no call for that. Maybe it warranted his killing; maybe not, but I reckon there's not much difference between her taking a knife to Ring and me taking a handgun to Lidia Fernandez. We both did what we felt we had to do, and I'd do it again, and I suspect Jo would too. Doesn't make it right; doesn't make it wrong. But I have my own ghosts to answer to every night, and it's not for me to cast stones in her direction.

I haven't heard any more from the ACLU or that Jackson fellow. Powder Graham says that Washington's so shook up about the president that we're way down on the Justice Department's list of things to tend to right now. He's reasonably sure that we haven't seen the last of it, and until we do, I'm still suspended. I have no idea how long that'll be, but it's probably just as well, given that most days it's about all I can manage to do to get up out of bed in the morning without swallowing more pain pills than I need to be taking. But, with

Ricky laid up indefinitely, and maybe not coming back at all, it means that Split Tree's without a working police department. Ben Cooper has assumed jurisdiction for the present; I'm told there's some sort of town ordinance or state law that allows the sheriff to step in like that. He'll do fine, and he'll keep the peace. After all, next year's an election year for him.

I finally crashed and slept most of Saturday, the pills helped with that, and I got up the next morning reluctantly. I didn't want to go to church. I didn't relish sitting there with my leg aching like it was, but mostly I didn't want to be around all those people, asking me questions and slapping me on the back for shooting a woman. After all that happened, church was close to the bottom of the list of things I wanted to do, but after all that had happened, it was close to the top of the list of things that Ellen Mae needed to do. She'd held up well, but it was plain to see that she'd gotten quieter over the last 24 hours, and I detected a dark shadow around her eyes. That doesn't always mean she's about to tumble into one of her spells, but it's a sign I've come to understand that I can't completely ignore. I could tell she was on the lip of the crater, and I needed to make sure she didn't slip into it. And so, I took a handful of pills, and waited for them to kick in well enough that I could bend my leg without too much pain, and then I drove us to church.

The chapel was full. Even most of the town's more prominent sinners had turned out. What happened to the president seemed to make everyone take stock of their souls, and I reckon they all felt the need for a spiritual cleansing. Everyone knows about Mr. Kennedy. Terrible thing. I didn't think much of the man, and I won't pretend now like I did, but I didn't wish that on him either. Or his family. And now we've got Johnson as president. Another damn navy officer.

There was a gap on the front pew, where Carl Trimble normally sits. He wasn't there, and like I said, nobody has seen him since he got out of the hospital and took up company with a pint of George Dickel. Grace was in her new normal spot, near the back, where she'd sat as a girl with her parents, but Jimmie Carl wasn't with her. We hadn't seen much of him either; even my two boys said that he'd made himself scarce since that night.

It was a long service. Exceptionally long. Reverend Webb mentioned Gervais and Lidia Fernandez; vile creatures, he called them, and he reminded us that we should all pray for the swift recovery of Ricky Forrest and Brother Trimble. That led to him spending some time thanking God for all his mercy in keeping the sheep safe from the wolves; although it didn't lead to him spending any time questioning who allows the wolves to prey on the sheep in the first place. He lost me at that point, and my mind began wandering back to all the signs that I'd missed with Gervais. When I finally checked back in on the preacher, he was still feeling the spirit and was still going at it, and he'd somehow tangled that length of yarn into a bigger knot that included Mr. Kennedy and all of the foul vessels who prowl the earth, tempting God's wrath. Before he was finished, he'd gotten around to talking about *End Times* and waded knee-deep into the *Book of Revelation* more than I thought we really needed to do. I just wanted to get it over with. It was bad enough that I can't stomach his message, but sitting for any length of time is difficult with my leg; for that matter, so is standing for any length of time. The only relief I get is for the short minute it takes me to change from doing one to doing the other, and his sermon didn't allow for that.

I'd assumed that Reverend Webb would cancel fellowship this week. I think a lot of people did. For my way of thinking, I figured he'd already taken a pretty good run at us, and I could tell that most people just wanted to get home and watch the news on the television. Kennedy's body was going to be taken to the Capitol to lie in state, and people seemed to think they needed to see it as it was happening. But I was wrong. He no sooner finished with the Apocalypse when he announced that fellowship was still on the program, and that we were all to gather the sheaves in the side yard as soon as the service was over. The world might have been turned upside down, but there was no reason that Split Tree had to be, he said.

Ellen Mae was looking exhausted, and I was seriously uncomfortable. Besides, she hadn't fixed any food to share, which she normally does, and I knew she wouldn't want to show up in the side yard empty-handed. So, instead, we both decided that we'd shake the pastor's hand and then excuse ourselves and get back on our road to perdition. It's not like he could really say anything about it, and even if he did, I didn't care. As we were walking out, I saw Grace Louise ahead of us in the handshake line. It didn't look like she was planning on any fellowship either.

We caught up to her on the sidewalk. "Grace," I called.

She stopped and turned and smiled. "Ellen Mae. Ray," she greeted us. "I see y'all aren't stayin' either." She smiled. "Now I don't feel so bad about skippin' out. I'm afraid I'm just not much in the mood to sip tea and make conversation today."

"Can't say that I blame you," I replied.

"You look better. Still limpin' though. Does it hurt badly?" She smiled again. "I'm sorry, Ray. I guess that's a silly question."

"How's Jimmie Carl?"

"He's alive," she replied, suddenly serious.

"Thank God," Ellen Mae said.

Grace smiled again. "Yes. Thank God, and thank Ray Elmore. I'm not sure who deserves the most credit." She paused. "Ray, I think I need to apologize. I . . . I don't recall all of the things I said the other night, but I think I may have said some things that were uncalled for, and . . ."

"You didn't say anythin'," I said. "Nothin' you shouldn't have."

"I hope that's right. I hope you're not just sayin' that. You promised you'd get him back, and you did. I never doubted you, you know. Not really. How could I? I don't know all of what I said, but I never doubted you. I want you to know . . ."

"I'm sorry he had to go through that," I said. "Both of you. I'm sorry. I should have figured it out sooner. It should never have happened. It was my fault, and I'm so sorry, Grace. That boy had to see . . . He saw and heard things that I'm sorry for. I never intended for any of that . . ." My own apology trailed off. I didn't really know what else to say.

She nodded. "I know. But you don't need to be sorry. You're the last person in this world who needs to apologize for anythin'. Yes, it was hard for him, but he'll be all right. And he'll be all right because of you. And Ricky Forrest. But mainly you. I may never know all you had to do, I probably don't want to know, but I know this, Ray Elmore, I know he's alive and he's home, and that's all that matters. And yes, he heard a lot of things that I wish he never had to hear or could have heard another way, in another place. That'd be a lot for anyone to handle; it'll take some time. And yes, there's a lot that he has to make sense of; a lot to understand. He knows what Carl is, he's known that for a long time, but this . . . he just . . . his whole world just came crashin' down on him; all at once. That's a lot for all of us to deal with."

We both went quiet.

"Where is he?" I finally asked.

"At work. At the store. I asked him stay home and get some rest, but he says he wants to work. He says he needs to earn some money. He thinks he needs to leave Split Tree."

"Grace—"

"*I think I'm goin' to go to the car. You two keep talkin',*" Ellen Mae interrupted me. "Grace, I'm so thankful that Jimmie Carl's safe. Please tell him that we miss seein' him around the house." She reached out and touched Grace's forearm. "Anythin' you need, you know to call."

"Thank you, Ellen Mae," Grace replied. "Yes, I will. I'll tell him. I know he misses y'all too. He just needs some time."

I nodded at Ellen Mae. "I'll be right there," I told her.

Grace and I watched her walk away, and then we looked at each other.

"Ray, you need to talk with Jimmie Carl," she said.

"I don't know that he wants to see me. I don't blame him."

"You'd be surprised," she said. "He's just very confused. He may not know it right now, but he needs you, Ray. We all do, but right now, he needs you the most. Now more than ever. I've no right to ask you this, but do you have another promise in you? Can you promise me you'll go to him?"

I told her that I would. That I'd try anyhow. We talked for a few more minutes, and then I offered her a ride, but she said that it was a nice day to walk; a good way to clear her head. She said she was in no hurry, and there was no one waiting for her at home. She kissed me on the cheek and thanked me for Jimmie Carl's life, and we said goodbye.

I took Ellen Mae home. I apologized to her. We'd planned to spend the day together, but I told her that I needed to talk to Jimmie Carl. I guess she understood; she said she did anyway. She's a good woman. I'd try to make it up to her later.

I took a few more pills, enough to last me through the afternoon, and I loaded my dog into the back of Donnie's truck, and I drove to the Western Auto. There weren't many customers in the store, and the few who were there were crowded around a couple of television sets watching the news about the president. A handful of them stopped me when I limped in, and they congratulated me on catching Gervais and asked about Ricky Forrest and when I was returning to the job. I thanked them all and told them that Ricky was mending and that it hadn't been worked out whether I'd return any time soon. I finally got free and made my way to the back of the store. Jimmie Carl was at the sporting goods counter, and I could tell he'd seen me, but he wouldn't look at me.

"Jimmie Carl, how you doin', boy?" I asked as I got to the counter.

"Okay," he replied. "Can I help you?" He still wouldn't look at me. He was nervously picking at his thumb.

"Funny to not see your nose in the middle of an auto parts catalogue."

He shrugged. "Goin' to sell that piece of shit car."

"Aw, now, you don't want to do that. Just needs a little more work. You've done a good job on it."

"I need the money. I'm goin' to get out of here."

"That right? You got any idea where you're goin'?"

"Far as I can."

"Far's a long ways. Believe me. I've been there, and I couldn't wait to get back here."

"That's you. I'll go to college maybe. Maybe the army."

"College would be a good choice. It'll be hard on your mother, but it's just for a few years. She'll be proud of you. All of us will be."

He didn't respond right away, but then he asked, "You need somethin', Mister Elmore?"

I watched him pick at his thumb for a moment. "Yeah, actually I do." I pointed at the nearby rack of fishing poles at the other end of the counter. "Thought as long as I'm suspended, I might as well do some fishin'. Nice afternoon. I got the dog and a couple of poles in the truck, but I need some sinkers and a box of night crawlers."

He nodded and moved down the counter to a small refrigerator where the live bait is kept. "One carton?" he asked.

"Not sure. What do you think? Tell you the truth, I was hopin' you'd go with me. Trip and me are fixin' to head on out to McKelvey Lake and see what we can get to bite. I was thinkin' you might go with us. There's a spot out there, it's hard to get to, but it's got the best bluegill on this side of the state, and not many folk know about it. My great-grandfather showed it to his son, and my grandfather showed it to my father, and he showed it to me and my brother forty years ago. That's where I taught Ray Junior and W.R. how to bait a hook. Sort of the place where the Elmore men have learned fishin'. How about it?"

"I'm workin'."

"My guess is you can get the afternoon off. Business is pretty light today, and your boss doesn't seem to be around."

"I already know how to bait a hook."

"Yeah, you probably do," I said. "I'm sure you can, but I never showed you how. I figure I'm way overdue."

ACKNOWLEDGMENTS

Poor, poor Split Tree, Arkansas. For a small delta town that prides itself on nothing important ever happening, it seems to have an astounding per capita murder rate. (The city council actually voted 6-1, with 1 abstention, to amend the signs that you see coming into town to read "The *Little* Town Where Nothing *Big* Ever Happens," until the public works director told them it'd cost $255 to do it. After that, the mayor decided that it could wait until the current ones are so shot through with bullet holes that they have to be replaced anyhow. It won't take long.)

Fortunately, for the inhabitants of the town and insurance actuaries everywhere, Split Tree is fictional. Locust County is as well. (Arkansas is real—you can google it.) I wanted a locale in Arkansas in which to set these stories, but I also spend a lot of time driving across the state, and I didn't want to have a flat tire on a real back road where a real deputy sheriff might say, "Wait, boy, now ain't you the one who wrote about us . . ." So, Split Tree was born, at least in a literary sense.

Obviously, the inhabitants are figments of my mind as well, though I'll admit that Ray Elmore (I've learned better than to call him Big Ray) shares a number of my father's traits, and not just his penchant for smoking at all times or his ever-rosy outlook on life. My father was one of those rare men who was never at a loss for what to do when everyone around him was paralyzed with fear or indecision. Ray Elmore is like that. I didn't listen to my father enough. I reckon few sons ever do. I probably listen to Ray Elmore too much.

The other person I don't listen to enough is my wife. I reckon few husbands ever do. In addition to advising me on all the important things in life, she also patiently reads all these Split Tree stories. Draft after draft. As with my life in general, her comments and observations always lead to improvements.

When this series started, I was living and working in Washington, DC. I had a small group of friends there, and two of them used to meet me for dinner on occasion and discuss writing. Marilyn London and Sarah Wagner are both top-notch writers in their own right, and I learned a great deal from them and their readings of "Big Ray" manuscripts, even if it isn't reflected in the final stories.

Lastly, lastly, lastly, and lastly: This started with a disclaimer at the beginning (that no doubt went unread), and it will end with a similar disclaimer: *This is entirely a work of fiction and any resemblance to persons living or dead — except for the occasional historical reference — is purely happenstance.*

TURN THE PAGE FOR A PREVIEW OF:

THE EVIL TO COME
A Big Ray Elmore Novel

The Evil to Come

A Big Ray Elmore Novel

Thomas D. Holland

A Work of Fiction

"The righteous perisheth, and no man layeth it to heart: and merciful men are taken away, none considering that the righteous is taken away from the evil to come."

Isaiah 57: 1

PROLOGUE

Bonin Islands, Japan
February 19, 1945

G rady Ricketts bit off a quarter-inch of the tip of his tongue. He didn't intend to. You don't intend to do something like that; not if you got half a brain, and Grady Ricketts prided himself on having half a brain. His momma always said he was the smart one in the family, and he believed her.

But he bit off his tongue anyhow.

He wasn't quite sure how it happened. One minute, he was laying in the sand, on his belly, taking care to not get his head shot off, watching a big man dragging bodies around on the beach. Grady thought the man was crazy; shell-shocked maybe. The Japs were shooting at anything that moved, anything that stuck up more than a foot off the ground, and here was this crazy nut running around in the open, dragging bodies behind him. It took Grady another full minute to realize what the man was doing with them; dang if he wasn't building a wall out of them, stacking them two or three high like they were odd-shaped sandbags. Jap bodies. Marine bodies. Parts of bodies. Parts that weren't even recognizable as parts anymore, but the man didn't seem overly particular about what he picked up, and Grady was thinking about how crazy the whole thing was when his own body lifted a foot off of the ground, and hung in the air for a second, and then slammed back into the sand.

And everything got ringing quiet.

That's when he bit off his tongue.

It didn't hurt at first, in fact, he hardly felt it, and his first thought after he realized what he'd done was to wonder if he'd ever be able to whistle at girls again. He was a good whistler, his momma always said so, and of all things that he could have been wondering about at that minute, he thought about whether he'd be able to manage a respectable wolf whistle again. Then he decided it didn't matter; he had himself a pretty young wife waiting at home, and she wouldn't want him whistling at girls anymore.

All around him, he could see other Marines, on their bellies, like rows of green dominoes toppled along the beachline, each one trying to bury up in the sand. All yelling. At least the live ones. *Get low. Get down. Oh God.* And all sorts of words that his mother wouldn't tolerate back home. Their faces looked like they were screaming, but Grady couldn't hear anything, just the ringing quiet. He spit out a mouthful of blood and turned and lifted his head slightly. That's when he saw the crazy man, the same one who'd been stacking bodies a few minutes earlier, kneeling over him, pawing at him and turning him onto his side and back. *You're going to get your rear end shot off, buddy,* Grady thought. *Get low. Get down.* But the man just kept rolling him back and forth. And poking at him oddly. The man's mouth was moving, in fact, he seemed to be yelling at Grady, just like the others, but Grady couldn't hear a thing. Grady couldn't feel a thing.

And then the crazy man grabbed Grady by the forearms and dragged him fifty feet into a shallow bomb crater ringed by the wall of bodies the man had built. All the time the Japs were shooting at them, and the sand was erupting into little spits and fountains on either side.

All quietly. Grady wondered for a minute if he was going to be added to the man's wall, but instead, the man rolled him onto his side, and cleared a mass of clotted blood from Grady's mouth with two fingers, and then he jabbed Grady in the thigh with something.

And then jabbed him again.

Grady felt sleepy.

And peaceful.

And everything went black.

CHAPTER 1

Split Tree, Arkansas
Wednesday, October 28, 1964

I was looking out the window of my office. The weather had taken a turn the last couple of weeks; it wasn't cold, at least compared to how those people up north measure it, but it was cool enough that the few trees we have in our county had packed it in for the winter, and now the yards needed some raking. Hank Jensen's two teenaged boys were working on the courthouse lawn, though neither of them showed much enthusiasm for their job, and I reckon I spent more energy watching them than they spent in getting anything accomplished. Most of their time went into goosing each other with their rakes and jousting like a couple of medieval knights.

I tend to watch people. Probably too much. I suspect it comes with the job. I'm the chief of police in Split Tree, Arkansas. When I tell people that, their eyes sometimes get big, like that's something important. It's the sort of job that sounds more important when I say it at the high school career day than when I think it to myself every morning when I look in the bathroom mirror. That's not so much a criticism of my town as it is simply a statement of fact. The truth is that Split Tree doesn't have much to recommend it anymore, if it ever did. It hit its high point a hundred years ago, and then coasted along for a while, but it never really recovered from the big flood of '27, or the collapse of the cotton market in the early thirties. That's the excuse we tend to use anyhow, brown floodwaters and poor crop yields. I don't mean to sound overly critical; I don't get paid to cast stones. I know all too well that I stand on my own two feet of clay, and I have even less to recommend about myself than the town does. I grew up here, as did my father and my mother, and their people before them, but I never did hit a high-water mark, and I can't blame my personal failures on broke levees and hungry boll weevils. But this is my home, and I'm not going anywhere, and I try to make it the best I can.

The police department here consists of four of us, which most days is more than adequate for a town of 506 people, who, by and large, don't have either the imagination or interest in breaking the law or aspiring for more than the average. There's me, chief of the tribe, and then there's my three Indians. My secretary, Jewell Faye Ivey, works three days a week and is now on her third police chief in thirty-six years. There's no doubt in my mind that she'll outlast me as well. Then I've got an officer who's been with us for a couple of years now. Charley Dunn Skinner. He's next to worthless in my opinion, but he's related to the head of the town council, and I had no choice but to hire him. He managed to get enrolled in a two-month training program at the state police academy in Little Rock, so I'm enjoying a bit of a break from him, even if it won't last. The remaining member of our department is Vic Straight. He's a young kid, twenty years old, skinny as a hank of empty sausage casing, and with the complexion of a freshly shaved housecat. He's working hard to get people to call him *Dang* as a nickname, presumably because he thinks it sounds manly but knows that *Damn* is too much to ask for in a town made up mostly of immersion Baptists. He's not meeting with much success on the matter, and most folk call him by his Christian name. At least I do. Everyone in a small town ends up with a nickname sooner or later, but what Vic doesn't seem to understand is that you don't get to pick what other folk call you, or when they start calling you that. He's been here since last April; he's the fourth officer I've had in seven years. He's originally from over in Oklahoma somewhere, but he came to us from doing a couple of years with the sheriff's department up in Lee County. When my former officer, Ricky Forrest, left us last year, the town insisted that I hire a replacement, and Vic Straight was the only one who answered the announcement. Truth is, I'd have been happy to keep the position open till the right person came along, but the town council thought I needed some help, and I was forced to bring him on. He's no replacement for Ricky, who left to join the state police last January. Ricky's going was a big loss for all of us, but I don't blame him one bit; he came close to dying when I botched up an arrest last year, and a Cuban woman that I was after cut him bad with a straight razor. My ham-handed, incompetent attempt to render him aid only made the injury worse, and thanks to me and that woman, Ricky's right arm doesn't work the way it should anymore. But he's smart, and the state crime lab offered him a supervisory job that doesn't require two strong arms. It's mostly a desk job, and it came with the promise of not getting himself cut up again, which was a decided bonus. It was a smart decision for him and his family, but I miss that boy every day; I had real hopes that he'd replace me. I don't have similar hopes for *Dang* Straight.

I was watching the two boys across the street chase each other around a magnolia tree when I heard the sound of a newspaper being folded with a purpose behind me. I resisted any urge to turn around.

When I didn't, Cecil Ben Cooper cleared his voice and issued a pronouncement directed at the back of my head. "Well, it's a damn awful joke, that's what it is. Ain't right. Just ain't right," he said. "Not if you ask me."

"Probably why they didn't ask you, Ben," I said. "Don't need you applyin' some of that common sense you're so well known for." I kept looking out the window. I really had no interest in where the conversation had been, or where I saw it was going now.

"Probably right about that, don't you know. Damn Swiss knuckleheads," he continued.

"I think they're Swedes. Norwegians in this case, Ben."

"Well, them too. Like it much matters. Ain't nobody but Big Ray Elmore likely to know the difference twixt them."

I continued looking out the window. I still didn't swing around to face the sheriff. "I reckon their wives can tell the difference. Mothers probably get suspicious of their accents from time to time too," I said, against my better judgment.

Cecil Ben Cooper is the Locust County Sheriff. He got himself elected right after the war and has managed to get re-elected every two years since. He's adequate for our needs and generally exceeds our rather low expectations. His office is on the second floor of the courthouse, overlooking the lawn where the two Jepsen boys were now launching their rakes at each other like javelins, but he spends two or three mornings a week sitting across from my desk, drinking Jewell Faye's coffee and reading the newspaper and cadging free smokes out of me. He had his feet up on the corner of my desk and was folding and refolding the paper forcefully, as if to express his low opinion of the Swiss. "Well, I don't see nothin' *noble* about it. That's all I got to say. Since when did stirrin' up trouble get to be *noble?*"

"He doin' that?" I asked. I knew I should have just let that dog sleep, but it got off the porch before I could stop myself.

"What? You don't think?" Ben replied. "You read the papers, same as me."

I finally swung around to look at him and shrugged. I really didn't want to get into it with him, and I lit up a Lucky Strike, as much to avoid responding as to feed my habit for nicotine.

"Now, don't you look at me that way, Big Ray," Ben continued.

"Been apologizin' for the way I look my whole life. Don't take anythin' from it," I replied.

"Well, I see how you're givin' me the old mean eye. You know it ain't just me. I'll bet you diamonds to dimes that you can head over to Gene's right now, right this very minute, and you'd hear the same thing. You know you would."

"Not sure the barbershop's the best yardstick to use in these matters. Besides, the boys over there probably have got more weighty matters to discuss than who got the Nobel Prize from the Norwegians this year. Hogs play the Aggies this Saturday."

"They do at that, but . . ." He made a face, as if he was unwilling to let the matter go that easily. "Well, it ain't just me; that's all I'm sayin'. It's hard enough for men like us to keep the peace without troublemakers stirrin' the pot. That's all I'm sayin'." Ben dropped his feet to the floor and opened the newspaper up again. "And I'm tellin' you, it ain't just me. Here. Now, you listen to this. That police chief over there, he says the very same thing I am. And he'd know." He found what he was after in the paper and read. *"They're scraping the bottom of the barrel*, Bull Connor says. Them Swedes, or Norwegians; that's who he means when he says they're scraping the bottom with that one. Them's his words; not mine. He says, the Reverend *King has caused more strife and trouble in this country than anyone I can think of*, he says. Now, that's him talkin'. That's a quote from the dang paper. A quote, mind you."

"Must be true then."

"Right about that. *More than anyone*, he says. *Anyone*. So, see, I ain't the only one."

"Bull Connor one of your heroes now? That can't be his real name? *Bull?*"

"I ain't got no heroes but Coach J. Frank Broyles and Jesus Hisself Christ."

"In that order?"

He smiled and tilted his head to the side. "Well, I guess we'll see how this weekend goes. Christ never went undefeated."

"Never could beat Texas."

Ben Cooper nodded at the truth to that.

I thought for a moment that we'd gotten the conversation diverted.

"And just what kind of *Reverend* is he anyway?" Ben started up again. "*Reverend*, my ass. Not like any reverend I ever seen in church."

I sighed. "Well, I reckon you go to a different kind of church," I replied. I started to stand up. I needed to hit the head, and I also really wanted Ben to go back to his own office.

"You know dang well what I mean, Ray," he continued. He wasn't planning to budge. "Just too much caterin' goin' on. That's all I'm sayin'. What with this presidential election comin' up and all."

"That right?"

"You know it is. Damn politicians fallin' all over their damn selves. Caterin'."

"Guess you can't blame a politician for wantin' votes," I replied. Ben was up for re-election himself and spent a good deal of his day reminding folk to turn out to the polls.

"*Wantin'* votes and *caterin'* are two entirely different things." He paused, and then smiled. "Hey, you know what the shiniest thing in the world is?"

I turned back to the window and didn't respond directly. I didn't know where he was headed, but I knew I wasn't in a particular hurry to help him along the way. "You the one hired the Jensen boys to rake leaves?" I asked instead.

"It's a Colored's ass dipped in Goldwater and shined with Johnson's wax," he delivered the punchline.

I took a deep breath but kept looking out the window. "You make that up yourself?"

Ben Cooper laughed. "I wish. Naw, heard it at the lodge. But dang if it ain't true. At least until the election's over and done. That's *caterin'*."

"Hmm."

"You ain't laughin'."

"Didn't realize it was a joke. Thought you were puttin' it forward as another quote from the newspaper."

"Well, I probably could. You know, Big Ray, it just don't seem—"

He was interrupted by the phone on my desk ringing, which is a bit unusual. Most calls go to Jewell Faye's desk.

"Police Department. Ray Elmore speakin'," I answered the telephone. I looked at my watch as I did. It was 7:27. I thought I was going to be glad for the distraction; events would prove me wrong. "How can I help you?"

"He's dying," a man's voice said. It was even, and flat; not a shout, but it was loud enough. "He's been shot."

"What? Who's been shot?" I asked. "Who is this?" I looked at Ben Cooper. He'd gone back to reading the newspaper and was shaking his head at the lack of common sense being exhibited by the Swiss.

"He's bleeding out. Pretty bad," the voice said. "You best do something quick, or he'll be dead."

"Who? Who is this? Who's bleedin'? What—"

"Dave Tucker. At his farm. He's dying. Dave Tucker. He's been shot. Better be quick."

And then the phone went dead.

ABOUT THE AUTHOR

Thomas Holland was raised in Arkansas and yet lived to tell about it. He was trained as a painter and printmaker in Salzburg, Austria, and at the University of Missouri, where he earned his BA in fine arts before taking an MA and a PhD in anthropology, also from Missouri, and later, a JD from the University of Hawaii. For almost 25 years he was the scientific director of the Department of Defense laboratory in Hawaii that searches for, and identifies, missing and unaccounted-for American military personnel. He led recovery missions in Vietnam, Laos, Cambodia, China, Iraq, Kuwait, and the workers' paradise of North Korea. During his tenure at the lab, the remains of over 1600 missing men were identified and returned home, including the Vietnam War Unknown Soldier. He is a licensed attorney in Arkansas and the District of Columbia, and is one of only about 100 active board-certified forensic anthropologists in the whole known universe. He is a consultant to numerous national and international groups, such as the International Committee of the Red Cross, and is the author of five previous novels and numerous, opaque, scientific and legal articles and book chapters. He currently is the Director of the Forensic Institute for Research and Education at Middle Tennessee State University, and his wife, Mary, split time between their home in Fort Smith, Arkansas, and a tiny apartment in Murfreesboro, Tennessee.

Made in United States
Orlando, FL
18 November 2024

54089295R10248